SCOUNDRELS

SCOUNDRELS

VOLUME THREE
HER MAJESTY'S
PLEASURE

1972–1986

BY

MAJOR VICTOR CORNWALL
AND
MAJOR ST. JOHN TREVELYAN

EDITED BY

DUNCAN CROWE AND JAMES PEAK

Black Door Press
2 Windmill Street
London
WIT 2HX

British Library Cataloguing in Publication Data.
A catalogue record for this book is available from the British Library.

blackdoorpress.com

DEDICATION

To Mike Crowe,
a *Scoundrel*.

FOREWORD & DISCLAIMER

When we founded Black Door Press in 2016, our hope was to provide a voice for Britain's unsung military and espionage heroes, whose stories were in danger of being forgotten. So many tales of bravery were waiting to be told, and readers appeared eager to hear of selfless acts carried out for Queen and country.

Who could have foreseen that five years later we would be reduced to nothing more than a mouthpiece for the horrific life story of our very first clients, Majors Cornwall and Trevelyan? For while the Majors' reputations go from strength to strength, our humble business has foundered. Black Door Press is now so mired in a multiplicity of legal action that Moody's gave it an unprecedented *F* rating and printed a tiny skull and crossbones next to our listing.

Desperate, we heaped together all of our remaining assets and hired Massingberd Q.C. for ourselves, to turn him upon the Majors and unravel us from the publishing contract we'd unwittingly signed. Unfortunately, it was Massingberd who had raveled the contract in the first place and so the task was as unfathomably complicated as it was expensive. He began acting against himself in a series of actions and counteractions that went as far as Strasbourg, and all at £1,750 an hour. As a result, we have lost our homes and are on the brink of bankruptcy. However, we have secured an agreement that upon publishing this third volume, we'll be free from the Majors' shackles forever. We therefore warmly welcome them back to the Black Door stable for this climactic volume, which is enforceably final under UK and European law.

The Majors have provided the following (unedited) blurb:

Scoundrels: Her Majesty's Pleasure *is an urgent and vital call to arms for anyone who has ever been screwed over by a repressive state apparatus, like, say, the police, the government, or the Queen. Provocative and intensely erotic, it is written so powerfully it's like looking back in time using a telescope that makes things that happened ages ago appear as if they happened only yesterday, but things that happened only yesterday appear as if they happened only yesterday as well. It's a primal scream of fury, and a wake-up call for a post-millennial Britain that doesn't realise how close it was to everything going to shit. Even though we now live in a time when things have gone to shit, it would have been so much worse without us. We hope you enjoy our book.*

Majors Cornwall and Trevelyan will resist requests for comment on their work. Readers are strongly discouraged from attempting to visit either Hellcat

Manor in Devon or Nimbu Towers in Gloucestershire. Several recent newspaper reports in the *Western Daily Press* ('Man Trapped in Man Trap'), *The Daily Telegraph* ('Camping Brownies Flee for Lives') and *Guns & Ammo Magazine* ('Five Ingenious Minefield Designs') speak more eloquently of the dangers than we ever could.

Doubtless the publication of this last volume will unleash another onslaught of legal action against the Majors. Bullish new plaintiffs thinking about launching libel claims (which must be served on the Majors by way of their legal representative Massingberd Q.C.,) should pay heed. Due to a novel and unprecedented argument accepted by the High Court in R. v Massingberd (2020), any letter of claim that he receives at Rapier Chambers, Inner Middle Temple, automatically confers upon its author, indictment on charges under the Treason Act of 1351 and an instantly payable invoice for the exact value of the plaintiff's entire estate.

Despite the furious arguments, the threats of violence, the actual violence and the many typographical errors, we find ourselves delighted that this third volume is now hitting the bookshops. It means our nightmare is finally over and we may begin to rebuild our lives.

Duncan Crowe & James Peak, London, November 2021.

CONTENTS

Hellcat Manor
Great Trundleford
Devon
March 11th 2021

Dear Major,

I'm writing to you as a matter of urgency.

Have you tried to contact the Club since we were freed from our shackles?

I have:

Hellcat Manor
Great Trundleford
Devon
March 4th 2021

F.A.O. Club Archivist, Scoundrels Club, Piccadilly

Dear Sir / Madam,

As one of your longest serving and most esteemed members, I was wondering whether you could furnish me with some information. I wish to know the name of the current Stair Luge Champion. Is it still a certain Major Victor Montgomery Cornwall? *

Yours faithfully,

Major Victor Montgomery Cornwall,
Scoundrels Stair Luge Champion, 1955

*I am aware that Miss Summerville technically completed the course three seconds quicker than I did, but she was not a member at the time and therefore should not appear on the honours board.

A few days later I received this reply:

SCOUNDRELS CLUB
Piccadilly, London
March 8th 2021

Dear Major Cornwall,

Thank you for your enquiry.

It seems there has been a mistake in our records.

I can see from our archives that you were indeed a member of the Club, from 1938, various black-ballings aside, until 1986. But our records show that you were killed on active service during that year, at which point your membership expired along with you.

Please accept my apologies. I don't understand how this could have happened. I have checked our Door Book, which suggests your last visit was in 1986.

Any information about how this error occurred would be greatly appreciated. Again, please accept my sincerest apologies. I will of course reinstate your membership immediately and I look forward to your return to the Club.

Yours sincerely,

Gwyn Johncocktosen.
Archivist, Scoundrels Club.

P.S. Sad to say, Major, you no longer hold the stair luge record. Our member, April Summerville, completed the course this season in 1 min 33 seconds, and her new record is expected to stand for some time. That said, if you fancy having a crack at it upon your return this can be arranged.

Do you see now, Trevelyan? We MUST finish our story. The Club was told we were dead! *Killed on active service*? We've been wiped from history! This is the warning, if we needed one, that we cannot dally any longer. It's time to get on with it and finish our story and reveal EVERYTHING.

Yours sincerely,
Major Victor Montgomery Cornwall

Nimbu Towers
Pullen-under-Lyme
Gloucestershire
March 14th 2021

Dear Major,

So, it looks like your stair luge record was not only beaten by Stephanie Summerville in 1955, but by her grand-daughter, I assume, over sixty years later. This makes me very happy indeed.

But as for the nonsense about the Club thinking we are dead; I am in complete agreement with you. It is an absolute disgrace. The Crown has clearly pulled the wool over their eyes. I have just written to Scoundrels to inform them that I am still alive too. I enclosed a photograph of me bench-pressing Cacahuete while he reads a copy of today's *Times,* so this is irrefutable.

This has annoyed me so much that after quite some time, I suddenly feel galvanised to push on and get our story told. Immediately I finish this letter I will head to the Library and start on my adventures in South America.

Perhaps you could begin by adding a bit of context. You'll recall that I wasn't in the best frame of mind.

Yours sincerely,
Major Arthur St. John Trevelyan

Hellcat Manor
Great Trundleford
Devon
March 18th 2021

Dear Major,

I really couldn't care less about the stair luge record. I was just curious. But what I will say is that when it comes to descent sports, women have a natural size and weight advantage over men. Also, I'd remind you that Knighthorn gave me a faulty tray that day, which was covered in rust. In addition, I caught a nasty carpet wrinkle around the balustrade turn, which cost me two seconds at least. And Summerville stiffed me at the start of the race, cheating by pushing off early. Anyway, it's not important and I couldn't give a stuff.

Glad to hear you're writing again. I thought I'd pick things up shortly after Titus tore Periford's head off:

CHAPTER 1
THE MOUNTAIN
THAT EATS MEN

SOUTH AMERICA, 1971

The dusty, windswept town had never seen a great ape before, let alone a mountain gorilla. And certainly not one wearing a tatty, stovepipe hat, set just so at a rakish angle. Titus was causing heads to turn as we strolled down the centre of the dirt road heading for the saloon.

On either side, low wooden stores lined the road, but their owners said nothing, keeping a safe distance from the two strangers who emanated trouble. This place had seen some weird things over the past few weeks, and they'd learnt not to interfere.

I reached into my pocket and pulled out a *Bad Hombre*, a hostile blend of rough shag *nicotiana rustica* infused with coca leaves that I'd had the Scoundrels tobacconist whip up for showdowns in high altitude South American towns. I offered one to Titus. He shook his head and waved it away. Titus was all business when it concerned Trevelyan. And today concerned Trevelyan.

A shop door suddenly swung open on our left. Instinctively, my hands flashed to the Colt Diamondbacks that sat on my hips. I'd had my man Baxter cut and recrown an inch off each barrel to give me a faster draw but *Fang* and *Fuffy* remained holstered. It was a small child who ran out, chased by his frightened mother. She was a dusky, fulsome woman wearing a loose, low-cut top, and her proportions were generous in all the right places. I caught her eye and made a mental note to return. I wagered she'd remember me. I was head to toe in Harris tweed, inspired by my great grandfather whose portrait hung in the east wing of Hellcat Manor. Colonel Gerald de Montford was an anthropologist known for his sartorial flair, and for being the man who introduced influenza to Papua New Guinea. I'd taken a leaf out of his book and dressed for the occasion. And what was the occasion? An intervention. Titus and I would snatch Trevelyan out of this hellhole and drag him back to England whether he liked it or not.

The problem was, we were already too late.

Trevelyan was dead.

SIX MONTHS EARLIER

The world around me was collapsing. Everything was ablaze. My chest burned. I retched, blinded by the wall of impenetrable smoke. My skin charred and blistered. Trevelyan lay in a bloody heap, bleeding out rapidly from a gunshot wound to the chest. His eyes desperate as he grabbed me and implored, "Cornwall, just bring my girl back to me." The weight of those words. I had to find her. I staggered back inside the warehouse and dragged Anais free from the inferno. The warehouse falling in on itself. Trevelyan struggling to breathe. Anais in my arms.

Too late. I was too late. I had failed.

I had failed Trevelyan.

I had failed Anais.

I awoke with a start and sat bolt upright in bed. I was drenched in sweat. It was the third time this week. The nightmares were getting worse. I took a moment to let my breathing return to normal and gather my bearings.

It was early morning. Blue moonlight streamed into the large, unfurnished room. I was in my new London residence, a Grade I listed John Nash townhouse that I'd bought a month ago after my physician suggested that I needed a change of scene.

"You need a break, Cornwall," Hoffenhaus told me, "perhaps some time away from zee Club. A little holiday might do you zee vorld of good."

"I hate holidays," I said. "Honestly I'm fine. They're just bad dreams."

"Zen perhaps," he said gently, "you can tell me vy you are crying?"

Hoffenhaus was no quack. He was the most expensive doctor in London, and probably the world. Why did I pay him if I wasn't going to listen to his advice? Maybe I did need a break. His suggestion that I might join him on a Nordic cruise was met with my stony silence. Instead, I'd bought the London house. It was somewhere quiet, unconnected to my life at the Club or Hellcat. The perfect bolthole in the city.

I'd also enquired about obtaining the adjacent land, *Regents Park*, with an idea I might turn it into a hunting plain where the Big Five of African lion, African leopard, African elephant, south-central black or southern white rhinoceros and Cape buffalo could roam freely, just yards from London's West End. Annoyingly, when I set out my plans, the Crown Estate wasn't interested in selling.

Apart from the strange dreams I felt I was dealing with things quite well. I'd had many traumatic experiences in my life and coped with them all in exactly the same way: by pretending they'd never happened, and simply getting on with it. It always worked a treat.

The low winter sun broke through the trees of the park and lit up my bedroom. I reached across the bed for the warmth of Chi-Chi but felt only cold Egyptian cotton. I reached over to the other side for Miss Natasha, but both girls must have already departed, taking their money. Nowadays they rarely stuck around to rest after I'd closed the show, usually just an hour or so before dawn. I'd asked them why. They'd explained that in sleep I'd often become agitated, thrashing around, as skittish as a stallion before a big race.

Gingerly, I swung my legs off the bed, and onto the tiger skin rug. My back twinged from being gouged with stilettos all night. My pleasure and pain receptors were inextricably linked these days, like crossed telephone wires, and I winced as the scalding shower pummelled the fresh bruises either side of my spine. The pungent scent of the soap steered my mind back to the spice markets of Tangier and the choking black smoke of the warehou–.

NO. Not a memory I wanted to revisit now, or ever. I rinsed off and dried myself. The phone rang. It was Summerville, our new M.O.S., enquiring after my health.

"I'm fine," I told her. Summerville asked about Trevelyan. She didn't know where he was.

Neither did I, I said.

Then she asked me if I was avoiding the Club.

No, I'm not, I said.

No, I don't know when I'm coming in next, I said.

Summerville told me she needed us for something important. "Find Trevelyan and get back here," she ordered. "We have a lead."

I hadn't heard from St. John for several months. I had tried to call him at Nimbu several times, but Cacahuete had given me one implausible explanation after another about why he couldn't come to the phone.

I knew why of course. Trevelyan had been hit hard by the death of Anais. At first, he'd been a regular visitor to Hellcat, bringing fresh flowers for her grave several times each week. But behind his firm handshakes, stoic nods and clipped speech, it was obvious he was papering over the cracks. This charade continued but with each visit Trevelyan's mood was darker. Then a warning sign.

At breakfast, which I insist on taking in absolute silence, he suddenly piped up. He wanted to dig a hole for me somewhere on the estate. I looked up from my devilled kidneys with red-pepper jelly and apricot stuffed mushrooms and told him I didn't need one.

He asked if I was sure. He was really happy to dig a hole, he said.

Clearly this was grief management. He wanted a punishing, repetitive activity with which to block out unwanted thoughts.

I couldn't see the harm. I even thought it might do him a bit of good to get a sweat on and push through the hurt in a way that meant we wouldn't have to talk about it. So, I agreed to a new trench in the south ornamental garden, that would improve drainage around the rose beds.

Within a month I had a well, a new aquifer, an icehouse, a grotto, an outdoor swimming pool and the foundations for an unspecified subterranean structure which Trevelyan could not explain, and which would never be built. When he offered to "give the hill on the edge of the estate some ski moguls" I took the spade from him.

After that the visits dwindled – weekly, fortnightly, until finally they stopped altogether. It was as if he'd given Anais up. This was upsetting, but I knew he needed space to properly grieve for his daughter.

So perhaps now was the right time to reconnect with the big guy? Give him a once-over, check he was somewhere near the straight and narrow, emotionally speaking.

I would find Trevelyan and get his life back on track. I looked over towards the phone. It sat on the polished wooden floor of my unfurnished room. I could do with a table for that phone I thought. And some curtains. And maybe a chair. Maybe a trip to Selfridges, or…

My eyes turned to the bedside drawers.

The top drawer was tantalisingly ajar.

I looked at my watch. It was still early. Trevelyan wouldn't even be up yet. I'll call him later, I decided. Perhaps a little something to relax me and get the day underway?

I opened the drawer and removed a leather roll-up case. I placed it on the bed, unfastened its string binding and rolled it out flat, releasing a breath I hadn't realised I'd been holding. It contained a rubber tourniquet, a spoon, a lighter, a syringe and a set of hypodermic needles. And a big lump of brown.

Yeah, I thought, I'll definitely call the big fella later on today.

Then I wound the rubber belt around my arm, gripped one end in my mouth and began tapping my arm for a vein.

"Put some clothes on."

My eyes took a moment to focus. When they did, Summerville was standing above me. "Where am I?"

"Fourth floor guest quarters."

"What am I doing here?"

"Titus dragged you across the park, and all the way down Regent St. You didn't even notice," she said, stiffly. "You were too busy riding on your magical dragon, or whatever ridiculous metaphor covers your drug abuse. Get your bloody act together, Victor, right now. Get dressed. There's a set of clothes in the wardrobe." Summerville was in full school-maam mode. I had always found her extremely attractive, but when she was giving me a bollocking this attraction reached another level entirely.

An hour later and I was in her office, as smart as a Guardsman and twice as hard. "Talked to Trevelyan yet?" she asked.

"He never answers the phone."

She gave me a dismissive look. "Then you're going to Nimbu."

"Gloucestershire? Bugger that." I picked up the phone on her desk. "Let's sort this out now."

I dialled Nimbu's number and waited. Summerville

leaned back in her chair. I smiled airily. It actually felt good to be back at the Club.

Cacahuete answered.

"Cacahuete, it's Cornwall. Again. Put Trevelyan on."

"Errrr…" Cacahuete stumbled, "…ees not possible, Meester Cornwall. Meester Trevelyan is eel in bed with a… fever."

"Fever?" my eyes met Summerville's. Another palm off. "What kind of fever?"

"Er…"

"Well?"

"Ees the rabies."

"Rabies?"

"Si, Meester Cornwall. He get bitten by…" the phone went quiet. I heard muffled noises, as if he was listening to an advisor. Then he said, "big bat."

"Trevelyan's been bitten by a big bat?"

"…"

"And he has rabies now?"

"Si."

"Okay," I said. "And while you're there, how's his river blindness? Has that cleared up yet?"

Cacahuete sounded embarrassed. "Errr… So-so. Ees a little better."

"And the beriberi?" I said, scornfully, "that Major Trevelyan caught from…" I had to contain myself, "… eating some berries."

"All gone."

I drew in a deep, deep breath. "Listen Cacahuete," I said. "I don't know if he's feeding you this guff or you're making it up for him because he doesn't want to speak to anyone. But tell him he must come to the phone. Now."

I heard another voice in the background. "Put him on!" I shouted. "Tell him it's Club business."

"Ai! Sooorry, Mr Cornwall. Is no heem. Is just the… television noise."

I made out a gabble of rapid Spanish in the background, then, "ee says 'ee will call you back. Lo siento."

The phone went dead.

Summerville frowned. It was all the instruction I needed. "Baxter!" I yelled, out of her office door, "fire up the Bentley. We're going to Nimbu."

AN HOUR AND A HALF LATER.

The second we pulled through the vast iron gates of Nimbu's grounds I could see something was wrong. The manicured lawns had been laid completely to waste. Huge mounds of Gloucestershire clay sat piled up next to deep holes. Trevelyan must have been digging hard to silence his demons.

Baxter sensed my shock and tried to sympathise. "One imagines that Major Trevelyan has found himself on a few sticky wickets in his time, sir, but perhaps it would be prudent to put on a few runs for him, hit a few boundaries, sir, while he holds up the other end until close of play."

I was about to reply when Titus started huffing excitedly. Barely out of his teenage years, he was now a full-size silverback, and although his ardour for Trevelyan had mellowed into something less intensely sexual, he still held a candle for the big man. And there were times when he couldn't hold his passion back. It was only last month that he'd been overzealous with a jolly-looking plastic mannequin which stood outside a butcher's shop in Yeovil and bore a distinct resemblance to Trevelyan. Titus had jumped on top of it from behind, smashing it to pieces with his revved-up pelvis. I had to talk the butcher down from a call to the RSPCA and spent £400 on sausages just to appease him.

As my boy made the transition to adulthood he behaved like any young man. Every so often he would act out, challenging my alpha status, and I'd be forced to show him who was the boss by denying him the things he loved, like swinging on the ballroom trapeze or stamping on the hens that clucked around the kitchen garden. He'd also become prone to mood swings and would spend hours alone in his room listening to show tunes. He'd recently seen the musical *Oliver!* and now seemed to be modelling himself on the character of Bill Sykes. I consoled myself that he was just trying to find his place in the world. I confess, I wasn't the best parent, often dispatching poor old Baxter to deal with the latest drama emanating from his room. "Dear Lord, Baxter. What do you think he's doing up there?" I'd say, unable to ignore the heavy banging from upstairs as fine particles of plaster dust fell about us.

"I can't imagine, sir," he'd reply, although we could both imagine only too well.

"Do you mind just poking your head around the door and telling him to keep it down?"

"Not at all, sir," he'd say, minding a great deal. And moments later he'd return with news of some horrific act Titus was performing on my childhood teddy bear. Poor old Mister Bigglesmith had been singled out for special attention. With his tiny beaded eyes and downturned mouth he had a strangely sad face for a toy. For years, he had a slight rip in his tummy where the stuffing was coming out, but now it had been torn into a glory hole where Titus had been hammering at him. Mr Bigglesmith's desolate eyes would stare back at me, conveying a sense of terrible betrayal. It was at times like this that I wondered if I should have left Titus in the jungle.

Baxter pulled up outside the front steps of Nimbu. I closed the Bentley's door behind me and bade him keep Titus busy by showing him the ducks in the pond.

As Baxter drove off again something caught my attention. What the hell is that? I craned my neck up towards Nimbu's Bell Tower and squinted. Trevelyan was flying the Mexican flag. What on earth had got into him? I rapped hard on the front door and leaned on the doorbell impatiently, already spoiling for a fight.

The door opened and standing in front of me was an old Mexican woman in her eighties. "Si?"

I took a moment to register. "Who are you?"

"Que?"

"Where's Trevelyan?"

"No se."

She stared blankly at me.

"Where's Cacahuete?"

"OH, CACAHUETE! Si, si, si." She motioned for me to enter. I removed my topcoat and gloves and handed them to her. Rather than hang them neatly for me she just held on to them, holding them up admiringly as if I'd given her a great gift. She shuffled away towards the living room expecting me to follow. This was a rum old do if ever there was one. I was ready to give Trevelyan a dressing down for mucking me around so much. And his judgment had clearly gone if his new staff were anything to go by. This one needed sacking for a start.

I followed her, expecting to meet St. John loafing around in his underpants, drinking gin. Instead, I walked into a room full of Mexicans of all ages draped across the furniture. A clutch of elderly ladies cackled, pointing at me. A middle-aged man took his hat off and stood up. It was as if Cacahuete had invited his entire extended family to come and live with him.

And that was exactly what he had done.

He appeared sheepishly at the door. "Meester Cornwall, I ees glad you have come today. I need to talk with you." He stood aside, beckoning me into the snug, where Trevelyan kept his really good scotch.

"Yes, Cacahuete," I replied, through a forced smile, "I think you do."

Once we were in the snug, I turned off the charm. "Listen," I said, "there's two ways we can do this, and one of them involves Titus breaking your arms. Where is Trevelyan?"

Cacahuete composed himself. "Meester Trevelyan ees very sad because of…"

"Anais," I said.

"Si."

"We're all very sad."

"Meester Trevelyan, 'ee try to dig holes to make himself feel better but it no work. He need to dig bigger holes, he say."

"So, where is he?"

"He made me promise no' to tell you."

"Break that promise or Titus breaks your arms."

"Señor, please."

"I'm losing my patience," I said, raising my voice to call my boy. "Titus! I have a job for yo–"

"Okay, okay, he tell me he go to place where he can dig forever and ever. And ever."

"And where is that?"

Cacahuete's eyes filled and his bottom lip began to wobble.

"Pull yourself together and tell me where he's gone," I said.

"He no come back, Majoor Cornwall," he said fighting back the tears.

"I'll fetch him back if you tell me where he is."

Cacahuete nodded and wiped his cheek with a sleeve. "He say he go to dig until he die."

"Where?"

"Bolivia."

"I see," I said. "Whereabouts?"

Cacahuete's lip began to wobble again. "Hee probly dead already."

"Trevelyan can look after himself."

"No. You don' understand, Majoor Cornwall."

I placed my hand firmly on Cacahuete's shoulder, eyeballing him. "WHERE. IS. HE?"

Cacahuete cleared his throat. "The Mountain That Eats Men."

The mountain of Cerro Rico in Bolivia was so named because the locals once thought it to be made entirely of silver. The *Rich Mountain* overlooks the small city of Potosi and sits upon the largest reserves of silver ore in the world. During its heyday in the 16th Century, its mines funded the Spanish Empire making Potosi one of the richest cities in the world. But the silver is paid for in blood. In its 500-year history it's estimated that over eight million people have died there. Working conditions are horrendous. Deep in the bowels of the mountain the shirtless miners rely on brute strength, using hammers, pickaxes and shovels to chip away at the rock face, with only the light from their headlamps to guide them. The warren of tight tunnels is a giant death trap. There are no safety regulations. There is no piped-in oxygen. Deaths from cave collapses, over-work, and lung disease are common. Knowing this, miners pray not to God, but to the Devil to keep them safe.

Whether he realised it or not, Trevelyan had gone to labour in hell. He was literally digging himself to an early grave. I had to get him out before it was too late.

I'd been tracking down Trevelyan for two weeks. His name was all over town. Named so for his furious digging technique, as well as his leathery skin, *El Armadillo* was the strange, burly, wild man from Europe who used his hands like shovels. Trevelyan hadn't exactly made himself popular among the locals. I followed the messy trail left in his wake: a series of unpaid bar bills, street fights, and confused prostitutes. A man possessed, they said. A man full of sadness and rage, prone to borrowing guitars from *Mariachis*, and then smashing those guitars to splinters when he found he couldn't play them. The locals' descriptions of *El Armadillo* were spot on. "*Si, el hombre del cuello gordo!*" – Yes, the man with the fat neck – one bar owner said angrily, pointing to the broken tables and chairs that had been swept into a corner, good for nothing now but firewood. He ushered me to a downscale brothel on the edge of town where the stern-looking Madame proved very helpful. "*Si, el hombre con el pene de un conejillio de indias,*" – Yes, the man with a penis shaped like a guinea pig – she said, as the girls standing around broke into laughter.

The Madame directed me to a barber's shop, where an elderly, trembling gentleman described how Trevelyan had insisted on a full body wet shave, so that his back hair didn't snag on the rocks of the mine. "*Hablar de eso me da ganas de vomitar,*" – Talking about it makes me want to vomit – he said.

"Yes, that's him." I'd said, stuffing a wad of cash in the old man's hand, "For your blunted razors, señor." And then another wad in his other hand, "and for your dignity."

The latest intelligence was bleak. Word was Trevelyan was dead. Killed in a brutal fight by a group of miners who disapproved of him mining naked.

If this was true, then there was no reason to be here anymore, other than to settle the score. Killing his killers was the least I could do for St. John.

I'd been told I'd find them in the bar, the last building on the street. I asked Titus to wait around the back and walked up three creaking steps to the veranda. Steeling myself for trouble, I stepped through the swinging saloon doors.

I waited for my eyes to adjust to the dim room. It was mostly empty. The only patrons were a couple of old gents playing cards at a table to my left, and three stocky figures sat at the bar with their backs to me.

The barman looked up from wiping the counter and greeted me with a short nod. The men didn't move an inch, although I was sure they would have spotted me in the mirror. Priming myself for action, I walked up to take a seat next to them.

"Singani," I growled, ordering a shot of the potent local liquor distilled from Muscat of Alexandria grapes. The bar owner nodded and poured me a glass of the clear liquid. I downed it in one and gestured for another. Then

I tapped out a *Bad Hombre*, lit it and filled my lungs before blowing the toxic smoke up to the ceiling. The three figures next to me still didn't look over. I produced a faded photograph from my pocket and handed it to the stocky little barman.

"Seen this man?" I asked.

The barman examined the photo. Unfortunately, it was the only one I could find. New Year's Eve, 1961, fancy dress night. Trevelyan dressed as a Dutch milkmaid, holding up a pair of jugs.

The Bolivian studied the image. His eyes widened, but he handed it back to me and shook his head.

I turned to face the others. "Gentlemen, perhaps you've seen this man?"

The hombre nearest to me leaned in and leered, revealing a set of crooked black teeth. He looked at the photo and suddenly broke into laughter. And then they all began to laugh.

"Something funny?" I asked.

"Si, es El Armadillo Loco."

"Crazy armadillo man?" I queried.

"Si. Crrrazzy. Mucho, mucho crazy armadillo man."

"Where can I find him?"

The mine worker shrugged and took a slug of beer. "I don't know."

"How about you, gaucho?" I said to the next one, "have you seen the crazy armadillo man?"

The bar owner looked on nervously.

"No, Señor," he said. He'd stopped laughing. He'd caught sight of Fuffy and Fang at my belt. "I just wonder," he said, "why does a man walk into a bar carrying weapons like these?"

"Making you nervous, amigo," I said. "Got something to tell me?"

He held my gaze and said nothing.

The saloon doors swung open. Another voice broke the silence. "It's not wise to upset the locals, stranger."

A tall figure stepped inside, his boot heels puncturing the stillness. He was expensively dressed in cowboy boots and a pale Stetson. He had a jaw like a skip but covered with the kind of stubble that farmers burn after harvest.

I turned to face him. His pale blue eyes regarded me as a couple of North Atlantic icebergs regard an ocean liner. The temperature of the room dropped a couple of degrees.

The three men grabbed their drinks and moved to the other end of the bar. My gaze didn't leave the lone figure, but my right hand dropped onto Fang, and my index finger slipped inside her trigger guard.

The man spoke, not with a local accent, but Afrikaans. "I don't know who you are, fella," he said, "but you've no right bothering the local gentlemen with questions like this."

"I'm just looking for someone," I said, before draining my glass. "Gimme another."

The barman hesitated. He looked nervously over to the South African, who nodded. He poured me another drink.

I held the photo up. "Seen him?"

He regarded it with narrowed eyes and sighed. "This

is a dangerous place, stranger. I'd hate for you to come to any harm. You're not going to find your friend here. It's probably safer for you to get on back home."

I drained my glass again and slammed it down on the bar in satisfaction, smacking my lips. "That is very bad news indeed," I remarked, "for you."

I began to whistle the opening bars of Consider Yourself, the jaunty tune from Lionel Bart's *Oliver!*

The saloon doors opened. Titus strolled in on his knuckles, his stovepipe hat at the exact same angle as Olly Reed's in the film.

"Jesus Christ!" exclaimed the South African, taking a few steps back.

"Quite the opposite actually," I said, flicking my lit cigarette into his face while drawing Fang from my holster. I fired her three times in quick succession, downing him and two of the burly drinkers who had been so bloody rude.

I didn't need the fourth bullet. By the time, I'd drawn a bead on the last man, Titus had twisted his head round so it faced the other way.

The big South African was lying on the floor, blood dribbling from his mouth. I aimed Fang at him for a second time. "This is for Trevelyan, you son-of-a-bitch."

The man tried to speak, but blood bubbled out of his ruptured lungs and I could see he was done for, so I fired twice more into his chest to put him out of his misery.

I dumped a thick brick of local currency on the bar, and murmured, "you saw nothing, understand?" The barman nodded and scooped up the money.

Titus and I were taking our leave when he stopped me. "Señor!"

"Yes?"

"Your fren', the man you looking for."

"Yes?"

"He no dead."

"What?"

"He no dead, Señor."

"But… I've just killed those men!"

"Si. You killed the Mayor."

'The Mayor?"

"And the mine manager, Señor."

My mind was spinning. The old drunk in the previous town must have lied to me. And all for a few thousand US dollars. But this was huge news! Trevelyan was alive!

"Why didn't you tell me he was alive when I asked you?"

"Ees complicated."

"Where is he? Still in the mine?"

"No, Señor. He go to the big jail on the hill."

"Jail? Why is he in jail?"

The barman winced. "Eeeeeeee… ees' done lots of things, señor…"

"What kind of things?"

"No es importante now."

"Spit it out man! Where the hell is Trevelyan? I was told he was dead. I've just killed four people because of that. Well, one was the gorilla's doing."

"I don' know, but ees no' normal jail, 'ees special jail."

"Special? Special how?"

The Bolivian wiped his sweaty brow with the bar towel. He hesitated yet again, trying to form his next words carefully. Then he said, "Ees jail for mucho dangeriso offendas de sexualidades."

I sighed.

Well, Major, you'll agree that I'm on absolutely raging form. Whichever way you slice it, that was a brilliant opening chapter. Sometimes I think it's a pity this third volume will conclude our tale, just when I'm really getting my eye in at this writing game. I'll probably concentrate on poetry after we're done.

That said, I suppose you ought to take it on a bit from here, if you're able. But say the word and I'll just finish it all off and you can just read it when it's in the shops.

Yours sincerely,
Major Victor Montgomery Cornwall

Nimbu Towers
Pullen-under-Lyme
Gloucestershire
March 23rd 2021

Dear Major,

Last night I opened a bottle to toast a big-hearted man whose life was brought to a violent close by your itchy trigger finger. You shot Jakob Allerbak in the face, mistaking him for the sort of bullying tyrant who used to run your father's diamond mines. You also gunned down Mayor Rosital and two chaps from the Potosi Rotary Club who had been so supportive of my rehabilitation. Yet another example of your failure to grasp the reality of the situation, ending in needless loss of life.

As I sipped the V.S.O.P. by the fire, I thought about Jakob. I remembered the free clinics he set up for the Potosi mineworkers and the way he'd spend his Saturdays teaching the local children to read. I remember the anguish of his pregnant wife – they'd only been married a year – when she heard Jakob had been shot, as the barman put it, by "a spindly dope fiend with a bad suit and a gorilla for a son."

Face it, Victor, you killed Allerbak for no other reason than your fetish for Westerns. You got over-excited and decided you were in the middle of one, forgetting that not all square jawed chaps with Stetsons should be dealt with as in *High Noon*. Thank you for finally admitting responsibility for his death. Now please settle the matter of £168,745, which my accounts book tells me I spent on sending his son, Ambroos, to Eton and Imperial, where he took a degree in metallurgy to honour the father he never met.

Here are the parts of the story you missed when you swaggered into town with that ridiculous gun belt, that ridiculous hat, and that ridiculous ape:

CHAPTER 2
THE BEAST

POTOSI SILVER MINE, BOLIVIA, 1971

I swung the pickaxe. I scooped up the ore. I put it on the pallet. I swung the pickaxe. I scooped up the ore. I put it on the pallet. I swung the pickaxe. I scooped up the ore. I put it on the pallet. I saw her face, a mask of concentration as she galloped through the forest of Nimbu on Angry Thunder.

Why had I not been stronger?

Why had I not been able to save her?

Don't think about it. I swung the pickaxe, scooped up the ore, put it on the pallet. I saw her by the lake in spring. She was calling the leopard in for tea. No. NO.

Think of something else. Anything else. Anything at all.

It's been said before that I'm a tough, unyielding lump of gristle who doesn't know his own strength. Back in London, lounging around the Gaye Bar the chaps would joke that I was only half-tamed, a riot in human form. My nicknames riffed on this theme: The Gloucestershire Sausage, The Thug in Velvet, Trevanderthal Man. It was true. I was a handful. I would often break armchairs by simply getting up out of them. As a matter of course, my tailor reinforced all the pinch points of my suits with the same leather used for shire horse bridles, or I would simply trash the fabric within days. For a laugh, Maurice had once added a new dish to the bar menu – *The Trevelyan*, thirty-two ounces of skirt steak, served *bleu* with a dental saw and a tenderising mallet.

And after three solid months of work, deep underground in the Potosi silver mine, I was more robust even than usual. There was not an ounce of fat left on my body. I'd banged my head against the rock walls so much that my skull looked like a normal skull, but with another skull smashed to pieces and glued on top of it. My hair had absorbed the rich cadmium and zinc of the mountain, and stuck straight up into the air, magnetised. I was from the third circle of hell, maybe the fourth. I suspected I was being poisoned by the mercury fumes from the refining pits. Tongues were wagging about me as I slaved away. The *mingas* were scared of my massive musculature, and the fact that I produced the same amount of silver ore as eight of them, each day, without fail.

Rumours about me grew. New nicknames stuck. Sin Jon Loco, The Beast with Three Backs, The Silver Bear, The Gringo Who Cries, and bizarrely, Mr Ice Cream. After a while though, the nickname shortened, and I was referred to by everyone as, simply, The Beast.

D'you know, they'd say, The Beast is digging to find his lost love.

No, you fool, The Beast is digging to find his lost daughter.

I was working the Devil's Seam. I smashed the pickaxe into the rock over and over again. Each strike as hard as I could possibly make it. My heart rate was up where I needed it to be, at one hundred and eighty beats per minute. I'd taken no bread or water. I worked in a hard-pounding rhythm that was so physically painful, second by second, that there was no room for anything else in my mind. If I was foolish enough to seize up, or succumb to a cramp, or even to wipe the sweat from my brow, the memories of my girl would flood through me, an uncontrollable torrent of pain.

I swept my static-shocked hair back and twisted it into a filthy bun as I hollered for the *mingas* to come and collect my latest full pallet. That made thirteen today – twenty-six tonnes. So far. And I was just getting going.

Jakob Allerbak, the South African mining manager, was standing in the entrance to the seam. He rubbed his oversized jaw with concern. He could see the pain I was in. Knowing the value of hard physical labour as a salve to extreme grief, it was he who had given me the job in the first place. But that didn't mean we were friends. I had no friends in this godforsaken place.

"Get me a new pallet," I bawled into Allerbak's face.

"Awww, come 'uff it, Beast. Tek a brek for tin mins, ya?"

"Get me a new pallet, now!"

"Not until you tek some wadder."

I saw red. Redder than red. I slammed Allerbak into the rock wall and turned away shouting for the devil to take him, to take me, to take everything. One of the passing *mingas* put down his barrow and approached, palms up, in a foolish attempt to calm me. I headbutted him on the bridge of his nose, and he fell down unconscious, and was dragged away by his terrified colleagues.

"Ahh, heck. Simmer tha' tempa down, Beast," admonished Allerbak, "ya can smik me arand all ya want, but ya cannot smik the fellas arand. Carlos will be on his bik for weeks nah."

"Give him my pay," I spat, loosening my tug-rope arms. Flakes of my dried sweat skittered down onto the rock floor. "Give him all my pay since I started here. And tell him I'm sorry."

"OK, Beast. Whitiver ya say," shrugged Allerbak, handing me a new bottle of river whisky. "D'ya want me to lock you in hya tonight, as usual?"

I nodded, smashing the neck off the whisky and taking three deep swallows of it.

"Ya sure ya won't come to the pub for a beer, Beast?" he said, hopefully.

"Just leave me," I snarled.

Allerbak sighed. "Okay. Don't overdo it, ya?"

I slammed my pickaxe into the glittering rock wall, where it sparked like something from Vulcan's foundry. "I've barely begun," I snarled.

I was alone for the night. I swung the pickaxe at the rock wall, once, twice, again, again. As I settled into a steady rhythm, my mind quietened. Soon, the bright metal edge of the pickaxe was all that I could see, clanging hypnotically against the silvery seam. The candles flickered in the stale air. A couple puttered out, and the memories began to form in the gloom. Over time I'd learned to shut down *anything* that featured my darling girl. I'd raise the tempo until my physical suffering became excruciating and wait for a tolerable memory to form.

I swung the pickaxe, scooped up the ore, put it on the pallet.

My mind began to drift. All I needed to do was dig.

Dig.

Dig.

Dig.

THE PALACE OF WESTMINSTER, JUNE 1940

"I need you to dig, Trevelyan," said Winston Churchill.

"Sir?"

"Dig around in that big noggin of yours. You're supposed to be good with words, the Club tells me." He threw a much-thumbed notepad onto the desk. "I've got to deliver this speech to Parliament in an hour's time. It's not quite working."

With a confidence I did not feel, I picked up the notepad and strode over to the leaded window for more light. Outside, a red double decker bus was trundling its way around Parliament Square.

Although I'd met many impressive men since I'd joined Scoundrels a couple of years back, this was a big moment for me. Churchill was the P.M. His time wasn't just money, it was blood. He was in charge of the whole flipping War.

I scanned the text, as fast as I could, hoovering up the references to the Rifles' last stand at Calais and the Dunkirk evacuation. "Looks good so far, sir," I ventured.

"Keep going with it, lad," Churchill snapped. He took a swig from his brandy and waddled around the room. I kept reading. Royal Navy... straining every nerve... hospital ships targeted by Nazi bombs.

"I need to get these bastards onside," Churchill ruminated.

I stopped reading. "Do you mean the House of Commons, sir?"

"I heard you were a quick study, Trevelyan, so don't state the bleeding obvious."

"Sorry, sir."

He grimaced. "I cannot allow Lord Halifax to put appeasement back on the table."

"That would be a disaster, sir."

"Quite so!" he muttered, and then as if the idea caused him physical pain, he suddenly dashed his brandy glass into the fireplace. "Quite. Bloody. So. It won't do! Fix it!"

I went back to Churchill's speech. More stuff about Dunkirk. The endless strafing from the Luftwaffe. I began to feel the power of his words on the page. With his brilliant turn of phrase, he was mobilising the entire English language – to War! Was there a rhetorical trick he hadn't used? He'd harked back to the Knights of the Round Table as the 'great opportunity' for British youth. He'd repurposed Napoleon's famous 'bitter weeds in England', but now these bitter weeds were Englishmen and women: steadfast against the Nazi threat, hardy, impossible to get rid of. The speech built and built. What a writer! What an orator! I could imagine him smashing his fist on the chamber desk, as he rolled on to a thundering crescendo.

"Well?" roared Churchill, "do you see the problem?"

I scanned the final paragraph. Ouch. "I think I might do, sir."

"Tell me! Quickly now, so I know you understand."

"It's this last bit," I cleared my throat, "where you say, 'even though large tracts of Europe and many old and famous States have fallen or may fall into the grip of the Gestapo and all the odious apparatus of Nazi rule, we shall not flag or fail.'"

"What about it?" Churchill turned to face me, grinding his cigar with his teeth, the old bull in the delicate china shop of Westminster politics.

"To speak frankly, sir…"

"I wish you would," he bellowed.

"It's wishy-washy."

The cigar drooped in his mouth. He stood, breathing heavily, fists clenching and unclenching. "Wishy-washy?" he whispered, "depressing?"

"Afraid so, sir."

"Tell me more," he said, quietly.

"It has the wrong ending, sir. It's depressing. It finishes with an image of Nazi might and power. How about something much more stirring at the end? Something about us. The Britons."

Churchill's head went down, settling comfortably into his many chins. He was suddenly lost in thought. So was I. Suddenly, bingo! It popped into my brain – the perfect metaphor with which to help Mr Churchill in his darkest hour.

"I've an idea," I said, padding over to the desk and grabbing a silver pencil. "I don't know why, sir, but I'm reminded of the dorms at Winstowe. Often, we'd be raided by bigger boys, you know, trying to grab themselves a bit of swag – extra pillows, chocolate bars and the like. It got very violent at times."

"Where the devil are you going with this?" Churchill regarded me with his porcine eyes.

"I came up with a perfect strategy to repel a dorm attack, sir. They're still using it today, apparently."

"What are you blathering about?"

"In the dorm we'd station chaps at every possible ingress. D'Arcy up front to defend the door with a hockey stick. Gunt Minor stationed behind him with a bucket of cricket balls for bombardment. And if they tried to come across the San roof, Cornwall would ambush them with his catapult. I'd have two or three boys ready to take over from anyone that fell. We'd defend with all our might, sir, never retreating. We'd fight them in the doorways. We'd fight them in the kit cupboards. We'd fight them on the beds, and in the communal showers. We'd fight them, whatever the cost might be. We'd even fight them on the…"

"…whatever the cost might be," Churchill repeated, slowly nodding his head.

In my excitement I was pacing around the room. "We'd even fight them on the landing! Even…"

"Trev–"

"…outside Dr Wimsey's office, it wouldn't matter a damn! We wouldn't give an inch!"

"Trevelya–," said Churchill, but I was in my stride now.

"Why not paint a picture about what Britons would do if the Nazis did invade? Talk about how we'd fight them absolutely everywhere and never surrender."

Churchill snatched the pencil from my hand. "Right. Good. Bugger off now, Trevelyan, I've work to do."

As the memory faded, I smashed the pickaxe into the seam and wrenched it out again. Frantically I searched my mind for another memory, one that didn't feature my girl.

Suddenly, Cornwall's face was leering at me.

That'll do, I thought, swinging the pickaxe into the never-ending rock.

THE PALACE OF WESTMINSTER, 1965

"Who are we having a quiet word with?" Cornwall asked me.

"A chap called Arnold Hunther. New boy. M.P. for Richmond-on-Thames," I said. "What d'you want to use as a prop?"

Cornwall looked down at the slivers of fried potato wrapped in yesterday's newspaper that he'd bought from a Parliament Square stall. "These'll do," he said.

I shrugged. "As you wish."

Just then, the bar door opened. "You're Arnold Hunther, M.P.," I said, brightly, to the man exiting.

"The same," said the young fellow, as he marched out of Annie's Bar, the rowdiest of the pubs inside the Parliament complex. Hunther checked his stride, puffed out his chest and looked down his nose at me. We've a right one here, I thought. Cocksure.

Hunther said, "and you are?"

"We…" said Cornwall, looming out of the shadows, "…are a couple of chaps."

Hunther frowned.

"Your first week on the job, isn't it?" I queried.

"That's right. What's this about, Mr…?"

"You poor, poor bastard," I said, conspiratorially. "Working twenty hours a day, forging connections, getting to know these ancient corridors of power." Ever so subtly, just by shifting our weight, we began to crowd Hunther, backing him into the stone ingress behind him. He didn't like that at all.

"Listen, I must get on," he said. "As you say, I'm terribly busy." He turned his shoulder to push past.

Cornwall dropped the newspaper parcel of chips at Hunther's feet.

"Oh," said Hunther.

I clapped him hard on the shoulder. "Arnold, you're more vulnerable than you've ever been before."

"It won't be long before you make a mistake," continued Cornwall.

"Overstep the mark…"

"Find yourself in a compromising situation…"

"Have you been down to Charlie's Oubliette yet?" I asked Hunther.

He swallowed and shook his head.

"The secret bumhouse below the Clock Tower? You can really let your hair down there. You'll love it!"

"You'll absolutely love it," agreed Cornwall, "but what if an aide spots you coming out of there, flies undone?"

"Your little fella poking out," I whispered.

"Or worse still, *inflagrante*."

"Whoops."

"Whoops, indeed," smiled Cornwall, indulgently.

"Difficult to square that with Mrs Hunther," I cautioned.

"And maybe that aide wants a little assistance with something… hmm?" whispered Cornwall.

"Maybe a little off-the-books favour for a trade envoy…"

"And then, before you know it, you're handed a twenty-four-carat fountain pen, just for meeting a Russian industrialist," I frowned.

Cornwall leaned in. "Your racing debts paid off…"

"Maybe you look the other way while those banknotes tumble into your briefcase."

"Whoops again!"

"Whoops indeed! Cheeky! Ha, ha," I enthused, "and nobody needs to know."

Hunther's face was a study in confusion. He couldn't decide which one of us to look at. His hand tugged at his collar. He needed more air.

Just then, an older Member walked past. Dunwell Clusters, M.P. for Ruislip South, a good egg who'd given the Club concern only once, over a brown envelope from the Moldovan bacon lobby, and quickly learned his lesson. He hurried past, eyes to the floor.

"God forbid you'd get all snagged up in any traitorous business of that ilk, Hunther," I said. "That wouldn't do."

"Wouldn't do at all," Cornwall echoed.

My tone hardened. "Pick up my colleague's chips, please."

"What?" said Hunther.

"Pick up his chips." I pointed at the mess of scrunched newspaper at his feet.

Hunther finally located his backbone. "This is ridiculous. He can pick up his own bloody chips! I don't know who the hell you think you are, but goodnight." Hunther attempted to barge past again.

I thumped him in the midriff, as if I were a prefect dealing with a mouthy third former. Not hard, almost casual, but enough to make him wheeze in surprise.

"Pick. Up. His. Chips," I ordered.

Hunther was properly rattled now. Gasping, he bent down and scooped the morsels of fried potato back into the newspaper. He stood and handed the whole lot to Cornwall.

"Thank you very much," said Cornwall.

"I'm so sorry I punched you in the stomach," I said, straightening Hunther's tie. "But also, at the same time, I'm not sorry at all."

Hunther was totally flummoxed now. "But... but... I... I haven't done anything."

"We know you haven't done anything." I smoothed his lapels down, my voice as soft as a caress, "but you will."

"You definitely will," Cornwall agreed. "Almost everybody does."

"But when you do, and you feel there's nowhere to turn, remember there's a lifeline."

"A... a lifeline?"

"A London number just four figures long," I said. "It's good from any telephone in the Commonwealth. One. Six. Three. Five. Repeat that please."

"One. Six. Three. Five," he stammered. "Good man. One. Six. Three. Five. And then you say..."

Cornwall cleared his throat theatrically, "Scoundrels, please!"

"The 'please' is nice to hear, isn't it?"

"It's nice to hear a please," Cornwall agreed.

Hunther nodded. "But... who... who are the Scoundrels?"

"We fix problems that nobody else can fix. You may not have enjoyed meeting us tonight, but one day you'll be glad you did," I told him. "We're on your side."

"So, don't forget the number," said Cornwall, "which was?

"One. Six. Three. Five." Hunther stammered.

"Have a pleasant evening." And with that, I released the Right Honourable Member and sidled off with Cornwall.

Job done.

My pickaxe swung again and again. I was hammering away at an unsustainable pace. Another memory surfaced, and this time I couldn't control it.

NIMBU TOWERS, CHRISTMAS DAY, 1965

"Come on Eustace. You always have lunch with us all on Christmas Day. It's the one time of the year we see you." I had been reasoning at Eustace's locked door in the attic of Nimbu for twenty minutes.

There was no reply.

"Eustace, please." Silence inside his rooms. "Look, Marjorie isn't even here. She's gone to Paris, if that's what's worrying you."

I heard my brother crossing the room. A bolt slid back. The door opened.

Eustace peered out, as nervous as the first rabbit to stick his head out of the warren.

"She's not here. You're safe."

Eustace, flushed and tense at the mention of my wife's name, shuffled after me. Poor chap, he'd never got over my parents suffocating to death in a priest hole under the Grand Fireplace during a game of sardines. Even the slightest thing could set him off, sending him scurrying away up here. He spent his entire life in the attic painting portrait after portrait of our parents.

But on Christmas Day he'd steel himself and come down for lunch. He followed me into the steaming kitchen, as Bernard-Bernard busily sieved wild turkey gravy into a pan on the Aga. "Joyeux Noel, Monsieur 'Ustace," he called, smiling broadly.

"Eustace!" shrieked Anais," jumping up from the table, where she'd been shelling snow peas. "You're having lunch with us?" She rushed over to him and threw her arms around his shoulders. "You'll sit next to me, won't you?"

Bashfully, my brother nodded. He loved Anais. In fact, there'd been a few years when I'd first brought her to Nimbu when Eustace looked like he was making a full recovery. They'd play together for hours, devising secret languages and leaving messages around the house.

Lunch was served. Eustace and Anais, pulling a cracker. Anais coaxing him from under the table, promising there would be no more loud noises. Henry the leopard purring at her feet. Bernard-Bernard's toque catching fire where Anais had sprinkled it with brandy. A toast to celebrate 1965. Anais graduating in astrophysics, well done my darling, don't know where you got those brains. A perfect year.

Not perfect. Not by any means. A screech of brakes outside. Speak of the devil and she will appear. Eustace, frozen to the spot, rushes for the stairs. Marjorie has come home. An icy mood descends on the household. Another Christmas ruined.

NO. Work harder Trevelyan. Don't think about Nimbu. Don't think about Anais, or any of it. Don't let the memories in. Just dig.

Dig.

Dig.

Dig.

After another hour my back finally spasmed. I dropped the pickaxe and fell onto the rough-hewn floor, oblivious to the sharp stone chips that pressed into my exhausted body. I fought for breath. At nearly three miles high, the air here contained only two third of the oxygen at sea-level. I stared up at the low rock ceiling. My heart hammering in my chest. Perhaps it was trying to burst its way out, and end me, forever.

I really had no care whether I lived or died, and as I slipped into the blackness, I wondered which it would be.

LATER

I glimpsed Anais, a little girl again, playing at the edge of the trees of Nimbu with her bow and arrow. She was laughing as she drew a bead on a wood pigeon. I could see her elbow was too high for the shot. I should walk in there and join her. I stood on the edge of the forest. Something caused me to turn, and in the field behind me, I saw the figure of Gruber Hansclapp, standing alone, utterly silent, regarding me. He picked an ear of wild grass and began to tear the seeds from the panicle, throwing them to the ground.

I felt my cheeks being slapped hard. Someone was pummelling my chest. Someone else was shouting. I was carried, jolting, bouncing off the rock walls, into the bright sunlight...

I was blind. Thick black bandages were wrapped around my head to obscure the sun. After months underground, even the weakest shaft of sunlight would sear my retinas, the doctor explained.

I'd been found, collapsed, dehydrated and exhausted almost to the point of death by Allerbak, who'd performed chest compressions on me, and, after a fraught hour, had brought me back from the dead and transported me to the tin shack clinic that served the mineworkers.

Later that afternoon, when I was properly alive again, I was visited by a deputation from the town. They persuaded me to drink a pot of thick black coffee and hear what they had to say.

Allerbak was the spokesperson. "Listen, my friend," he said, "things can't go on like this, ya? You're going ta kill yirself. Ya DID kill yirself."

Mayor Rosital and some members of the local Rotary Club nodded their heads in sympathy. They told me about an emergency meeting at the town hall an hour ago, that was attended by almost all the townsfolk. The only item on the agenda was the question of what to do about The Beast.

The miners of Potosi lived a dangerous existence that could end at any moment in a collapsed shaft or a pocket of poisonous gas. Maybe that was why they found the idea of a man putting himself through such pain voluntarily so difficult to understand. Their wives talked of nothing else but the Englishman with the silvery hair, whose screams of anguish echoed down the mountain, even as he slept. Their children had become obsessed with the stories of the man who was digging to get himself into hell.

There were plenty of points of view: banish the Beast from the mine, and send him back to London, called one furious miner. Or perhaps just wait? The Beast would be dead soon anyhow, suggested a shopkeeper. Then another, a friend of the man I'd headbutted, asked why they didn't just drive a pickaxe through The Beast's brain one night? This idea gathered steam. Suddenly, Mayor Rosital told me, pitchforks were being fetched. Torches were being lit. A mob was beginning to form.

It took Allerbak to stand up and speak from his big, soft heart. The Beast's mental anguish was heartbreaking, he said. And besides, he knew the truth. The man had lost his daughter to a terrible villain. Murdered in cold blood. The Beast is fighting the sort of demons that can never be overcome, Allerbak said, and that was why he was working himself to death. We aren't the sort of town that murders good men, Allerbak reminded them. The Beast needs care, and love, and kindness. Could the town rehouse him somewhere secure, Allerbak pleaded, where he could rest and regain his humanity, and perhaps, finally, see that working himself to death was no way to honour his daughter.

The townsfolk remembered they were good people who believed in salvation. They put their pitchforks down. Yes, came the answer. But there was only one place that could hold a man like The Beast. A place with thick steel bars.

It wasn't a perfect solution, but there would be solitude and time, and three meals a day, and no more river whisky, and no more digging.

Allerbak sat down. The town voted on the motion to send The Beast away to a special place – but not for the usual reasons of oversexualised dancing in church or interfering with the chickens.

It was settled. The motion carried.

All this Allerbak explained as I lay on the cot in the tin shack clinic, still weak with exhaustion. And as his light blue eyes stared kindly into mine, I began to feel woozy and lightheaded. Into the coffee, Allerbak told me, they had slipped an anaesthetic – enough to stun a bullock. When I awoke I would be in a different place. A place where I could heal.

"Where am I going?" I slurred.

Allerbak winced. That was the only snag, he said. I was destined for *La Boca De Hombre Malo* – The Bad Man's Hole – the prison for mucho dangeriso offendas de sexualidades, where the worst criminals in Potosi were detained.

LA BOCA DE HOMBRE MALO, POTOSI MUNICIPALITY, A WEEK LATER

Jesús ran things around here. He was a bad hombre indeed, and head of the *Chicos Muy Traviesos,* the Very Naughty Boys. Only four feet nine inches tall, he was psychotic, mercurial, lithe, and lightning quick. He kept a nasty little blade whittled from a conch shell, in his *bolsillo de la prisión* – his prison pocket. He liked the look of me. As I was wrestled into my cell for the first time by six guards in full riot gear, I heard the three worst words you can hear in a Bolivian prison: Jesús loves you.

I learned from a guard the week before I arrived, that he'd dropped a concrete block on the head of a prisoner who'd failed to blow him a kiss and sliced an ear off a cook who'd refused to serve his refried beans in the shape of a heart. Jesús was serving out a sentence for stealing washing from the local nunnery, which, under Bolivian law was punishable with the same severity as murder, arson, gun-running and interfering with the anus of a mule, for all of which, incidentally, he also had convictions.

Jesús had taken a shine to me alright. It was my cross to bear. After the powerful prison showers had rinsed away the months of mountain grime the common consensus amongst the troubled deviants of the prison was that I was absolutely fabulous. A peach. My weight had come down to one hundred and seventy pounds, and most of that was lean muscle. I was a snowy white colour, almost translucent from my three months underground, and my metal infused hair glittered like spangles in a Rio discotheque. Even better, or worse, I'd been allocated a pair of rough denim jeans, a tight white T-shirt and a pair of Brogan leather boots. I looked like the hitchhiker who raped James Dean.

So here I was, cornered in the rec room. All the other prisoners had vacated it upon receiving some hidden signal. And now Jesús, flanked by two of his largest patsies, was sizing me up. They were looking for a way to make me join their gang. And the initiation ceremony for that was something I was not okay with.

"Hola," Jesús said, smiling ravenously as he looked me up and down.

"Good day to you," I replied evenly, scanning the room for weapons.

"*Eres una exotica encantadora…*" whispered Jesús, throatily.

"I beg your pardon?"

One of Jesús' patsies had some faltering English. "Ee say you are an exotic lovely."

This would take some careful handling, I realised, so I set my jaw hard. "Tell him the last person to address me in such a manner lost his ears, and his lips and his nose, and found them all stuffed up his arse."

I reflected that perhaps it was a mistake to mention 'arse', so I decided to move the conversation on a bit. "What does this gentleman want with me?" I queried. Even that question sounded peculiar in the circumstances, so I decided to shut up and hear what they had to say.

After a certain amount of back and forth, and gesticulation, we established that Jesús wanted to shower me with kisses.

"You can tell Jesús that if he tries anything like that I will stamp on his head until it resembles *llajua*." This is a kind of light tomato and onion salsa.

Jesús pouted, and motioned to the patsy, who took a step forward. The man pushed me experimentally in the chest. I seized his wrist and with two quick cracks, broke his radius and ulna bones. Then I slapped him several times in the face with his own floppy hand until he began to squeal. Then I collapsed his knee with a brutal heel kick, so he went to the ground.

Jesús smiled and licked his lips. He was encouraged by my show of force.

I stared into the face of this terrible fellow. I don't know why, but all of a sudden, a flash of insight came to me. The clarity was shattering. What the hell was I doing here, fending off Bolivian sex offenders? After spending three months trying to kill myself in a silver mine. After weeks digging holes at Hellcat Manor. After losing my daughter. Anais would not want this for me. Anais would be ashamed of her father if she could see him right now. My Anais would want revenge.

That was what I should be doing – or die trying. Not giving my life to a mountain or a gang of perverts.

"Ee say that you cannot escape him," said the patsy, as Jesús looked on, coquettishly. "Trus' me, you may as well give yourself to Jesús."

I fixed him with a glare. "You'd better tell Jesús that I am here because I am in tremendous pain. Pain he could never understand in a thousand years. You better tell Jesús that I don't have time for him and his silly fancies. You'd better tell Jesús that I have a job to do. I seek revenge on the man who killed my daughter, Anais Soulla Trevelyan. And you better tell Jesús he figures so little, that in ten minutes time, when he's dead by my hand, I won't even remember his name."

There was a quick, Spanish conflab. Jesús stamped his foot and crossed his arms, looking away.

The patsy turned back to me. "Jesús asks eef perhap' you consider modelling for the life drawing class instead?

"I can spare him an hour," I said, "but then I need to get back to England."

"*Ai! Inclínate sobre la silla, y mira hacia atrás con sorpresa,*" said Jesús, gesturing wildly.

"Jesús ask," offered the henchman, "eef ees possible you honch over the chair, and put finger on the leeps, and look back at us, as eef…" At this point there was an animated discussion as Jesús tried to articulate what he wanted.

"…as eef you have been captured stealing jam from the pantry."

Thankfully, at that moment, the governor's secretary walked into the classroom. He looked perplexed. "There's a gorilla here to see you, Señor Trevelyan. And an Englishman also."

"Righto."

"The governor requests that you please hurry, as the gorilla is sitting on him."

I went to the office. Titus flung his arms around me. It took a while for him to let go. Cornwall and I shook hands. After my recent adventures, I had surprisingly little to say to him, but I was touched that he had bothered to come.

"Is this man free to go?" Cornwall asked the governor.

The governor regarded Titus, who was making one of his faecal drawings on the office wall.

"Of course," he said.

"Good," said Cornwall, turning to me. "Let's get back to London."

When I reflect upon my time in Bolivia, I realise I'd pretty much given up. Hard digging was the only thing that gave me solace. I've always found it the perfect tonic for almost every malady apart from spine and pelvic injuries.

I still dig around in the Nimbu soil today. Just this summer I uncovered the complete skeleton of a Saxon warship in one of the curious mounds that dot the scrubland towards the banks of the Severn. There was a tremendous trove of armour and weaponry and gold whatnots, and I had a couple of archaeology pointy-heads over from the University of Gloucestershire to investigate, and they declared it the greatest find since Sutton Hoo – but they spent so long fannying around with their little trowels and brushes that I couldn't be bothered with having them on my land any longer, and I sold the whole lot to a scrap metal dealer.

Anyway, that is why I haven't been doing much writing recentl but I'm back in the kitchen now, trying to leaven your stodgy prose with my pithy, juicy wit and perfectly cut *bon mots.*

Over to you.

Yours sincerely,
Major St. John Trevelyan.

Hellcat Manor
Great Trundleford
Devon
April 5th 2021

Dear Major,

Thank you for that sanitised version of what happened to you in the Bolivian jail, but if you expect me to believe that Jesús didn't make you his prison wife then you also believe I was born yesterday. I saw his tormented reaction when you were released, hurling himself against the electric fence in tears, calling out your name over and over again. And as I put you in the car, he tore off his shirt, revealing a crudely inked image of your scowling face across his chest. That tattoo was not only his tribute, but a warning to others that you were one of his untouchables. Jesús sure did love you, and I think you loved him too.

Anyway, let's move on.

CHAPTER 3
THE CASINO UNDER THE SEA

Prison can change a man. I don't know what happened to Trevelyan in that cage, locked up for twenty-four hours a day with only Jesús and his sex-disciples as company, but there was a paler fire burning behind those eyes than in the man I used to know. I stared at his big bovine head, all brow bone and jowls, vibrating under the rotor blades, and I imagined myself as Dr Frankenstein regarding his monster. He was a mess. He was at least seventy per cent scar tissue. His hair was long, lank and greasy. His shaggy greying, beard was knotted in clumps, stuck together with what I hoped was old *salteñas* dough but could have been anything. He hadn't washed in weeks. He reeked. Titus didn't seem to mind, and spent the whole journey grooming him fondly, picking things from his scalp and beard, but as we helicoptered to La Paz I made sure to sit as far away as I could with the window wide open. Inhaling in his presence was like a smack in the face from a glove of ammonia.

"Old friend, what have they done to you?" I murmured. Trevelyan just stared out of the window.

"You look well," I lied.

"I'm fine," he lied back.

"But we'll need to get you cleaned up before we go to the Club," I said, "Aram Atsi won't let you in looking like that."

We spent the next day in the hotel suite where I'd stationed Cacahuete. Buffing Trevelyan up was a big job. I went down to breakfast and returned to a string of angry Mexican expletives coming from the bathroom. Trevelyan's beard was like wire wool. It had blunted three razors and Cacahuete's best machete. I could tell Trevelyan's manservant felt guilty for allowing his master to get himself into this condition. He stalked out of the bathroom declaring he was going to get a cheese grater from the market. I asked him why.

"For the cheese," he declared, darkly.

I decided to leave them to it and made contact with Summerville, who had been appointed acting M.O.S since Tiberius Lunk was shot by Sayonara Fang. Four years later, he was still in recovery, paralysed from the waist down. It was unclear whether he'd ever make it back to the Club.

Summerville had some new intelligence for us. Hansclapp had been spotted at the blackjack tables of the Casino de Monte-Carlo, our first sighting of him since the terrible events of Morocco. She gave us the green light to take him out.

I asked a lot of Baxter: he was to take Titus back to Hellcat without me. I couldn't bring him to an undercover operation at the casino because the lights and sounds would have caused him to have one of his wobbles. Also, he was underage. Also, he was a thirty-five stone gorilla.

Baxter reacted to this request with his trademark stoicism, but I could see he wasn't happy. I decided to get them, and Cacahuete, tickets on the Concorde flight from JFK as a special treat. To my knowledge, Titus remains the only gorilla to have travelled faster than the speed of sound, although the pilot had to slow down and drop altitude for the last part of the flight as Titus fractured a window when he wasn't allowed to wear the Captain's hat.

The following morning, I met Trevelyan in the hotel lobby. His hair had been washed and cut. His beard had been removed and he now sported a handsome moustache as thick as a lump of moss. He was clean, suited, booted and semi-civilised again.

I nodded my appreciation as he lumbered across the floor. "Good to have you back, Major," I said, shaking his hand.

Trevelyan cleared his throat. "When the time comes to put an end to Hansclapp," his voice sounded unnaturally light as if he'd practiced this, "and if circumstances allow, I would like to kill him myself."

After what happened to Anais, I felt this was a reasonable request.

CASINO DE MONTE-CARLO, JULY 1971

We arrived in Monte Carlo the following day. Now that I'd sorted Trevelyan out my attention drifted back towards my own well-being. On the face of it I was fine. But my affable, urbane disposition masked a dark mood that I couldn't shake. The moment the suite door shut behind me I dropped my bags, ripped my jacket off, tapped up a vein and began to sail the moon.

How had it come to this? In recent months, I'd become well acquainted with the Scoundrels Club pharmacologist, Porcelain Jim, a pale stick of a man, not a member, who spent much of his time in the lobby reading old copies of *Oz Magazine* and waiting for members to look him up. Jim had something for everyone. When Maurice Johncocktosen broke his wrist lifting weights in the Gymnasium, Jim gave him a semi-synthetic opioid he called *krokodil*, a homebrew of painkillers, iodine, industrial bleach and the red phosphorus from matchheads. Maurice was back pumping iron the very next day, achieving a PB on the snatch and jerk, despite his radius snapping and spearing through the skin of his forearm. It took him a further sixteen weeks in a Thai monastery to kick the krokodil habit. Similarly, Joan the Coat Check Lady complained of having 'a bit of a headache'. Jim appeared with a plastic funnel, some lubricant and a gram of an unlicensed scopolamine derivative. Joan's headache disappeared, but so did all feeling below her waist for the next eighteen months.

When I mentioned to Jim that I was experiencing some emotions after a difficult undertaking, he slapped me on the shoulder in solidarity and prescribed me some good, old-fashioned Horse. Heroin, as pure as the driven snow. At first it worked wonders, allowing me to take my mind off my lost goddaughter and function as the exceptional operator I was. However, when I later discovered that Jim smuggled the drugs intra-anally, injecting the sticky brown residue began to lose its sheen. It was too late though, I was hooked. But I promised myself that after this hit I'd start to wind it down. We had a man to kill.

If there was a list of the world's greatest casinos, the Casino de Monte-Carlo would be number one. This is where the real high rollers come to play.

I'd been once or twice before, most notably in '62, in the company of a certain Mrs Marjorie Trevelyan. St. John had asked me to chaperone his new wife, who wanted to indulge in a shopping weekend. I'd agreed as I was anxious to try out my new Cessna 205 and the 1000km trip was right at the edge of the aircraft's range. Besides, I could hardly refuse. I felt sorry for the poor bastard. Those first few weeks of marriage to Marjorie hit him like a ton of bricks, and he needed the weekend off.

As we touched down, Marjorie demanded we head for the casino immediately. I'd had no idea gambling was her poison, but I soon learned that she was terrible at it. It was almost as if she was trying to lose. We sat down at a Fr. 5000 blackjack table, and within twenty minutes she'd racked up a colossal loss and only quit when I called Trevelyan to check if he was happy to underwrite Nimbu against her mounting losses. When I explained to him that she kept hitting on 19 they had an angry exchange, and her credit was cut. Marjorie karate-chopped the pit boss in the windpipe and stormed out in a rage to go shopping instead, where she spent over three million francs on fur stoles – all of which she ended up leaving on the beach. It was a very entertaining weekend all round, but I came back from it feeling even more sorry for Trevelyan.

We entered the casino around nine. The central gaming room was stunning, a Belle-Époque monument to the god of greed. Marble pillars, dark wood panelling, gilded mirrors and elaborate frescos adorned the walls and ceiling. It was like the Sistine Chapel, if the Sistine

Chapel had been designed to wow you into emptying your pockets of everything you had.

Four chandeliers framed a vast stained-glass window that looked down from two storeys above the baize tables, covering everything in a glittering, sparkling light. Shapely hostesses glided around with trays, while discreet security personnel drifted, posing as guests. And all under the watchful eye of the Director of Operations, a burnished chap with a suntan darker than his dark suit. His easy smile and open demeanour were draped over him, a lie as thin and smooth as silk, masking the ruthlessness of a system which would fleece you before handing you concrete boots in exactly your size and directing you to the quayside.

The centre of the room was dominated by a roulette wheel where a chunky fellow in loose fitting robes was playing to the great excitement of those around him. A stack of ten thousand franc plaques were piled up on his table, a sign of a successful session. He was surrounded by beautiful women and nervous flunkies, who flittered around him like butterflies. He was clearly a regular, some kind of powerful potentate or sheik.

We watched as the man shunted his entire stack of plaques across the table, indicating he wanted all on red. The croupier moved the silver dolly to confirm his choice. The wheel turned once more. All eyes were on the small white ball as it rattled around, skipping from one pocket to the next. A moment's pause and then a few sharp intakes of breath, followed by a smattering of applause. The croupier smiled warmly and handed the man twice the chips back, before apologising as he pulled a black cloth over the table to suspend play while the table was re-stocked. The man had broken the bank, well, at least this table's bank, but he barely reacted, as if this happened most nights. Perhaps it did. He picked up his highball, like a fairground bauble in his hairy fist, and downed it.

"A big fish," I murmured to Trevelyan. "If Hansclapp's making connections, it would be with a man like him, don't you think?"

At the mention of our adversary's name Trevelyan's eyes flashed, but he shook his head, and gave me a broad smile to show me he was on point.

"Agreed. A good place to start."

The Director of Operations appeared at our side. "Bonsoir, Messieurs," he oozed. "Is this your first time at the Casino de Monte-Carlo?"

"Alas, it's been too long since we were here last," I said.

"Well, I'm sure you will make up for it today. Is there a game that I can direct you towards? Perhaps the roulette wheel?"

"If you can guarantee us the same luck as the last gentleman."

"Ah, Mr Badda Ladin, one of our most esteemed guests. If you have only a fraction of his success, you'll leave here happy."

"Perhaps his good fortune might rub off on us." Trevelyan was jovial. "And how would one sit down with Mr Badda Ladin?"

"I'm afraid that is not possible tonight, sir. Mister Badda Ladin is on his way to our private rooms."

"Perhaps another night," I said.

"Enjoy your evening, gentlemen." The Director of Operations bowed and walked away. Oh well. Time to put some effort in. Trevelyan and I needed to start thumping down some significant chunks of change if we were to be taken seriously.

"Let's get cracking," I slapped Trevelyan on the back, and we took a couple of high stools at the nearest vingt-un table. I pulled out a handful of plastic chips, each worth Fr. 500 and a smaller stack of plaques, of Fr. 2500 each. I ordered a gimlet and nodded to the croupier that I'd be opening two boxes. Trevelyan pulled out a thick wad of French banknotes and tossed them in casually. The croupier spread them out neatly across the table and pushed a tower of chips over to him.

Playing in tandem over four boxes, we stayed at the table for an hour, our chips and plaques steadily stacking up. Trevelyan was at the last two boxes, and had been employing a simple, low-level card count, the sort of thing that's easy to do while talking loudly, joking and flirting with the waitresses. He kept a mental note of each shoe's low value cards, subtracting this count from the picture cards and aces as they were dealt. Whenever the count reached +8 with only a few hands left to play, we'd quadruple our bets, knowing that picture cards favour the gambler. Done over an hour or two this technique would turn a small profit. More to the point, it would grab the house's attention. I made sure to clap Trevelyan on the back and celebrate boisterously whenever he won a lump – and when he doubled down on a quadruple bet, I hooted loudly and sloshed gin all over the tubby American to my right.

Our cheating and exuberance were designed to make us just enough of a pain for the house to move us on. Sure enough, a demure lady in a little black dress placed a gentle hand on my shoulder. "Your luck seems to be in tonight, Messieurs. The Director has asked whether you will play at one of our more exciting tables?"

Trevelyan was tallying up our winnings so far – Fr.500,000. About fifty thousand in sterling. Not a king's ransom, but a lump the casino wouldn't mind having back.

"How kind. I think we would," I grinned.

"Then follow me," she said.

We moved through double doors into a *salon privé*. Elegant plasterwork, lots of gilt. A red carpet so thick it was like walking through a summer meadow. A stunning, blonde hostess stood by with a fresh pair of gin and tonics for us on a silver tray, which we ignored, demanding instead a bottle of Krug '58 if they had it, and '61 if they didn't. A croupier with slicked back hair and a firm jawline was already standing at our personal table. "Bonsoir," he smarmed, "the table minimum is ten thousand francs."

"In that case," I said, "we'd better bring out the big guns." From my trouser pockets I pulled out sheaf of bearer bonds, which were spirited away, and within three minutes, they'd been replaced with a stack of chips worth three million francs.

The croupier cracked his knuckles and dumped four virgin packs of cards onto the baize, smushing them around the table with his hands in random sweeps. He then stacked the cards up again and proceeded to execute the house shuffle. He must have learned this in the womb, so quickly and efficiently was it performed.

"*Alors,* 'ow many boxes would Monsieur like to open?" he enquired.

Trevelyan looked at me, frowning. I shrugged noncommittally, lighting one of a small stock of *Double Downs,* a sweet aromatic borazjan tombac blended with sugar, which the Scoundrels tobacconist had knocked up for chancing one's arm.

"I think tonight we will play just one hand."

"Just one hand?" asked the croupier, surprised.

"For everything we have," I confirmed.

The croupier gave us a wolfish smile. "You are all-or-nothing gentlemen," he observed.

"You are quite correct," said Trevelyan, pinching a cigarette from me.

The croupier dealt the cards.

Ace for us.

Ten for the dealer.

Another ace for us.

Tricky.

To properly play this hand against the house's ten, I would need to split the aces and hope he drew tens on top of each. But this would cost us the same stake again.

"Split the aces, please," I said.

"But you have already staked all," said the croupier. "'Ow will you cover this bet?"

I held his gaze while Trevelyan rummaged in his pocket for a small velvet drawstring bag. He loosened the string and upended the bag. A waterfall of sparkling rocks fell soundlessly onto the baize.

The croupier nodded to an unobtrusive gentleman who was standing in a corner of the room. This man disappeared and came back presently with a tiny, balding appraiser, who screwed a loupe into his eye and plucked a diamond from the table with a pair of long tweezers.

"For ze same bet again, I suggest twelve of these diamonds," said the little man.

"I suggest something else," I said.

"Oh?" said the man.

"I suggest all of these diamonds as the second part of the bet," I eyeballed the man, "and if we win, you take us to the real salon privé."

The appraiser shrugged. "But Monsieur, zis is ze salon privé."

Trevelyan chipped in, scoffing, "don't take us for fools," he said. "We're not American tourists. Stop pissing around and show us where the real action is."

The appraiser's eyes burst into life. Trying to keep the smirk from his mouth, he replied, "Monsieur is well informed. There is one other room we keep for very special players…"

"We rather thought so," said Trevelyan.

"…and so let us see what happens." The appraiser slipped out from behind the table and stepped to the side to observe. The croupier counted out twelve diamonds, and then the other eighteen. He smoothed his hands together as if washing them and then held them apart to indicate to the closed-circuit television monitors overhead that he was holding nothing back.

He split the aces and placed the pile of diamonds behind the second ace.

He drew us a card – a king – and placed it on the first bet with the mountain of chips.

"Vingt-un," he called.

He drew another card, a queen, and placed that on top of our second ace. "Vingt-un," he said again, this time with a note of congratulation in his voice.

He flipped over the house's second card, a ten. "And vingt for the 'ouse," he said, evenly. "And 'ow would you like your winnings?"

I scooped up the diamonds and dropped them back into the velvet bag. "Biscuits, please," I said, smiling. The croupier began to tally up million-franc plaques.

It was only then that the champagne – the '58 – arrived. While it was opened, and a couple of glasses poured, a statuesque redhead in a silver Yves Saint Laurent cocktail dress approached. The dress only went down about as far as the girl's waist, revealing a pair of impossibly long legs in six-inch stiletto heels.

"Sirs, for le *vrai* salon privé," she said, coquettishly.

"That's right," I said, devouring her with my eyes.

"Then follow me, please," she said, over her shoulder, as she headed for a heavy velvet-lined door.

Trevelyan went to scoop up my winnings – a magnificent pile of thick discs – but the girl had other ideas. "Oh no, sir, we'll cash that out for you. You can collect it later from the desk."

"But we'll need a stake, surely?" he queried.

The woman only smiled. "Not necessary. Just follow me."

The velvet door led us out of the casino and into the warm Mediterranean night air. As we descended the steps a smart black golf buggy pulled to a halt for us. Trevelyan and I got into the back. The driver, a lithe Korean girl in a peaked cap and stamped on the accelerator. We sped away, negotiating narrow paths and tunnels at a breakneck pace until we arrived at a jetty just south of the Monaco Yacht Club. Here a host of luxury yachts were moored, and at the very end of the quay an impressive grey superyacht stood alone.

We could hear the muffled sounds of a party, but not on deck. The noise was coming from deep inside the vessel. This was where the real action was happening. The buggy stopped in front of a gangplank.

We were led onto deck and down a flight of stairs into an access corridor on the maintenance deck. I could detect the stench of marine diesel. We passed a galley stuffed with bawling chefs. Steam billowed out along with the aroma of boiling lobster. Our redhead ushered us down a steel staircase. As we descended to the hull, I noted a subtle shift in the sound. Our footfalls began to echo off the steel walls. We were now under the waterline.

"This way please," she said, leading us along an access corridor, narrow and unadorned. Every few metres we stepped through openings in the bulkhead each sentried by a heavy steel door, reminiscent of a submarine. Incongruously, we stopped at a plush red velvet curtain draped across the entire corridor. A broad gentleman in black tie unclipped a red velvet rope.

Our host turned to us and smiled, "the *real* salon privé, gentlemen. I do hope you enjoy yourselves." She parted the curtain and rotated a large locking wheel. With a metallic grind the heavy door opened.

I crossed the threshold with a swagger, wanting to make a strong impression, straight into a tiny, dimly lit chamber with curved walls of polished steel, like an elongated egg standing on its end. Trevelyan cannoned into me, expecting the space to be larger than it actually was, pushing me against a seamless curved window of toughened glass. Through this window, the water was faintly illuminated, allowing us a view of the sea life outside. But the fish might well have been gawping at us, for we were penned into this tiny room, while they had the whole ocean in which to swim. Our whole space was barely a metre and a half in circumference, entirely bare except for a battered wooden chest on the floor. The floor itself was a tight steel mesh that creaked as we shifted our weight. There was a conspicuous lack of gaming equipment. Surely, we were in the wrong place? I scanned the room to see if it led anywhere else. It didn't. This was it.

Trevelyan had already turned back to leave, but the door was immovable. "Cornwall," he gasped, "we're trapped."

I didn't answer.

Somebody else did. It was a horribly familiar voice. "Major Cornwall, Major Trevelyan, welcome to my gaming room."

At that moment, a light came on to reveal that the top half of our chamber formed a glass viewing gallery two feet above our heads. The design was ingenious, it sloped inwards to allow for a perfect view down onto us.

Gruber Hansclapp gazed down. "What are the odds, gentlemen, that you should find your way to my casino under the sea?"

Trevelyan could barely contain himself. His fists were squeezed so tight they were bloodless.

"You came here to gamble for high stakes," Hansclapp sneered, "and now we will gamble for the highest stakes of all – your lives." He lifted a coupe of champagne to us and called out. "Place your bets please!"

Now we could see Hansclapp was hosting a party of his own. More faces appeared looking down at us, and soon it was as crowded as the Royal Box at Ascot. Hansclapp's guests were glitzy and glamorous. Fabulous bare-shouldered blondes on the arms of flubbery-lipped aristos, braying and swilling Krug as they leered down at us. Chips began to change hands with great enthusiasm. From our low perspective, it was tricky to see exactly, but I thought I recognised one or two guests.

There was Idi Amin, chuckling merrily with Warren Beatty, as if they hadn't a care in the world. Which they hadn't. My old friend General Manuel Noriega was there. As younger men, we'd once spent a glorious day at Lords watching Len Hutton smack the Aussies around for 145, yet here he was, mad-eyed and gee'd up, snorting angel dust from the cleavage of a horse-faced gal who may have been Princess Margaret.

"No more bets," sang Hansclapp, and I could see how much he was enjoying himself. Frantically I looked for a weak spot in the design of our egg-like prison, but there was nothing to break, and nothing to break it with.

The lights in the viewing gallery dimmed and a silence descended on the party above. Then there was an odd sound, as if a cork had been removed from a bottle. A sudden spring of water, an inch across, issued forth from the wall at fantastic pressure, and swilled around our feet. Trevelyan immediately put his hand against the flow, but the water spurted from beneath it. I could hear laughter from the viewing gallery. Sammy Davis Jr. raised a glass to us, wobbled his head and winked.

We scanned the room for inspiration. The chest on the floor must have been there for a reason. I kicked open the lid. Inside were several wooden wedges and a mallet.

"Here!" I chucked Trevelyan a wedge, and he jammed it into the crack. I hammered it firmly in place.

The water stopped.

There was applause from above.

"We've got to get out of here," I said.

"Win the game, gentlemen," Hansclapp's voice said from above, "and you win your freedom. Lose the game, and you drown."

To my left, a second water jet opened up, wider this time, perhaps three inches across, punching me in the chest. Trevelyan scrambled for a larger wooden wedge and threw it to me, but before I could jam it in the gap another leak had sprung from behind us. Then another. And another. And another. How many wedges did we have? Trevelyan and I worked quickly to bung up the holes but soon we were standing in ankle-deep water. Each time we thought we'd done it, another hole appeared, until we'd used up all the wedges.

Another jet. No more wedges. Trevelyan looked at me, aghast. The water had reached our calves. "Shoes!" I suggested.

He was already twisting his leather brogue into the gushing hole. But the pressure was too much, and the shoe was forced back out. "It needs to create a seal, or it won't stick," shouted Trevelyan above the noise of the torrent.

In desperation, I waded across and jammed my left hand deep into the hole, right up to the wrist. The water stopped flowing.

Immediately, another jet opened up, and Trevelyan stuffed his right arm into it. Now we were both stuck fast to the walls of this unspeakably devious drowning pit, unable to move our arms. Another jet opened up, this time spurting across the rising surface of the water, which was now at our knees.

Gritting my teeth, I balanced on my left leg and jammed my right foot inside it, making a seal just above my ankle. Then another jet opened up, near Trevelyan's left side, requiring his left fist through it. Another. Trevelyan jammed his right foot into this one. We were both now pinned, with no free limbs, in this horrific game of *Twister*.

I looked up to the viewing gallery and the faces leered back. Was this it? Had the game finished? We'd bunged up all the holes. Everything was being utilised.

But then another leak burst through, a couple of

inches in diameter, at Trevelyan's waist. The water fired in a powerful jet straight at the crotch of his trousers. He let out a cry of alarm. He looked at me desperately. "Do something, Cornwall!" he called.

But I couldn't do anything. I was trapped, just as he was. The water cannoned into his crotch, raising the water level higher. The game was obviously rigged so we'd lose.

Or was it?

I had a glimmer of an idea. It was so grim that I barely dared suggest it, but… "There is one option," I shouted over the rushing water. Trevelyan was never one to catch on quickly, but I knew he'd get there eventually…

And so it proved.

His face rumpled like an untacked carpet and a pained expression advanced across it. His mouth contorted and he roared. A full blooded, 4.7 litre twin-turbo V8 engine holler of despair. The kind of sound I'd not heard since racing *Busty Barbara,* my AC Cobra at Le Mans.

"There's no other way, Trevelyan," I grimaced. "Drop your trousers! You're going to have to stick your old chap in."

Above us, I saw Hansclapp clinking glasses with the lady who definitely could have been Princess Margaret. He was laughing at some private joke she'd made, her magnificent front teeth glinting with the same brilliance as her diamond earrings.

Trevelyan swore and unplugged his right hand to undo his fly. Water spurted from the hole he'd been covering. After releasing himself and positioning his hips over the waist high aperture, he jammed his hand back, stemming the flow once more.

Nothing changed. The water level continued to rise. Trevelyan seemed troubled.

"What's the problem?" I asked, awkwardly.

He cleared his throat. "I'm having some trouble," he said. I could barely hear him over the sound of the gushing water.

Then he murmured something else.

"Say that again?"

He looked to the floor and winced. "I said it's not big enough!"

There came the sound of laughter from the gallery above. I turned my head, to see what was going on. The water was still jetting out from the hole in Trevelyan's crotch, billowing through his trousers and forcing them down, revealing his bare arse.

"Look, it's nothing to be ashamed of, but if you need me to do it…" I said, earnestly, trying to keep the strain out of my voice.

"No! No. If we swap, we'll let too much water in. I've got this. I just need to focus."

I waited expectantly as the water level crept up. I didn't want to interrupt his train of thought at this critical juncture. After a while Trevelyan cleared his throat and said, rather sheepishly, "No. That hasn't worked. I think I'm going to need your help."

I went numb for a moment.

"It seems to me we've got no option, Victor," he said. I did not enjoy him suddenly using my first name, "And I know you're not going to like it."

I kept silent.

"I wish there was another way," he lamented, turning his massive, thuggish head, streaked with grime and sweat, fixing me with blood-shot eyes, "but you're going to have to arouse me."

I've never been a religious man, but I beseeched the Lord, asking him, "hath I done something to anger thee?"

To his credit, Trevelyan was resolute. He'd been man enough to blurt out his plan, however horrendous it was, and he was suddenly overcome with a manic intensity I'd only ever seen in him once before, years ago when I uncovered his lie about de-flowering Big Maureen, the dinner lady who worked the Winstowe pudding hatch.

"Arouse me, man! Our lives depend on it!" he screamed.

"Tell me there's another way!"

The water continued to rise. "Listen," he pleaded, "this is a survival situation. Like on Dartmoor manoeuvres, when Captain Shelldrake got into Archie Bennett's sleeping bag against the threat of hypothermia."

"They were lovers, you fool! That was a ruse," I said.

"Oh, whatever. Just get this done. Arouse me!"

The water was now lapping my thighs, and still I hesitated. I simply didn't know where to start.

"Look, Cornwall," he said, "if this freezing water gets any higher, it's going to prove impossible to achieve a sustained erec–"

"–Dear God, I cannot believe it's come to this," I cut him off. "Very well."

I reached across to take hold of him. Water gushed out from the hole my hand had been plugging.

"Keep your hand in the hole!" he said.

"Then how?"

"You're going to have to do it aurally."

I misheard this and shook my head. "Never going to happen."

"No, I said 'aurally'."

"What!?" At that moment, I welcomed the prospect of drowning.

"Look, I'm revealing a lot about myself here, Cornwall," he said. "So just go with it. I need you to talk dirty. It gets me going like nothing else."

"I see," I said.

Then he added. "Talk to me in the earthy accents of North England. I like brassy, Northern women. Like the ones on television who wear tight, leopard-skin print."

"I understand," I said.

"There's one more thing."

"Go on."

Trevelyan was suddenly bashful, conscious of the spectators above us. This was clearly some admission he was about to make. "You'll have to insult me. Make me feel small."

"You've got to be kidding." There was more laughter from the viewing gallery.

"Come on, Cornwall! I need you to make me feel pathetic."

I sighed heavily. This was a truly dreadful way to check out. Drowned while trying to maintain Trevelyan's lob-on. The Times obituary writer would have a field day. I couldn't let it happen... I'd rather die.

And yet I did have form in this area. My sweet nothings were the stuff of legend. During the War I was famed for my saucy radio exchanges with bored WAAF radio operators during the long flights back to Blighty. These interference strewn dialogues would often result in cross-channel frig-offs, earning me the nickname *The Minge Whisperer*. But this wasn't a winsome gal in a tight-fitting uniform I was talking to. It was Trevelyan. A lump of dunce about as erotic as a bowl of vegetable soup. Moreover, I wasn't really in the mood, but in the spirit of saving our lives:

"Ooooh, by 'eck," I said unconvincingly, "yerra big fat twat."

Trevelyan opened his eyes. "What was that?"

"Northern."

"No, no, no. You'll have to be much more specific. Raise your game Cornwall," he shouted over the rushing water, "or we're dead."

Above my head glimpsed Hansclapp chinking glasses with Ernest Borgnine.

I realised I needed to separate myself from the process and treat it as a role. A memory popped into my head. I was back at Winstowe in the Upper VI, performing in the final year revue. We'd put on a daring modern version of *Othello,* set in a Scunthorpe builders' merchants. My Othello sent a shockwave through the school, not least because of my refusal to wear blackface. Instead, I subverted the role, opting to *white-up* in Chanel's *Le Blanc* foundation, and played the Moor as a middle-class albino hod-carrier. If I could just channel that sort of intensity into this new role, then I might just be able to save us both. I cleared my throat and started off somewhere around Birmingham.

"C'm 'ere, yow big saft babby," I said in my best Black Country accent. Trevelyan wasn't amused.

"That's the Midlands, Cornwall! I said Northern!"

"Where exactly?"

"I'll know when I hear it."

I closed my eyes and visualised a map of England, until the image was strong enough to navigate around the industrial towns and cities that make up our great Northern powerhouse, the proud heart and pumping lungs of the nation. Somewhere on the stark moors, windswept hills and rolling, fecund dales lay the secret to giving Trevelyan the stonker that would save us from drowning.

I stamped an imaginary red cross on Birmingham to rule it out and scrolled north-east, towards Sheffield. I leaned in towards him until our heads were almost touching, then whispered breathily into his ear.

"I've been tekkin it from t'purrstie when yuv been owt t'werk, yer big fat bass-tad."

Trevelyan made a peculiar groan.

"Yuv nivver dun 'arf wh't 't' big fooker does to us, ee's a real man, and no mistek…"

Trevelyan went quiet for a bit. I made a few guttural moans and groans as a placeholder while I thought about what to say next.

"Well done, keep going," said Trevelyan, before adding, "but go further North."

This was a nightmare. I moved across the map north-westwards, until I settled on Liverpool. "Ayy lad. Wa' do yous' call dat? Me gran's gorra bigger chopper than da'! There's nott'n there!"

"That's Scouse! Not Scouse!" he said, angrily shaking his head.

I scrolled right to Manchester and gave it a shot. "You don't get 'owt for nowt so put wood int' 'ole and jiggle it about yer big fookin' lummox!"

Trevelyan murmured. "Further North, damn you!"

I scrolled north-east until I landed on Newcastle. "Why aye man! Am gannin' doon the toon tha' neet. Yas can bang us roond back a tha' Tesco, if yee leek…"

Trevelyan made a slight facial movement. "That's it! What was that?"

"Newcastle."

"I think you've found it. Now insult me."

"Yas' pathetic, man! Yas a reet mammy's lad."

"Go on!"

"Yas' a useless fat wanka, man."

Trevelyan went very quiet. The water flow started to slow. It seemed to be working, so I channelled my inner Geordie lass. "How'way man! Why yer still on tha' slack? Ai've gorra reet doonsterrs treat fer yer when yer fookin' good ta go."

Trevelyan's hips began to move rhythmically back and forth. It revolted every single fibre of my being, but I had to keep going. "Ahm ganin tuh invite a load iv squaddies owor ta uurrrs, an' myek yee watch while ah nosh 'em aaaaalllll."

The water stopped rising. Trevelyan was in the zone and panting heavily. The question was, how long would

I have to keep him going like this? I looked up to gallery for any sign.

"COME ON!" I pleaded, to the spectators. "WE DID IT!"

There was no reply from the viewing gallery. The braying and champagne guzzling had stopped. The people I could see looking down on us were now stony-faced.

Trevelyan made a desperate sound, "Cornwall, I'm losing it…"

"Yer a shandy-drinking Suthern shite, an ah sometimes frig me-sel off, proper mint, thinking aboot aaal yor friends from wark."

I looked up again and yelled to the heavens, "WE'VE STOPPED THE WATER. LET US GO!" before turning back to Trevelyan, "Ahm preggars, an' ah divvint evan knar if yas'es the fathar."

Nothing from the viewing gallery.

I was running out of material and piled into Trevelyan with whatever I could think of. "Ahm leavin yee fo' a bord cos hor dick is biggor than yoors."

With that, there was the sound of a gear releasing below us, and the water drained away through the grille on the floor. Within seconds it was gone. I pulled my arms from the holes and collapsed panting with the exertion of the last few minutes.

There was the sound of slow clapping from above. The lights blinked back on. The guests had departed, but Hansclapp was alone at the window, with a glass of champagne, which he raised malevolently. "You can put yourself away now, Trevelyan," he said, with the hint of a smile behind his shark-like eyes. "Thank you for a wonderfully diverting evening's entertainment."

I looked over at Trevelyan, spark out in the dregs of water, trousers still around his ankles. My eyes were drawn to his nether parts. I didn't know if, as he collapsed, he'd snagged his old lad on the lip of the metal hole, but it looked in terrible shape – bruised, battered, a drowned rat that had been beaten to death with a length of rusty pipe.

Above us the lights went out again.

And like that, Hansclapp was gone.

Major, in the spirit of accuracy and objectivity that informs all of my writing, I know you won't begrudge me detailing your most private inclinations. Besides, it was life or death in that terrible undersea casket, and it was your *membrum virile* that got us through. In fact, and you'll enjoy this, you might even say that we were saved by your bell.

Yours sincerely,
Major Victor Montgomery Cornwall

Nimbu Towers
Pullen-under-Lyme
Gloucestershire
April 20th 2021

Dear Major,

Oh, how you have seized with both hands the opportunity to make my personal predilections public. Just what I expect of you. Yes, I find northern brassiness powerfully erotic. Yes, I respect strong women who can drink ten pints of bitter and stand up to relieve themselves at the men's urinal if the queue for the ladies' is too long. Big deal. Move with the times, man! It has probably passed an old codger like you by, but we now live in an age where the only sin is embarrassment.

Besides, that incident furnished us with some very useful intelligence. Hansclapp's mistake was to let us get a sense of the social circles he moved in, and when you're dealing with sharp bastards like us, that's fatal. We were back on his trail…

…to Maljeria.

CHAPTER 4
THE FIRST XV

SUMMERVILLE'S OFFICE, SCOUNDRELS CLUB, 1973

Summerville was puzzled. She rubbed her eyes wearily. "So that's the whole story," she queried. "There's nothing you've missed out?"

"Er, no. I think that covers it. We used all of the wooden bungs, won the game and the water drained away," I said.

Summerville knew we were keeping something from her but had decided it wasn't important. "Very well. Your adventures gave me some interesting insights – especially the famous names you mentioned. I've liaised with the French Immigration Office to confirm they were in Monaco that day."

Cornwall chipped in, "Noriega?"

"Yes. He was there. Visiting his aunt."

"Idi Amin?"

"Plays golf with Warren Beatty. Thick as thieves."

"And Sammy Davis Jnr?"

"Just loves to hang out with dictators, apparently."

"So very different from his stage persona," said Cornwall, who was a huge Sammy fan.

"Anyway, this means I have a new undertaking for you."

"Sign me up," said Cornwall bullishly, but

Summerville ignored him. She was looking at me. "I understand you used to play a bit of rugby?"

I shrugged. "Loose head prop forward."

Cornwall snorted in derision. "If he ever made the team."

Summerville slipped on a pair of tortoiseshell spectacles and picked up a yellowing newspaper folded to the sports pages. "At yesterday's Winstowe-Eton match," she read, "'front row replacement Arthur St. John Trevelyan made a notable impact late in the game when he received a skaddling ball on the halfway line and ignored his own sprained ankle to beat six men and heave himself over the try line. The final score was 22-20 to Winstowe.' Sounds like you know your way around a rugby field."

"I had my moments, I suppose," I said.

"Wait a minute, I was captain for that game," whined Cornwall. He looked thoroughly put out. "Trevelyan only played the last ten minutes! I passed him the bloody ball that led to the try!"

"Well, it's quite telling that under your stewardship Winstowe was losing," remarked Summerville.

Cornwall spluttered. Summerville ignored him. She reached under her desk and spun a rugby ball at me. I reflexively trapped it with one hand against my forehead.

"A lot is going to rest on your shoulders," she said, "now that you are captain of the Scoundrels First XV."

"What?" Cornwall was incredulous. "C'mon, Summerville," he railed. "It's ridiculous to put St. John in charge of a rugby team. He doesn't even know the rules."

"Laws," she corrected, "and I can't see your name anywhere on this report, Cornwall. As I was saying," she turned back to me, "your little gambling trip gave us a lead." She held up a photograph of the North African high-roller we'd seen at Monte-Carlo.

"Mr Badda Ladin," I said. "Who exactly is he?"

"He's a good, old-fashioned dictator – of the People's Republic of Maljeria. A real piece of work, he likes to experiment with chemical weapons on his own people."

Summerville produced a folder of aerial photographs and spread them on her desk. "We think these funnels here," she explained, "pin-point the underground lab where he develops new concoctions. Now that we can put him with Hansclapp it starts to resonate."

"Bosphorus Phosphorus," I breathed.

"Precisely. My working hypothesis is that this lab has been purpose-built for express manufacture."

Cornwall was still a little huffy. "So why not just borrow a B52 from the Yanks and bomb it to smithereens?"

"We can't afford to start a war, Cornwall. Whatever we do needs to be on the quiet. It can't look like the UK is behind it."

"So, what are you thinking?" I asked her, "Poison? A riding accident? A disloyal bodyguard shoots him in the face?"

"We're certainly going to do for Badda Ladin," she confirmed, "but Whitehall's feeling is an assassination will make him a martyr and there'll be an instant replacement from his extended family, cut from the same cloth. That won't do. We must make it seem as if the Maljerian people have risen up and overthrown him, so the F.O. can step in and help form a new democracy."

"You want to stage a revolution?" I'd never fomented a revolution before, not since I was in the Remove at Winstowe, when Mashie-Niblick and I got onto the roof of the Tuck Shop to campaign for larger helpings of mashed potato. It hadn't ended well. He'd fallen through a skylight and suffered a sucking chest wound after landing on a box of liquorice sticks.

Summerville swept back a lock of raven hair that had escaped her Alice band. "I've an idea how to light the touch paper with the people of Maljeria," she mused, "but it's risky."

"Any thoughts on how we get into the country?" I asked. "If we don't have a good cover, we'll be snatched by his secret police in the arrivals lounge and fed to the desert gophers."

"Yes, you're right. Badda Ladin's a paranoid bugger. If I sent the pair of you in as oil executives, he'd see through it, but he does have one weakness."

"What?"

"Rugby. He's an absolute fanatic. He became obsessed with it since he was up at Oxford. He wants to make it the national game of Maljeria. Trouble is he's got some way to go before the grassroots game takes off, on account of all the malnutrition and disease his people contend with." She gestured to the same photograph. "Now look at this."

She pointed out an oval structure close to the funnels.

"What is it?"

"Badda Ladin's new rugby stadium. He's inviting first string clubs from all over the world to play the Maljerian XV."

"And that's where I come in," I said tossing the rugby ball into the air.

"Exactly," nodded Summerville. "I've secured a fixture between the Maljerians and the Cavaliers."

"The Cavaliers?"

"Your team, St. John," smiled Summerville. "Surely you've heard of the Old Cavaliers. The Jolly Prancers. The Lucky Boys. Established in 1868. In 1932 they beat Harlequins sixty points to six. In 1954 they clobbered Saracens eighty-four to nothing. An impressive record..."

"...which you invented?" said Cornwall.

"Quite so. Ruff Puff has been inserting a long string of honours into rugby history," she said. "Last week he broke into Twickenham to carve the Cavaliers onto the boards as English Club Champions in 1917 and 1943, He's inserted fake match reports into all the newspaper archives. The Cavaliers are go," she said, sitting back in her chair. "They just need a captain. What do you say, Trevelyan? Are you up for leading this operation?"

"Of course, on one condition."

"What's that?"

"Total freedom over who is on the team sheet."

"You're the captain. It's your call," Summerville smiled. This depth charge sucked all the energy from the room.

Sudden negative pressure, with the epicentre to my left. Cornwall looked like he was going to burst as it occurred to him that he wasn't necessarily even in my team. After what seemed like an aeon, he turned to me. "Listen, old man," he said, his voice soft and passive, "you'll need a decent blind-side flanker. Happy to oblige." The look of expectation on his face was priceless. His moustache hunched up like a slug that was about to do a highdive. I couldn't resist.

"I'll get back to you," I said, and broke his gaze.

"Major Cornwall," Summerville said, "you'd better give Trevelyan and me the room. I'd like to discuss a few details. I'm sure he'll be in touch," she smiled, "should you make the cut."

Cornwall's dignity deserted him. He flounced out, slamming the door behind him. We were alone. Summerville glanced at me conspiratorially. "I rather enjoyed that," she whispered.

I offered her a *Hospital Pass*, a filterless white burley, grown near the All Blacks training station at Rangiora, that I'd had the Scoundrels tobacconist whip up for picking the best man for a job.

She opened a drawer, pulled something out, and tossed it to me. "A prototype," she said.

It was a silver medallion about the size of a thruppenny piece. I held it up to the light. On one side was an etching of a rugby player. Me. I was starring directly outwards, chest puffed out, rumpled collar, rugged and handsome but for a tight-fitting leather skull cap squashing down my brow. The obverse was perfectly smooth and slightly concave. "This is a commemorative medallion."

"I can see that." I examined the glinting circle of silver on its thin chain.

The medallion spun slowly in the shards of late afternoon sunlight slicing in through the high windows.

"I've commissioned thirty thousand of them to hand out to the stadium crowd," she said.

Suddenly it hit me. I'd always thought nobody was a match for Tiberius Lunk in terms of strategy and cunning, but Summerville had been audacious.

"D'you think you can pull it off, with only a rugby team for back-up?"

I mulled it over in my head. "Start a revolution, destroy a chemical lab and kill a dictator, while on a jolly boys' tour?" For the first time in a while I found myself enthused. "Almost too easy."

"Good," she said, licking a pencil. "So, who d'you want as your hooker?"

I leant back and considered all of the blunt instruments at my disposal.

AN HOUR LATER, SUMMERVILLE'S OFFICE, SCOUNDRELS CLUB

I left the office, team sheet in hand. Scoundrels are often pretty useful sportsmen, so there was no shortage of men who were experienced rugger players, but I needed chaps who were also proven in behind-the-lines operations, and steady. They also had to have iron constitutions and be able to sing in tune. After all, there's no good banging out a rousing chorus of *Lily the Pink* if your tenors are flat. It can really dampen the mood of a fifteen-man communal bath.

I began to reread the names as I moved down the corridor to the Gaye Bar, planning to pin up the team sheet on the fixtures board. But I felt somehow fenced in. I looked up. There were members everywhere, practically hanging from the chandeliers. Cornwall must have let the cat out of the bag. Decent undertakings had been thin on the ground recently and every Scoundrel wanted a piece of this one. I counted Duckworth, Kemp, Wazzlehurst, Vogel, Ruff Puff, Osmond Biggidy-Grid, Popsy O'Doherty, Mackelhose, Duncannon Stormington III, Ferdy Gunt, Davy Vebster-Webster, Andrew Handd-Shanddie, Eddie Klovacs, Lonnie Wilberforce Hide, Geoffrey Fastnet – I didn't know he was back from Texas, how splendid – Gar-Gar Mason, Jules Moosejoy, plus loads of younger men I hadn't bothered to learn the names of. There was even Fantohm-Waxwell, our infamous unidexter, leaning unsteadily on the banister, raising his ever-present glass of neat gin to me.

"Hullo! It's only Trevelyan," called Batty Bratwurst, barging out of the Trophy Room in an unnecessarily jovial manner. "How are you, chum? Off to the Bar? Let me stand you one." He slapped me on the back much too forcefully, as if I was choking on a lump of fillet. Batty had been a useful prop forward in his day, but he was a good five stone overweight now. Not in my team. Too fat. And too short a fuse. Why only last month he'd lost his rag at the Albery Theatre, when his mishearing of a line in Hamlet: *Tubby, or not tubby / That is the question* had caused him to leap from the stalls and smash the offending actor in the face with the nearest hard object, which happened to be Yorick's skull, causing the performance to be abandoned.

"Sorry, Batty," I said, ruefully. "Next time, eh?" The big lump's face fell a thousand miles.

As I made my way to the Gaye Bar, Sebby Lauzier, an elegant Frenchman and pretty useful fly-half, suddenly mentioned that he'd been meaning to invite me out to his gaff in Chamonix for a weekend's heli-skiing, and was this Friday any good? He gave me a playful slap on the arse and wandered off, leaving it to the fates. Maurice Johncocktosen, the tenacious soul who'd once broken into Windsor Safari Park to settle a bet about the rectal temperature of an African lion, reminded me that I owed him one hundred thousand pounds because of it. "But not necessarily," he murmured, breaking into a crude haka.

There wasn't a single Scoundrel who didn't rise to greet me with a kidney punch, back-slap or brotherly fondle. I struggled through the throng of hopefuls, into the Gaye Bar, and over to the fixtures board. I made a bit of a show at tidying away the old notices. I tore in half a pencil-drawn diagram about the best way to garotte a swan, and scrumpled up some old Meat Raffle results, giving them to Ruff Puff to put into the wastepaper basket.

I found four little pins for the corners of the sheet.

The jostling behind me settled into a tense silence.

Then I had a wicked and slightly shameful idea.

"Is Cornwall about?" I asked the room, without turning around. There was no reply.

"Victor?" I called, loudly. You could have cut the atmosphere with a knife. I turned to the room to see that a path had cleared all the way to the bar, where slouched Cornwall, nursing a brandy in one of the ridiculous balloon glasses he favoured.

Slowly, he turned around and peered at me. "What is it?" he said, sulkily.

"Team sheet's going up," I said, innocently.

He sighed and placed the giant glass carefully onto the bar, where it glinted in a shaft of afternoon sunlight. The sunlight snagged on my thoughts. In my mind's eye, I could suddenly see myself all those years ago, hurling brandy from a similar glass at a Nizari Hashashin swordsman in the Long Room, as Jack Dempsey, George VI and Lunk Snr looked on. And there too was Victor, callow in his Winstowe blazer with its slightly too short sleeves, kicking a cigarette ember up at the screaming aggressor to set him on fire and complete our membership ordeal.

Cornwall stalked over and held out his hand for the team sheet. His face was expressionless, but his poker tell, a pulse in the side of his neck, beat once, twice, three times.

I studied his face for a long moment, noting the deepening lines, wrinkles and scars, some of which I was responsible for, some from the kicking that life gives everyone.

I realised this tour wouldn't be the same without him.

"One sec," I said, and whipped out a pencil. I made a scribbled addition to the bottom of the team sheet before pinning it up.

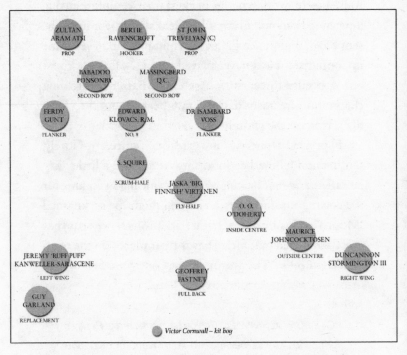

ZULTAN ARAM ATSI
PROP

BERTIE RAVENSCROFT
HOOKER

ST JOHN TREVELYAN (C)
PROP

BABADOO PONSONBY
SECOND ROW

MASSINGBERD Q.C.
SECOND ROW

FERDY GUNT
FLANKER

EDWARD KLOVACS, R.M.
NO. 8

DR ISAMBARD VOSS
FLANKER

S. SQUIRE
SCRUM-HALF

JASKA 'BIG FINNISH' VIRTANEN
FLY-HALF

O. O. O'DOHERTY
INSIDE CENTRE

MAURICE JOHNCOCKTOSEN
OUTSIDE CENTRE

DUNCANNON STORMINGTON III
RIGHT WING

JEREMY 'RUFF PUFF' KANWELLER-SARASCENE
LEFT WING

GEOFFREY FASTNET
FULL BACK

GUY GARLAND
REPLACEMENT

Victor Cornwall – kit boy

The room clamoured behind me. After a few pregnant seconds, there were the usual whoops of joy and roars of anguish familiar to any school changing room when the team sheet is published. I steeled myself, and nodded to Masterson at the bar, who gestured to the fresh bottle of Ardbeg that he'd already put out for me. I strolled over to the bar, took a seat and waited for the onslaught to begin.

"I can't believe you left me off the team, you rotten f-," screamed a spittle-strewn Mackelhose as he was hauled away by Aram Atsi, who, with his usual sixth sense, had come upstairs to provide security. Gripping Mackelhose in his patented shoulder-anus clamp, Aram Atsi slung him down the back staircase, only pausing long enough to nod his thanks. He'd always wanted to be sent on an undertaking, but the right job had never come up, until now. He'd never played rugby, as far as I knew, but a twenty-three stone Armenian hammer-throwing champion obviously had the raw beef required to keep my scrum on the straight and narrow.

Popsy O'Doherty, my inside centre, a lovely, sentimental fellow, began to sing *extempore* a little ditty he called *The Ball Buster*, which became my nickname for the entire tour, rather as a General might be nicknamed 'Monty' by his loyal troops. It had a rousing chorus that everyone belted out, almost as if their places on the team depended on it. The words of the song have faded with time, so I won't reproduce them here.

NOTE FOR CORNWALL: Do you have a record of Popsy's song lyrics as I've never seen them written down, and can't quite remember how it went, but I remember it as a stirring call to arms, our own take on the All Blacks' Haka or the Fijian Cibi. Perhaps you'll find a way to squeeze them into your next chapter. Many thanks.

Before long, those who'd not made the cut sloped off to lick their wounds. Only the Cavaliers XV remained in the Gaye Bar. I opened a tab, stood on a table and made a rousing address, pint of Black Oyster in hand. I told the lads that we were going to save a brave desert nation from destruction at the hands of an evil man, which turned out to be true. I told the lads that we'd probably not all make it back in one piece. This turned out to be true as well. Finally, I told them that the man we were going to kill was in league with the man who'd killed my daughter. The room became solemn, but I rode this out. Then I locked Anais away in my heart once again, ordered fifteen pints of Black Oyster and started the business of getting totally hammered.

Later, just as Maurice was wheeled away to the San to have his stomach pumped, I spied Cornwall, ever a man apart, staring out at the London dusk, ruminating. I expect he was thinking of his goddaughter.

He turned and raised his glass to me in salute. Then gave me the wanker hand signal of which he has always been so fond.

I had a vague inkling that he'd put Summerville up to this whole wheeze, so I raised my glass to him, just in case I was right.

PRESIDENTIAL PALACE OF MALJERIA, APRIL 1973

Cornwall had got to RAF Northolt early. As kit boy, he had a lot to think about: boots, studs, spare studs, laces, spare laces, Vaseline, ear tape, muscle heating gel, muscle cooling gel, anaesthetic gel, shower gel, jockstraps, sun hats, mosquito paste, flyswatters, gumshields, blackboard and chalk for my team talks; not to mention flags and rugby balls. I was pretty impressed with how seriously he was taking things. He'd even brought along a string bag of two hundred Seville oranges. He'd stowed it all in the cargo hold and then baggsy'ed the seat next to the pilot. He'd never lost his schoolboy fascination for aircraft, and I didn't have the heart to tell him that it was my seat. After all, what did I care? Much better for the skipper to be in the back with the lads, rucking and joshing and generating a bit of team spirit.

The pilot, an affable, long in the tooth Wing Commander called Dander, was, unfortunately, a betting man. While I drilled the team on the law changes since we'd played at school, Cornwall told him a few stories about his 1949 world tour for the Commonwealth Secretariat, when he'd been commissioned to flit back and forth across the world in a horrific inversion of the Miss World pageant, making love to the world's most hideous women in the most fly-bitten outposts. Dander thought this was sensational and offered Cornwall a little something from his hip flask. I was told later that, in the normal run of conversation, they got onto the topic of micro-gravity. It was Cornwall's contention that in a zero-gravity environment one could smoke a cigarette in the normal manner. Dander disagreed. Before long they'd shaken hands on a £10,000 wager.

Dander threw our Hercules into a series of massive parabolic climbs and dives, which saw the plane cavorting across the skies from 12,000 to 36,000 feet and back again, every twenty seconds. Cornwall apparently found that it was impossible to smoke a cigarette in the state of weightlessness that the steep dives produced, but only because the cigarette kept being knocked from his mouth by loose oranges. He lost the bet on this technicality and wrote Dander a cheque there and then.

In the back of the plane, the team spent this time vomiting all over each other. The evening before, a few of the lads had been to a Keralan seafood curry house in Soho, and soon the rear cabin was a revolting miasma of semi-digested squid vindaloo.

As if that wasn't bad enough, nearing Maljerian airspace, Cornwall put it to Dander that he couldn't perform an E.I.C.L. for double or quits. The evasive inverse corkscrew landing is commonly used by the military when ground-to-air missiles are a factor around the destination airport. Dander took up the challenge and spiralled our plane down to the runway at 400 MPH, covering Ruff Puff, who was using the lav at the time, in liquid effluent that had risen up from the tank beneath.

Ruff Puff was the first to admit that Dander's landing had been first class, but during it he'd caught his best mahogany hand under the loo seat and cracked two fingers off it. When we'd taxied to a halt I broke Dander's nose for pissing us about, and I also tore a serious strip off Cornwall, who protested that this sort of harmless prank was exactly the sort of thing rugby tours are made of, and how we'd all be laughing about it later.

Major. It is over fifty years later, and I'm still not laughing.

We made it through Maljerian Border Control and were met by a luxurious, air-conditioned team bus, complete with listening devices, which took us to our hotel for the week-long run-up to the big game. I allowed the team a little R&R for the evening, but as punishment I made Cornwall accompany me to the Presidential Palace, to meet Badda Ladin himself. I was expecting only a handshake and a few promotional photographs, but Badda Ladin had other ideas.

Cornwall and I sat side by side on a plush velour sofa, shielded from the powerful evening sun by parasols, waiting for our host. We'd been served plums with sherbet on crushed ice, while a bare-chested man wafted us with a fan made from the tail-feathers of the Maljerian ostrich. Two serving girls, faces demurely covered, plump buttocks cocooned in silk, stood holding platters of figs. A band of colossal turbaned guards, their thick cypress pikestaffs held a single inch from the floor, stood to attention, while a young man was expertly disembowelled by Badda Ladin's court torturer in front of us. The torturer, smiling broadly, wrenched ropes of intestine from the young man's flayed abdomen like a magician pulling handkerchiefs from a hat.

The victim expired with a whimper, at which point Badda Ladin made his big entrance. Ornate double doors burst open, and in he strode. "Mr Trevelyan! My honoured guest! Welcome to Maljeria, my desert jewel, as forward-thinking as it is steeped in history and tradition."

"Thank you for receiving us, Your Excellency," I said carefully. "And may I present Mr Victor Cornwall, the Cavaliers' Assistant Coach."

"My house is your house, Mr Cornwall," he said, as Cornwall bowed low.

"And how did you enjoy the little entertainment I laid on for you?" He stared at us expectantly.

I broke into my broadest smile and clapped vigorously. Cornwall proclaimed it the finest disembowelling he'd ever seen. The court torturer smiled bashfully.

"And what had the young man done to deserve his sentence of death?" I queried.

Badda Ladin looked briefly confused. "Nothing. He was just passing by. All of our young men clamour to die for the honour of Maljeria."

An awkward silence quickly developed, so I blurted out some more praise for the torturer.

"Yes!" Badda Ladin enthused. "We are lucky to have Zakash the Barbaric. He's the best at this! I bought him from the Shah. Would you like to see him garrotte someone?" Badda Ladin's eyes swept the room. He pointed at one of the serving girls. "You! Come here!"

"No! No, really. Not on our account," I interceded, quickly.

Badda Ladin shooed the girl away and turned to answer his question. I watched as the girl trembled with relief. How long would she last at the Maljerian court? Months, maybe? Weeks?

Badda Ladin, the self-styled People's Protector of the Republic of Maljeria, was one of the most black-hearted fellows I'd ever had the misfortune to meet. With more family money behind him than the Vanderbilts, he was as puffed-up as a peacock's cock, as ruthless a dictator as ever gave orders for his entire cabinet to be hanged in the Main Square. He was a despicable, nailed-on, ocean-going psychopath. A psychopath with a new Bosphorus Phosphorus lab and very poor taste in friends. After seizing power in a bloody coup, Badda Ladin's very first act was to make Rugby Union the national sport. He had fallen in love with the game twenty years before, as a student, where he had simply bought and endowed Ladin College, Oxford after failing the entrance exam. His second act was to destroy the ancient city centre to make space for a lavish new rugby stadium. He liked to keep his people downtrodden and banned the building of hospitals and schools. He restricted access to food, even though the country's oil reserves could have made every citizen as rich as the Saudis.

"Your Excellency, we are looking forward to playing in your new stadium," said Cornwall

"I am glad to hear it, Mr Cornwall," our host boomed, leading us to a table covered with a silk cloth. "This is the Maljeria of tomorrow!" With a theatrical flourish, he pulled away the silk to reveal a fantastically detailed architectural model, gleaming white. It was a cool, pale, modern oasis in a sea of desert. At one end was the Presidential Palace, surrounded by ornamental gardens and low sandstone buildings. The centre was framed by a sparkling dual carriageway with junctions peeling off to a sprawl of airstrips, artificial lakes and parks. On a roundabout stood a bronze statue, perhaps modelled on the Colossus of Rhodes, showing Badda Ladin in heroic pose, scimitar in one hand, rugby ball in the other.

We peered down at the model of the city, with its fresh green trees and tiny figures strolling in the wide boulevards. It bore no relation to reality whatsoever. We'd just been driven through the real Maljeria on our way here. Where on this architectural model were the slums and the filthy huts? Where were the leperous figures huddled desolately around the single, ramshackle clinic? Where were the forced labour camps?

At the far end of the model stood the venue for our match – a gigantic sports stadium, all sweeping struts of white steel. Inside it was a lush green pitch. "Behold! The Badda Ladin International Rugby Stadium, just completed, at a cost of over one hundred and twenty million dollars," he crowed.

"A wonderfully modern development, Your Excellency," simpered Cornwall. Badda Ladin inclined his head in agreement as he ran a smooth finger over the stadium's curving roof.

"And what are these?" I asked, pointing to a group of massive steel drums, low funnels and irrigation channels clustered around the rear of the stadium. I watched Badda Ladin's reaction carefully.

"Ah! The stadium complex contains a state-of-the-art laboratory. A little investment in Maljeria's future. Research and development in new sports medicines and, ahem, the biological sciences…" His eyes wheeled madly at some private joke, "…along with other *innovations* that may one day change the world."

"Maljeria is lucky to have a leader who invests in the future," I said.

"Indeed!" Badda Ladin was pleased with this. He clicked his fingers to another serving girl. She raced to offer up a mirrored tray, upon which lay a mound of powdered cocaine. The girl had laid out a fat line the length of a pistol barrel. He hoovered it up in one aggressive snort. "But where are my manners?" he said. "Gentlemen, do have some cocaine. Its purity is 100%."

I hoovered up a great big furrow of it. It was pretty spicy. My synapses started firing at a trillion miles an hour. I fixed my attention on the model stadium, in all its riveting detail. Godlike, I hovered over the rugby pitch with its two H-bars at either end. I zeroed in on a tiny referee in black, frozen in the act of blowing a whistle. The stands were filled with a crowd of cheering figures, thousands of them, their arms raised in celebration. I looked even closer. And what was this? At the edge of the pitch was a figure that could only have been Badda Ladin himself, holding a teardrop-sized rugby ball in one hand, and a grand silver trophy in the other. On the 22-yard line were a row of players, kneeling before him, their necks exposed. A little barrel-chested man in a leather jerkin was positioned behind the players. It looked a lot like Zakash the Barbaric. He was raising a long blade above his head.

I nudged Cornwall, who had also noted this horrid scene. "How many does your stadium seat?" he asked.

"Thirty thousand!" shouted Badda Ladin, snuffling up another line of cocaine. "Nearly ten percent of my whole population will be there to watch our game next week!"

"The world has never seen such an impressive sports venue!" Cornwall declared bombastically. "It makes Twickenham look shabby! This is the new home of rugby!"

"Yes!" Badda Ladin seized Cornwall's hands,

clutching them in excitement, "from your lips to the ear of God."

There was a lot of love in the room. Now was the time. I fished the silver medallion from my pocket and held it out to Badda Ladin. "Your Excellency, we'd like to distribute these commemorative medallions to the crowd, if it pleases you."

Badda Ladin glanced at the medallion dangling from my fist. "Of course, of course," he waved this irrelevance away. "And if any of my citizens fail to cheer for the Cavaliers, I will have them strangled."

Soon after that, Cornwall and I made our excuses, pleading fatigue. We wished our host, and Captain of the Maljeria International XV, the very best of luck in what we were sure would be a game full of incident.

"And may the best team win," called Badda Ladin, as we took our leave.

Cornwall, although I was calling the shots and making all the running, it's undeniable that you were there, and you've probably a few things to add about whether you sliced up the oranges lengthways or into chunks and about how difficult it is to keep track of fifteen different gumshields.

Can I ask that you jot down a few notes about the week leading up to it, before I get onto the actual substance of the match? Thank you.

Keep it brief though.

Yours sincerely,
Major Arthur St. John Trevelyan

Hellcat Manor
Great Trundleford
Devon
April 25th 2021

Dear Major,

There are a few home truths about the tour coming your way, I'm afraid, which will probably knock you for six, to mix my sporting metaphors. I've checked my old diaries for '73 and dug out the lyrics for the song you mention. Popsy was an excellent songwriter. I believe that after the tour he flogged the rights to a popular guitar band named *The Sweet*, who adapted the lyrics and made it a big hit later that year. But what you took for an anthem about your rugby prowess was actually a sideswipe at your weak captaincy and poor on-field skills:

BALL BUSTER
POPSY O'DOHERTY (1973)

Ahh-Ahhhhhhhhhhhhh!
Ahh-Ahhhhhhhhhhhhh!
You better beware,
You better take care,
Of St. John Trevelyan
And his ludicrous hair.

When you're in a maul,
With a hold of the ball,

You know that the Ball Buster
Contributes fuck all!
Ahh Ahhhhhhhhhhhhh!
Ahh Ahhhhhhhhhhhhh!

There he is in the dirt,
Blood all over his shirt,
Ball Buster's gameplay's
Completely inert!

Nobody knows,
Where Ball Buster goes,
He'll give four points away
Right under your nose!

Does anyone know the way
To get him to stay away?
(He hasn't got a clue WHAT to do!)
Does anyone know the way?
There's got to be a way!
To sub Buster.

I suggest that you take a seat and pour yourself something conciliatory, because this is going to hurt more than your wedding night.

CHAPTER 5
THE KIT MAN AND HER

MALJERIA, APRIL 1973

I had to hand it to Summerville. Presenting Trevelyan with the captaincy as a way of putting a spring back in his step was not only clever but rather thoughtful. It's what made her tenure at the Club so successful long term.

I'd met her privately the day before our meeting with him and gone along with her suggestion. I knew it meant that my natural flair for gutsy leadership on the field would go to waste and I'd appear to be little more than his gofer, but Summerville was persuasive. "Take a back seat on this one, Cornwall," she said, "when I mention it in the meeting it's the first you've heard of it, understand?"

"No chance," I'd said, straight off the bat. "I'm the man for the job. At Winstowe the touchlines were packed with mothers of students who'd only come to watch *me* play."

"I'm serious, Cornwall. It's not always about you."

This comment confused me and struck me as entirely unreasonable. "C'mon Stephanie. He's got cack-hands and a squiffy eye. At school his nickname was The Nursemaid, because of all the hospital passes he made."

"I don't care," she said. "He needs something to go his way. My decision is final."

Summerville looked devastating when she was taking me in hand like this. How could I resist? "Very well," I sighed.

Then she added the kicker. "And while we're being frank, you're to quit the junk before I put you in command of anything."

Ouch. I shrugged this off with one of my trademark soppy grins, but she'd got me where it hurt. I was getting genuinely worried about my heroin intake. The stuff was so bloody moreish. This was the second time she'd mentioned my dalliances with the white dragon, and I knew there wouldn't be a third. I needed to get my little habit squared away, and that meant facing a demon I'd ignored far too long.

HARLEY ST, LONDON, THE NEXT DAY

Dr Hoffenhaus' eyes glazed over, and he sucked his upper lip. "As ever, you're an enigma, Victor," he murmured. "Cough."

I coughed.

"How is it behaving itself?"

"Well," I said, taking a deep breath, "I've had absolutely no complaints, I want to be clear on that."

"Of course. But…?"

"The pain is getting worse."

"It does appear a little swollen," Hoffenhaus grimaced and turned his head torch up for a more detailed examination, "after what you've put it through,

I'm hardly surprised. You still feel a dull ache at the base?"

"Now it's a dull ache all over."

"Hmm, the legacy of your damaged *vas deferens*, of course," he mused, concluding his examination, "but perhaps there's something more." Hoffenhaus seemed to be thinking it over.

"Ahem," I tried to get his attention. "Dr, may I...?"

"..."

"Dr?"

"What? Oh, of course. Feel free to put yourself away."

I sorted myself out and sat down.

"Are you sure you've told me everything, Cornwall?" he asked.

"There is something else," I admitted, "I've been having this recurring dream."

Hoffenhaus frowned. He took out a pen and note pad from his drawer.

"Talk me through it," he said.

It had all started a while back, I explained. A horrifying nightmare of that night at the Plaza Hotel in New York, where I barely escaped with my life, let alone my manhood. It would begin with Sayonara Fang's lithe body thrashing around on top of me, grinding her pelvis until I was deep inside her. But then, as she locked me in, the sudden feeling of extreme, unbearable pressure all around my shaft, and a numbing sense of impending doom – but a doom that bore agonisingly down on my glans. I'd scream out as the pain became unbearable, before she'd wrench the whole root out of me, like dental pliers seizing a stubborn wisdom tooth. The remains of my cock were spat out onto the silken sheets, a decapitated King, bleeding out onto the castle cobbles. At this moment I'd wake up, drenched in sweat, but alas, my ordeal would not be over. Because despite being awake, the excruciating pain would continue and my cock would start to spasm violently, chucking itself around like it was in the mosh pit of a heavy metal gig.

At this Hoffenhaus looked up from his notepad, intrigued, "So it's as if your penis is trying to commit suicide by smashing itself against your thighs?"

"I've never considered that, Doc, but yes, I think it is," I said.

"Interesting. And then what happens?"

"I just grab it with both hands like a pilot controls the joystick of a helicopter in heavy turbulence. And after an hour or so, the pain and spasms subside."

Hoffenhaus finished writing on his pad and let out a low whistle.

He lit a cigarette and offered me one. I declined. He blew out a thick plume of blue smoke. "Victor, I am a doctor of the body. I'm not qualified to speculate on the workings of the brain, but I do have a theory."

"What is it?"

"It seems to me that Fang has not only put a kink in your vas deferens, he said, "but a kink in your mind."

I was taken aback. "How the hell did she do that?"

"I think you have something called DO–PTSD–OTP.

"...?"

"Delayed-onset post-traumatic stress disorder," he said, "of the penis."

"Go on," I said.

"If it hadn't been for the mammoth tusk condom, she would have taken your manhood away and you'd have been a dead man, right?"

"Yes," I breathed.

"That kind of close call is the very definition of trauma. Your penis has undergone a near-death experience. And it is manifesting itself as real, physical pain. You are expecting to be castrated every time you remember the encounter. To control the pain, you've been taking a pinch of heroin, and unfortunately those pinches are getting bigger."

"Is it all in my mind?" I asked.

"No. The kink in your vas deferens is real. You're all backed up! Your testicles are three times the normal size, and your restricted pipework is causing a dangerous pressure build-up of seminal fluid. May I speak frankly?"

"I thought you were speaking frankly."

"May I speak even more frankly?"

"Please do…"

"You've got bunged-up balls. The dreams are making them worse. Your brain keeps telling you you're being castrated. Nothing will change until you sort out that kink in your vas deferens."

"Okay," I said, "so how do we fix it?"

"It needs fresh trauma to undo the previous trauma. Something brutal like a sharp kick from the hind legs of a donkey. Or a wallop in the knackers with a kettle-bell."

I swallowed hard. "And my heroin addiction?"

"Stop taking it."

I nodded sagely. Sometimes the answer is staring you right in the face.

Hoffenhaus passed me my usual fresh prescription pad, blank, but with his signature on each page.

"That said," he added, "if you want to get through this rugby tour – and I can't believe I'm saying this – you'll need more heroin. Just go to the chemist and ask them to give you as much as you can fit in your suitcase."

"Thank you, Doctor," I said.

"Enjoy the tour. And, Victor, next time please consider leaving your ape at home." I looked over to the corner of the office, where Titus was face down on the bed, arse cheeks spread skywards as he waited, hoping for a rectal examination.

"Come on, Titus, there's nothing wrong with your prostate," I sighed. "Thank you, Doctor, for your candour."

MALJERIA, NORTH AFRICA

Summerville's meeting had gone off without a hitch. I did my best to look aggrieved when she handed Trevelyan the captaincy and he was too blinded by power to see it for what it was. He took on the role with zeal, parading around the Club changing rooms like a jumped-up lieutenant. He'd bark out orders left, right and centre, putting a few noses out of joint in the process. It became clear early on that he had little conception of what a captain actually did. He took to wearing a red tracksuit and holding tedious meetings in front of a magnetic whiteboard covered in coloured disks. Sometimes he'd arrange them like he was playing draughts. Other times he'd get angry and sweep them off the board in one go, berating the players for not listening to him properly.

Trevelyan liked to order me around in front of the others, getting me to run basic errands: making the tea, cleaning boots, ironing socks. Every day after training Trevelyan would come back into the changing room and yell "Kit Boy!" take off his stinking rugby shirt and throw it on the floor for me to pick up.

"On my way!" I'd reply, gamely jogging out of the kit room.

Rather than find these tasks demeaning, I found them energising, because what Trevelyan failed to understand is that the kit man is the most vital component of any team. He is the eyes and ears of the dressing room, always watching, always listening. A good kit man asserts his authority with cunning and guile. To some, he's *consigliere*, a trusted friend and confidante. For others, he's a teacher or even a father figure. He can make and break sporting careers, become a player's greatest champion, or the architect of their downfall. He can pull the strings with a quiet word in the coach's ear or a subtle remark in the bar. In many ways, it is the kit man who picks the team.

I resolved that I'd be the best damn kit man the Club had ever seen. The model for this was Tug Malone, the incumbent at Scoundrels Gym, who had a mystical ability to get under the skin of any opponent. He'd masterminded the Club's win over the All Blacks in 1967 by barbecuing fifteen endangered kakapo parrots on the touchline while they performed the *Haka*.

So, I got on with observing the players, taking notes, and asking questions. Who was fully fit? Who was sweating too much? who wasn't sweating enough? Who'd been up until four with the Palace kitchen girls? At the end of each training session, I'd collect a bag of dirty kit to wash. But before it went into the machine, I'd conduct a thorough analysis of it. You can tell a lot about a player from the state of their kit and I learnt to read the signs like a Cherokee tracker reads the wilderness. Each item told a story, and I kept the notes in a diary to record my findings.

TRAINING SESSION
TUESDAY 11th APRIL

PLAYER: RAVENSCROFT, Bertie
POSITION: Hooker.
SHIRT: *Slight lateral soil-smears down left flank. Small contusion of fabric beneath right axilla. Suggests player is vulnerable to grabbing beneath armpit within scrum. Complex aroma profile: Sweet notes of fresh sweat/ cologne. Hints of mint, lavender/ tonka, top notes of mace, neroli, bergamot – probably Brut. Dominant acrid notes of Newcastle Brown Ale.*
SHORTS: *Soiled. (Inside.)*
UNDERWEAR: *See above.*

SOCKS: N/A

BOOTS: Lightly scuffed. Minimal mud residue. Traces of flesh and blood around toecap and studs. (See Johncocktosen's back.)

NOTES: Shirt analysis confirms suspicions that Ravenscroft did not pull his weight today. Only moderate soiling, fabric rich in alcohol-infused sweat. It is my assertion that he was hungover and forgot to put his socks on. Ball park estimate is that he consumed nine pints of Newcastle Brown Ale. His soiled shorts contribute to this assertion but could also indicate a degree of anal laxity. Conclusion: Referred to team doctor to be fitted for a match day butt-plug.

PLAYER: SQUIRE, Sheldon Ray
POSITION: Scrum-Half
SHIRT: Gross right-side discolouration. Soil and sweat. Severe abrasion down clavicle intersection. Fabric across right pectoral smoother, suggesting he can only pass the ball to the left.
SHORTS: Torn pocket, mud marks.
UNDERWEAR: Lemon curd residue around gusset.
SOCKS: Lightly soiled in keeping with a moderate session.
BOOTS: Encrusted with salt stains – sweating from feet?
NOTES: Squire performed well today. Salt residue in boots indicates good effort, but he needs to work on passing the ball to the right. Conclusions: Bespoke session reminding Squire he has a right side as well as a left, and quiet word about appropriate lubricant choices.

PLAYER: TREVELYAN, Arthur St. John

POSITION: Tight Head Prop (Captain)

SHIRT: Moderately soiled. Blood spatters down back of neck indicating player is entering the scrum facing the wrong way.

Two raised 'bull's eye' injuries to fabric around pectoral region suggest that subject has unnaturally large areolae. No action, simply a point of medical interest and a bit weird.

SHORTS: Traces of hair and saliva. Initial analysis suggests both belong to Ponsonby. Possibly due to Locard's Exchange Principle during rucks. Maybe another reason? Recommend moving Ponsonby to other position or tell him to behave himself.

UNDERWEAR: N/A. Subject refused to relinquish post-match.

SOCKS: Structural integrity compromised. (Broken elastic). Possibly they were too small for the player or his calves are just too big?

BOOTS: Traces of mud. Traces of Ponsonby's saliva.

NOTES: Player needs bigger socks. Player to learn how to enter a scrum properly. Player advised to keep away from Ponsonby.

I knew every detail.

I was prepared to use anything to gain an advantage. I had trebled-up on Hoffenhaus' prescription recommendations, and my doctor's bag was a pharmacopeia of depth and range. The players thought I was giving them daily vitamin injections but in fact it was a carefully prescribed cocktail of whatever I felt they needed. A couple of the lads were on clenbuterol to boost their metabolisms. I had the second row on steroids to increase their muscle mass. Gunt was on EPO to improve his stamina and Ruff Puff was on Human Growth Hormone. I knew it was a longshot, but I hoped his hands might grow back.

There is a lot of negativity surrounding doping in sports, but my take was that it works bloody well. I noticed a significant uptick in training capacity as the game got closer.

It was the day before the game. In the changing rooms Stormington was his usual garrulous self, towel-flicking 'Big Finnish' Virtanen on the arse to get a rise out of him. Soon those two big men were wrestling naked on the tiles as Babadoo Ponsonby watched on silently, clenching and unclenching his fists.

I went around collecting soiled kit. As always, I offered each player a kind comment or a nugget of advice during my rounds. "Good hands today, Geoffrey," I said, thumping Fastnet on the shoulder, "but don't be afraid to take it on yourself once in a while. You'll cause them problems, so draw them in and don't feel you've got to offload straightaway."

'Righto, Cornwall," he said, "will do."

I moved on, picking up Ravenscroft's kit and stuffing it in my dirty linen bag. "Careful on those line-outs, Bertie. You're still telegraphing it too much, okay?"

"Gotcha Victor, I'm working on it."

I dropped another filthy pair of shorts into my bag as I spied Ruff Puff trying to leave in a hurry. "Ruff Puff!" I called after him. He turned. "What the hell do you call that performance?"

He tried to explain himself, but I shouted over him, "I know you're in a wheelchair! And you've got wooden hands. But if you don't start pulling your weight in those rucks, you'll be on the next flight home! We've no room for baggage in this team!"

The poor guy had had a tough day. His nose was broken, and he sported a fresh black eye where Voss had lamped him. "Thorry, I've justhed not been on it thoday. I'll remember my rubber handths tomowwow."

I gave him a hard stare. "You do that," I said, "now go and sink a few pints and forget about it, you silly bugger."

"Thanksth, Victor," he said, "I pwomith I'll do better."

I moved on. Next was Trevelyan. He was sat on the bench by his locker with his head in his hands. I bent down to pick up his discarded shorts. He'd had another dreadful session and was quietly fuming. He tended to take criticism badly, so I needed to be diplomatic. "Quick word, St. John," I said.

"Bugger off, Cornwall, not today."

"Fine," I said, "But just remember in rugby we pass the ball *backwards*, yeah?" He just stared at the ground. I turned to the rest of dressing room and clapped my hands hard three times, "COME ON PEOPLE! REMEMBER THE BASICS!"

The dressing room door swung open and one of Badda Ladin's sinuous consorts came in. The room froze. She was ravishing, beneath her patterned gown and veil. She made us all feel like the hairy, ill-smelling, lumpen thugs we were.

The room fell silent, and she spoke. "Tonight, gentlemen, you are invited to celebrate the inaugural Maljerian Invitational between the Cavaliers XV and Badda Ladin's World XV. Please accept our hospitality and enjoy the evening." She stopped at the door, and turned back, dropping a bare shoulder. "It should be fun," she giggled.

THE PRESIDENTIAL PALACE, LATER THAT EVENING

Say what you like about Badda Ladin, but he knew how to throw a party. The evening began with a 'ceremonial purification' – every member of the team endured a hard scrubbing with desert thistle loofahs from the muscly wenches who ran the palace *hammam*. They were certainly thorough. I've never had my eardrums and the inside of my eyelids buffed before, and I probably won't again – an experience to be treasured. They were incredibly attentive. Ruff Puff had his hands removed and polished with an aromatic oil and Ravenscroft finally got rid of a deep-rooted blackhead between his shoulder blades that he'd had since the War.

A great start to a memorable evening. Once cleansed, we were given matching raw silk *jebba* to wear and escorted into an ornate marble-pillared hall in which curtained loungers had been set in a wide circle. There was no sign of Badda Ladin, or for that matter, any of the opposing team, but most of the lads couldn't have cared less.

At first, I saw this feast as a clumsy attempt to undermine our readiness for the game. Get out the best champers and the Cavaliers would make merry, arriving at the stadium the next morning, hungover, listless, and flatulent – and it would be a rout for Maljeria. The oldest trick in the book, more or less. In British club rugby this kind of chicanery is almost a mark of respect. As I tucked into the excellent *peacock al pistache,* I ruminated on this.

As it turned out, I'd undersold our host. He was playing a whole different ballgame.

The centrepiece of the room was a round table laid out with a sumptuous banquet, the likes of which I'd never seen before, not even at the Club's Nelson Dinners. There were whole honey-glazed pigs, deep bowls of ink black caviar, freshly shucked oysters on crushed ice, joints of rolled wagyu short rib, lobster thermidor, flagons of ice-cold German lager-beer, hashish burners and opium pipes. The players relaxed into the scene immediately and soon the room was abuzz with activity and laughter. In one corner a band played traditional Maljerian music with instruments hewn from unidentifiable animal parts. I watched as a serving girl approached Trevelyan with a bowl of olives. He tilted his head in anticipation, his carotid artery bulging under the strain of lifting his prize-winning swede. His salivating maw opened slowly and the girl dropped an olive into the black pit below. I don't know quite what it was about this, but a foreboding thought wormed its way into my mind.

I regarded another teammate, the giant Aram Atsi. Somehow, he'd managed to secure *three* serving wenches. One of them was straddling his chest and giving him a pectoral massage while the others worked a thigh each. He had a chicken leg in each hand and a big smile on his face. It was as though Obelix had died and gone to heaven. The next man along was Ferdy Gunt. He was a man with a proper appetite, granted, but the way he was being spoonfed pints of caviar was obscene, bringing to mind both French geese and Christmastide at an old people's home.

All of a sudden, I felt the familiar dull ache at the base of my groin. Was my early warning system alerting me that trouble was brewing? Something certainly didn't feel right about this evening. I levered myself upright and waved away my serving wench as she offered me another devilled swan egg. Everywhere I looked my teammates were being treated to their every whim. It seemed we had the palace to ourselves. Most odd.

I strolled over to Trevelyan's lounger. "A moment, captain?"

Trevelyan grumbled a bit then dismissed his serving girls. "What is it?"

"Having a good time?" I enquired.

"I was."

"Don't you think this all feels a bit too good to be true?"

"What's not to like, Cornwall. This is fantastic!"

"Where is our host?"

"Who cares. Let's worry about Badda Ladin tomorrow. Relax and enjoy yourself."

"And what about the other team? Don't you think it's a bit strange we're the only ones here?"

Trevelyan didn't seem at all concerned. "Not really, I think you're being paranoid. Bugger off back to your *chaise longue* and leave me to it, will you?"

"Okay, but keep your eyes peeled," I cautioned. "I've a feeling we're being fattened up for the kill."

I returned to my chaise. I accepted another glass of champagne and some glistening black grapes. Maybe Trevelyan was right. Perhaps I was being paranoid. I popped a grape into my mouth and tried to relax but the dull ache at the base of my groin became a throb.

The music stopped. A guard struck a massive bronze gong and the double doors to the great hall opened. The tender fruit ruptured between my teeth. A lithe figure dressed in diaphanous silks swept into the room with a graceful whirl. Another one of Badda Ladin's veiled dancing girls here for our entertainment, no doubt.

Except she wasn't.

As she pirouetted across the room towards us, I recognised the woman beneath the mask.

Her name was Death. At once all of my fears were confirmed.

We *were* being fattened up for the kill.

No one moved like Sayonara. She was like mercury. The lads were spellbound as she leaped across the floor, twirled, swayed and gyrated. They had no idea how much danger they were in. Sayonara Fang was once my lover, but she had shot Tiberius Lunk and broken one of the sacred tenets of any healthy relationship by trying to bite off my penis with her fearsome vagina. I knew she needed to be brought to justice, but also that she'd never be taken alive. I wasn't sure that, after all we'd been through, I could be the one to do it.

Even now, as I watched her roll her jewelled belly as effortlessly as the winter swell off the North Devon coast, the throb in my groin became a Def-Con One klaxon, with my jammed vas deferens as the clapper. Fang had wrecked my entire genital ecosystem and haunted my dreams but still her allure was irresistible.

I forced my mind away from my own feelings, and back to the sit-rep. What was she up to? Did she know I was here or was this a coincidence?

I picked up an embroidered fan and fluttered it to obscure my face. Fang continued her dance, pulling out long red silks which she trailed through the air in a complex series of manoeuvres involving flick-flacks and somersaults. The boys burst into hearty applause. She was Olympic standard, but Olympic gymnastics routines don't usually end with someone being stabbed in the eye with a sharpened ribbon pole.

Fang glided up towards Jaska 'Big Finnish' Virtanen. The great man was grinning from ear to ear as she extended a seductive finger and gestured for him to come forward. Jaska stood up, swept back his thick mane of hair and took a pace towards her. She made a coquettish faux retreat and then shyly reached out for his hand. Virtanen turned to us and punched the air in triumph and all the lads responded with raucous cheers. Fang led Big Finnish out of the banqueting hall.

I was up and off my lounger like a shot. None of this made sense. What was Fang doing at Badda Ladin's palace? Protecting the Bosphorus Phosphorus lab? Or was this an assassination? And what did she want Virtanen for? Surely she hadn't just chosen him for pleasure? Over me? I cast that ridiculous thought from my mind. There had to be something else. He was in danger, no doubt about it. I needed to act fast. I moved in pursuit, but Trevelyan was in front of me, blocking my path.

"Lucky, lucky, bugger eh?" he blared. "Mind you, if she wanted a big lump of gristle to chew on, she could have chosen me. Big Finnish even looks a bit like me too." Trevelyan fiddled with his bouffant, which tonight was swept back with so much glistening lacquer that it resembled a tidal wave at a sewage farm.

"Suddenly, the pieces clicked together. "She thinks he *is* you!"

I pushed Trevelyan aside, sprinted across the floor and crashed through the double doors. Jeska Virtanen was about to be killed – horribly. And he wasn't even the target.

Trevelyan was.

I sprinted out of the hall and into the anteroom, shouting for Virtanen. My mind was racing. Fang must have been sent here by Hansclapp. Perhaps this was the next phase of his plan? They had a minute's head start but I had no idea which way they'd gone. The palace was a labyrinth of corridors and reception rooms, going off in all directions. Suddenly Trevelyan was behind me, huffing with the effort of hauling his body faster than a prop-forward commonly would. He was still clutching some kind of savoury donut. "D'you mind telling me what the hell is going on?"

"The dancing girl is Fang. I think she's here to kill you, but she's got the wrong guy."

"By god, Jeska's a dead man. Which way?" he said.

We didn't have long to wait before we found out. A guttural scream echoed down the corridor. It was an awful sound. The sort of cry a man might make after, say, having his penis chomped off. Trevelyan looked at me in disbelief and I nodded sagely back, conveying the two things we'd just learned: Virtanen had moments to live, and those moments would be very unpleasant.

Trevelyan offered me a pathetic little knife, procured from the cheese table. "Take this," he said, "it was all I could grab." I waved it away, turned and ran, kicking open doors on either side of the corridor. Trevelyan followed me. We had to find Jeska before he bled out.

Then, sylphlike, Fang emerged from a door up ahead, gently closing it behind her. I was amazed at her calm demeanour. She looked as if she was just on her way back from the ladies' room.

"Sayonara!" I shouted, and she turned, surprised. Our eyes met. She was every bit the deadly beauty I'd last seen on the banks of the Thames. Fang saw Trevelyan standing beside me and her face betrayed her. She *had* got the wrong guy. I expected her to run but I was wrong. She flicked her wrist and a thin blade dropped into her hand. She started moving quickly towards us.

"Ahhh," Trevelyan said.

We were in big trouble. "She's coming for you, Trevelyan," I called. "Get behind me. I'll keep her occupied." Fang was running now. The knife, a *tanto* blade, glinted as she passed through the shafts of light streaming in between the pillars of the corridor.

"Go, Cornwall, or she'll kill you too!" Trevelyan cried.

"She won't," I replied.

"Take the knife," he urged, offering it to me again.

"I don't need it."

Fang was nearly upon us.

"Just take the bloody cheese knife man!" Trevelyan stuffed it into my hand. Fang was almost at striking distance. With only ten feet to go I suddenly blurted out, "SAYONARA! I LOVE YOU!"

She skidded to a halt in front of me. Her eyes locked onto mine. "That's right, my *sakura*," I said, "I love you. I always have. Put the blade away."

Trevelyan seized the initiative. Moving slowly in a wide circle around her, he raced to the room where Virtanen lay injured.

"Put the knife down, my love. You can't kill me."

"How can you be so sure?" Her voice was ice cold.

"Because without you, I'm dead anyway." I dropped the cheese knife. And once again my vas deferens began its dull throb. For the first time, I realised that it was throbbing in time to the beat of my heart. There was a flick of her wrist, too quick to follow, and scchhhting! The tanto knife's blade was suddenly buried deep in the wall behind my right ear, and her lips were on mine.

We raced to find a room – any room – tumbling along the corridor, our hands on each other's bodies, our tongues wrestling like a pair of greased-up Turkish taxi drivers settling an ancient feud over parking infringements on each other's turf. She kicked open the door behind her and pulled me headlong onto the bed, ripping off my clothes with a ferocity of a Kansas twister. Suddenly I was naked, and entirely vulnerable. She tore her own clothes off, and stood directly above me, on the bed, a tiny Colossus of Rhodes, but with perfectly sculpted pubes. She had changed and yet she was the same, my Sayonara. Here and there a new scar. Her muscles finely honed from the exertions of a thousand murders. Magnificent. I stared up at her taut thighs, slightly parted, and deep into her glistening weaponised fandango. I knew, such was the passion of our reunion, that if I slipped inside her she'd never be able to control such a potent charge. She'd bite me off at the peak of our ecstasy. Yes, maybe she'd keep her prize in a trophy cabinet as a perverse memento, but it wouldn't matter. I'd still be a dead man with his cock bitten off.

I was considering whether this would actually be worth it, but Fang had a better idea. She took a pace back and dropped cat-like to my hips. She began to perform a slow, lazy, intimate investigation with her parted cherry lips. "Last time, I hurt you," she whispered.

"I remember."

"Now I will heal you." Fang bent to the task. She wrapped her hands around my manhood as delicately as if she was taking delivery of an unpredictable ice cream cornet on a scorching August day. Her tongue darted and flickered around the edge of my meatus, licking and slurping, as if catching the drips. And now her perfect tongue and ruby lips were fluttering over me like butterflies, but butterflies that really, really loved ice cream.

As she nibbled and guzzled away, the dull ache in the base of my groin throbbed with powerful intent. Such was her immense sexual magnetism, I began to feel my testicles unfurling in their pouch. The pressure in my shaft began to build as my doglegged vas deferens held firm. On and on she licked and sucked and kissed and nibbled and slurped and guzzled and swilled and chugged and noshed. The pleasure and pain receptors in my brain were vying for attention with each other. It was exquisite. It was unbearable. It was delectable. It was agonising.

I gripped the sheets and looked down. The purple veins on my shaft were standing out like the flood plains of the Amazon seen from a small propeller plane. I found myself in a delirium, crying out as the logjam in my tubes became unbearable, my imperfect plumbing raising the bar pressure way into the red. I knew something was going to blow, but Fang never faltered. My pipes were entirely in her hands for this delicate investigative work. She was an expert plumber, charging £85 per hour and Corgi registered.

And now her technique changed. Nestled between my thighs, she glanced up at me, and fluttered her long lashes once, like a curtsy, before sliding the rest of my shaft into her mouth, chowing down, gorging upon it, rolling my length around as if it were a stick scraping wisps from a candy-floss machine.

Then she began to roll her head from side to side, forward and backwards across every ligament in my groin. This way. That way. Sounding the depths of my tensile strength. Straining and stretching with ineffable skill. I understood that I was wrong, she was no plumber. Fang was now an osteopath, an osteopath of the groin. Flexing it, bending it, with each movement, loosening its moorings. With a dread shudder, I realised that she had rooted out my kinked duct, and now she was going to make amends, to repair all the damage she'd caused me at the New York Plaza, when my cock had been the plaything of her vicious downstairs fanny-ratchet.

Our eyes met. "Obbb-wwoobb-woobgghh," she gasped.

"What?"

She spat me out and gasped, "hold still."

There was a devilry about her. I couldn't tell if what she was doing would kill or cure me. My sweating, gurning face, at the very limits of tolerance for pain, confirmed that we were in this together. I nodded an assent. She pulled in a long breath through her flaring nostrils and in one fluid movement drew every inch of me down her throat. Her chin came to rest on top of my ballsack, her nostrils to just above my thatch of salt and pepper pubic hair, giving her, for one fleeting moment, an uncanny resemblance to the late Albert Einstein.

I cast that image aside. Now I was locked in her mouth, as secure a prison as her legendary lady-garden. Suddenly I felt her tongue, freakishly long, slide snake-like around the circumference of my glans, over and over, turning like molten toffee. The hands that had hitherto been teasing my outer thighs were suddenly planted firmly on the mattress and with incredible athleticism she lifted herself off the bed into a perfect handstand. My entire shaft was still down her throat and her lips now clamped tight, forming an airtight seal. Fang's strength and balance was incredible. With a power that belied her size, she began pushing out a series of vertical press-ups, using her throat like a plunger.

At the same time, she started to hum, and inside her mouth my imprisoned penis began to vibrate. Round and round her tongue went, a rotor blade beating against my alarmed beacon. Faster and faster. My sperm ducts were screaming, over-pressurised way beyond their limits. I could feel my penile ligaments thinning to breaking point, as taut as the catgut in an expensive tennis racquet... but still there was more! With astonishing dexterity, she began to roll her neck in the *opposite* direction to her magnificent rotating tongue. The gyroscopic effect was astounding. Faster and faster, generating friction which penetrated deep into my roiling shaft like an infrared massage. The temperature became too much to bear, and just as I felt my penis would catch aflame, she carried out the *coup de grace*. Her teeth closed firmly around my glans, the enamel tips holding it firm. Faster and faster and faster again, she turned me on the spinning lathe of her mouth, changing the very shape of my corona, whittling my bell-end into something new. Would it be knurled, chamfered or threaded? I couldn't tell. I thrashed around on the bed in a rapture. I saw fireworks, a kaleidoscope of colour. I heard marching bands, alpine horns, William Blake.

BRING ME MY BOW OF BURNING GOLD!
BRING ME MY ARROWS OF DESIRE!

And still Fang held fast.

Then, just as the pleasure and pain in my shaft reached it's zenith, she let her arms go slack, and the full weight of her body was jackhammered down onto me, compressing my penis like a stamped-on concertina. All the breath left my lungs. Gravity kicked in, and she crashed down onto the bed, my manhood still locked tight in her throat. I felt a tremendous CRACK, and an instantaneous feeling of release. Pleasure and pain smashed together in one moment, and suddenly I pumped and pumped and pumped a full yard of man ale. I continued to spurt uncontrollably – as if an apprentice fireman had been given control of the big hose, until at last, after what felt like hours, the pump ran dry.

My body began to fit with this orgy of release, and I twitched spasmodically as the last crackles of electricity earthed themselves onto the bed. Panting, I stared at the ceiling, utterly spent. I couldn't lift my arms. My legs were of lead.

Fang spat me out and dusted her hands together with all the tenderness of an Australian sheep farmer. She was, if nothing else, pragmatic. Job done. She disappeared into the bathroom while I recovered. I was a husk of a man. An exoskeleton, an insect that had had its innards sucked out by a deadly spider.

As I lay there, gasping, I realised the pain in the base of my groin had gone. My murderous lover had undone the damage with this astonishing display of *fellatio virtuoso*.

My vas deferens was straight as an arrow.

Sakura, my cherry blossom girl, had healed me. I was born again.

As you know St. John, this was another significant turning point in my life. Once again, I was able to make love without having an epidural or passing out. That is why I thought I'd include my poem *The Tunnels of My Love* from my third poetry collection. Although it's ostensibly about a brief affair I had with a lady architect who came to evaluate the structural integrity of Hellcat's reservoir in the 1990s, it was, of course, about Fang all along.

THE TUNNELS OF MY LOVE
(1991)

The tunnels of my love
Have been impassable for years.
Blocked by the limescale
Of my calcified heart.

But now you've brought
A high-pressure hose,
To swill out my depths,
And repoint my tunnels,
Sometimes even replacing the original Victorian brickwork,
With other bricks you sourced
From the salvage yard of your love.

And now
Suddenly the whole thing drains away properly,
As per the original design.

PRESIDENTIAL PALACE, MATCH DAY

I awoke the following morning in the deserted palace. It was as if I was King of Love, with my Queen at my side. I immediately felt the folly of harbouring such romantic notions. I was, in fact, still in danger. By even falling asleep I'd been playing with fire, but I just couldn't help myself. After so many years of Fang's absence, I realised I'd been yearning for her.

We lay for a while in each other's arms. My clothes were in tatters where she'd ripped them from my body and lay strewn all across the floor. One of Trevelyan's medallions had fallen out on the carpet. Fang spotted it too. She got out of bed and picked it up.

"It's beautiful," she said, "so polished. What is it?"

"Oh, that? Just a souvenir," I said, offhand. "We're going to give them out to the crowd before the match. Something to remember us by."

The medallion dangled from her fingers. The surface caught a shaft of light and reflected onto a point on the wall. She gave me a sideways glance, suddenly understanding. "I think they'll remember you," she said. "And how many of those are you giving out?"

"A few thousand."

She raised her eyebrows. "Whose idea was that?"

"I forget."

"You are such naughty boys," she laughed. "I wish I could stick around to see it."

She passed me a glass of water. As I took it from her, I caught her wrist and stared into her black eyes. Impenetrable, unknowable, and yet, was there, at last, some softening in them? Some hope that we could yet be together.

"Hansclapp sent you to kill Trevelyan?"

She let the glass go and looked away. After a moment she said, "not to kill him, to incapacitate him."

"And you've failed. Hansclapp doesn't tolerate failure."

She lay on her back on the bed, looking up at the ceiling. "It's true," she whispered. "I have failed him. And now I must disappear."

"Where can I find you again, my *sakura*?" I took a sip from the glass of water.

Bugger.

I knew I'd made an error when she turned to me, a tear in her eye. The room began to spin and close in.

"Sleep well," she purred, and kissed me softly on the lips. Before I passed out I remember thinking how inconvenient it was to be slipped a mickey now, of all times. We had a regime to overthrow, a Bosphorus Phosphorus factory to destroy, and a rugby match to win.

Major, thanks to your quick thinking and willingness to hold his penis for so long, Jaska Vertanen survived his ordeal. Although his life was saved, his penis wasn't, and for the rest of his life he had to make do with a pathetic stub only eight and a half inches long, the poor bastard. But it was a valiant effort, nevertheless.

With Big Finnish out of action we had to put Guy *Judy* Garland in as fly-half, leaving us without a single replacement for the entire eighty minutes of the game.

I'll let you detail the match itself, and the astonishing events at its conclusion.

Yours sincerely,
Major Victor Montgomery Cornwall

Nimbu Towers
Pullen-under-Lyme
Gloucestershire
1st May 2021

Dear Major,

After a lifetime of self-aggrandisement, you have developed a fine ability to shoehorn yourself into any story, rebuilding it around you, like the groupie who claims she was the fifth Rolling Stone because she once gave Keith Richards a hand-shandy. Quite different from my recollections of your time as Kit Boy. You were forever shuffling around offering people weak tea that they didn't want, and you couldn't even cut an orange properly in half. You were not some Svengali pulling the strings of the team, you were the kit boy who kept giving everybody poorly laundered shorts that weren't theirs.

And you expect me to believe you spent yet another night in the arms of Sayonara Fang? I suspect she knocked the shit out of you while I was saving Jeska's life, and simply locked you in a cleaning cupboard for the night. You nearly missed kick-off, you bloody fool. And I had to clean my own boots.

Still, the whole enterprise had a happy ending, as long as you weren't Badda Ladin:

CHAPTER 6
DEVASTATING MATRIX OF DEATH

THE BADDA LADIN INTERNATIONAL RUGBY STADIUM, APRIL 1973

The Maljerian sun was high in the sky and burned with a brutal intensity. We entered the stadium to the kind of flat, joyless cheering forty thousand subjugated people produce when corralled by shock troops armed with truncheons. At each corner of the stands, there was a Kliment Voroshilov tank, barrel aimed straight into the terraces. I'd not been at the Berlin Olympics, but I bet it had this kind of feelgood vibe to it.

I jogged the lads out onto the pitch for a warm-up. At the other end of the field, the Maljerian backs were already drilling in tight formation. We hadn't even clapped eyes on our opposition yet. Badda Ladin had kept them well away from us for the duration of our stay. He hadn't even published a team sheet.

The Maljerian XV sprinted out onto the pitch. I watched them from the corner of my eye. My first impressions? They were lean, fast, tough, fit, big and hard.

Babadoo Ponsonby, second row, didn't like what he saw either. "I say, he's a bit of a unit," he murmured pointing at a shaven-headed thug doing press-ups with another man on his back. Bloody hell! Basto Staalcox, the South African flanker who had been banned from international rugby for biting off an opponent's ear and swallowing it whole. And stripe me if that wasn't Jonah Mussa, the Yeti of the Serengeti, a six-foot seven Tanzanian winger, who grew up on a farm and trained by pulling his father's broken tractors through the desert.

What the hell was going on?

I set my boys some drills, and went to speak with the referee, the diminutive Parisian Alain Floose. He looked rather tense. "A teamsheet of the Maljerian players please," I demanded

He handed it over with a flourish, "Voila! I sink eet will be a very interesting game, non?"

I read through their teamsheet with increasing dismay. As well as Staalcox and Mussa, there was Tinker McKendrick, the Scottish stamping legend, and Gladwell ap Neith, the angriest Welshman in Wales and the world. The list went on, and on, and I noticed the inclusion of Manasi Ratuva from Fiji, a squat fellow with demonic blood-red eyes from all the punches he'd taken. His party trick was opening coconuts by head-butting them.

"Every single man here is a banned international!" I said.

"Zey are not banned 'ere, Monsieur," he said, then added in a low voice, "Zis is not what I signed up for either. I tried to leave, but zey said zey'd keel me. Eef I werz you, I'd let zem win, and try not to become, 'ow you say… dead." Floose shrugged. It was good advice, I suppose, but advice I could not take.

I headed back to our boys, who were stretching each other's thighs, like I taught them. Cornwall jogged up to me with a tray of misshapen fruit slices. "Want half an orange, skipper?" he asked brightly.

"No, I bloody don't want half an orange," I snapped. "Can't you see what's going on? They've fielded a world class side of psychopaths."

"I don't see why that matters," Cornwall countered. "We're no angels ourselves."

I slapped the tray of oranges out of his hands. I must admit I was rattled, as our plan was bigger than this game of rugby. It was complex, requiring clarity and focus. And not being stamped to death by bigger boys. "What the bloody hell are you doing down here, anyway?" I hissed at him. "You know the deal. You should be up in the stands giving out the souvenirs."

"I'm off to do that now," he said, defensively, nodding to a hessian knapsack in which thousands of shiny medallions clinked together "Listen," he said, suddenly serious, "the weather report is dicey. Cloud cover due from the west. We'll have a smaller operational window than we thought."

"Well, it has to work," I said, "or we're dead."

Just then, a chorus of trumpets heralded Badda Ladin's entry onto the field. A phalanx of troops spread out to protect him as he waved triumphantly to the dejected crowd whose response was muted to say the least. Badda Ladin scowled, and nodded once to one of the troopers, who turned around and fired his rifle into the crowd. A circle of space cleared, to reveal a fellow bleeding profusely, his little son wailing in anguish.

The trooper took aim again. The crowd got the idea and began to cheer madly, "Ladin! Ladin! Ladin!" suddenly rabid in their enthusiasm for not being shot.

I turned to Cornwall. "Right, get up on the terraces and start doling out the medallions, quick smart."

Things went wrong from kick-off. The whistle blew. The ball was punted by Badda Ladin himself, their captain and fly-half, in a high parabola. It landed in our pack of massed forwards. Massingberd Q.C., with the enthusiasm and innocence one's first ever game of rugby brings, jumped high, caught the ball and smiled at me on the way down. "Easy!" he quipped, on landing. Then a truck named Staalcox collided with the small of his back. As Massingberd hit the grass he was instantly piled upon by six other Maljerian forwards, each of them digging, gouging, pinching, thumping and stamping on whatever part of his body they could find. The ball skittered loose and was scooped up by Tinker McKendrick, who sent it down the long tail of Maljerian backs, as effortlessly as a stone skimming across a lake.

My forwards set off in hot pursuit. I gazed down at Massingberd. He was not a pretty sight. "Alright?" I asked him, pulling him to his feet, where he wobbled around like a newborn foal.

"I'm going to pursue every single man in their team through the courts until they have nothing left," he vowed. "There will be no survivors."

The referee's whistle blew. A try to Maljeria in the corner, worth four points, back then. We'd been playing for less than two minutes and it was four-nil already.

Kick off again. The ball came sailing across the African sky towards us. This time, Massingberd didn't jump for it. He couldn't because his left kneecap had twisted the wrong way around. The ball fell to our other rugby virgin, Aram Atsi who tucked it casually under one arm. A colossal Maljerian lock led their charge but Atsi was like quicksilver in a hot pan, melting through the tackle. He began to make his way upfield with a thundering run. Atsi was our secret weapon, naïve in the laws of the game but a sensational specimen and natural athlete. With him in our team we'd always have a chance. Staalcox sensed it too, and with only yards to go from their try line ended his run with a brutal punch to the throat.

"Referee!" I called, "Surely that's a penalty!"

Floose was about to blow his whistle, when, "no foul, referee," called Badda Ladin, as he jogged past, drawing his finger across his neck.

"Pl-pl-play on," stammered Monsieur Floose.

The ball trundled back to me, I grabbed it and bullet-passed it out to our backs. But Ferdy Gunt's unnaturally elongated head got in the way of my inch-perfect delivery. The ball pinged off his forehead, stunning him like a clubbed salmon, and bouncing straight into the arms of

Mussa, who'd steamed into the melee on a speculative basis. Mussa cantered along for a bit, casually lamping Voss across the jaw as he went, and booting Eddie Klovacs in the stomach. He manoeuvred the ball to his left side, and then, realising he had a spare right arm that wasn't doing anything useful, used it to clothesline Squire, our plucky little scrum-half, who hit the deck and stayed there.

I looked down at Squire. He wasn't moving. "Come on ref!" I said, "You can see the swelling on his throat! That's the sin bin, surely?"

"No foul! Play on. Any back-chat from you, and I'll penalise for dissent," said Floose.

The ball skittered loose. Bertie Ravenscroft tried to pick it up, but as he stooped he was kneed in the face by a marauding Maljerian centre. It was easy for their outside half to grab the ball and break for our try line, and then convert the try: Ten-nil.

It soon became clear that the referee felt unable to penalise the Maljerian team, no matter how brazen the infraction. We were in for a very rough ride. Badda Ladin had bought together the worst bastards in rugby and given them national shirts. The game became lawless. Everyone was in danger of attack at all times, whether they were in possession of the ball or not. The crowd had warmed up too, cheering every kick, headbutt or punch to the kidneys. This was even more significant than it seemed. For our wider plan to work, we needed Badda Ladin to panic at the prospect of an embarrassing loss. The crowd had to see that he wasn't invincible. Instead, his team were scoring with impunity, while we were racking up horrible injuries.

With ten minutes to go before half time, Geoffrey Fastnet, our full back, caught the ball from a high kick. He jinked beautifully through three lumbering forwards and made twenty yards in an open sprint. He had Popsy O'Doherty on his right and Stormington on his left, and their try line was getting closer and closer. Their last line of defence was the Welsh maniac Gladwell ap Neith, a man who grew up tearing the wool off sheep in the Black Mountains. ap Neith broadsided Fastnet with the force of a juggernaut. It happened so swiftly that Fastnet didn't have time to stop running, his legs still pedalling as he tumbled, which accounted for their unnatural position as he hit the ground. There was a sickening, twisting crunch as something structural gave way. Fastnet was splayed like a run-over cat.

I got to him quickly. He was gasping for breath, his left leg severely misaligned. He let out a strangled groan. I called our doctor, Isambard Voss, over to examine him.

"Help me," begged the deathly pale Fastnet, who had begun a long shuddering fit on the grass.

"The leg is dislocated. It's come out of the hip socket," Voss said, grim-faced, rubbing his vast handlebar moustache. "We need to get him to a hospital right away."

Badda Ladin stepped forward. "We have a saying in Maljeria," he leered. "When the lame camel stops producing milk, smash its skull in with a rock."

Fastnet had gone a shade of puce. His forehead was slick with sweat.

Badda Ladin continued, "He is weak and near death. I'll get one of my guards to dispatch him."

I nudged Voss to do something, he was a bloody doctor after all.

"We may be able to avoid that," Voss said, "if... well, it's been a while since I did one of these, but it should just pop back, I suppose."

Voss took hold of Fastnet's leg. "It's a simple matter of angles. We need to ram the ball joint at the top of the thigh back into the hip socket," he explained, as he grappled the leg into the right position. Fastnet cried out in agony.

"Trevelyan, get behind me and shove hard when I say," the doctor continued, "we'll have this fixed in a jiffy," said Voss, in his best bedside manner. "One, two..."

-CRAAAAAACK-

"...three! Excellent!" Voss announced immediately, "it went straight back in."

I was expecting to see a look of sweet relief upon Fastnet's face. Instead, his soul broke in two. He began a low keening noise that rose smoothly through his entire vocal range, before he hit a piercing top-C. It was the sound of a solitary wolf. The last of a species crying alone in the forest. The sound of loss. The sound of Pain itself. The terrible echo filled the stadium, silencing it. And then the noise died away to nothing.

"Ahh," Voss gulped.

"What's the matter? What's happened?"

"Something went wrong."

"What?"

"Ummm. Well, errrr, I think that when I performed the, er, relocating of the thigh ball back into the, er, hip socket, I may have, er…"

"Spit it out man!"

"I may have, ahhmm, forgotten to evaginate his testicular pouch from the manouveral theatre."

"What the hell are you talking about?"

"His left nut is trapped inside his hip joint."

"What?"

"It's now under intense pressure. If he moves even an inch it'll probably burst and be ground into a paste." Voss began to warm to the theme. "Imagine a clove of garlic crushed inside a pestle and mortar."

I looked at Fastnet. He was smashing his fists against the turf, as if he were having an epileptic seizure and giving birth to a two-stone baby at the same time. "Kill… me!" he whispered. "Please, someone! Just… kill… me…"

Badda Ladin motioned to one of his guards to finish Fastnet off.

"No, no, no," I stepped in. "We'll simply dislocate his thigh again and his scrotum will drop back out, won't it?"

"Er…yessss?" said Voss, uncertainly. And then, remembering that he was a doctor, repeated more definitely, "yes."

Getting Fastnet off the pitch was not done well, the kit boy's fault. Cornwall tripped on his laces, dropping his end of the stretcher. Fastnet tumbled off it onto – terrible luck– a bag full of boots. Seeing as he was already back on the ground, Voss decided to get on with re-dislocating the thigh, and after some manoeuvring, Fastnet's mangled scrotum was released from its bony prison. It flopped out of his shorts like a reject from a chicken escalope factory.

We relocated the hip joint for a second time. Then we were forced to re-dislocate it once more as, sod's law, exactly the same thing had happened again. Finally we crunched it back into position once more to Voss' satisfaction.

"Are we ready now?" said Badda Ladin, holding the ball, and keen for the restart.

Luckily at that moment Floose blew up for half time. Twenty-eight points to Maljeria. Zero to the Cavaliers.

We trudged off the field and back to the changing rooms for a very hard look at ourselves.

We took stock.

Three of the wooden fingers on Ruff Puff's hand had cracked off. "I can't catch the ball like this," he reasoned, "so I'm going to make some alterations." He picked up a clasp knife and began to whittle his hand. Soon he'd fashioned it into an evil wooden spike.

I shrugged. "Fair enough. We're not really playing Union laws out there, are we?"

I checked on Fastnet who Cornwall had put into a medically induced coma. It dawned on me that I couldn't send this man back on the field. And though I knew he couldn't hear me, I still made a show of bawling him out for letting the side down. Who the bloody hell else could take on the full back duties, I raged, kicking over a box of ice.

Inevitably, an argument ensued about how wise it might have been to bring more than one replacement player, until Cornwall cleared his throat. "I've a little experience at full back," he said. "Might as well put me in."

I scowled. "Fine. Get changed. But don't make a hash of it and remember the plan." The look of delight on Cornwall's stupid face was almost enough to make me smile. But not quite. "There's one more thing," I said.

"What?"

"Get your medicine box out. We need it for the second half."

Cornwall emptied his knapsack onto the physio table. A bewildering range of ampoules, pills and creams.

"Chaps, gather round," I called. "We're going to do things differently for the rest of the game, so pay attention." The team huddled around us and switched on.

I picked up a pouch of lozenges. "Tell us what these do."

"An anti-psychotic for chimps," said Cornwall. "Haloperidol. It makes them forget they are chimps."

"Good," I grabbed a tiny vial with a quarter-inch syringe, inside which was a dark blue concoction, "and this?"

"Hydromorphone with gabapentin. The Japanese

use it to subdue sumo wrestlers. Side effects are rough though," he warned.

"What are they?" asked Stormington.

"Prolonged projectile defecation, then deep sleep for seventy-two hours."

"Perfect. And this spray?"

"That's not mine. It was in Gunt's locker. It's for premature ejaculation…" Gunt nodded sheepishly. "One squirt causes total muscle paralysis."

Cornwall gave us a whistle-stop tour of his stocks of propofol, pyrantel, tramadol, levetiracetam and bethanecol. He had quite the collection. Drugs from every corner of the earth, for human and veterinary use, licensed and experimental. He had uppers and downers, drugs to make you cry, to fight, to sleep, to mate, to piss less, to piss more, to raise your heart rate, to make you temporarily blind, to stop feeling pain or to feel pain a lot more painfully.

"Right, we're going to start dosing these bastards with one thousand percent of whatever the recommended daily allowance is. Pick your opposite number," I said, "and get something pharmaceutical inside him, any way you can. Mission critical."

"But what about Badda Ladin?" asked Cornwall.

"Leave him to me," I said. "Captain's privilege."

We marched back out to the field of play. We had a rugby match to win.

At the start of the second half, Maljeria were in front by twenty-eight points to nothing. They'd scored five tries and converted all but one of them. It wasn't long, though, before we started levelling the playing field.

Staalcox was brought down on our 22-yard line by an elbow to his windpipe by Ponsonby. A punch-up ensued, and while Floose sorted that out, Aram Atsi grabbed Manasi Ratuva, and I stuffed three lozenges of haloperidol into his mouth and choked him until he swallowed. At the ensuing scrum Ratuva stood stock still and then pitched forward, his forehead hitting the ground first. While he was dragged from the field, Duckworth and O'Doherty stuck a line of LSD tabs onto the back of Mussa's neck, and another behind his knee. He skipped off the pitch and began to kiss and cuddle the floodlight post.

We dosed and spiked our way through the entire Maljerian team. We finally bagged Staalcox in the middle of a ruck, when Maurice split open the back of his shorts with a razor blade, and Gunt rammed a gabapentin suppository into his rectum. As it melted into his bloodstream, Staalcox became more and more pliant, until Squire was able to simply topple him over and stamp on his face.

The scores changed rapidly. Maurice pranced over the line for a showy try in the corner, and Stormington touched down under the posts after blowing a cloud of powdered tramadol into ap Neith's eyes. I scored in a quick and efficient sixth phase rollover, then Klovacs bundled the ball over just as Popsy slapped a handful of propofol paste onto the side of McKendrick's neck. He slumped to the grass, curled up, shat himself and began sucking his thumb. 28-24.

By now, Badda Ladin was losing his rag. His side had been decimated, and there was still six minutes left to play. I chose this moment to jog up to him for a bit of a chat. I put my arm around on his shoulder, as if I was discussing a technical point. "I know all about the work you do for Hansclapp," I said, cheerily. "Enjoy this last five minutes of rugby before we burn your stadium to the ground." He gaped at me. I jogged off before he could reply.

Scoring our last try was a piece of cake. By this point they only had three players who could walk, and that included a slew of replacements that Floose should not have let come on. After their restart, I caught the ball and evaded an ambitious tackle from the one remaining Maljerian flanker, who was struggling against the effects of an equine anti-psychotic. I ran over to Ruff Puff on the wing and stabbed the ball onto the end of his hand spike. He trundled himself over the try line and plunged his arm into the turf, to level the scores as the timer ticked eighty minutes. Twenty-eight points to twenty-eight.

We had a conversion attempt left.

I stood with Cornwall in front of the posts.

We were watching the sky carefully.

This was the tricky bit. The instant we took those points, and victory, we'd be signing our death warrants. But for our plan to catch fire he needed to be unmasked in front of his people as a petulant, foot-stamping child, unfit to rule. And for reasons that would become clear, the weather needed to be perfect.

"You ready?" I murmured, under the guise of doing up my bootlaces.

"Just say when," replied Cornwall.

I scanned the skies again. The scudding clouds were beginning to clear, revealing the powerful Maljerian sun. "Delay, half a minute," I said.

Cornwall began to carefully build a little mound of earth for the new ball to sit on, so he could take the conversion. He took an age. Badda Ladin was marching up and down his try-line, incandescent. Something inside him snapped, "Trevelyan, if your man converts that try, the Cavaliers will all die," he screamed, foam flecking his lips like a rabid dog.

The crowd began to stir, but not enough. Yet.

I kept a careful eye on the skies. The clouds were beginning to clear.

As Cornwall continued to draw out his kicking preparations, Badda Ladin rushed over to his personal guard, ordering them to strip off their uniforms and join the team. "There are a full ten minutes left," he screamed in Floose's face, "the game will continue after this kick."

Floose chose this moment to develop a backbone. "I'm afraid zis is ze last kick of zer game, Your Excellency," he shrugged, motioning to the game clock. Floose turned his back on Badda Ladin and blew his whistle for Cornwall to take the kick.

Badda Ladin had never been told 'non' in his life. He snatched a scimitar from a guard and ran after Floose. With a single devastating stroke, he buried it into the top of Floose's skull. The curved blade protruded from the referee's head, like a coxcomb, in a gross facsimile of his nation's Gallic rooster emblem.

Floose fell to the grass, dead.

This was so brutal and unsporting that the crowd actually began to jeer and boo their President. And right on cue the sun began to shine brightly in the azure sky.

"Right," I said to Cornwall, "two points please."

Cornwall took a single step back and tapped the ball cleanly between the centre of the uprights. Two points, and a final score of 28-30 to the Cavaliers.

Killing the referee had sated nothing in Badda Ladin's black heart. His face was livid. His beloved team had been beaten. He called a stream of aggressive commands in his native tongue, and I was seized by two burly guards. Cornwall got the same treatment.

Badda Ladin drew his forefinger across his throat. "The Cavaliers have cheated at this great game," he announced. "They will now be beheaded! Guards, carry out my sentence."

The team was immediately surrounded by guards, who corralled us all to the half-way line. Two more guards jogged out with a scarred chopping block, rimed with blackened blood. The portly figure of Zakash, Badda Ladin's court torturer, strode out onto the field holding a scimitar. This was looking dicey.

The crowd's dissent seemed to be growing in volume, as the preparations for our summary execution continued. If our plan was going to work, it had to be now. I only hoped the crowd would play ball.

Zakash offered his weapon to Badda Ladin, who

seized it. He had evidently decided to cut our heads off himself. Brandishing the scimitar, he gave a few practice swipes through the air. "You will not live to regret the day you dishonoured Maljeria," he snarled at me.

Suddenly a speck of concentrated sunlight appeared on Badda Ladin's chest. He looked down at it, perplexed. A lone brave soul in the crowd was taking a stand and reflecting a ray of sunlight onto him, using a little silver medallion.

The bright speck was joined by another, dancing across Badda Ladin's jersey. A third beam fell on his shoulder and another one flashed across his eyes, making him flinch. Another beam of light, this time from the northern end of the stadium, struck his neck. Then a fifth and a sixth. Suddenly, the idea caught on and everyone realised they could join in. In seconds, medallions appeared from everywhere, as people in the crowd directed slashes of sunlight towards the man who had persecuted them for so long. Soon thousands of beams of light were firing down on him from all sides of the stadium.

Badda Ladin started to panic, as more glinting beams lanced his eyes. He tried to shield himself, but the rays of reflected sunlight were increasing with every passing second. He dropped the scimitar and began to wriggle frantically, swatting the beams away as if they were a swarm of invisible bees, but the crowd had only to tilt their convex medallions infinitesimally to find him again.

The thick black hair on Badda Ladin's chest began to smoulder, as every part of his body began to cook. He started to run, but he couldn't rid himself of the rays that tracked him around the field. His shirt smouldered at the back, causing him to wheel around, slapping at himself. Panic-stricken, he called for his guards, but they backed away from him, throwing down their weapons. Now, from all sides of the stadium, the stream became a river became a Niagara of concentrated light pouring down upon him, a devastating matrix of death from which there was no escape. Badda Ladin began to scream. His jersey burst into flames. I watched as the meat of his thighs blistered and blackened.

In seconds his turban became a beacon of flame and his fingers were melting and dripping fat, like sausages on the world's most unpleasant barbecue. Inside the fire, I saw his will break. It does me no credit, but I confess I rather enjoyed it. I smiled at him, meeting his eyes, even as his beard sizzled to nothing, exposing the glowing white of his superheated jawbone.

I wanted him to know with his last breath that I was responsible for his demise.

"Twenty-eight points to thirty," I crowed, shaking my head as if I were terribly disappointed. "And, just so you know, we're not even a real rugby team."

His skull melted. Within thirty seconds it was over. Badda Ladin resembled a waxy stump of candle grease, surrounded by charred bones.

Once the crowed realised their tyrannical leader was dead, things got a bit hectic. There was a sort of unleashing of spirit, an instantaneous festival of violence, that sometimes happens during times of sudden revolt.

The whole scene reminded me of our retreat from Wan Booli camp in '45. The crowd tore up the structure of the stadium and beat guards to death with railings and bricks.

"We should move to phase two now, skipper," shouted Cornwall, as a dot of light appeared on his chest.

"Agreed," I said, as a dot appeared on mine. "Off we go."

I motioned to the team. Running together in a tight pack, we hustled our way off the pitch, and out of the stadium as quickly as we could.

Now we had some real work to do.

We descended into the bowels of the stadium, no longer a marauding rugby team, but a disciplined unit. The guards had already vacated their posts, so our progress was unimpeded. We found what we were looking for. A set of steel double doors led to a corridor which led, under the pitch, to a bunker. We entered a state-of-the-art weapons lab configured in much the same way as Veck Mangal's factory in Istanbul. We located stockpiles of dried algae, used in the production of Bosphorus Phosphorus, and a cabinet of lab notes which we began to load into bergens. There was a single gunshot from a corner office, and a jagged spray of blood leapt up onto the inside of the window.

Maurice and Squire rounded up the lab technicians and scientists.

"Cooperate quickly and you'll survive the next few minutes," I explained to the group. "Don't and you won't. I need an English speaker."

Silence.

Maurice fired his pistol above their heads. One scientist panicked and tried to make a run for it, but Aram Atsi tapped him lightly on the chin and he fell to the floor.

"I need an English speaker," I repeated, "or this idiot dies." I raised my weapon, hoping that I would not have to pull the trigger.

A young scientist raised her hand and stepped forward. "I speak English," she said.

"Where do you keep the refined product?"

"It's all in there," she said, pointing to a refrigeration unit.

Cornwall opened the fridge door. Inside were the vials of glowing green liquid that Hansclapp had managed to get away with from the Orient Express years before. "Is this all of it?"

The scientist nodded. "That's all the Bosphorus Phosphorus."

Cornwall picked up the vials and dropped them on the floor. Some shattered. Others were stamped on by the Cavaliers' boots. As arranged, Cornwall palmed one of the vials, slipping it into his pocket.

I scanned the lab. It looked like a fully functioning production facility to me. "I was expecting to find tons of Bosphorus Phosphorus here, not just these vials. What else are you making?"

The scientist hesitated. She was weighing up her options, which, given that she worked for Gruber Hansclapp, were not good ones. "*Catilansanthropaltic bosothoncantalene* – what you call Bosphorus Phosphorus – was not something we could make here."

"Explain."

"After the destruction of our Istanbul facility we had to find another source of algae, which led us to a region of Northern England."

"Where?" Cornwall asked sharply.

"Newcastle. Specifically, the southern banks of the Tyne."

"Bloody hell, Bosphorus Phosphorus is being made on home soil."

"Not Bosphorus Phosphorus," the scientist corrected. "The English algae has a subtly different structure from the algae in Istanbul, which changed everything."

"How do you mean?"

"For a long time, we didn't understand how dangerous it was. It's uniquely unstable, and we suffered many setbacks."

"Setbacks?" asked Cornwall.

"With the Tyneside synthesis we recorded a GHS toxicity class of I+ and a similar exothermic reaction profile to Semtex, as well as dramatic new functions."

"When I asked you to speak English, I meant English," I warned her.

The scientist let out a long breath, trying to keep her panic under control. "It no longer functioned as a mind control drug," she faltered. "It functioned as a bomb."

"A bomb?"

"The new algae created a new compound, at a genetic level, unlike anything we'd ever seen. Once ingested, it can't be excreted."

"It accumulates in the body?"

"Yes," she gulped. "A sudden movement, or a loud noise even, can set it off."

"How did you find this out?"

"One of our researchers, Dr Adrian Briggs, discovered it…" and her voice rose an octave, "…by accident."

"What happened?"

"Part of his job was to take microdoses to build up a tolerance. The compound forms a hard bolus and lodges in the stomach wall. It's metabolically bisturbile."

"Get to the point," I said.

"It turns out each gram, once ingested, has the same potential energy as a hand grenade," she explained. "Dr Briggs was buying a snack from the vending machine, and our best guess is…" She pulled off her glasses and rubbed her eyes, "…his chocolate bar got stuck in the little curly metal bars." She made a tight circular motion with her finger as she relived the memory. Briggs was angry. All he did was thump the glass to try and dislodge it, but…" she started to sob.

"Tell me," I said.

"The compound performed a rapid unscheduled disassembly inside his stomach."

"Come again?"

"Briggs blew up. He went everywhere. It was disgusting."

"Bloody hell," said Cornwall.

"So if you can't make Bosphorus Phosphorus anymore," I asked, "what's this stuff called?

The scientist looked sheepish. "Tyneside Cyanide," she said.

"On whose orders did you make this? Badda-Ladin?"

"No, we report to a German lady."

"A German lady?" Cornwall rummaged around his bag looking for something. "Is this her?" He held up a raunchy photo of Marjorie in lingerie. I didn't remember taking that photo and made a mental note to quiz him about it.

She nodded.

We quizzed the scientists about other factories, but I knew that Hansclapp would have told them nothing of his network. I explained that Badda Ladin was dead, and that they had thirty seconds to leave before we started shooting, and that ten of those seconds had already elapsed. They ran for the exits.

Then we relaxed a bit and used some of the science equipment to brew a really excellent pot of Yorkshire Gold. It was a real luxury to be able to keep the brewing temperature at exactly 94.6 degrees for four and a half minutes, while we waited for the crowd upstairs to fully disperse. We didn't have long to wait. People were desperate to spread the word of Badda Ladin's demise and were flowing out of the exits. The Maljerian Revolution had begun.

Furdy Gunt rigged the lab with the three pounds of nitroglycerine he'd been keeping in his boot bag. He slapped on a fifteen-minute fuse and we double-timed it north out of the city, commandeering a bus to get us to the desert.

Three miles out of the city, we pulled over to the side of the road, to watch the stadium blow up. I felt a curious sense of pride as I watched it burn. The Palace was on fire too. Evidently, the Maljerian Revolution had begun.

Our Hercules was waiting at the R.V., propellers already spinning. We bundled into it, eager to get home. "Baggsy the cockpit," called Cornwall.

"Not a chance," said Massingberd Q.C., slapping a piece of foolscap paper with a lion and unicorn crest onto his chest. "You've been served, Victor. At Trevelyan's bidding I applied for an injunction against you sitting up front," he explained, so get your arse in the back."

Massingberd nodded to me. "Cockpits are for captains," he said.

I've always thought it a shame that we'd stage-managed a first-class revolution and rid the world of a despicable tyrant, but that the real story had been hitherto lost to history. Until now! How apt that the world will finally know the true origins of the statue with its magnificent flowing locks, dressed in full rugby garb, that stands in Revolution Square.

It was cast, the taxi-drivers say, from the metal of thousands of tiny medallions.

Yours sincerely,
Major Arthur St. John Trevelyan.

Hellcat Manor
Great Trundleford
Devon
May 10th 2021

Dear Major,

That game was won on the rugby fields of Winstowe College, which you'll remember is where we first used magnifying glasses to laser frogs at lunch break.

I regret to inform you that the statue that you commissioned in your likeness is no longer standing in Maljeria. It was torn down after a few days and the sculptor hanged for colluding with a foreign power.

Since then, Maljeria has gone from strength to strength. Its young, hopeful democracy now provides over 35% of the world's pornographic actors and its poppy fields are the envy of the world.

Upon returning to England, I made a concerted effort to kick the heroin into touch. Baxter built a monastic rehabilitation retreat in the grounds of Hellcat, and put me on a daily routine of yoga, meditation and purging. His purge required me to drink a foul liquid that caused me to projectile vomit many times a day, until I'd lost two-thirds of my bodyweight. He then resolved to rebuild me, sending me out on dawn runs and hunting me down on his quad bike. After a few weeks, I started hitting the gym hard, took salad with my steak, and indulged in nothing stronger than a good 18-year-old single malt. I was fifty-three, but looked thirty-three.

I was off the *horse* but the good times wouldn't last.

CHAPTER 7
AN UNFORTUNATE TURN OF EVENTS

DOVER, NOVEMBER 1974

It was a cold, clear autumnal morning in October, when I found myself taking part in a ding-dong*, on a breezy Kent clifftop. We were here to commemorate the long life of Frederick Bilkingson, a well-loved, affable old Scoundrel who as a young man spent the First World War undercover, running the Kaiser's morning bath and reporting his chit-chat back to Whitehall. Arguably, Bilkingson laid down a lot of track for modern espionage techniques used today. He also ran the Club's Meat Raffle throughout the 1950s, and was remembered fondly for his diplomacy and tact, always presiding over this high-stakes evening with hardly ever a controversy. I asked him once how he did it. He said that hosting the Meat Raffle required an iron hand in a velvet glove holding a sledgehammer. He once pitched both Andrew

---

*   A ding-dong is the collective noun for a meeting of Scoundrels. This can be
      traced all the way back to Sir Robert Walpole who came into the Club as a guest
      of George II. Walpole was being given the grand tour and put his head around
      the corner of the Long Room where some of the chaps were boisterously re-
      enacting the early death of a Scoundrel who had been backed over by a cannon
      whilst making love to his mistress in a Green Park laurel bush. "Some kind of
      ding-dong taking place in there," he remarked, and the name stuck.

McGuthrey and Conrad Barber through a window, after they disturbed the peace about 10lbs of zebra fillet, won by ticket 16, or 91, depending on whose side you took. Bilkingson was also an innovator. He introduced typewritten tickets and the refrigeration of the prize meat, after the infamous Burmese python casserole of '36, which claimed so many innocent lives.

My father once told me that you could measure a man by his taste in Burgundy, and today, in celebration of a life well led, we were drinking the finest. In the weeks before his death, Bilkingson simply would not accept that his powers were waning. The end came when he absconded from his nursing home to visit Heavy Betsy's. When the paramedics arrived, Betsy directed them to the basement where they found him bent over a table dressed as a traffic warden, cap and all. His shorts were still around his ankles and he had light cane marks on his buttocks. Betsy herself was dressed as an angry lady motorist in twinset and pearls. The paramedics reported that his heart didn't stand a chance, but also that his smile was worthy of a toothpaste commercial. The death was recorded as caused by misadventure, which was ironic because Miss Adventure was one of Betsy's other popular personas. And at £30 an hour, better value too.

Bilkingson's last will and testament stipulated that his body be placed inside the barrel of a Howitzer and fired in the general direction of France. The head of the Royal Artillery was an old pal and he had wangled it. The regimental brass band played a maudlin Grieg funeral march, before we were instructed to put our fingers in our ears. There followed a giant whump, and a shockwave felt in the chest, and we were shrouded in a thick cloud of Howitzer smoke. Somehow, I found myself next to Hendricks. I thought briefly about shoving him off the White Cliffs, but we were at Frederick's funeral and I didn't want to cause a scene. It was an awkward encounter.

"Fine chap," he remarked, coughing and waving away the fug.

"One of the best," I replied. "Terrific way to go, too."

"Yes, splendid." He shifted uncomfortably then said, "shame Trevelyan couldn't make it. Bit off don't you think, to miss a chap's funeral?"

"I'm sure Fred would understand," I said. "Trevelyan's had his fill of funerals for a while."

"Quite so." There was an ugly silence. "Well cheers to Frederick then."

"Cheers."

We raised our glasses.

"Are you sticking around for the fireworks? I hear the Navy will be scuppering his old yacht. Might be worth seeing."

"I have to get back to London. I have an appointment at Purdey's this afternoon."

"New gun?"

"For the boy."

"The gor-..." I could see Hendricks struggle with this question, "...you've ordered a Purdey for a gorilla?"

I turned to face him, squaring up. "Yes, I have," I said.

Hendricks grunted and looked out to sea.

James Purdey & Sons was one of the finest gunmakers in the country. I was picking up Titus' first gun, now that he was old enough to come shooting with me. It was, if I was being true to myself, a last gasp attempt at turning him into a proper Englishman. Due to his oversized hairy fingers, and poor impulse control he'd need a leg up if he was going to make a success of life in our fusty old culture. He'd struggled with some of my instruction of the traditional country pursuits. I'd tried to teach him to ride, but the only thing that he could saddle was a shire horse – but Titus pulled his tail off after he was dismounted at a low stile. So instead I tried to make a hunter of him, utilizing his natural cunning and stealthiness honed in his early months in the Congo rainforests. But when we tracked a fox back to its den, he simply stamped the whole thing in, and paraded around with it like a sock-puppet on his hairy fist. I despaired. I mean, he was no worse than some of the chaps I'd grown up with, but I needed more than that from my firstborn and heir. I'd thrown money, no object, at the situation. A handmade shotgun from Purdey might give him the confidence he needed. At £162,000 it was an exquisite work of art, crafted from Damascene steel with a stock made from woolly mammoth tusk.

After that I was scheduled to meet Trevelyan at Scoundrels for our weekly catch up on our shared business activities. This was usually a dull affair where Trevelyan would struggle with a giant calculator and accuse me of siphoning off funds. But by the early evening we'd both be pissed on Scotch and all would be forgotten.

Baxter dropped me off at South Audley Street. Trouble was waiting. Purdey's manager, a weasel-faced man called Mellonshire, met me at the door. "I'm terribly sorry, sir, but there seems to be a bit of a problem," he said. His voice trembled with nerves, but I was in a garrulous mood.

"Why? You didn't drop it, did you Mellonshire?" I quipped, and then realised that actually wouldn't be funny so added, "you didn't, did you?"

"No sir, the gun is in perfect condition, but-"

"Good. Let's see it then!" I clapped my hands together and embarked on a rambling reverie, as was my wont. "Ah, Mellonshire, you can't imagine the joy I'll feel when I watch my boy tear open this gift for his birthday. The look on his face. His beautiful big brown eyes, like a couple of dark pools of dangerously deep water, looking back at me and saying, 'thank you, Father. Thank you for trusting me with a loaded firearm, even though I'm not sure which end goes bang'…" Mellonshire attempted to cut in, but I hadn't finished. "It's such a bloody delight to be able to enjoy sport, just a father and his son. I imagine you remain unmarried, Mellonshire, but trust me. It will be a very, very special moment."

"The cheque you wrote last week, sir," he grimaced, "I'm afraid it hasn't gone through."

I looked at him as if he'd spoken gibberish. I shrugged. Mellonshire tried again. "I'm afraid you won't be able to take the gun until it has."

I wasn't sure what he meant. "When you say hasn't, *gone through*, what does that actually mean?"

Mellonshire squirmed, "Er… well sir, usually it means that one doesn't have enough funds," then he added quickly, "although I'm sure that's not the case, in this instance."

My temperature was rising rapidly. "Of course I have the funds in my account. It's only £162,000! This is ridiculous."

"Well, sir, the bank… "

"The bank what?" I snapped. "Get Coutts on the phone this instant!"

I wandered off around the shop to pass the time while he called the bank. They may have been the finest gunmakers in England but this Mellonshire chap wasn't up to much. There was obviously some mistake.

I tried on a deerstalker and admired myself in a mirror while Mellonshire explained the situation. "Is that Gideon?" I shouted across the room, "tell him it's Victor!"

"Sir, the manager requires your password."

I bristled at this and snatched the phone from Mellonshire. I knew the manager well. Gideon Longhorn used to polish my shoes at Winstowe.

"What the bloody hell is this all about then, Gidders? Why can't I buy my gun?"

He asked me for my password. I checked no one was listening. "It's F – u – f – f – y," I said.

Gideon explained the hiccup. It was more than a hiccup.

"Yes. Uh huh... I see... oh, right. Yes. Uh huh... Is it? Ahhhh. And... is that normal? Of course... Right. And this was when? Okaaaaay...ah righto... I see. So... what you're saying is...Well, I never... Thank you, Gideon. That all makes perfect sense now."

I put the phone down gently.

I found that my hand was trembling.

Mellonshire looked at me and smiled hopefully. "All okay now, sir?"

"Not really, Mellonshire, I'd say it was just about the bloody opposite."

I staggered out of the shop and onto the street and was almost immediately knocked over by a black cab. The horn blared out as it skidded to a halt. I looked up just in time to receive a mouthful of Cockney invective from the driver. I stumbled away still not believing what I'd just heard.

Apparently, my Coutts account had been stripped of everything.

Everything.

In cash terms, I was penniless.

I wandered around the streets of St James's trying to piece it all together. I couldn't figure how it might have happened. Had I been gambling much lately? No. Had I got completely pissed and bought something really expensive, like, say, the Isle of Wight, without remembering it? Don't think so. I trudged about for hours, light-headed. Then, somehow, I found myself standing outside Scoundrels, its immaculate Regency exterior looking more elegant than usual in the cold November sun. Aram Atsi had his greatcoat pulled tightly around him. He held open the door for me. More than ever, I craved the welcome of the Club's warm bosom.

It was still early so I knew the drawing room wouldn't be busy. I needed a stiff drink. I found my favourite chair by the open fire and slumped down waiting for one of the staff members to bring me something very strong and very Scottish.

Just then the door swung open and in came Jonty Pulvertaft, pushing Ruff Puff in his wheelchair. His head was badly cut and there was blood all over his face. He was furious.

"Ged me back in there Puwlvertaft! That thun of a bit'th ith gunna get a thucking good hiding."

"Steady now," said Pulvertaft, who had a thick red welt across his face. "Come in here and cool off."

"He thwu a vase at me," Ruff Puff spat.

"Please calm down, Jerry," said Pulvertaft, "we need to attend to that wound."

I got up from the chair. Ruff Puff seemed both relieved and angry to see me. "Juth'd the per'thon! Cornwall, you're gowin to luv thith."

"Trouble?" I said.

"Twuble? That fwend of yor'th hath gone bertherk He 'ith smathing up the Juwels Verne woom. That'th twuble."

I looked at Pulvertaft for confirmation. He nodded, "Trevelyan has gone a bit bonkers, I'm afraid. He's locked himself in the Jules Verne room."

"He'th ath'olted a dith'abled man, that'th what he'th done!" Ruff Puff was pointing to the cut on his head.

Pulvertaft said, "I've never seen him like this, Cornwall. You need to talk him down."

I suddenly felt tired. It wasn't like I didn't have my own troubles to worry about. I made my way through the Atrium, past the Stuffed Frenchman and up the Lower Grand Staircase. I stopped by the sporting memorabilia cabinets, helped myself to a couple of items and continued up the stairs.

A crowd had gathered around the door to the Jules Verne room. Joan the Coat Lady was loading her tranquiliser rifle. Thankfully, Summerville was there too. When she saw me, she told the others to clear off.

"I don't know what's got into him but he's causing havoc. See if you can talk him down before he does any more damage." I nodded, put on the scrum cap, popped in the gumshield and banged on the door.

Eventually the door opened half an inch. Trevelyan's massive head was behind it, but I could only see an eye and a bit of wonky nose.

"Hullo, St. John," I said, evenly. "Feel like letting me in?"

The door slammed shut and there were a few more crashes and bangs, then the door opened slowly.

The room was wrecked. Trevelyan had demolished everything, and in the process it looked like he'd demolished himself too. His knuckles were bleeding and I could see ragged holes in the plasterwork where he'd been punching the walls. He regarded me with desperate, wild eyes and slumped down on one of the Chesterfields. "It's gone," he said. "All of it."

"What's gone?"

"My money. Every penny. I've been taken to the cleaners, Cornwall." He sagged into the seat. "I just don't understand it," he said.

I thought about Purdey's and things started to make sense. Both of us had lost our money. That was no coincidence.

"I understand it," I said, stony faced. "I've been cleaned out too."

Trevelyan's eyes met mine.

"We've been robbed, old friend," I said. "Who could have done such a thing?"

Not only had our personal fortunes been stolen, Cornvelyan Enterprises had been stripped of all assets. Someone had done their homework. We literally had nothing. Our estates had even been seized and donated to the National Trust. We discussed the prospect of hiring Massingberd to get everything back for us through legal channels, but a finger in the air calculation showed we couldn't even afford enough of his time to tell him what had happened.

Summerville found us, looking sombre. "I need you both to come to my office, now," she said.

We climbed over the smashed furniture and followed her downstairs. She led us at funereal pace. I noticed several members couldn't make eye contact as we passed. The air felt negatively charged, as if a terrible event was about to occur. Only Maurice, when we crossed him on the stair, gave me a thump on the shoulder. But it was a thump of sympathy, and I could see by his face that some very bad news had broken.

Sitting in her office was the last person in the world I wanted to see. Hendricks. After Periford's death, he'd been made General Secretary, and he was clearly here in an official capacity. He had a dusty black book in front of him, from the archives by the look of it.

Summerville closed the door behind us.

Hendricks offered us a thin smile.

"What's going on here?" I asked him.

"A serious infraction, I'm afraid." I could see that he was relishing every moment of this.

Summerville sighed. "Ancient Club Rules. Hendricks has been doing some research, apparently." Summerville looked at him with undisguised dislike. "I've yet to understand why."

"I've always been fascinated by Club history," Hendricks countered. "And it's astonishing what you can find in these old books." He opened the tome to a pre-marked page. "This is the Club's original Rulebook. Containing every Rule passed since 1642. There are some crackers in here. The game of conkers, for instance," he ran his finger over the spidery text. "It is against Club rules to use a conker that has been soaked in mead," he read, and tilted up his punchable face to us, raising his eyebrows in mock surprise. "It's deemed *ungentlemanly*."

"Every schoolboy knows that a conker needs to be passed through a pig and then cured for a year before it's battle ready," Trevelyan replied.

"Why are we here, Hendricks?" I sighed. "Trevelyan and I could do with a drink."

"I'm sure you could," Hendricks fired back, "but that may not be possible." He held my gaze for a moment before reading from the book again. "You'll like this. It is instant expulsion for any Scoundrel caught sodomising the Monarch's swans."

"You must be heartbroken," I said, eyeballing him.

Summerville repressed a smile.

"I think you'll find this one most illuminating," Hendricks turned the page again, "because it says here that: *All memberes must be able to guarantee and paye all debts upon the demande of any other membere at any time, including bar billes, annual subscriptions and contributions. Failure to pay on demande will result in revocation of membership.*'"

Hendricks looked up, brightly. "I don't think I'd ever read that one before."

The air in the room was stale. Hendricks somehow knew we had no money and he was going for the jugular. He removed a black billiard ball from his pocket and placed it on the table in front of him.

Blackballed. Thrown out of the Club. By one of the few men who I truly detested.

Hendricks now had the bar ledger open in front of him. "Cornwall. You have an outstanding bar bill of £82,645.49."

I shrugged. Ordinarily I would have quipped "loose change" or "ring my accountant," but I no longer had the conviction to do so.

Hendricks turned the page. "Major Trevelyan, your bar bill for this month so far stands at £197,462."

Even I was a little surprised by that and shot him a quick look. He whispered something about Virtanen and Ponsonby and a couple of bottles of 70-year-old Macallan Lalique. By now, though, Hendricks was in full flow. "These bills must be paid upon request by any Club member. And I'm requesting it. Settle your bills, here and now."

Summerville interjected, "Come on, Hendricks, don't be such a prig. This isn't practical, and–"

"Is the Membership and Operations Secretary really telling me the Club Rules are incorrect?" Hendricks mock-horror was difficult to take. "Well I never. I should report this to the Committee."

Summerville held her tongue. Clearly, she'd been broadsided by this. Club Rules were Club Rules. Sacrosanct. But this wasn't cricket.

"Well?" Hendricks sneered. "Are you able to settle or not?"

Whichever way I looked at it the answer was the same. No. I swallowed my pride. "I cannot pay the bill here and now."

"How about you Major Trevelyan?"

Trevelyan shook his head.

Hendricks smiled. "In which case, and of course I say this with deep regret, I have no other option than to revoke your membership with immediate effect," he smiled, slamming the book shut.

Summerville spoke. "For the time being."

Hendricks shifted in his seat, visibly annoyed at her addendum, but Summerville continued, "I don't doubt the Majors' will find their feet in due course and be back here in short order."

Hendricks opened his repellent mouth to speak but she shut him down. "The door to Scoundrels Club," her voice was firm, "will remain ajar."

Hendricks didn't like this, but he pressed on. "I'm sure you'll remember," he said, "that upon joining Scoundrels, you're obliged to provide the cellar with a notable bottle, which remains unopened until the day you die," he paused, "or until you're dismissed."

Trevelyan rolled his eyes.

"Major Trevelyan, you provided us with a rather special claret."

"My father gave it to me on my fifth birthday."

"And Major Cornwall, you laid down a Melchizedek of Krug '28."

I don't know how I resisted diving across Summerville's desk to place my hands around his spindly throat. "That's correct," I said.

"I understand," Hendricks continued, "that it is a thing of extreme rarity. Forty bottles in one. A titan among mortals."

There was a timid knock at the door.

"Enter," called Hendricks.

In came Reverend Dr Tristan Blunders-Hatch, Scoundrels' Master of the Cellar. The old boy was sweating heavily as he pulled along a tin cart with a squeaky wheel. Inside the cart our bottles were nestled on a bed of straw.

Blunders-Hatch was a Club oddity. He had an encyclopaedic knowledge of wine, and spent his entire life roaming our vast vaulted cellars, staying blind drunk for weeks at a time, and rarely coming up for air. With some difficulty, much brow wiping and huffing, he tipped the cart up and got the Melchizedek on its end. Then he placed Trevelyan's bottle and some degustation glasses on the table.

The Melchizedek was a monster. Thirty litres of vintage Krug. It weighed upwards of 100lbs and was four feet long. It was more naval cannon than bottle.

"Gentlemen," he began, "it is with great regret that, as Master of the Cellar, I must open your membership bottles here today." Blunders-Hatch bowed his head solemnly as if the weight of this news was too much to bear. This was poppycock. The spiders-leg blood vessels in his cheeks seemed to glow purple in his anticipation of a vintage as yet untried. There was not one iota of regret in his voice. The man was yearning to get at our booze. "It is customary for ex-members to wet their lips and then remove themselves from the premises."

"Here, here!" Hendricks brayed. "Let's get them open, eh?"

I'd had enough of this humiliation. I resolved to take matters into my own hands. "Fine," I said. "But the Melchizedek was a gift to my father from Oscar Wilde. Nobody opens it but me."

Summerville's eyes narrowed. She nodded her approval.

The Reverend looked at Hendricks, uncertain as to the protocol. Hendricks clearly wanted to object but couldn't come up with a reason quick enough. I stood and heaved the Melchizedek onto the desk, where it crouched malignantly.

I turned to Blunders-Hatch. "Reverend, I'm sure you'll agree that a bottle of this quality must be sabered."

The Reverend nodded his agreement. He fetched a cavalry sabre from its place on the wall over the fireplace and handed it to me.

"My father was a pious man," I lied. "Reverend, would you be so kind as to read us the Lord's Prayer?"

"If I can remember it," muttered Blunders-Hatch.

We all bowed our heads and closed our eyes as the Reverend racked his brains for the opening lines.

> *Our Father, who art in heaven,*
> *Hallowed be thy name.*

I opened my eyes, as if cheating at hide and seek. I grabbed the Melchizedek by the neck and bottom, took the weight and lifted it silently from the desk, tilting it off-balance. I heaved it this way and that, giving the champagne inside a jolly good swill around.

> *Thy kingdom come.*
> *Thy will be done, in earth as it is in heaven.*

Now I pivoted my hips and swirled the massive bottle in the opposite direction. The Krug was churning nicely, building up pressure. Everyone's eyes remained closed.

Give us this day our daily bread.
And forgive us our trespasses, as we forgive those
who trespass against us.

As the prayer continued, I agitated the contents of the bottle even more. Summerville opened her eyes slightly and gave me a half-smile. Silently, she began to edge her chair away from Hendricks. "Stay strong," she mouthed to me, and in a gesture I've always remembered, put her right hand onto her heart for a moment.

But deliver us from evil.
Amen.

They opened their eyes.

"That would have meant a lot to my father" I said, unwrapping the foil. Hendricks sighed impatiently. Somehow, I'd taken ownership of my own dismissal and he didn't like it one bit. Slowly, I unwound the wire muselet which held the cork in place. It was critical that I was careful with this. I could feel it straining for release. As gently as if I were defusing a bomb, I discarded the cage.

"Reverend," I queried, innocently, "the seam should be on the top?"

Blunders-Hatch ummed, and ahhed, smacking his distended lips together and agreed that yes, that was correct.

"I thought so," I said, rotating the bottle to ensure the seam was facing up, and at the same time, angled it at forty-five degrees. "Cheers!"

I sliced the blade along the seam up the neck of the bottle until it caught the annulus. At this exact moment, Hendricks guessed what I was up to —but a fraction too late. The neck of the bottle fired like a cannon, shearing off in a billionth of a second.

The cork hit Hendricks right between the eyes with the force of, well, forty champagne bottles opened at the same time. His head jerked back which toppled his chair backwards, crashing him onto the ground. He was knocked out cold.

The champagne foamed out of the bottle in an unstoppable torrent. I grabbed two tasting glass and let the froth fill them, passing one to Trevelyan. We drank deeply.

"An excellent vintage," I declared, wiping my chin on my sleeve.

"Enjoy the dregs, Reverend," I said, unsmiling, as Trevelyan grabbed his claret from the table and tucked it under his arm.

We picked up our coats and marched out of the office. "We should probably go and see Marcus now," Trevelyan mused as we strode towards the stairs.

"Victor! St. John!" called Summerville.

We stopped and turned to hear what she had to say.

"Fix this mess, and get back here, P.D.Q," she said.

We stepped out into the bright afternoon sun. As always Aram Atsi, stood on the pavement, a monument to steroid misuse. Since his inaugural undertaking in Maljeria, he seemed to have hardened still further.

We descended the steps and bade him farewell. As we were about to walk away he called after us, "Mister Corn-whorl, Mister Trev-hellian."

We stopped and turned. He reached into his great coat and then produced two crisp £50 notes.

"Pleaze, sirs, not think me rude. This come from me with all love and respekt. Safe travels, sirs," he said, extending the notes towards us.

Trevelyan and I looked at each other and then at the money. Tentatively, we took the notes. This was the only ready cash we had in the world.

As we walked away from the Club, even we couldn't have imagined how difficult our lives were about to get.

And so begins our descent.

I remember when I was a child once asking, "Will I always be rich, Farver?" And my father replied, "You are, and always will be, richer than Croesus. And for that you should be thankful, because the rich are terrible at being poor."

How right he was.

Yours sincerely,
Major Victor Montgomery Cornwall.

Nimbu Towers
Pullen-under-Lyme
Gloucestershire
May 16th 2021

Dear Major,

Dash it, I am almost weeping at the memory of Aram Atsi's kind act. With no estate or private income of his own, he was one of those peculiar coves for whom cash was actually quite important. He sent almost every penny he owned back to his family's wrestling school in Nakhchivan for the training of local prodigies. That hundred quid would have paid for thirty little lads to throw each other around for a year. He was a fine man who, when he wasn't calming down angry Scoundrels or defenestrating intruders, danced a fine *dudek,* and made his own pomegranate schnapps.

Anyway, that kind act heralded an absolutely awful period in both of our lives, Victor. A period where we realised what life is like when you're without even the steam off your piss to warm you:

CHAPTER 8
ZEROED

FORTNUM & MASON, NOVEMBER 1974

Sir Marcus 'Crassus' Saxpence's genius was for economics. He began the war as an eighteen-year-old pencil-pusher in the Cabinet Office and finished it with the rank of Lieutenant Colonel, with command over military logistics in the capital.

Late one evening, Churchill found him at his desk rejigging routes for delivery vehicles around London – an exercise that proved to save 30,000 gallons of petrol per week. When quizzed by the P.M, he explained that his new routes would bring his auxiliary truck-driving girlfriend home on average 58 minutes early, enabling him to bang her an extra 3.38 times per week.

Churchill, whose genius was for talent spotting, set Marcus on a problem of national importance. Within a week, Marcus had come up with the data to support a radical three-pronged solution to Britain's food scarcity.

One: control how much food people could buy with special 'rationing cards'.

Two: stop eating pigs, and instead spread layers of their fertilising effluent *inside* people's living rooms, creating special indoor allotments that would increase national vegetable production by 40%.

Three: make gluttony a treasonous act and begin

sending all fat people with waists over thirty-eight inches on dangerous missions behind enemy lines.

Churchill went with only the first of these brilliant ideas, but Saxpence's future as an economic thinker was assured. By 1945 his ingenious policies were keeping the British economy grinding out cash for bombs, tanks and very big cigars. Knighted, celebrated and then asked to manage assets by pretty much everyone with more than seven zeroes to worry about, Saxpence's clients included the Mountbattens, the Saudi Royal Family and the actor Ernest Borgnine. We'd grabbed him as our Chief Accountant. There was nothing he didn't know about the great British art of tax avoidance. Cornwelyan Enterprises was in safe hands.

But right now, those hands were nervously fiddling with a silver spoon marked F&M. We were here to talk about cash. Our cash.

I didn't really think about money at all. It had always attracted itself to me effortlessly. Cornwall too. We'd raked in so much of it through Cornwelyan, that it had ceased to have any meaning. We couldn't possibly spend it all, however hard we tried. And we tried hard: bespoke racing cars, the finest wine, helicopters that could fly upside down, West End theatre productions of absolutely no merit, skiing, prostitutes, skiing prostitutes. Why, Cornwall had just commissioned a Congolese themed log flume in the grounds of Hellcat so Titus could discover his cultural roots, using only the interest on the interest of his monthly dividend. Wealth was a burden which we had always shouldered happily. But all that was about to change.

"I'm… I'm not sure how to explain this," Saxpence stammered, "but something rather rum is going on that I have never seen before."

"Rum, Marcus?" I asked, sourly.

"I need to go back to basics I'm afraid, so please bear with me. Your company, Cornwelyan Enterprises, was incorporated formally in the United Kingdom in 1946, and you dumped several million pounds into it, from…" Saxpence consulted a manila file that was dusted with icing sugar.

"The Pine Cone Club. Our Japanese wartime casino," said Cornwall, proudly.

"So, when the Labour government levied the Excess Profits Tax in '46, aimed at chaps like you who'd had a good war, you didn't pay a penny to the Exchequer."

"Should bloody well think so too. War heroes don't pay taxes," Cornwall said.

"Indeed," nodded Saxpence, "and thusly, we found it prudent to squirrel your assets away from Switzerland to Swaziland. All the money was shielded, some of it offshore in gilts, shares, trusts, seed capital for new companies. We diversified into vineyards, bullion and racehorses. Some of it was hanging in the National Portrait Gallery in the form of a couple of Gainsboroughs."

I took a slurp of Darjeeling. "Was?" I queried.

"This is not about lack of income," Saxpence said. "The monies from the palace Hirohito gifted you, the Tackle Chappie profits from your wholly owned subsidiary Soho Dandy Ltd, and the license arrangements for your Turkish bread empire," he faltered, have all, simply…" Saxpence fingered his collar, which must have suddenly felt rather tight.

"Simply…?" I prompted.

"Disappeared."

"HOW?" I thundered, slamming a fist on the table.

"I don't know," he said sombrely.

This was met with the loudest silence I have ever heard.

Saxpence was now digging the silver spoon into the palm of his hand. "You've got to understand, chaps, that diversifying a portfolio is always a good idea. If property crashes you've got cash in the bank. If the gold standard crumbles, who cares? You've got a boatload of platinum in a vault somewhere. And a boat. With diamonds in its hull. Done well, diversification becomes a mechanism for profit itself. And I did it very well."

"Of course you did, old man! None better," I said, encouragingly. "And, Marcus, I promise we won't be angry, but would you mind immediately telling us what the hell has gone on with all our cash?"

Marcus winced. "Somebody knew where every last penny was. And last Friday, in the last hour of business, well…"

"Last Friday in the last hour of business, what?"

"Someone trousered the lot."

TEN MINUTES LATER

We'd known Saxpence for thirty years, but we did not feel squeamish about dangling him upside down, one leg each, from Westminster Pier, as a perfect Turner sunset smeared itself over the water.

His head was only a few inches from the icy Thames, and he didn't want to go any closer than that. We had little doubt he was telling the truth, or as much as he knew of it. But why take a chance?

"Nothing personal, old man," I said, affably, "just checking your mind is focused. Run us through it again. Top line only."

"Righto," Saxpence's thick grey hair was slapped by an oily wavelet, and he spat out a gobful of dirty water. "At four o'clock GMT on Friday last, a series of synchronised events occurred across the globe, with, it seems, pinpoint accuracy. Your bank accounts in four continents were cleared of cash, and the contents of your safety-deposit boxes, at Hatton Garden, Coutts, and Lombard Odier were removed by various gentlemen with the correct passcodes."

"What about your fees?"

"The safety deposit box I've been using at Coutts to take my ten percent has gone too."

"We'll have to owe you," I said.

"Every single one of your properties, even if you only part-owned them, had their building insurances cancelled at four, and fires started by five. Razed to the ground in all cases. The various bits of intellectual property and royalty-earning products were sold off to other companies for a single unit of the smallest denomination available, using lawyers who haven't the foggiest what was really going on. For instance, the Tackle Chappie is now owned by Debenhams, who got it for a penny."

Cornwall laughed out loud at this. I let go of Saxpence's ankle to hold my head in my hands, and his head plunged into the Thames for a second, before Cornwall pulled him up again.

"In Antwerp," he gasped, "every stone from your diamond cutting concern was collected by the usual courier with forged paperwork, driven to the Belgian coast, loaded onto a tugboat and then simply dumped at sea. In Macau, the board of your import-export company was arrested at four, found guilty of sedition at half past, and shot by firing squad at ten to five. Your assets were seized by the Chinese government, and the case closed."

Cornwall made a slight tutting sound and pulled at the side of his moustache with his free hand.

"At the National Gallery, thieves locked the doors, bound the guards, pulled both Gainsborough's off the wall, snapped the frames, covered the pictures in oil and lit a match. In Swaziland…"

"Why?" I cut through Saxpence's agonising detail.

"To bankrupt you, of course! As things stand, you haven't got a bean."

"But what about Hellcat?" Cornwall asked.

"And what about Nimbu?"

"Nimbu Towers has been transferred to a woman called…" Saxpence struggled to remember as the wind whipped spray into his face. "Kreutz!"

"WHAT?"

"Well, Marjorie is still technically your wife, I suppose," mused Cornwall.

"Ahhh, she's your wife? I didn't realise," said Marcus. "Makes sense…"

"Why?" asked Cornwall, sharply.

"Because she now owns Hellcat Manor as well."

Cornwall uttered an expletive that I'd seldom heard him use and let go of Marcus' leg. Unfortunately, I wasn't quite over my own shock, and I hadn't grabbed hold of him again. He plunged into the Thames, head first.

A few seconds passed. Marcus surfaced, gasping. He began to tread water while removing his tie and undoing his top button. "What I find astonishing," he said, "is that it must have taken years of planning to pull this off. Whoever is behind all this must really, really have it in for you. They haven't even taken the money for themselves! Everything you own has just been…" Marcus searched for the right word, "…zeroed!"

I threw Marcus a life ring. Not to him, at him.

We hauled him out of the river and put him in a taxi, apologising for the rough stuff. He was very gracious about it. We said goodbye, and hoped it was not for the last time and all that. Then we strolled along the Thames in the pale light of the evening.

"A penny for 'em?" said Cornwall.

"You haven't got a penny to give me."

We walked towards Berkeley Square in silence. Cornwall stopped at the flower girl's stall and selected a crisp chrysanthemum for his buttonhole. He handed over a £50 note.

"Keep the change," he said to her absent-mindedly, as he always did. She smiled and thanked him.

"That was half our cash," I reminded him as we walked on.

Cornwall grimaced. "Bugger," he said, patting his pockets. "I've never had to think about this sort of thing before."

"How hard can it be? We'll simply live on our wits," I said, confidently.

"Being down-at-heel for a bit will sharpen us up," he agreed.

"We'll pick ourselves up, dust ourselves off, start all over again," I serenaded, experimentally.

Cornwall didn't reply, which was his way of agreeing with me. "Where does one actually *go* when one is dirt-poor nowadays?"

"Waterloo Bridge."

Readers may wonder why on earth we didn't just tap up some of the other Scoundrels for loans to tide us over while we resolved this nonsense. But asking for credit simply wasn't the done thing. There was no chance we'd be going around cap in hand for a few hundred grand here and there to put us right. That was not the Scoundrels way. Scrounging from friends was as big a social crime as talking behind a fellow's back, drawing a gun on anyone under ten years old or agreeing to pay parking fines. Not in the repertoire.

It began to rain. I hailed us a black cab at the corner of New Bond St and Bruton St, jumped in and told the driver Waterloo Bridge. He set off into the heavy London traffic. I settled down with my thoughts, and Cornwall with his.

Through the toughened glass screen, I could see our driver staring straight ahead. The traffic was grinding along at a snail's pace. But something was odd. What was it? Then it hit me. There was no hole in the glass to hand over the fare. In fact, the glass was a solid sheet a couple of inches thick, and brand new, not battered and scratched as one would expect.

Alarm bells. A trap. Too late.

Both doors locked. The speaker system engaged. Our driver, his eyes on the road ahead, was talking to us.

"Major Trevelyan and Major Cornwall. It is my pleasure to drive you to your destination. And of course, there is no charge for ex-Scoundrels."

With a lurch, I realised who the cab driver was.

My first reaction was to kill him. I jumped forward and smashed my fists into the glass at the points most likely to give, but it was as unyielding as the ape enclosure at London Zoo. At the same time, Cornwall was trying to kick the door lock into submission, but it refused to yield.

After our fruitless attempts, we sat back down.

"You're a dead man, Hansclapp," I said.

"Oh, come now, Major Trevelyan. We're old friends. Call me Gruber."

"Go to hell."

"I am hell," he said, flatly, eyes on the road ahead.

Cornwall leaned forward. "You can't stay behind glass forever, Hansclapp," he said. Cornwall might have appeared calm, but I could see his moustache had gone rigid, and his eyes had assumed the peculiar scarlet tinge that invariably precedes extreme violence. "We'll catch up with you soon enough. And when we do…" he looked out of the window dismissively, "…we'll take our vengeance."

"Vengeance? What do you know about vengeance?" Hansclapp sneered. "I've made a study of it! Who do you think it was who tipped off the Club about Monte-Carlo? He caught my eye in the rearview mirror. "That was excellent entertainment, by the way, Major Trevelyan."

The anger inside me had built to a point where I could barely speak. We'd been outplayed. Again.

"You are puppets, gentlemen," he continued, "and you haven't even realised that it's me who has been pulling your strings."

I slammed a fist against the glass once more, "I repeat. You are a dead man, Hansclapp."

"Major Cornwall," Hansclapp said, "only a few days ago you were nearly killed by a taxi as you left Purdey's, correct?"

Cornwall's troubled expression told me this was true.

"Did you not recognise the taxi driver? Perhaps you were a little preoccupied. Shame, I could have given you a lift back to Scoundrels."

Cornwall rubbed his forehead and sighed, "If you know us so well," he said, "then you'll know we've spent our lives flushing away little turds like you."

Hansclapp laughed at this.

"Just tell us what the hell you want," I exploded.

"I want you to suffer!" he said, "I want you to suffer like I have suffered."

There was silence. I slumped back in my seat. Cornwall stared out of the window, deep in thought. We were nearing Waterloo Bridge.

For now there was nothing we could do. A hissing noise came from a thin pipe laid into the ceiling of the cab. A sweet smell: the anaesthetic halothane. I elbowed the side window as hard as I could. It didn't give in the slightest. My lids felt heavy and I struggled to stay conscious. As I looked across to Cornwall I could see he was already out cold.

I awoke shivering underneath Waterloo Bridge. My head throbbed and I felt a little sick, a side effect of the halothane. Cornwall, by my side, was stirring too. Only now did I see that we'd both been stripped down to our underpants. Through the fug, I registered that Cornwall had completed his new back tattoo of the scales of Truth and Justice, held in the talons of an eagle, its wings spreading across his shoulders. I had no idea that truth and justice were so important to him.

Cornwall staggered to his feet and vomited onto the pavement. He began to spasm and with a mournful groan, released his bowels, shitting all over the kerb.

Conspicuous by its presence nearby was a bundle of appalling clothing – a couple of sparse woollen jumpers, and some threadbare trousers that Hansclapp must have left for us. With no other option, we got dressed. As I shrugged the damp, mouldering garments on, I pictured taking Hansclapp's neck in my hands and slowly wringing it.

Cornwall looked at himself, then me, and scrunched his face up. "I'm not sure about these clothes," he said, missing the point completely and yet somehow hitting the nail on the head at the same time.

I suddenly felt dreadful. I heaved up my guts onto the ice-cold paving stones and, as my body shuddered involuntarily, I realised my underpants were filling of their own accord.

"At least I had the good sense to do that before I put the clothes on," joshed Cornwall. I didn't care. It meant my body was ridding itself of the halothane.

Even as I evacuated my bowels and retched over and over, I was planning our next move. Homeless. Fundless. So what? No point in grousing. We had to play the cards we'd been dealt, that was the Scoundrels way. Except we weren't Scoundrels anymore.

Nevertheless, with a bit of nimble thinking and hard work we'd be back in the black soon enough, and then we could get on with the business of stamping on Hansclapp's face until he was entirely, completely, irrevocably dead.

Besides, the Major and I had already extended our fortunes many times over and there was absolutely no reason why we wouldn't be back in the gravy inside of, what? A week?

Two weeks at the outside.

I have nothing to add to this.

Yours sincerely,
Major Arthur St. John Trevelyan

Hellcat Manor
Great Trundleford
Devon
May 25th 2021

Dear Major,

Your initial optimism that we'd be back on our feet within days was rather endearing if not a little stupid. Hansclapp had well and truly rogered us, Winstowe-style.

CHAPTER 9
THE DIRTY RAGAMUFFINS

THE SOUTH BANK, LONDON, NOVEMBER 1974

There was a moment on the first evening, as the late autumn sun lingered, when our predicament didn't seem that bad. Trevelyan and I sat on a bench on the South Bank looking out over the Thames. The sun's rays cast an orange glow upon us and the romantic in me began to wonder if I was well suited to owning nothing. Maybe it would be liberating. I'd always harboured ambitions of being a sort of literary vagabond roaming the streets, living on my wits and having adventures that I'd document in verse. Most artists were penniless at one time or another and it didn't do them any harm.

Trevelyan wasn't as adaptable. I wouldn't say I was worried about him, but he got tetchy if he didn't chow down on a *cote de boeuf* at least three times a week. Also he hadn't twigged that we could no longer afford Heavy Betsy's, where he did most of his loving these days. I'd save that news for later.

I pulled my tatty jacket tightly around me and lit a cigarette of my own design – a *Dirty Ragamuffin* – an acrid blend of used fag-ends sourced from the pavements of Lambeth, compressed and rolled in the printed lyrics of a Ralph McTell song. It was a hostile smoke that burned my throat and made me retch. Inevitably, my thoughts turned to the Scoundrels tobacconist, a gentleman so committed to his craft that he had taken a vow of eternal chastity so the *cohibas* he rolled on his own thighs were virginal. I longed to fill my lungs with a smoke less obnoxious than this.

A light drizzle began to fall. We left our bench and wandered off, looking for cover. We waited for a while under Blackfriars Bridge. I watched as the rain droplets bounced off the paving slabs, forming puddles. I had a flash of poetic inspiration: "Pitter-patter, pitter-patter" – the words just formed in my mind. A pretty nice way to describe rain, I thought. I made a mental note to write it down then realised that I couldn't afford a pen. Or paper.

"Cornwall?" Trevelyan said.

"Yes?"

"What *is* poverty?"

I allowed myself a gentle smile. His question was asked with all the innocence of a child who was recovering from a kick to the head from a horse. What should he know of poverty? He'd led a life of extreme privilege, as had I. The difference between us was that I was a man of the world, as much at ease amongst kings and princes as bus drivers or yoga teachers. And I was a natural traveller. Wherever I laid my hat was my home. It so happened that I always laid my hat in the finest Jacobean estate ever built, and seldom bothered to put it on again except to pop up to the Club.

So instead of tearing a strip of him, I merely patted Trevelyan on his shoulder. He'd learn. "We're about to find out, old friend," I said, "we're about to find out."

An hour later, we were ensconced under Waterloo Bridge, colloquially known as Cardboard City, although that was doing it a favour. It was a sleeping place for London's down-at-heel, a shanty town of damp cardboard and wooden pallets. A few small fires flickered in the half-light, circled by swaddled figures bending to the flames.

My first reaction was shock. I couldn't believe how many people were there. I'd spent a lot of time in London, and seldom seen anyone homeless.

As night drew in, the temperature dropped. I slumped down against a concrete pillar and pulled my legs in, hunching myself over to preserve my body heat. We'd been destitute for less than a day and it was already starting to annoy me. Not only that, so was Trevelyan. He was pacing up and down, gesticulating and talking urgently to himself. I think he may have been in shock, a delayed reaction to what had become of us. I tuned into his gibbering and I was surprised to hear a non-stop stream of positivity.

"We're a couple of resourceful chaps," he muttered manically, "for goodness sake, if we can survive Wan Booli, we can survive this. How hard can it be?"

"Save your energy, St. John," I said. "Try to calm down and get some sleep."

"Sleep? There's no time for that. I'll forage for berries in the park. You gather some firewood. Once I'm back we can build a lean-to for tonight and when we're up and running we can collect water in a solar still."

I regarded him through narrowed eyes. He was approaching this as if it were a Duke of Edinburgh Award. I excused myself and went for a walk. I needed time to think and to work out how to get us out of this mess.

I leant on the Thames embankment and gazed out at the beach which edged the low tide. My eyes fell upon a discarded fluffy toy covered in mud along with all the other detritus. My mind turned to Titus. What would become of him?

TITUS, DETRITUS (1974)

There is my boy,
Down in th' mud,
How could this happ'n
To my flesh n' blood?

We're both thrown away,
With the other debris.
It's only November,
Shalt we see Feb'ry?
Who'll care for thou,
If without thee I be?
For ye'll tear th' head off
All nursemaids 'cept me,
So vow this, I will,
For thou art my blood.
Daddy won't leave ye,
Down in th' mud.

The poem came to me, fully formed. Perfect. I longed to see those big, brown limpid eyes and hear my son huffing once again in my ears.

And what of Baxter? I needed to warn them of my terrible fate.

I walked to the public telephone box at the end of Waterloo Bridge, and dialled the operator.

"I'd like to reverse the charges to Hellcat Manor in Great Trundleford please. Say it's Cornwall."

The line went quiet. It felt like an age. As I waited my attention was diverted by the colourful business cards that papered the walls of the phone box. Two in particular caught my eye. One advertised the services of a well-endowed masseuse who also appeared to be a nurse. It was a poor-quality image, but she looked remarkably like Tikki Takka, my own masseuse. Perhaps this was the sideline she'd told me about, that brought her up to London so much.

I noticed the other card because it had the words, 'MAKE MONEY FAST!!!' written in bold letters with just a phone number underneath. It was tempting to take that one too, but common sense told me that it would be some sort of scam. I waited a moment longer before Baxter's calm voice came down the receiver.

"I'm afraid I have some bad news, sir," he said. "Hellcat has been given by Mrs Kreutz to the National Trust. Their people are here now, sir, boxing up your possessions."

I punched a fist through one of the glass panels in the phone box.

"And what about Titus? Where is my boy?"

Baxter cleared his throat. "I'm afraid he was taken away this morning, sir, to London Zoo."

It was like I'd been slammed in the gut. The phone receiver felt like lead in my hand. I dropped the handset and slowly sank to the floor. As the tears rolled down my face I heard the faint sound of Baxter's voice coming from the dangling receiver. "You don't need to worry about me though, sir, I've got some small savings and a sister in Toxteth with a spare room. I'll be alrig..."

A zoo.

My boy. In a zoo.

In a cage.

After a while I stumbled back to my new home in Cardboard City. Trevelyan was now wearing a tabard he'd fashioned from a piece of blue tarpaulin, tied in the middle with boat rope. He had built an enormous fire from some pallets he had stolen from a building site, and the roaring blaze that resulted had already spread to the advertising hoardings at the back of Waterloo. Some of the other residents were looking out from beneath their shelters and muttering their disapproval. It was going to be a long first night.

And so it proved. The fire was eventually doused by the fire brigade, and the entire community under the bridge was now soaking wet. It was a cloudless, clear evening and bone-chillingly cold. Trevelyan and I had scavenged as much cardboard as we could to keep us off the concrete floor, but even after snuggling against each other the frigid temperature took hold. I drifted in and out of a fitful sleep. Visions of my boy in a cage haunted my dreams. Several times I woke up screaming only to realise that it wasn't a nightmare after all. We really were homeless.

At around three, I awoke to the sight of Trevelyan bent double, vomiting up the berries he had foraged earlier. His face was a pallid green and even though it must have been minus five he was sweating. Who knew what he'd ingested, but his pronouncement that the railway sidings were 'a veritable larder of natural produce' now looked way off the mark.

The next morning brought no reprieve. Sometime around ten we dragged ourselves off our unyielding cardboard beds and twisted our numb limbs back into shape. Thankfully, Trevelyan's stomach had nothing else to reject. His tank was now empty and he'd need feeding soon. I noted that his trousers were saturated and he admitted that he'd wet himself on purpose to warm himself up.

I reflected on how our descent into savagery had been so alarmingly swift. It was only a few days ago that we had shared a bottle of 1946 Petrus. Now I was watching him trying to stamp on a pigeon for his breakfast. It was disturbing.

We washed on the fetid little beach by Blackfriars Bridge and wandered into the West End looking for anything that might aid us: dropped change, discarded food, stuff to keep us warm at night. We rummaged in bins and loitered outside cafes but yielded next to nothing. The hours passed. By five thirty the only sustenance I'd had was from a chocolate bar wrapper I'd sucked, and Trevelyan had swilled back some minty shower gel he found around the back of the Oasis leisure centre on Endell St. Nobody would give us anything.

We needed money, dosh, moolah. And there was only one way we'd get it. We were going to have to hustle, do a bit of wheeling and dealing. Stick our dirty fingers into a few pies, etcetera.

I came up with a plan. Trevelyan wasn't going to like it but the more I thought about it the more it made sense. I glanced across to the big man who was lolloping alongside me with his mouth gormlessly open. How much would he be worth on the open market? He was definitely *niche* but could earn us a few quid if put in the way of those seeking a bit of rough trade. And with everything he'd been through, they didn't come much rougher. It didn't take a pervert to realise his mouth alone offered an intriguing proposition. Even though he had a head like a sea container and a body like a Norfolk dumpling, in a sleeveless stonewash denim jacket and a studded leather cap, he'd go down a storm with the bear market. I kept my own counsel for the time being, figuring it would be better to suggest this when he'd hit rock bottom.

The evening was drawing to a close and once again the cold began to numb our bones. It was obvious that the clothes we had were pitifully inadequate, and as ten o'clock approached again, I suggested that we mug some people for their coats. Trevelyan said he would do anything to improve our situation. We didn't have to wait long. Sure enough a couple of guys in long overcoats emerged from the door of a pub. They held newspapers above their heads as they hailed a cab. Except they never made it to the cab. Trevelyan hit the first chap at full tilt from behind taking him down. I came behind the other one with a forearm choke-hold that subdued him enough to drag him into the shadows. Within a minute we had their clothes and wallets. There was no question of feeling any guilt. The rules out here were different. It was dog eat dog and I was an alpha: half Doberman, half Rottweiler. St. John was a bloody great big hairy St Bernard who could sit on your chest and slobber on you.

"The frigging zip's stuck," Trevelyan cursed, as he fumbled with his new coat. We checked the stolen wallets – surely we'd have enough money for a steak sandwich and a cup of Earl Grey. Simpsons would still be open and I knew the maître d' well enough to ensure a table, even in our reduced state. But the wallets were pathetically thin – a fiver in one, and diddly squat in the other. We must have mugged a couple of actors or students. Trevelyan lost his patience. He threw the wallets to the ground and took a swing at me that I only just managed to duck. He was becoming increasingly agitated.

"I'm hungry, Cornwall!" he wailed. "How many more people do we have to mug before I'm back on the fallow deer sausages?"

He had a point. Mugging people would only get us so far. It wasn't enough.

That evening, as we loafed on a park bench, I thought the unthinkable. We might have to get jobs.

"Do what?" said Trevelyan, as if I'd asked him to shit in his hat.

"Just to get enough money to eat."

"We can't get jobs. I don't know how to have a job."

"I've got an idea of a job you could do, easy peasy."

"Go on," said Trevelyan, his stomach rumbling.

The Beefy Centurion was one of Soho's oldest gay porn theatres. Situated just off Wardour Street, it didn't look much from the outside. Or the inside. But it did serve the best steak tartare in the whole of London – minced expertly by their Michelin-starred chef, Claude Bamber-Gascoigne. Because of this, and only because of this, Trevelyan and I used to be regulars. Outside the theatre stood a life-sized plastic mannequin of a Roman soldier in tiny leather briefs and what I suspect was non-regulation armour. I'm no historian but I doubted the real legions left their buttocks exposed to attack. I'd already put in a call and made the suggestion to Slippery Mick, the owner, that he should replace the mannequin with a walking, talking substitute. Mick seemed enthusiastic about my idea, and even more so when I pitched Trevelyan for the gig.

"All you have to do is stand there being friendly to the gentlemen who use the club. It's a cinch!"

"Why can't you do it?" he asked, petulantly.

"I don't have the right look. They need a swarthy type like yourself, all brow bone and biceps. The punters will love you."

"How much do I get paid?"

"*We* get paid, £1.50 an hour! Or more," I enthused, "…if you sit on the occasional lap." I murmured this last bit under my breath.

"That's nearly enough for two pints!" Good. He hadn't heard.

"Exactly!"

"And what are you going to do while I'm slaving away?" Trevelyan asked, suddenly suspicious.

"I'm going to get another job."

"Where?"

"London Zoo."

Dr Mandy Lahore, Director of Mammals, Zoological Society of London, sat across the desk from me, looking down at a file. She was a smart looking woman in tweed. I guessed she was in her mid-forties and well established within the world of zoology. Her accent told me she'd spent time in Australia, probably Perth. A woman in her position must have met plenty of animal experts over the years, but I was banking on there being one expert she'd never met, Dr Alan Fanshawe, the renowned primatologist who I'd fallen out with in the Congo. As luck would have it, she hadn't.

Until now.

"Well, Dr Fanshawe," she said, looking up from the file on her desk, "your credentials are impeccable, but I'd heard you'd given up primatology after a nasty experience in Africa." She closed the file and stared at me, wondering whether to bring this up. "Didn't you... lose a finger to a baby gorilla?"

There was no way I could fake this. I held up my right hand, "stitched it back on myself," I said, smiling.

"Resourceful," she flashed me a smile, "but we just don't have a vacancy here for someone of your experience. And besides, our gorillas need only very simple husbandry. A bit below your pay grade."

"Kind of you to say," I smiled, "but I've spent years studying gorillas in the wild. There's really nothing else for me to learn." Dr Lahore raised her eyebrows.

"What I'm trying to say, I suppose, is that what interests me now is studying apes in captivity."

She nodded. I could see her weighing me up. Damn. I'd overplayed my hand here, and it would cost me dearly. It went without saying that Dr Lahore found me devastatingly attractive, and she was probably already looking forward to having a tumble with me behind the camel house, but she was also switched-on and ambitious. She knew that if she hired a man with Fanshawe's credentials, she'd have brought in a rival who might get in the way of her inevitable plans for the zoo directorship.

She made her decision. "I just don't think we have a position like that here at this time. I'm sorry, Doctor," she shrugged.

I tried to keep a lid on my emotions. I'd got this far. I'd managed to purloin a suit from a delivery truck, and I'd researched and set up the meeting with Lahore all from a pay phone. I'd gained an interview for a job that didn't exist. I couldn't leave now. I had to see my boy.

"I quite understand. But may I at least take a look at your gorilla facility here?" I said.

"Oh, of course, Dr Fanshawe. I'd be delighted to show you around."

My heart was racing. How would Titus react to seeing me? How would I react? Dr Lahore led me from her office across a lawn, through a gate and into the public area of the zoo. We followed a paved path, past the Reptile House and toward the Ape House.

"How many gorillas do you currently have?" I asked.

"Well," she said sadly, "for a while we had five. Two adult females, an adult male, and two younger ones. But we recently acquired a new adult male, which made it six. He was rescued from a private owner…"

My blood began to boil. Rescued? What a joke that was! I missed a large chunk of what she said next because it took all my will power to stay in character, but I kept a straight face and played along. I just managed to catch the last bit where she said, "…it was a great shame. Bobo had been at the zoo for over twenty years. He didn't deserve to be strangled to death with a tyre swing in front of all those children…" Her voice broke a little. "Still, the new dominant male seems to have calmed down, so we have five again."

She led me into the Ape House.

The anticipation was almost too much to bear. We entered through a fly-screen door into an artificial grotto. It took a moment for my eyes to adjust. "The apes are not always inside at this time of day," the director explained. "They'll be around the corner."

The Ape House had panoramic windows built into fake rock walls to allow the public to see into the enclosure. We passed the first window which revealed a simple climbing frame of telegraph poles and heavy ropes. A tyre hung from the ceiling and the floor was covered in thick straw. There were no gorillas. We kept walking.

"They'll probably be in this one," she said, leading the way.

I followed, turned the corner and then I saw him. He was less than two feet away, just on the other side of the glass. My boy, Titus! My big, beautiful boy, humping another gorilla like his life depended on it. A lump caught in my throat. I just managed to say, "incredible."

"Isn't it just?" the director said. "Since he killed Bobo this is pretty much all he does every day."

"Good for him."

"He's very highly sexed," she said. "We'd never seen gorillas engage in threesomes, until he came in. Is that something you've ever witnessed in the wild?"

I sucked in air, knowledgeably. "No, not really. I think that might be unique. What are you feeding him?"

"Fruit, seeds... nothing you wouldn't expect."

"Maybe try him on a burger once in a while. Might calm him down."

"A burger? Oh, we couldn't possibly give him meat. You know gorillas are vegetarian."

"Most are," I countered, "but not all, I've seen hi–... a gorilla eat an entire joint of ham."

Dr Lahore was confused.

"You must remember," I said, adopting my best scientific tone, "that gorillas are pretty much human. I'm beginning a study that suggests that gorillas in captivity, surrounded by humans, will take on human traits. So, if they see the children eating sweets, they want to eat sweets. If they see the adults smoking, they want to smoke."

"You're not suggesting we let the gorillas smoke tobacco, are you?"

"I am," I said, pointing at Titus. "This one looks tetchy. Could probably do with a soothing ciggie." The poor bugger was on forty a day before he was kidnapped. No wonder he'd killed Bobo. I pulled out a packet of twenty Benson & Hedges that I'd brought along as a present. "Try him on these," I said.

Titus dismounted, stood up on two legs and swung around to look at us, pizzle out. Our eyes met. Titus hurled himself towards the glass, smashing into it headfirst. The director shrieked and jumped a few steps backwards. Titus' face was level with mine. I reached out and slowly raised my hand to the glass. He shadowed my movement. Our hands were almost touching, just an inch of tempered glass between them. Tears formed in my eyes.

"You have an incredible connection with him," Dr Lahore said, moving forward again.

"I can read gorillas better than anyone," I said. "And with your permission, I'd very much like to come back to observe this one again. You won't have to pay me anything. I'd just like to come and go during opening hours, informally."

Dr Lahore thought about this for a moment. "I don't see why not. We like to associate ourselves with the world's leading experts. When would you like to return?"

"I'll be here first thing tomorrow," I said.

So there you are, Major. Life on the streets was tough to begin with, but once I made contact with Titus, it became a little more bearable.

Perhaps you'd like to move on to what happened when you popped down to Nimbu?

Yours sincerely,
Major Victor Montgomery Cornwall.

Nimbu Towers
Pullen-under-Lyme
Gloucestershire
June 2nd 2021

Dear Major,

You were lucky to make contact with your boy so easily. I remember being jealous of the structure that visiting him at the zoo gave your day.

That first winter I spent much of my time when I wasn't working the early shift at the *Beefy Centurion* wandering aimlessly around the West End, gazing into shop windows and thinking about all the money I used to waste on fine wine and well-insulated jackets. Dark times.

CHAPTER 10
HOME TO NIMBU

WATERLOO BRIDGE, LONDON, DECEMBER 1974

The maniac they called Fagin Derry raised his anvil of a fist and boxed the back of Cornwall's balaclava three, four, five times. His head reverberated off the kerb like a speedball. Cornwall tried to arch his back, but he couldn't buck the horrible fellow off. With surprising agility for such a barrel of a man, Fagin jumped up and stamped on the back of Cornwall's left knee. Cornwall gave a yell and rolled out of the way. He grabbed the edge of an overflowing bin while the big man showboated to the crowd of shambling wrecks who'd assembled, strutting around like the biggest cock in the yard.

Cornwall hauled himself to his feet, he made it look painful. "Fagin Derry," Cornwall shouted, pointing at the man. "I'm calling ye out, ye feckin' shitehawk." He spat on the ground. "An' I'm sayin dat all the Derrys is shitehawks, y'heed?" He was speaking *tramp vernacular*, a shadow tongue rooted in Gaelic, Cockney and Scots, used by London's gentlemen of the road. Most mistake it for mere drunken rambling, but it has its own stark poetry. "Ye feckin' gimme wha' I ask or ays tha' end of youse."

"Ye'll get nothin' from me, ye big ballbag bastard," drawled Derry. The crowd of fetid men jeered along with him

Cornwall rushed him, but Fagin Derry had been here before, many times by the look of him, and let loose a beast of a swing that wouldn't have shamed James Rube Ferns. If his fist had connected it could have been game over, but thankfully Cornwall ducked it and slammed into Fagin Derry's chest, rushing him backwards to the far side of the alley. Derry rabbit-punched his ear and Cornwall made an excellent feint of losing his footing and falling onto his back. Years ago, I had fallen for Cornwall's sneaky brand of combat trickery, and I could see what was coming next.

"Now ye'll meet ye maker, ye feckin' spaff-cart," shouted Derry, who loomed over Cornwall like the villain in some Victorian melodrama.

Cornwall lurched upwards and wrapped Derry's long, greasy beard around his fist. He pulled hard over his shoulder, guiding Derry's head onto the corner of the iron fire escape with a CLANG.

Nasty.

Derry slumped into unconsciousness, blood gushing from the temple. Cornwall unwound the beard from his fist and staggered to his feet. The other tramps jeered and shuffled back to their places. Victorious, Cornwall picked up the victor's spoils – a bag of stale donuts – and booted Fagin Derry hard in the midriff. Then he stamped on one of his ankles a few times to properly immobilise him. Winter was tough here. You didn't leave a chap with a grudge any room for a comeback.

Cornwall sat down next to me, and I handed him back his semi-tame rat, Nana, whose gaze was firmly on the brown bag of pastry. Nana was clearly the closest thing he could get to a replacement Titus, and I didn't begrudge my old friend the solace he got from keeping her fed, even if it was most unsavoury that he kept her in the warmth of his jockstrap. Tenderly, he passed her a morsel of jammy donut. Then he handed me a whole one. "Would you have waded in, if that had gone worse for me, old man?"

"I could see you had him on the ropes."

"Never in doubt," he grunted. In fact, that fight had been Cornwall's third of the day. I'd had two myself and the results were increasingly in doubt. Street living was getting to us both. We were lacking in energy and losing our taste for the startlingly violent melées that would blow up at any moment in our cardboard city under Waterloo Bridge. Put a rag-tag band of unlucky, unhappy, unstable chaps somewhere damp and cold without enough food and this is what happens.

We got into our box. "What shall we do tomorrow?"

"I'm going to visit my boy again," said Cornwall.

"I'm going to go busking to earn some dinner money. I'll see you at the statue of Eros in the afternoon."

We each settled down with our thoughts. Mine were bleak. It was minus five degrees last night. I wasn't sure how much more of this I could stand. The same awful scenarios keep replaying themselves: new chaps would arrive; they'd clock the pair of us speaking English properly and assume we were a couple of soft ponces; they'd steal something or say something to test our boundaries; we'd then have to go through the rigmarole of mixing it up with them until they realised we weren't to be trifled with. Just this morning I'd had to stab a young chap in the eye with my sharpened thumbnail for trying to make off with my collection of plastic bags. Two nights ago, Cornwall threw a Geordie into the Thames for moving in on our sleeping place near the generators.

I'd never known how debilitating having absolutely nothing was. Every moment was a fight for survival. The creature comforts at Scoundrels Club were a dim and distant memory. I dredged up wisps of Crozier's cream horns, and the Macallan 40-year-old in the Gaye Bar. I thought of Tuesday brekkie, and the fallow deer sausages. Soon I was drooling like a bloodhound with a leg of lamb. This was a mistake. It made my cardboard pillow soggy.

I sat up. In the dark glass of the opposite building I caught a glimpse of a wild-bearded fellow, rocking back and forth, muttering, like a wankered John the Baptist. Then I realised it was me. In just a short time, homelessness had nearly broken my spirit.

Cornwall was sleeping fitfully. I tried again to doze off. But I couldn't because of the cold, and the feeling of isolation, and desolation, and the fleas, and the weird buzzing in my ears, and Cornwall snoring. And farting. I ached all over and wanted more than anything to be in my study at Nimbu, the floorboards creaking quietly as Cacahuete came in with something delicious on a tray. "That'll be all, Cacahuete," I'd say to him without even looking up from my book.

I should face facts. I'd never see Nimbu Towers again.

Dawn punched me in the eye. I'd got through another night. Now I had to get through another day. Perhaps I could close my eyes for just a few more minutes. Beside me, the tatty, slumbering lump of Cornwall grunted and belched. He smelt like yesterday's anus.

No. This would not do. Overnight, something had clicked into place. Somehow, I'd woken with an iron resolve. I was determined to prove the glum, near-broken Trevelyan of last night wrong.

I was going to Nimbu. I'd have a word with whoever was running the place and make off with something valuable. Cornwall and I would regroup, scrabble together a bit of cash from here and there, sell a painting or a horse, get ourselves into a decent hotel and back on our feet.

It was a plan. It needed to happen immediately, before I found a reason to lie back down on the cold stone of Waterloo.

I'd go alone, I decided. I left Cornwall sleeping.

I walked to Paddington Station. On the concourse, I swiped a trenchcoat and an unattended suitcase and, just as the whistle blew, jumped on the 7:58 to Swindon. In the suitcase was a present wrapped in shiny wrapping with a ribbon. I ripped it open and devoured every last one of the box of chocolates inside. I charmed the buffet girls into giving me coffee and as they giggled over my compliments, a brace of cheese sandwiches disappeared from the tray.

I found an engaged washroom and waited until I was alone. I tapped on the door. "Tickets, please", I called, "just pass them under the door." The occupant proffered their ticket, which I swiped. Then I spirited myself away three carriages down.

I wedged myself into a corner seat. If I stayed sitting, I looked like a slightly down-at-heel antiques dealer or perhaps a low-selling writer of fiction. I dozed off, and the guard shook me awake at Stroud, wrinkling his nose as he got close to me.

I walked the nine miles to Pullen-under-Lyme in just under three hours. I didn't want to bump into anyone from the village, so I approached Nimbu from over the fields. I tramped down an old poacher's track that ran through the woods towards my ancestral home.

I used to play in these woods with Eustace. Ma and Pa would often bring us here for picnics in the springtime. The familiar trees seemed to break me from my dolour. A popular song that I'd heard while skulking in a cafe implanted into my mind and wouldn't leave. It was a happy one, something about picking yourself up and dusting yourself off, and starting all over again. I found that I was whistling the melody as I marched along, ignoring the flea bites rubbing at my collar, the hole in my right boot and the ache in my hip where I'd slept on a broken grille.

It was a crisp, clear autumn afternoon. The horse chestnut branches were bare, spread out in supplication to the wide, grey Gloucestershire sky. How funny, I thought. These branches have been stripped of everything too, but they don't seem to mind. They'd only to ride out the winter and before they know it, the sun would come out again, and they'd be bursting forth with bud. By autumn it would be conkers galore.

Stepping out of the trees, I reached the 20ft. high stone wall that marked the boundary of the Nimbu estate. I ran my hand along its rough surface. This wall was probably the best thing my Uncle William left behind him. The Victorian entrepreneur had lost much of his fortune trying to establish badger-racing as a commercial concern, before raking it all in again by switching to greyhounds. Winning and losing fortunes was in my blood, I reflected.

The wall stretched as far as the eye could see. Folded into its sweeping grandeur was a quaint little gatehouse crafted from the same Cotswold stone. I walked across the stone bridge that led over the drainage ditches and rapped bullishly on the door.

A burly man in a black flak jacket opened the door wide and looked me in the eyes. Buzzcut. Slavic cheekbones. Polish, maybe? Lithuanian? Perhaps German. Definitely military. Not a regiment to be proud of, I bet. He jutted his lantern jaw my way. A question.

"Good day to you," I said. "Ring the house for the Land Rover, please, and get them to draw a bath. It's been a hell of a few days."

The guard's eyes narrowed. "State your bissniss please." Aha, German then.

"I'm Major Trevelyan. This is my estate, and I'll thank you to ring for a lift immediately."

"Vait." The door slammed in my face.

I did vait. For twenty bloody minutes. My repeated knocks had no effect.

Then the door opened once more to reveal a tiny blonde woman in immaculate twinset and pearls, contrasting with her ancient, scrunched wax jacket. Her riding boots were from another generation, perhaps her grandmother's. Here was a classically English woman of the English countryside. She stepped smartly out of the gatehouse and barred my way. "Major Trevelyan, I presume?"

"Indeed," I put out a hand, which she pumped enthusiastically. Her eyes were shining and her dull pink lipstick was freshly applied.

"Lovely to meet you, Major, at last! You should have rung ahead."

"I wasn't sure when I'd arrive."

"Of course, of course," she breezed. And, may I say, how generous is your gift. Gosh, honestly, we at the National Trust have seldom come across such unbridled generosity. It really is quite unparalleled."

National Trust? If these people were from the National Trust, I was a Dutchman with three cocks. I smiled at her, nonetheless.

"Well, Miss…?"

"Ayrshire, Eleanor Ayrshire."

I was suddenly conscious of my trousers held up with string, my lank hair, unshaven cheeks and the unsightly smears of blood on my cuffs, but I powered on unabashed. "Well, Miss Ayrshire, I just need to pop up to the house for a couple of documents."

"Now, now, Major, you know the terms of the agreement." Miss Ayrshire waved a finger at me, a saucy smile blooming on the pale rose of her face. "Is this some sort of test, you naughty fellow? Har-har! Ayrshire's not falling for it! You'll remember your instructions were to refuse you entry at all costs."

"…"

"So no Nimbu Towers for you!"

"Ahh, yes, jolly good. Well done," I smarmed. "But this is no test, Miss Ayrshire, I simply need to biff on over to the house and grab a few bits from the study. For the solicitor. All quite simple–" I shifted my weight to slide past her, and through the gatehouse door. Miss Ayrshire's arm came out like a striking cobra, slamming into the doorframe in what, I could have sworn, was not the languid movement of an English rose, but a full *asako* breakhand smash, much favoured by the KCIA, the secret service of Korea.

"You can't fool me that easily, Major! I cannot let you in to Nimbu today or tomorrow, or any other day. By the terms of your very generous bequest, you are *persona non grata*. For your own good! The National Trust will be keeping the house exactly as the Trevelyan family left it, as a piece of living history. You can't disturb that by coming in, even for a second."

"Yes, even so, I–"

"Nimbu Towers will open to the public next month, just as soon as the front drive has been tarmacadamed to make a coach park. We're all so excited to be able to conduct guided tours around the finest Palladian manor in England, with your personal effects displayed just as you left them. Simply wonderful. We're to open six days a week!"

I was stymied. "Glad to hear it," I said. "And my brother. How's he getting on?"

"Eustace is still holed up on the top floor, as arranged. Quiet as a lamb. You mustn't worry about him."

"And Cacahuete?"

"Your little manservant fellow?" Miss Ayrshire winced slightly. "He did cause us one or two problems, but he's safely back in Mexico by now, I expect. I'm sure he'll adjust."

I'd been dealt an unplayable hand, but I hadn't hitched all this way for nothing. I decided to force the issue. "Madam, I really must insist that I come in and check on your progress." I put my hand firmly on Miss Ayrshire's shoulder to move her aside. In one fluid movement, she snatched it away, squeezing the medial point of my palm, dropping to one knee and sweeping her foot across the flagstones to my Achilles tendon. At the same time, she executed a perfect Z-arm throw of the *hapkido* school, which confirmed my suspicions about her time in Seoul. I cartwheeled across the bridge and into the drainage ditch, which someone had recently filled with slurry.

I staggered up through the filthy stuff to see the statuesque Miss Ayrshire, standing on the bridge, looking down at me. She was re-zipping her wax jacket.

"Mr Hansclapp mentioned that you might not be able to resist popping by for a visit," she cooed. "The National Trust has been taking over estates for generations, although none so fine as this. Don't worry, Major Trevelyan, everything Mr Hansclapp specified has been achieved. Your family home is in safe hands."

With that, Miss Ayrshire's eyes hardened. "Your ex-home, that is."

She crouched down and spat in my face.

Then she stood, turned a delicate calf, and marched back through the gatehouse door, slamming it behind her.

I was seized with a cold, seething fury I had not felt since my worst days at the Potosi mine. But this time I knew what to do with it.

I walked back down the poacher's track and made my way into the village of Pullen, and the house of the fellow who used it most. I sat in his parlour and drank his tea, and reminded him of the times that I, and my father, and his father before him had let him and his father, and his father before him make off from Nimbu with rabbits and pheasants and the odd bit of silver plate.

I told him what I wanted, and he gave it to me. I asked for a hacksaw, a shotgun and as many cartridges as he could spare. I went into his shed and sawed the twin barrels of the shotgun down as short as I dared. I went to the quarry and test-fired the weapon.

At five minutes to nine in the evening, I shinnied over Nimbu's wall, and made my way inside the perimeter back to the gatehouse. I rapped hard on the door. The guard from earlier opened it, expecting to see the fellow who would relieve him.

I shot him in the face with the first barrel of the poacher's twelve-bore, then walked smartly through the hall and blasted his companion in the chest before he'd even managed to get out my leather armchair.

I took two Sig Sauers from the hips of the dead guards along with a flak jacket and black cap. I left the lodge and walked across the courtyard to a quadbike that had keys in the ignition. Sloppy stuff. I did not rate these sentries one bit.

I rode fast to the main house. I got another two men on the way there, point blank in their Land Rover, after hailing them as one of their own and shooting them through the driver's side window. I took their walkie-talkie and called for a comms check. This told me just three remained. Seven in all. Non-standard. You'd expect a squad of ten, or maybe eight for this kind of guard duty.

I slid through an unlocked door into a mullioned greenhouse my father had added to the sunny, western side of Nimbu. The lavender plants crowded each other and looked to be doing well, especially for this time of year. I was pleased about that. Someone had also cut the plum tomatoes back for the winter. At least the place was being properly looked after.

I checked the doorway that led to the Library.

A guttural voice. Authoritative. Used to being obeyed. An officer. "Come out, Major Trevelyan. Come out."

I knew better than to reply. Far too easy for this chap to draw a bead and let fly with a machine pistol that would go right through the plasterwork. I crab-crawled to the abutting scullery, knowing I'd be better protected by the thick stone walls in this part of the house. From there I jumped up, steamed through the scullery and into the parlour beyond. I was expecting to find it empty, but in fact one of the three remaining guards was there, facing the wrong way with a Kneisser 5 and half-sized cylinder mag. I pulled a Welsh dresser down on top of him and put three rounds through the wood into his guts.

Black blood seeped out from the dresser onto the stones. I must have nicked his liver. I heaved the dresser off the poor bastard. He was as white as a ghost, coughing up more black stuff. He wouldn't see morning. "How many more?"

He gasped, "two."

"Your officer's name?"

"Vandar," he gasped. "You met her."

"Where is she?"

To his credit, he wouldn't say, but his eyes flicked reflexively up to the ceiling. The first floor.

"I got your liver, I'm afraid. Don't fight it, just lie still," I said softly. I hid behind the door to listen, so I could get a sense of their whereabouts upstairs. There were no creaks or footsteps. I'd need to search for them.

If I'd have been in their shoes, I'd have done exactly the same thing. And I would already have called for reinforcements, so I took a chance and raced up the stairs. A dangerous moment, but I got to the top without drawing any fire. I ducked into the linen cupboard that was a favourite hide and seek place of Eustace's and peered from a crack in the jamb. Nothing. No movement.

After ten minutes, I moved again. I found Miss Ayrshire, or Vandar, in Cacahuete's quarters, taking cover in his bathroom. She took a swing at me with a pair of brass knuckles, but I caught her wrist and threw her against a wardrobe. With the wind knocked out of her I twisted her arms behind her back and tied them up quickly with a cord from one of the robes. I pushed her down back into a chair and drew my pistol.

"I don't like interrogating women," I said, "but I will."

Miss Ayrshire kept her mouth shut and looked at me with contempt.

"It's a credible accent," I said, "but you're not British, are you? German? Austrian? Where did Hansclapp hire you?"

There was a subtle change in the light from the doorway. Before I could move, I heard two silenced rounds at close range, and Miss Ayrshire slumped forward.

I turned.

Standing, with a Heckler & Koch dangling from her slim wrist, was my wife. Marjorie.

She'd had work done. Expensive work. Anais' knife had destroyed her left eye, which was now of glass, skilfully done and perfectly matched to the real one, which glittered as she regarded me down the length of her aquiline nose. Her thick hair was now bobbed and dyed black. Her jaw had been reset after Victor's timely intervention with my mother's brass teapot. A suspicion of crow's feet, and a thinning of the skin at her porcelain temples, but that was all. Still perfect.

"Why didn't you go for an eyepatch?" I asked, in the hope she might get cross and lose concentration, so I could launch off the bed and break that perfect nose with my palm. I shifted my weight in readiness.

She took a pace back and aimed at my heart. "Darling, how I've missed you," she smiled. "Now get your hands up."

She motioned with the barrel for me to turn around, which I did, although my legs felt rather weak. I thought she might just put a round into the back of my head and be done with it, but this didn't happen.

"Marjorie, I must just ask," I said as cheerfully as I could, "where the hell is my father's Wolseley?"

The kitchen table. I sat at my end. Marjorie at hers. She had made tea one-handed, warming the pot and spooning the Assam while keeping the Heckler trained on my centre mass. She instructed me to take my mug down from the mug shelf. It was the one Anais brought me from a school trip to Walton-on-the-Naze. It said 'The Boss' on it in big block letters.

"Do you still drink tea, St. John?" she said.

"What sort of question is that?" I replied, evenly. I was actually dying for a decent cuppa but didn't want her to know it.

"You look… changed," she said. "Is life on the streets terribly awful?"

I shook my head. "It's actually rather life-affirming."

"A biscuit?" She sat down and slid a tin of shortbread down the length of the table. I opened the tin and took one. I wondered if I could spin the tin lid at her and follow it with the tea, but even as these ideas occurred, I could see they'd end with a bullet in my heart.

"Been well?" I asked.

Marjorie's tinkling laugh, like a shark biting down on a crystal decanter. "A fractured skull, a dislocated shoulder, my pancreas removed. Not to mention hypothermia from six hours crawling around the grounds. Seven surgeries in all."

I shrugged.

"You should have killed me, darling," she admonished.

"There's still time."

That laugh again. "Ever the optimist, St John." She took a sip of tea, and the steam curled around her face. The brief humidity made her look suddenly ravaged, her soul laid bare. "No, after today you'll never see me again. Except perhaps on television or on the front page of The Times…"

"So, what's the plan then?" I goaded. "You and your brother having fun?"

"Quite so," she nodded, "and I bet you'd like to hear all about it."

"Not particularly."

"Well, it's my party, so you shall."

Marjorie settled back and rested the gun on the edge of the table. Scoundrels are taught the best time to strike is when an adversary is beginning a tale, as there is a subconscious expectation that one will simply sit and listen. I drained my mug and held it in my throwing arm, at the same time shifting my weight so I could launch myself towards the doorway. I was going to aim for her good eye and dive for cover – maybe I'd be fast enough to get my torso behind the wall before she…

CLICK.

She'd cocked the Heckler. "Your mug. Put it down. *Langsam. Jetzt.*"

I sighed, placing it back on the table. After a brief pause, Marjorie said, "she knew, didn't she? She always knew."

"What are you talking about?"

"Anais. She saw through me from the very start."

Instantly my hackles were up. I nearly cracked, but I didn't. I controlled my breathing and looked down at the mug on the table. The mug Anais bought me. The Boss. My girl. I let the fury charge in my body, like the paddles on a defibrillator. It built up in my chest, and fizzed along my arms, and settled in my hands, a weird ball of potential energy that had to go somewhere.

I looked up at Marjorie. "You should just kill me. If you don't, I'll never stop until you and your brother are in the ground."

Marjorie laughed again. "Oh, you'd love that, wouldn't you? An easy death. Well there's not a chance of that. Playing with your lives is Gruber's favourite hobby. He'd never forgive me if I spoilt it for him."

I snatched up the mug and hurled it at her as hard as I could. It slammed into her cheek, breaking the cigarette holder and knocking the cigarette into her lap. In a trice, I was across the table and my hands were around her neck and I was squeezing, squeezing, squeezing the life from her.

She tried a bent thumb *kapo ken* strike into my carotid. I saw stars and lost the sight in my right eye, but I did not let go. She scrabbled for the lit cigarette again and drilled it into my cheek, but I locked the pain away and kept on throttling her. I had a 100lbs weight advantage, and I used it all to hold her down so I could finish the job.

She was smiling as she looked deep into my eyes. I couldn't believe how calm she looked, so close to death. "Make love to me," she whispered.

For a fraction of a second I relaxed my grip. Big mistake on my part. A saucepan crashed against the side of my head, and her knee drove hard up into my groin at exactly the same instant. My stomach was a cauldron of boiling lead. The stars I was seeing became a billion explosions of light. She threw me onto my back and kicked me hard in the throat. Only then did I pass out.

"Thank you so much for coming so quickly," Marjorie said, in her cut-glass lady of the manor voice. "He's this way."

I opened my eyes. I felt woozy. I'd been drugged. Marjorie had spiked me with booze. I could smell it on me. I could also see lots of big black boots striding in, onto the flagstone floor.

"He turned up drunk. He was terribly angry. He said if he couldn't have me, nobody could…" Her voice wobbled. Marjorie wrote the rulebook on this kind of ruse. On cue, she burst into tears.

"Well, he won't be bothering you anymore, madam. We'll have him down the cells in a jiffy," said a pair of boots, stepping forward towards her.

"Thank you so much, sergeant."

"Did he…" the boots searched for the word, "… manhandle you in any way?"

"He struck me about the face," she said. "I rather think you can see the mark?"

"I can, madam."

I tried to interject, "taaakke aaa looook uppstaiiiirs," I slurred, "deeaad bodieeees …"

A new big black boot took a step forward onto my fingers. I could feel the full weight of the entire constabulary on top of it. "I'd take this opportunity to keep quiet, sir, if I were you," said the boot.

"He'll literally say anything to get back at me," she said. "He was always a jealous man, even before our marriage foundered," Marjorie sobbed. "He's come up with all these crazy ideas that I was sleeping with other people. He seems to have no grasp on reality. I'd thought I'd seen the last of him."

The boot shifted, crushing my fingers into the flagstones even harder. "Rest assured, we'll not let him bother you again, madam."

She moved closer to the boot. I presume she cried on his shoulder for a moment.

"There, there," said the boot. "It's all over now."

"Thank you," Marjorie said tearfully.

Six months, in the clink, Major. That's what I got for that little interlude. It's an absolute disgrace! I was hoping for at least three years. I actually wept the day I was released because I knew I was heading back to Cardboard City, a place far less hospitable than D-Wing at Holloway. And so it was that I was back with you all too soon, dossing down in a puddle of piss.

What can I remember about those awful days now, from the comfort of the four-poster bed with a hot toddy steaming on my bedside table and a Romeo y Julieta glowing in the ashtray? I remember how those Waterloo days ground on and on, into one another. How winter turned to spring, and spring to summer and then to autumn, and then onto winter, followed by spring and then into summer again, and into autumn, and then winter again and then spring and then summer, followed by autumn and then winter again, and after that spring – let me know if you're getting this – without ever an opportunity coming along to make our lives better.

And then 1978 became 1979, became 1980, became 1981, became 1982. All that time wasted just trying to survive the cruel mistress that London is, if you aren't able to buy her new handbags and seat her at the best tables. Soon she's kicked you out of bed, changed the locks and gone off to Ascot without you. A cruel mistress indeed, Cornwall, with none of the associated benefits of having a mistress. You never receive a surprise noshing off in the kitchen while making a crêpe suzette if you're a tramp.

I expect you are itching to tell all your tales of shoe-shining and renting out stolen deckchairs in Regents Park, but I'd urge you not to. Let's skip all that, Major and fast forward to the eighties, when it all got interesting again.

Yours sincerely,
Major St. John Trevelyan.

Hellcat Manor

Great Trundleford

Devon

June 8th 2021

Dear Major,

For once I agree with you. Those days were so mind-numbingly dull that I can barely remember any of it. There's not much more to be said than that. Nothing changes, and every day blends into every other day. And then suddenly it was the eighties.

CHAPTER 11
A POUND OF FLESH

MAYFAIR, LONDON, 1982

The hard London rain thrummed on the Mayfair restaurant window as I tucked into another succulent mouthful of Argentinian steak.

"May I speak frankly?" I said, wiping my mouth with a white cotton napkin.

"Please do," the President said.

"I've honestly never heard of them. Never. And please understand, I don't mean any disrespect when I say that. It's just, y'know, the sun never sets on us. We're a big Empire. There are places like these dotted all over the world."

The President raised his eyebrows and shook his head as if he couldn't believe what he was hearing. He was incredulous. "Well I must say this comes as a surprise," he said, regarding me over his glass of Malbec. "And you think that most people in the UK are equally ignorant?"

"Yep." I stuffed another chunk of steak into my mouth. "Let me put it this way," I continued, indicating how good I thought the beef was. "You've mentioned these islands several times now and I still can't remember their name." I broke into laughter.

President Galtieri wasn't laughing. "Las Malvinas," he said again.

"Right. And what is that? Spanish?"

"Si."

"Well, I can assure you that nobody in Britain even knows they're there."

Galtieri nodded slowly. "Are you sure?"

"I'm positive. And may I say," I said, swallowing the last piece of meat and placing my knife and fork onto the clean plate, "what a pleasure that was Mr President. Thank you again for inviting me to sample your most excellent produce. I declare Argentinian beef the best in the world. And as Britain's new Meat Envoy, I shall be reporting back to Whitehall that Argentina will be our number one beef importer from now on."

I raised my cotton napkin to my brow, dabbing away beads of nervous sweat. I wasn't Britain's Meat Envoy, I was a homeless fellow, not even on my uppers. I had no uppers. I'd tried everything to better my circumstances, but nothing had worked. Through a horribly circuitous route, involving months of preparation, faked signatures and doctored Government stamps, I'd lied my way into a meeting with the Argentinian President while he was on an official trip to London. And all just to get a decent meal inside me.

Now Galtieri was banging on about some islands I'd never heard of 8,000 miles away.

"You really think people in the UK don't know about the Falkland Islands?"

"Well," I said topping myself up with the Malbec, "I didn't know about them. And I know more than most."

Galtieri suddenly seemed preoccupied, his mind elsewhere, and he didn't speak for a while.

Obviously in hindsight, it's easy to look back and see where one might have done things differently. I'm not proud of the next words that came out of my mouth. "Let me put it this way," I said. "I bet we'd love to get shot of them, given half a chance." Neither am I proud of my follow up.

"The UK government would never go to war over a barren rock in the South Atlantic."

As I left the restaurant that evening with a belly full of beef, I felt happy for the first time in a long time. I couldn't wait to get back to Waterloo Bridge and tell Trevelyan about the terrific coup I'd pulled off.

By now we'd been on the streets for eight years and tried everything we could think of to improve our situation, but it's quite difficult to get back on your feet without a home, a bank account, any money, food, clothing or an uncle high up in the city. And so we survived on our wits. The odd scam here, the odd scheme there. We'd become versed in the arts of the hustle, a bit of bunco, flimflam and grift. We'd learnt what time restaurants throw their food out and which bakeries had dodgy locks that could be shivved. But how much longer could we keep this up? We were desperate and ready to do just about anything to make our lives better.

I tried to re-invent myself. First as a motivational speaker, then as a model for *Just for Men*. I even knocked around for a bit telling people I was Stanley Kubrick, a short-lived ruse that secured me reservations at the Savoy and Dorchester. But word soon got around that Kubrick always did a runner after the pudding wine and it all came to an abrupt end. Trevelyan had similar luck. After coming out of prison, he was convinced he could make a go of it on the professional darts circuit. Although he looked the part, he was terrible at darts, but also at mental arithmetic, spending whole minutes between each throw working out the score. There followed a period as a human statue in Covent Garden, but his jitters put paid to this. He also got excited about a gig as the relief *basso profundo* for *Showaddywaddy*, but the stylist couldn't get his hair to lie down so he was fired.

The only time we got any respite was when we were asleep, but even then our memories would play a cruel trick on us, duping us into believing that everything was back to normal. The only thing I had to sustain me was seeing my boy Titus at the zoo each day. Without that, I knew I would hit rock bottom.

LONDON ZOO, LONDON, SEPTEMBER 1984

"Dr Fanshawe? Might I have a word?" Mandy Lahore, now the Director of London Zoo, strode towards me as I sat at one of the outside café tables, enjoying a morning coffee. This was my favourite part of the day. I'd worked my way into being a quasi-member of staff since first masquerading as the primatologist Dr Alan Fanshawe. I had my feet firmly under the table, just enough to get access wherever I wanted, but not enough for anyone to call on my expertise, which was good as I didn't have any. I'd befriended the young lady behind the till, and it had become standard practice for her to give me my morning brew and a sausage roll free of charge. I savoured them after another frigid night under the stars. "Dr Fanshawe?" Mandy Lahore, now the Zoo Director, seemed uncharacteristically tense today.

"How can I help, Mandy?" I asked, looking up over the rim of my coffee cup. Only now did I see that she was she was flanked by two police officers.

"Dr Fanshawe, I don't presume," she allowed herself archly, "I'm afraid that you are not who you say you are. You've been deceiving me for the past ten years?"

"What?"

"Do you have any identification on your person, sir?" said one of the police officers.

"My wallet's in my other jacket, I'm afraid." My wallet wasn't in my other jacket. I didn't have another jacket. I didn't have a wallet.

"CORNWALL!" A figure came into view. It was Fanshawe. The real one. He'd aged badly. He sported a goatee and a heavy mullet haircut. He'd put on a ton of weight and lumbered across the café. "You've a bloody cheek, man!" He pointed a stumpy half-finger at me.

I stood up, drained my coffee and slipped the rest of the sausage roll into my coat pocket. "Oh dear," I said, feeling the blood rush to my fists. "Of course, I'm not Fanshawe. Guilty as charged, but the real crime here is that my boy is locked away in that cage 24/7. I only wanted to see him."

"Dr Fanshawe has filled me in on your story, Mr Cornwall. You took Guy from Africa when he was just a baby."

"His name is Titus."

"His name is Guy," insisted Lahore, "Guy the Gorilla."

"Come with us, sir, please," the policemen stepped forward.

"No need, no need," I said, all smiles. Acquiescing at the point of arrest was a textbook Scoundrels manoeuvre. Eight times out of ten it meant the officers would neglect to put handcuffs on. Which was, of course, a mistake.

I sidled around, nearer to Fanshawe, until I was close enough.

"You bloody idiot, Cornwall," he said. "Did you really think you'd get away with pretending to be m—"

-SMACK-

My perfectly executed right cross knocked Fanshawe out cold. A bit of a kerfuffle with the two law enforcement officers later, I was in the back of a police car being driven away from the zoo. I felt dreadful, for now I had no way of seeing my boy.

The sun's rays fell across my face as I slumbered, softly enveloped in the meadow flowers that were already in bloom. The pasture behind Hellcat was a postcard of bucolic Englishness during spring. That morning I'd been visited by Gabriela, the local postmaster's wife, a buxom Colombian beauty with proud, upstanding breasts and a penchant for tight linen tops who somehow found herself behind the counter in a village post office in Devon. Today she'd knocked on my door, deputising for her sick husband, and had remarked how wonderful the grassland looked in flower. I'd pronounced that the view was best enjoyed with a bottle of Krug and a tartan rug and she'd gamely agreed. Our innocent stroll soon became a lustful tryst of the most vigorous variety and we now lay spent in languorous fashion, with no sense of time nor consequence.

How long had Gabriela lived in the village? I couldn't remember. I thought that was strange considering her striking beauty. I looked down at her again. She was snoring loudly. The image jarred.

Then a memory nudged me. I was in a tent on the side of a mountain. Some of the other chaps were there, Fonzi Spriggenhorn, Jefferson, Meekins. Gabriela was there too, wearing a thick parka. She was shouting at me.

"I can't help it! It's my obstructive sleep apnoea," she yelled. "The doctor says I need to lose weight and drink less!"

"But you're keeping everyone awake!" I pleaded.

I was confused.

I was back in the pasture.

Titus, my ape-son, appeared from the long grass. He seemed troubled.

'What's up boy?' I said. Titus picked up the bottle of champagne. He held it to the light and swilled around the remains.

'It'll be warm now I'm afraid," I said, "I'll crack open a cold one for you when we get back to the house.'

Titus tipped the remains of the bottle over me. I felt the liquid trickling down the back of my neck. My shirt was saturated. "What? Why did you do that, son?"

I woke up.

My eyes adjusted to my surroundings. I wasn't in my meadow at Hellcat. I was underneath some railway arches at Waterloo. Nana, my pet rat, was urinating down the back of my neck. I swiped her away and cursed. Bloody hell. I'm still destitute. Nana scuttled back to me. She ran over to my chest and nuzzled in under my chin, trying to say sorry. I nearly hurled her against the wall out of frustration, but stayed my hand. Friends were hard to come by on the streets, and I could ill afford to lose Nana, we had become so close. This wasn't the first time she'd urinated on me though, in fact her general health had become a concern. On top of her irregular heartbeat and gammy hip, this was the last thing she needed. I was sure it was down to her appalling diet but no matter how much I tried to train her she continued to eat her own faeces.

My attention turned to the person lying next to me. Trevelyan. He was snoring so loudly that his throat was vibrating. Damn it all. Gabriela didn't even exist. She was just a composite of all the gorgeous women I'd ever banged. I dusted myself down and trudged off to the telephone box to get a better night's sleep – standing up. As I yanked open the door my eyes fell upon the array of business cards stuck above the phone. Many were barely readable now. They'd been here for years. MAKE MONEY FAST! I remembered seeing this one years ago when we were first made homeless, yet this one looked new. Had someone put it here recently? MAKE MONEY FAST! Surely a scam. Just get to sleep, Cornwall. My eyes pinged open again. There was a phone number underneath. What did I have to lose? I flipped the card over a few times in my hand and then before I knew it, my fingers were turning the dial.

Major, you know as well as I do that there is no such thing as easy money, but it was desperation that drove me to dial that number. I'm about to relate the terrible events that led to the enormous scar on your flank.

If you don't wish to relive it all, I suggest you skip the next few pages until you come to the line: <u>The surgeon tossed Trevelyan's rancid kidney across the room where it landed on the table with a meaty slap.</u>

The man on the other end of the phone call made it sound so simple. Twenty grand, cash, in one day. Easy money. I agreed to meet him later that evening outside a pub in Bermondsey.

Mr Bolatov was a heavy-set man with round spectacles. He had an Eastern European accent that I couldn't place, but I knew not to ask too many questions. Still, I did have a few. "Explain to me again," I said, "why a human being only really needs one kidney?"

"Iz no problem," he said. "yor fren' no feel a' theen."

"And he'll be able to live a normal life afterwards?"

The man put out the palm of his hand and rocked it back and forth, "more o' less."

"And the doctor performing the operation is fully qualified?"

"Yess, yess. No problem. He train many yeer."

"That's reassuring. Whereabouts?"

"Frunze."

"France?"

"No. Frunze. It's in Kirghizia."

I wasn't sure where that was.

"...near Uzbekistan." The man added generously.

"Ah, I don't think I'm aware of that University."

"Ees no Univerzity. Iz state-run vivisection research facilitee."

I had a few doubts about this but twenty grand was twenty grand. I said, "And I hope you don't mind me asking, but what will you actually do with his kidney?"

The man held my gaze. After a time, he said, "experiments."

We shook on it and agreed to meet the following evening at an old warehouse in Wapping. This time I was to bring the donor, Trevelyan. I chose not to tell him as I knew he'd only rail against the idea. But I was sure he'd understand when it was over.

Getting him to Wapping was easy enough. I'd slipped a special red pill into a bottle of White Lightning cider I'd shoplifted and he was even more pliant than usual. We arrived outside the warehouse and he soon curled up on the floor and fell asleep on the pavement.

I banged on the rusty iron door twice as instructed. There was a metallic grating sound as it opened a few inches. Bolatov's face appeared in the gap. "You av zer donor?"

I nudged the sleeping Trevelyan with my foot. "You have the money?"

Bolatov nodded and disappeared back into the shadow. The door opened. Several bulky men came out and hoisted Trevelyan onto a gurney.

I followed them down a dimly lit corridor and into a makeshift operating theatre. It smelled of bleach and death. A single lamp cast a harsh pool of light above the operating table, which looked like something from a Victorian asylum. It had been fitted with thick canvas straps and buckles.

Bolatov directed my attention to a steel bathtub full of ice in the corner of the room.

"When eets over, we put him in here. We cover him in ice. Then you call the ambulance. Understand?"

"Call an ambulance? But I've got to get to Simpsons. I've booked a table," I said.

Bolatov shrugged. "As you wish."

Trevelyan was stripped naked and carried on to the operating table. Bolatov's men proceeded to strap him down. One of them stood at Trevelyan's head. He placed thick leather cord between Trevelyan's teeth and held on to the ends.

"Are these men going to be carrying out the operation?" I enquired.

"No, no. Theze nurses izz just preparing him."

The medical team entered the room. There were three of them, all wearing surgical scrubs. That was good to see. I had been beginning to think this was a cowboy operation.

I stepped in front of the surgical team, blocking the route to their patient.

"I don't want to come across as pushy," I said. "But may I see the money?"

Bolatov pulled a black briefcase from under the operating table. He opened it for me. Stacks of fifty notes in sets of ten. I nodded in satisfaction and he placed it against the wall.

There was a metallic jangling sound as the lead surgeon fumbled around in a toolbox. I looked on as he laid out a series of hideous serrated instruments, well suited for medieval torture. He didn't seem sure about which one to choose, hovering over them as if they were a box of chocolates, but finally settled on a thin-bladed knife. He said something in his native tongue that brought everyone into focus. Bizarrely, all the doctors put on ear defenders, the kind I've used myself for grouse shooting.

The operation was about to begin. The nurse at the head of the table adjusted his grip on the cord in Trevelyan's mouth. Bolatov gave me a reassuring nod of his head. The surgeon placed the tip of the knife onto Trevelyan's flesh. Only then did I notice something troubling: there was no anaesthetist.

I coughed to get their attention. The surgeon's hand stalled.

"Is he not to receive an anaesthetic?" I asked.

My question was met with blank looks.

The surgeon shrugged. "Heez asleep, no?"

Bolatov moved towards me and whispered, "iz best not to deesturb the doctor. He needs concentrate."

"But Trevelyan needs an anaesthetic," I argued.

"Anaesthetic very expensive," Bolatov said, then added, "he had sedative already."

"Is that going to be enough?"

He placed a hand on my shoulder and gripped it. It was equally reassuring and menacing. "Let's see," he said.

The surgeon adjusted his stance and regained his composure. The narrow blade hovered again over Trevelyan's flesh. Then in one movement he brought the knife down and carved a foot-long incision down Trevelyan's side.

Trevelyan awoke immediately.

"YEEEARRGGHH!!!!"

The heavyset nurse at the head of the table pulled down hard on both ends of the leather cord in Trevelyan's mouth, forcing his head back down onto the table. "Bite eet boy!" he shouted into Trevelyan's face.

Trevelyan bit down on the leather, screaming through gritted teeth. The thick canvas straps that were buckled tight held him firm.

A surgical assistant stepped forward and applied a steel spreader to the wound, winding it back until the gash was several inches wide. Trevelyan's instinct was to thrash around, but his bindings held him firm. He just about managed to turn his head a fraction to see me. I gave him a quick thumbs up to lift his mood but his bulging eyes conveyed only terror, pain and anger. He was straining so hard I feared they might pop out. I wondered whether I should call Simpsons to put the reservation back half an hour or so.

Bolatov handed me a pair of ear defenders. "For the screaming," he said, kindly.

Every now and then, Trevelyan would raise his head and unleash a hideous cry only for his head to be yanked back into place by the nurse with the leather mouth-strap. I tried to pass the time by running through the menu at Simpsons from memory. I'd been really looking forward to spending a bit of Trevelyan's operation cash on a good feed. Would it be the kippers on toast? The kedgeree? Or perhaps a full English. I already knew what I'd order, but it was fun going over it in my head.

Snapping out of my reverie I noticed that the operation had taken a dark turn. The surgeon and his team were having a heated argument. I was annoyed about this hiccup, whatever it was. This was supposed to be a nice surprise for Trevelyan. I'd spent ages planning the whole thing out, from the moment he fell asleep to the moment he'd wake up in one of the banquettes at Simpsons. And now they were ruining it for him.

"What's happening?" I said.

"Zair ezz a small problem. Zey can't get to zi kidney. One of hiz ribs iz in ze way."

The surgeon shouted at one of the assistants who then passed him a small-toothed saw. Bolatov patted me again on the shoulder. "Iz fine. They find a zolution."

I turned my back on the surgeon as he began saw off one of Trevelyan's ribs. I'm not a man who is prone to self-doubt but I admit I was beginning to question whether this was going to be worth it. Trevelyan's screaming was distressing, so I filled the time with light chit-chat.

"How long does the operation normally take?" I asked, while facing the wall.

"Three hours."

I continued to face the wall. "And will he remember anything afterwards?"

Bolatov considered this carefully before answering, then said, "yes."

After a bit I glanced over my shoulder to see how

they were getting on. Not well apparently. They had a defibrillator out and were jolting him with it.

"Everything okay?" I asked.

"Yes, yes, yes. No problem. He dead for few minutes but he fine now."

"Riiight…"

I turned back towards the wall. Just let them get on with it, Victor, I said to myself. To take my mind off it, I started to daydream again, this time about what we'd do with the twenty grand. A night at a good hotel. That would put a smile on Trevelyan's face. And of course, we couldn't celebrate our upturn of events without a little trip to Heavy Betsy's. I'd even allow Trevelyan first dibs in the breast immersion chamber where he'd spend a couple of hours with a nipple in his mouth having his hair gently stroked.

I was lost in thought when I felt a tap on the shoulder. I turned around to see the operation was finally over.

"All good?" I said.

The surgeon and his assistants stood stony faced. Something was wrong.

I removed my ear defenders.

"Problem?" I asked.

Bolatov nodded to the surgeon.

The surgeon tossed Trevelyan's rancid kidney across the room where it landed on the table with a meaty slap.

"This organ is useless," he shouted. "Worthless!" I looked at the steaming lump of flesh. It was tar black.

I took a big gulp of air and let out a weary sigh. I should have bloody well known. Trevelyan barely drank any water. I could see my full English slipping away.

Bolatov wasn't smiling. "You've cost me valuable time and money, Meester Cornworll."

"Listen," I said, thinking on my feet. "He has two lungs. I don't think he needs both of them."

Bolatov was incredulous. "Sorry Meester Cornwall. Surgery is closed."

I lost my temper and grabbed him by the lapels.

"I want my money Bolatov. You asked for a kidney. I gave you a kidney."

Bolatov knocked my hands away, turned to the nurses and said, "kill them both."

At that moment the lights went out.

This was followed by a brilliant, blinding flash and a deafening bang that was so disorientating I simply dropped to the floor. Several more seconds of commotion, more gun shots and then the room fell into silence. I could hear nothing save for a faint ringing in my ears and my own heavy breathing. A blazing glare of torch light was aimed at my face. I raised a fingerless-gloved hand to protect my eyes. I was about to say, 'don't shoot,' when I heard a voice I recognised.

"May I suggest you're more careful with whom you do business, Major Cornwall." Stephanie Summerville directed the light away from my face and stripped off her black balaclava. "Events at the Club are way beyond my control. I need you both back and I may have found a way to help you."

This was a bolt from the blue. It had been almost ten years since I'd seen Summerville. She looked as magnificent as ever. I on the other hand…

"Turn your eyes away, Stephanie," I said, stepping back into the shadows dramatically, "lest they be forever burned with the image of my grim countenance. I am a beast, a cruel simulacrum of the Adonis you once knew…"

"Shut up and listen."

"Okay."

"What do you know about horses?"

"Lots," I said.

"Do you?"

"No, not really. Why?"

"An undertaking has crossed my desk. You and Trevelyan would be perfect for it. It's well paid, highly illegal, and if it goes wrong it's nothing to do with me."

I was excited at the prospect of work and finally getting some money. The money! My attention turned to the briefcase against the wall. Summerville hadn't noticed it.

"Cornwall, are you listening to me?"

I regained my senses. "Yes, I'm in," I said, and then looked over to Trevelyan who was still opened up on the operating table. "And he is too, if he lives."

"Good. You are to get your hands on a very expensive birthday present – a racehorse. The problem is that the horse is owned by someone who doesn't want to sell it."

"You need us to change their mind?"

"I need you to steal it. The horse is extremely valuable. Pull this off and there's £300,000 in it for you."

"Each?"

"No, of course not each. It's not a bloody Monet.

But it should just about settle your bar bills and then I can make you Scoundrels again."

Music to my ears, except, "I think Trevelyan might be dead."

Summerville rolled up her sleeves. "We haven't got time to get him to a hospital. Pass me that needle. I'm going to stitch him back up."

You have probably wondered why much of your lower abdomen looks like a piece of chewed dog meat. Summerville and I did our best with next to no medical training and only a rusty nail for a needle.

More widely, of course, I hold up my hands and say *mea culpa*. But the truth is you should be thanking me. That kidney was a ticking time-bomb. If it had stayed inside you it would have soon burst, dousing your insides with septic gunk and ending your days. Also, that briefcase full of cash went a hell of a long way and put us back on the road to recovery. It's not my fault you refused to take any of it through your sheer bloody-mindedness.

That incident marks the only time I've ever had to cancel a reservation at Simpsons. But the staff couldn't have been more accommodating. They completely understood and we even had a laugh that kidneys would not be on the menu that week, even though I knew that they would. They always are. It's Simpsons.

Yours sincerely,
Major Victor Montgomery Cornwall

Nimbu Towers
Pullen-under-Lyme
Gloucestershire
June 13th 2021

Dear Major,

I can still feel the ache where my kidney used to be. You're little more than a whoremonger, prostituting your oldest friend for a few grubby banknotes. I don't know exactly what you and Summerville sewed me up with (Catgut? Fuse wire?) but the scar is an angry purple and puckered up like your favourite rent boy's arsehole.

The entire enterprise was just another example of your feckless, giddy, ill-thought-out, finger-in-the-air, fly-by-night lunacy and if you were in my presence now, I'd put down my pen and strike you hard across the mouth.

Bloody lucky we caught that kidney cancer though, eh? Every cloud.

CHAPTER 12
HORSE TRADING

LONDON, SEPTEMBER 1984

As I staggered away from the scene of my unscheduled nephrectomy, I told Cornwall exactly what I thought of him, which wasn't much. I have never been angrier with him, and this is in the context of always, on some level, being angry with him.

I spent a fortnight convalescing behind a line of bins in a North Kensington alley, away from the river chill, resting up. He offered to use the cash he'd made to get me a suite at the Dorchester, but I told him to roll each banknote up very tightly and stick them where the sun doesn't shine.

He turned out to be, perhaps through guilt at what he'd done, a decent nurse. I was an obstreperous patient, haranguing him even while pissing blood and weeping a yellowy pus, but he was diligent in finding me fresh cardboard for my mattress and changing my bin liners twice a day. He never left my side apart from when fetching me food and medicine or spending the night in his suite at the Dorchester.

I was very poorly but I refused to die. Whenever I felt my heart struggling to beat and the darkness closing in, I would summon in my mind's eye the smug face of Gruber Hansclapp looking in the rearview mirror of his black cab. This image boiled my blood and kept me warm. It also gave me purpose. Just to spite Cornwall, I continued to live on the street. I suppose I didn't want to give him the satisfaction that he'd solved all our problems. Besides, he hadn't.

And yet, on Christmas Day, 1984, Cornwall, wearing a Santa hat, brought me a warm fruit pie and a gabardine trenchcoat from Cordings of Piccadilly. I took this as a final apology for stealing my kidney and, with a curt "Merry Christmas", let the whole thing go.

By March '85 I was right as rain. Physically, that is. For some reason, even though I could now afford a decent hotel suite, I'd become so acclimatised to roughing it that I elected to stay in my alley. I suppose on some level I didn't feel ready to re-enter my old life. I didn't belong any more, and for a Scoundrel that was a terrible cross to bear. Besides, I'd pioneered a workout based on short sprints up and down the alley and lifting full rubbish bins above my head like an Olympic powerlifter, and when Stephanie Summerville asked us to meet her at a greasy spoon by Victoria Station, I was ready.

She hadn't changed a bit in the years since I'd seen her. She stirred sugar into her mug of tea and wrinkled her nose as we sat down. Her eyes swept quickly over my grizzled beard and frayed woollen gloves. She grimaced as she took in Cornwall's over-extended quiff, electric blue flecked suit, thin leather tie and Armani winklepickers. Although the kidney money hadn't been enough to reinvigorate his account at 1 Savile Row, it had been good enough for off-the-peg at Selfridges. He'd taken to 1980s style like a duck to water.

"You two really do need to raise your game," she said. "St. John, you need de-fleaing. Victor, I have no words for whatever *that* is."

Cornwall was about to say something in defence of bri-nylon when the café owner came over. "You two, you're both barred," he said. I'd forgotten that during a freezing night last year we'd forced open his kitchen door.

He'd found us asleep the next morning, surrounded by empty bottles of vinegary house red. Cornwall took out an envelope and peeled two twenties from the thick sheaf inside. "Two teas. Keep the change," he said, enjoying feeling flash. The café owner went off grumbling.

"How's the Club?" I asked Summerville.

"Things are dreadful. In short, I need you back. That's why you need to get this horse-napping job absolutely right." She looked dubiously at us. "Are you sure you're up to it? It's been a long while since you were operational."

"Are you seriously asking if we can steal a horse?" scoffed Cornwall.

"Yes," she said, curtly. "And it's my neck if you get this wrong. Are you going to let me down?"

"We've never stopped being Scoundrels, Stephanie," I said.

She eyeballed us both in turn. "Right, get your arses to Ireland for tomorrow night. You're stealing a stallion from the Ballymany Stud. You've got to get him to Ascot to meet the buyer and conclude the sale within twenty-four hours."

"Does this stallion have any distinguishing marks?"

"He's a five-year-old thoroughbred colt."

As a gentleman of the road, I had developed a working knowledge of the turf. "Ballymany Stud?" I mused. "Fancy. He sounds expensive."

"Very."

"How much?"

"Ten million."

I let out a low whistle. "That's a lot of horse."

"That's only his insurance value. You couldn't buy him for ten million."

"Why not?"

"The Aga Khan says he's not for sale."

"What's his name?"

Summerville took a sip of tea. "Shergar," she said.

COUNTY KILDARE, IRELAND, THE NEXT DAY

It was five in the morning. Under a full moon, our Land Rover jounced along the country roads, scraping hedges and skidding on wet gravel. Cornwall crunched the gearbox as he took a long bend, his driving as erratic as ever. I wanted to tell him to be careful, but experience had taught me it'd be even worse if he slowed down.

In the rearview mirror I could see our horsebox, containing the most valuable racehorse in the world, swaying all over the road. There was a furious neigh and a hoof slammed against the side of the box.

"Shergar wants you to cool it," I said.

"Shergar's not driving," Cornwall replied.

And indeed, we needed to crack on. The Guardai took horse theft more seriously than they took murder, and the Aga Khan paid big bonuses to those who protected his interests. "Mind that tree!" I shouted at Cornwall, as he skidded past a crooked ash.

The heist had gone smoothly. Textbook. We'd delivered four kegs of doctored stout to the Ballymany grooms' quarters, with a note from the owner of a maiden that won the Punchestown 3.20. We'd sent a case of similarly doctored champagne up to the big house. We'd scoped out the neat row of stables as the horses were bedded down. We'd listened to the music coming on, and then the sound of raucous laughter and dancing, and we'd waited for the sedatives in the stout to take effect. We'd thrown hooky steaks to the guard dogs. We'd sapped the men in the sentry box and we'd disabled the closed-circuit television without appearing on it.

Getting Shergar out of his stall was a little trickier. He was a naughty boy with a mean streak. He'd kicked Cornwall in the knee and crushed me against the wall with his massively muscled flanks. Getting a bridle on him had been almost impossible, as he kept thrashing around and trying to bite us. I'd had to give his knackers a squeeze to show him I meant business.

Now we were hurtling along towards Broad Lough and with a fair wind we'd be through Wicklow Port and out to sea before anyone knocked on Shergar's stall door with his breakfast oats and raised the alarm.

Handling Shergar's magnificent testicles had got me thinking. Gram-for-gram, the most valuable substance in the world isn't uncut diamonds or beluga caviar, it's the seminal fluid of an Arabian-Turkoman thoroughbred stallion. A teaspoon would set a chap back over £50,000. And that was for a normal winner. Shergar's pony gravy was said to cost eighty grand a pop. As I'd gripped those priceless bollocks, I fancied I could feel the thunder of billions of spermatozoa galloping along the endless furlongs of his sperm ducts. Imagine the laurels in there, I thought. All the St. Leger champions, the Queen Elizabeth Stakes winners, the odds-on favourites destroying the Derby field by ten lengths.

Surely we were missing a trick.

"What exactly was your Club bar bill, Cornwall?"

"Pushing a hundred grand, give or take."

"Mine was nearer two hundred."

"This cash for delivering Shergar just about covers it, then."

"With not a lot left over," I said, "but I think I know how to cream a little more out of the deal."

"I'm listening." Cornwall's gingery moustaches bristled in the moonlight. He licked his lips, a wily old fox with his thoughts on the henhouse.

"This horse's knackers are an absolute goldmine. When I grabbed his bundle, I thought they were going to burst. He's got it to spare."

Cornwall liked this. "We'd need a buyer. Who has a load of mares that need servicing?"

"Rufus Felham?" I wondered out loud. Rufus owned an enviable patch of North Gloucestershire. His estate backed onto Nimbu, where his wife, Dame Harriet, ran Podolphin Racing, the worst stables in England. Rufus had to buy a majority share in Chepstow racecourse just so her nags could find races to run. "This is not just any old spunk, it's *Shergar* we're talking about. Top drawer jizz! Rufus will bite your arm off for it."

I took a swig from the hipflask I'd nicked from the stables. It tasted like the stuff they use to harden pony hooves. Maybe it *was* the stuff they use to harden pony hooves.

"What would they pay, d'you reckon?"

"Depends how many rounds he's got in the chamber," I mused.

"Well, you're the one who felt him up," said Cornwall. "What do you think is reasonable?"

There followed a spirited discussion about how often a fellow can be expected to fire and the corresponding loss in power with each reload, which took us as far as Croneybyrne. And by Slanlough we were deep into the logistics, which were problematic. "We've got to deliver him to Ascot by midnight," I mused. "And that's after the voyage across the Irish Sea. We haven't got time to stop and let him romance a load of ladies."

"You've seen him though, he's a proper shagger," said Cornwall enthusiastically. "It won't take him long. We'll call ahead and get Harriet's mares lined up in the yard. Bam, bam, bam – and straight back on the road."

"Too risky. If we miss the rendezvous, or we get pulled over by the police, the deal's off."

We rattled over a crossroads at seventy, both lost in thought, trying to crack what was essentially a scheduling problem. The Land Rover scraped along the side of an overgrown hazel hedge. There was another indignant whinny and a blizzard of furious stamping from our passenger in the back.

"There is a way," I said, tentatively, "but I don't relish it."

"Oh yes?" Cornwall looked over at me as he took a

cattle grid at sixty mph, his face briefly vibrating like he was plugged into the mains.

"If we could phone ahead, do the deal, and divert to Harriet's stables, I'm pretty sure we'd still make the rendezvous," I said, and winced. "But that means we're going to have to use the time on the boat…"

I gulped.

"To what?" asked Cornwall.

"To wank him off."

We lapsed into silence. "I suppose that from an animal welfare perspective, it might relax him a bit," said Cornwall.

I cricked my neck. "Finish your coffee," I said. "We're going to need that thermos."

Dawn had just broken, and Maurice Johncocktosen was waiting at the boat, a 37-foot fishing vessel, looking very nautical. It felt bloody good to have Maurice with us. Although he looked like he'd put on about sixty pounds since I'd last seen him, he remained a capable rogue, just the sort of Scoundrel for a jaunt like this. From the deck he saluted backwards, crossing his eyes and poking his tongue out the side of his mouth. "Hullo, you old bastards," he called.

Dawn was already breaking as we unhitched the horsebox and winched it down onto the deck. This accomplished, Cornwall drove the Land Rover back down the muddy track that led to the isolated jetty on Broad

Lough. I heard the whump of a petrol engine catching fire, and a minute later Cornwall came sprinting back. "Permission to board?"

"Permission granted," said Maurice, casting off the rope. "Brandy is in the cabin."

Getting through Wicklow Port was a doddle. Cornwall and I hid below deck, and Maurice manned the wheel and the radio. During our trip down the river to the sea, we'd stretched an oily tarpaulin and some lobster pots over the horsebox, so we could masquerade as fishermen who'd pulled in for supplies. The harbourmaster even gave us a Gaelic seamen's prayer on the shortwave.

As we motored out of Wicklow harbour, the sea was as smooth as glass.

Maurice was all for our enterprise, although there was a bit of confusion over the whys and wherefores. He initially thought Cornwall wanted the spunk for himself. "Terribly good for the hairline, apparently," he winked at Cornwall, "especially for the receding gentleman. Chock full of protein."

"Just get us to Wales, Maurice," replied Cornwall, sniffily.

Maurice shrugged. "Fine, but your captain is warning you we're about to have some weather," he remarked. "So if I were you, I'd start getting him in the mood, quick smart." With this, Maurice went off rather huffily to man the wheel.

Cornwall and I regarded the bolted horsebox door. I noticed that the sea was getting heavier, and the deck was beginning to roll. Then the door was kicked hard from the inside. A dent appeared in the steel panel, which shimmered in the cold sea air.

"After you," Cornwall said, firmly.

"Oh no. After you," I insisted. "Your wrists are stronger."

During the full and frank exchange of views which followed, it became clear neither of us wanted to grasp the nettle, so we tossed a coin to decide who would enter Shergar's horsebox first.

I would enter Shergar's horsebox first.

Cursing my luck, I paced around the deck and wondered exactly how I would get two and a half tonnes of skittish muscle, trapped in a steel box on a rolling sea, to ejaculate into a coffee flask. I am not ashamed to say that I was apprehensive. Fearful, even. Then I remembered animals can sense fear. This wouldn't do at all.

I paced to the prow of the boat and looked out at the rolling grey swell, and the wind spurring up choppy little waves that my Ma used to call *white horses*, which galloped alongside our vessel. I wondered what she'd think of her boy now, rolling up his sleeves to masturbate the world's fastest racehorse. I expect she'd be proud.

I thought for a moment and soon had a plan of action. I did some energetic shadowboxing, thirty fast press-ups, and then a minute of vigorous jogging on the spot. I sniffed under my armpits. Perfect. This burst of exercise on top of a night lying in a mossy Irish ditch meant I smelt like a side of venison hanging in a poacher's parlour.

"What the hell are you doing?" asked Cornwall.

"Working up a bit of a lather."

"Why?"

Wasn't it obvious? I wanted Shergar to get my scent. I wanted him to sniff my high testosterone tang and understand that I was the alpha. This is the smell, he'd figure, of an animal demanding respect. "Command and control," I told Cornwall, as I removed my trousers and rubbed the crotch area over my head and face. "I'm going to go into that box as an apex predator. I want Shergar to think I EAT horses. I want him to think I could chew him up if I wanted to."

Cornwall began to nod enthusiastically. He was getting it. "And, as an apex predator, if all I want to do is wank him off, he'll think he's getting off lightly." Cornwall continued to nod. He was sold on this as a bloody good idea, which gave me great confidence, as to be honest I had my doubts about it making any sense at all.

The rear of the horsebox was a giant door of hinged metal with only two positions: bolted closed or laid flat to form a ramp to the floor. I'd briefed Cornwall to lever open the door just enough for me to flip down from the roof, as smoothly as a lover slips between silk sheets. Then Cornwall would close it again. Once I was locked inside, I would start throwing my weight around, beating my chest and howling like a banshee, cowing Shergar into submission.

I clambered onto the roof of the horsebox and crouched, light and springy on my haunches.

Cornwall whispered, "ready?"

I nodded.

"Go!" He slid back the restraining bolts of the horsebox and opened it enough for me to swing down inside. I landed as softly as a cat in the darkened container.

Unfortunately, either through over-excitement or his usual ham-fistedness, Cornwall slammed the door closed with a deafening clang that reverberated around the inside of the box. This startled Shergar and he bucked wildly, slamming into the wall. I lost my footing on the shit-smeared floor and cannoned into Shergar's back legs, causing him to collapse on top of me. His tremendous flanks and thick thighs squashed all the air from my lungs, and I felt a couple of ribs pop. Shergar's next impulse was to scramble up again, so I took a couple of hard hooves to my abdomen.

As he regained his feet, he went berserk, shouldering the sides of the horsebox and braying like a mule. It was nearly pitch black in there. All I could see was his enormous rippling shape cannoning left and right off the steel walls, bucking and twisting as if he'd just been gelded. The noise of his neighing and stamping was indescribable. I couldn't see the hooves coming – CRACK! He caught me a lucky shot in the side of the jaw. One of my back teeth shattered into fragments.

The smell of my blood seemed to drive Shergar into a frenzy. He managed to turn himself around and trapped me against the hay holder with his withers, snorting fetid breath into my face. He was eyeballing me, and those eyes relayed a message. The message was: you are dead.

I'd underestimated this horse and needed to dominate him. I tried to waft some of my alpha pheromones in his direction, but this angered him further. He let out a furious neigh that perforated one of my eardrums.

"Trevelyan? Trevelyan?" Cornwall was calling me. "How are you doing in there?"

"Get in here," I yelped. "This is a two-man job."

"Are you wanking him off yet?"

"Just get in here!"

The horsebox was suddenly flooded with dawn light as Cornwall let the ramp fall to the deck. To his credit, he thought quickly, and stuck his thumb into Shergar's flared nostril. Shergar's eyes widened and he let out a bass whinny like the foghorn on the Trelawney lighthouse. I scrambled away from him and back down onto the deck.

Maurice chose this moment to take a souvenir photograph. "Say cheese," he shouted, from the deck. The Leica's flashbulb went off with a stunningly bright starburst, causing Cornwall to swivel around and release his grip on Shergar's nostrils. Shergar bucked and caught Cornwall with a hoof full in the throat. He was thrown out of the horsebox onto the deck beside me.

Maurice quickly slammed the door shut and bolted it. "Fruity bugger, isn't he?" he said, chuckling. "You need a bit of a rethink, chaps. I'll be in the cabin."

Cornwall and I made a cup of tea and sat down on the deck astern to count our losses. I had taken a real kicking. I'd cracked three ribs and lost a back tooth. Cornwall had a livid bruise along the side of his throat and thought he must have broken a couple of toes, but he refused to take his winklepickers off to check the damage.

"The problem is," Cornwall mused, "that Shergar thinks he is the alpha."

"The problem is," I replied, "that Shergar IS the alpha."

Cornwall's brow furrowed. Gulls cried and the dawn clouds scudded along. "I'm going to try something completely different," he said.

"What's the plan?"

"I'm going to speak to him in words he can understand."

Cornwall doesn't speak any foreign languages apart from a smattering of German and French. However, he has worked hard to assume a mastery of accents and dialects in English. It's no exaggeration to say that he can speak English a hundred different ways. He can do all the key ones you need in the espionage game: laconic Texan oilman, seductive Russian piano teacher, penniless Italian nobleman, cheeky Cockney wideboy, as well as a superb whining Glaswegian taxi driver. He can speak pidgin, *bislama*, butler-English and Jamaican creole, and listening to them is a rare delight.

Cornwall grabbed the thermos flask. "Roight den," he said, in a perfect Irish brogue. "Les' see whaat a liddle love-tark ken do fah' da big fella, ey?" He walked back over to the horsebox. He stood at the door and cleared his throat, wincing painfully as he did so.

> "Ohhhh, Shergar boy,
> da pipes, da pipes are callin', loike…"

He sang gently as he began to conjure up the character of a shy County Derry stablehand, a simple country boy, perhaps putting down his broom and fingering his flat cap, such was his embarrassment at being called on for a tune by the lads.

I nodded approvingly, and Cornwall continued.

> "Fro' glen ta glen',
> all down da mouhnten soide…"

Here he paused, masterfully. There was a scuffling noise inside the horsebox. Shergar was listening.

> "Da summer's gahhhhnn,
> an' arl da roses fallin…"

He continued, his baritone growing in power:

> "– Shergar, it's ye mus' go—ooooohh,
> An' I mus' bide."

Brilliant! Fancy introducing the horse's name into the song! That's probably exactly what used to happen back at Ballymany Stud. It would make Shergar feel right at home. From inside the horsebox, we heard some light gruntling as Shergar shifted his weight, most probably straining to hear this beautiful ballad, his ears pricked. Music was, quite literally, soothing the savage beast.

I gave Cornwall the thumbs up.

> "But come ye back, when summer's in da meadow!
> Or when da vaaaaaalllleey's hushed
> and whoite wit' snooooow…"

Cornwall's voice resonated across the sea. The gulls had stopped their screeching, and it felt as if even the waves had quietened, as he began to power through for the big crescendo.

> "It's I'll be heeeerrrrrrre!
> In sunshoine or in shaa-aa-aa-dow,"

And now he really let loose at the top of his lungs,

> "Oh Shergar-boy,
> ohhhh Shergar boy –
> I LOOOVVE!
> YEEEEEE!
> SOOOOOOOOOO!

And on the last word of the song, Cornwall crept forward and gently opened the horsebox door.

Shergar let fly a double hind-leg kick to Cornwall's chest, casting him backwards through the air like a rag doll. Shergar, looking over his rippling shoulder, let out a triumphant neigh, shook his lustrous black mane, farted loudly and went back to chomping hay.

Over the next couple of hours, we tried everything. Tempers frayed and I remonstrated with Cornwall for having left the horse tranquilisers in the Land Rover as they would have come in jolly useful.

We tried rocking the horsebox back and forth to create a sort of sexy rhythm that might get him in the mood, but Shergar seemed not the slightest bit aroused.

We tried cutting a hole in the roof to lower me down onto his back, hoping that once astride him I could harness the natural authority of the cowboy or jockey. He bit me on the ankle and clubbed my crotch with his giant glossy skull until I was forced to scramble back out of the hole.

I put on a couple of fisherman's jerseys for padding and, while Cornwall distracted him by shining a torch in his eyes, I tried to grab his old chap while it swung wildly around. I wrestled with it, trying to get it to go off – but to no avail. We came to the conclusion that, like many celebrities, Shergar was a very difficult personality– irascible, proud and malicious, with a clear sense of what he would and would not do.

And what he would not do, right now, was be wanked off.

Seven hours later, lunchtime, with the Welsh coast in sight, we were feeling dejected. We were both covered in all the varieties of racehorse effluent – faeces, sputum, sweat, blood – except the type worth thousands of pounds. We had almost given up hope of collecting the precious fluid that would begin to rebuild our fortunes.

Then I saw it, lying on the deck: the 24V battery pack for the catch winch. Suddenly I remembered a story I'd heard from Colonel Khumba, a Scoundrel who lived on the South African veldt, about rhino husbandry. He swore blind that a tranquilised rhinoceros could be made to ejaculate simply by ramming an electrical stun-gun up the rectum, until it reached the prostate gland. The first time this happened, Khumba recalled, he didn't believe it would work, and he had to catch all the rhino spooge in his pith helmet.

Maybe the same technique would work now? Working quickly, I fashioned a primitive electric pulser, using the battery, some copper wiring and a metal truncheon for fending off porpoise attacks. I gave Maurice a test shock on the back of the neck as he stood holding the ship's wheel, and he went down like a sack of potatoes. What's more, all the ship's instruments went haywire, but thankfully we could see the coast, so no navigational problems resulted. Maurice soiled his sou'wester and, although he regained consciousness almost immediately and laughed it off, he never recaptured the high spirits with which he'd started the voyage.

Time was short. I flung open the horsebox door one more time and marched up the ramp. Cornwall leapt past me, wrapping his arms around Shergar's neck in a vicelike grip. As Shergar tried to fling him off, I went straight to his rear end and pulled out the truncheon. Cornwall was now being smashed off the roof and walls of the horsebox and I knew I only had one chance to get this right. I pulled Shergar's tail out of the way, jammed the truncheon in as hard as I could and turned the battery on. Instantly, every muscle in Shergar's body, and Cornwall's body, tautened, and Cornwall fell to the floor. He staggered, almost broken, to the thermos, and dragged himself into position at the horse's nethers. "Here it comes!" he shouted.

Shergar's formidable old lad began to throb furiously. The emission began. The first spurt bounced off the lid of the thermos, which Cornwall had neglected to remove, spraying muck all over Cornwall's face and hair, and dripping in thick, mucal clumps onto his wax jacket. "Get the lid off, man!" I cried in exasperation. But Cornwall couldn't see for all the jizz in his eyes. I snatched the flask from him, twisted off the lid and got it back into position. In two or three mighty spurts, the thing was full to the brim. I twisted the top back on, but Shergar hadn't run dry yet. Hastily, I pulled out my cigarette case, shaking out the small stock of *National Velvets,* a batch of black paper Sobranie-Villancourts that I'd had the Scoundrels tobacconist whip up for masturbating racehorses. I held it up and managed to catch Shergar's dregs. Snapping it closed I chucked it in my pocket, swept up the Thermos, turned off the battery and dragged the battered Cornwall out of there.

I turned back to close the door of Shergar's box, but I needn't have hurried. He was standing there with a soppy look on his great long face. All the stress and tension had gone from his eyes, and he looked as happy and content as, well, anyone would.

The rest of the day went surprisingly smoothly. Maurice dropped us off on the Welsh coast and chugged off again to return the boat he'd stolen.

We picked up our new Land Rover and horsebox and drove through Wales like maniacs. By suppertime, we'd pulled into Rufus and Lady Harriet's farm in Gloucestershire, leaving the engine running.

The news of Shergar's disappearance had broken. Rufus was a little stressed that we'd brought him to his farm but didn't baulk as I passed the flask through the window in exchange for everything he had in his safe – a very useful forty grand.

We screamed up the M4 towards Ascot, just in time to make the midnight rendezvous with our buyer.

We met him in the lorry park of a disused motorway service station, probably the most down-at-heel place in Ascot. He was a rangy chap in a battered wax jacket and flat cap, who was wearing a disguise he'd clearly bought from a joke shop. He seemed very affable. To this fellow, buying a stolen racehorse was a great wheeze, and he wanted to know all the details of the robbery, congratulating us for a job well done.

He had a green Range Rover with horse box on the back and a few solid chaps in two other vehicles, ready to wrangle our naughty boy into his new berth. Shergar sliced the earlobe off one of these men with a well-aimed kick, and our buyer simply tutted and lit a Sobranie from a gunmetal case. He invited us to smoke and watch his men taking cracks, belts and bites from Shergar, finding the whole thing hysterically funny. He told us he was in hot water with his missus, again. He wanted to make up "for years of miscreancy", by giving her the sort of birthday present that money couldn't buy. The very definition of uxorious, he'd had Shergar 'napped just to please her.

I rather liked him and felt he would have made a decent Scoundrel. Cornwall later told me he felt the same. He had a relaxed, urbane, unruffled way about him, even when handing over a briefcase with several million pounds in it – including our three hundred grand delivery fee.

He'd handed over the cash almost as an afterthought, slapping each of us on the back, and remarking that he'd had "a bloody entertaining evening", and that he hoped our paths would cross again one day.

Which they did.

There we are, Major, a turning point for us.

Podolphin Racing dominated the Chepstow scene for the next two decades with a stunning series of bred stallions and mares that seemingly came from nowhere. Among them, Little Victor won the 1989 Juvenile Hurdle from odds of 150-1, and Sinjun's Delight won the 1991 Welsh Grand National by a clear furlong.

Perhaps you'll take over and deal with our triumphant return to the Club?

Yours sincerely,
Major Arthur St. John Trevelyan

Hellcat Manor
Great Trundleford
Devon
June 19th 2021

Dear Major,

I thank you for reminding me what it's like to have one's sternum cracked by the hind legs of a 600kg racehorse, although it was a small price to pay in the grand scheme of things. Not only did that escapade help get us back on our feet, but the scientific paper I subsequently submitted to the Royal College of Veterinary Surgeons ripped up the rulebook on animal husbandry. Although it was later banned for its claim that you could steer a horse most effectively by its testicles, I understand that it's now a cult classic amongst apprentice jockeys.

Anyway, after a *decadus horribilis,* we were back to the Club! But a dark cloud still hung over me and it needed to clear before I could do anything else.

CHAPTER 13

DADDY'S GUNNA BREAK YOU FROM THE ZOO TOMORROW

LONDON, JANUARY 1985

We were back. Sort of. The theft of Shergar had gone without a hitch and within a few weeks Summerville had set us up a couple of high street bank accounts and wired us the fee. Then, she signed off the debts on our bar bills and reinstated us back at the Club before anyone could object.

Just like that, we were members in good standing again. Plus we had a big fat juicy bonus from the sale of Shergar's big fat boner juices.

But Trevelyan and I were still in a terrible mess. It takes more than a quick shave and an off-the-peg suit to hide the evidence of all those years of street living. Now in my early sixties, I looked weathered and craggy, my once youthful visage had been replaced by a brutal, patrician replica, like the Lincoln of Mount Rushmore. And that was just the outside. Inside, I felt like a sucked orange, a mere husk of pith and skin.

Time had been even less kind to Trevelyan. His teeth were held into their sockets through memory alone.

He was now unable to wear shoes on account of his toenails. Unchecked, they'd not so much ingrown as completely encased his feet in nail, like the clogs of a Dutch milkmaid. On the frigid ground of Waterloo's cardboard city this had had its benefits but watching him clomp around the fitting room of a Jermyn Street bootmaker was painful. Eventually I presented him to the Horse Guards' farrier to sort him out.

Unable to return to Hellcat and Nimbu, we were forced to find temporary accommodation at the Dorchester. It was just the tonic we needed. Like schoolboys with their father's credit card, we giddily booked the two best suites they had. We ate in the restaurant that evening. It promised to be the best meal I'd ever had but was ruined by Trevelyan's table manners. I should have known he'd be excited. When the food arrived, he was clapping like a cymbal-banging monkey. And he devoured it with a bestial savagery that turned my stomach. I'd witnessed him do a number of unsavoury things over the years, but I never imagined I'd see him deep-throat a T-bone. When he finally came up for air it had been stripped clean. I raised a sardonic eyebrow and remarked, "Hungry?"

It took a moment for him to regain his breath. He grinned at me with watery eyes and said, "I'm ordering another one."

We stayed in the restaurant until late, testing the reserves of their finest Reserves. We eventually retired to our rooms with smiles on our faces and warmth in our hearts. My head hit the goose-down pillow and I began to drift off. Brief vignettes floated through my soused mind. I saw myself as a young child in hunting attire, stalking across the estate with Farver.

Farver had blooded my face. This was my first kill. A roe deer that he now carried across his shoulders. That memory drifted away to be replaced by another. Baxter being chased around the eastern lawns by Titus riding a sit-on lawn mower.

Ah, Titus. My mind swirled with more memories. Finding him on my old Triumph Bonneville dressed as Evel Knievel, sincere in his belief that he could jump the duck pond. Pinning me to the parquet flooring in the West Wing until I gave him one of my Cuban cigars. Dressing him down for pressing his pizzle against the Aga, on a cold January morning.

But then a more disturbing picture swirled into my mind's eye. Titus cornered by a man with a gun. Shot with a tranquiliser dart and heaved into the back of a van. Trapped in a cage at London Zoo, pacing up and down with nothing to occupy his inquisitive mind. Staring out into the distance, his big brown eyes, wet with tears as children goaded him with sweets and ice creams from the other side of the glass. Titus. My boy Titus.

I snapped awake. As I thought about my son behind those bars, a slow, boiling anger built within me. The last time I saw him was the day I was thrown out of the zoo. He'd been stuck in there long enough. My heartbeat quickened. It was time to get him back.

"Titus," I vowed into the darkness. "I'm coming to get you."

THE BLUE BAR, SCOUNDRELS, NEXT DAY

I was in no mood to piss around. I hadn't set foot in the Club for a decade, but as I approached the imposing figure of Aram Atsi by the door it was like I'd never been away. My muscle memory kicked in and, with little more than a polite nod to the big lad, I skipped up the five granite steps with the grace of Rudolf Nureyev at his peak.

I was in.

But before I could enjoy myself, I had an annoying job to do, on Summerville's orders. She was unmovable on the topic: "little birds, in their nests, must agree," she said, with a glint of maternal steel. I was to apologise to Hendricks for firing the cork from a Melchizedek of champagne into his face, concussing him and bursting an eardrum.

Hendricks had always been a creature of habit. I saw no reason why the intervening years would have caused him to change his tightly wound ways. Here was a man who opened his eyes at 05:45 every morning, did forty-seven minutes of *Tae Kwon Do* before having one off the wrist for the next thirty-five seconds. Here was a man who would throw breakfast eggs at the wall if they'd been on the boil for any more or any less than four minutes and thirty-two seconds, which is why I knew that at three minutes past four that Thursday afternoon, he'd be entering the Gaye Bar for his customary snifter, prior to sitting down for his high tea at four twenty-one.

Of course, Summerville's diktat directly opposed my own plan to drive his nose bone into his brain with a single palm strike, but I could see the bigger picture, and reluctantly assented. Hendricks and I would never be friends, but if the Club demanded we play ball then we had to put our differences aside. Nevertheless, I wanted to needle him a little on my first day back, so I sat on his favourite bar stool and ordered a whisky from Jervis, as if I'd never been away.

I was there for 16:01 and had timed it to perfection. He swept in at 16.03, just as I was setting my empty tumbler down and nodding for another. Hendricks stalled with a look of horror on his face, instantly disguised. All credit to the smooth bastard, he gathered himself quickly. I pretended not to notice but I still scored that as my point. *Fifteen – Love.*

Hendricks glided across the floor towards me.

"So, you're back. Summerville told me it was happening," he paused, then added coldly, "welcome."

"Hendricks!" I cried, congenially, "how lovely to see you." I let my face fall. "But you don't sound very pleased to see me after all these years."

"Some of the best we've ever had," he replied. "What have you been up to?"

"Oh, you know, just taking some time off, relaxing."

"I heard you were penniless and eating out of dustbins."

I held his eye. "That too." *Fifteen all.*

"You're in my old seat," he said.

"Old seat?"

"I gave that one up when they extended the bar into the atrium." Hendricks motioned to the far end of the room. I hadn't even registered the extension. "I prefer the light over there," he added. A shaft of soft afternoon light streamed in from above, highlighting a comfortable armchair. Now I looked at it, it stood out like an oasis in the desert. So confidently situated, away from through-traffic, perfectly placed for both privacy *and* sociability, with a direct eye-line to the bar. It *was* the best position in the room. Another point to him.

Fifteen – Thirty.

Hendricks looked me up and down. "I'd heard the years had been unkind, but-"

"Still upset I killed your brother?" I volleyed back, unsmiling. "Or will you spare me the pissing and moaning?" *Thirty all.*

"At least the rough sleeping hasn't affected your charm," Hendricks spat.

I caught the attention of Jervis, "I'll have four fingers of *his* finest single malt."

Jervis looked uneasily to Hendricks. Hendricks nodded. Behind him the door creaked open, and Summerville breezed in.

"Playing nicely, boys?" she said.

"Just getting reacquainted," I replied. "I'd forgotten how charming Hendricks can be."

"Listen, Cornwall," Summerville said, "now is the time to clear the air once and for all. Then we can move on."

"You want me to be honest about how I feel about Major Cornwall?" said Hendricks, through clenched teeth.

Summerville met his eyes. "Yes."

Hendricks shifted uncomfortably. This kind of folksy, soul-bearing honesty was not usual at Scoundrels. "Very well," said Hendricks, "if you insist." I may have imagined it, but the room suddenly fell silent. "I've always hated you, Cornwall," he said. His directness took me aback. The words seemed to hang in the air like the final chime of an old grandfather clock at midnight. Over at the bar were a couple of young Scoundrels, sipping their Campari sodas, intrigued as to how this would play out.

"Can you be more specific?" I replied.

"You're nothing more than a show pony. Style over substance."

"What I'm going for is timeless elegance, rather than style, but thanks all the same," I said, nodding.

"Frankly, you've always struck me as a bit of a ponce."

I faked a look of surprise. "Really? ¿Cuál es el problema?" I said, in Spanish.

"You're just so full of yourself aren't you, Cornwall? You think you're God's gift to women."

I shrugged. The numbers didn't lie. I *was* a handful around the ladies, and everyone knew it.

"And I don't like the way, even now, you're strutting around the Club, like some sort of returning hero." "Not to be facetious," I interrupted, "but I am *literally* a returning hero. Or is it that you're saying you don't like the way I walk?" *Forty – Thirty.* "Oh, come on Cornwall, you know what I'm talking about. You're always bowling down the corridors, dishing out high fives as if you were in a West End musical based on your own life. Well, not everyone is enjoying the show." *Deuce.*

I was about to give him both barrels, but then I saw how Summerville's eyes narrowed, and that I must keep my powder dry. A change in tactics was needed.

"I hear you Hendricks, I really do. But what can I say? I guess you're right. I *was* like that. But that was the *old me*. The *me* that existed before I'd been forced to live off my wits, scrabbling around like a street rat. The *me* who had never felt the frigid earth drain the heat from his bones. The *me* that had never had to slake his thirst with a discarded can of WD-40, who every night had to climb on top of Trevelyan while he slept and use him like a roll-mat."

Hendriks frowned. This was not what he'd been expecting.

"I suppose what I'm trying to say is…" I took a theatrical breath and jutted my chin out, "…is, *sorry*."

An Oscar-worthy performance. But it was not time to congratulate myself just yet. I had to address the biggest elephant in the room.

"And listen," I said, softening my tone, "I know I killed your brother."

I raised my hands in a *mea culpa*. "He was a good man." This was a blatant lie. "If only he hadn't challenged me to that knife-fight he'd still be around today. He couldn't have known that I'm probably the finest exponent of *hunga munga* combat this side of the Congo."

Hendricks said nothing.

"May I also say," I added, filling the silence, "that I thought you showed remarkable clemency in the way you handled it." This was also an outrageous lie. Hendricks had tried to kill me with a rhino, marmalising my anus in the process. It was a wound which nearly killed me, leaving me with a ringpiece that, even now, could only produce pine marten scat.

"My anus needed to be replaced by the way. I don't know if you knew that." I said this with a breezy charm, so that it didn't look like I was getting on his back about it.

"I didn't," he said.

"Yes, I nearly died. Thankfully they were able to replace it with the anus of a pine marten."

Advantage Cornwall.

"My pine marten?" Hendricks looked at me in shock. And then disgust. I don't think he could quite believe what he was hearing. "Chup Chunder was a gift from my mother," he said.

Deuce. Again.

"Oh."

"She was trying to cheer me up when I lost my brother."

"Ah."

Advantage Hendricks.

There was a long and awkward pause while we both sipped our scotch. "Anyway," I added, cheerily, "my anus was repurposed into a new set of lips for Trevelyan! His had dried out in the desert. I think they call that serendipity."

I was pleased with that one, and I wished Trevelyan had been there to hear it. It had been years since he could say words like *serendipity*.

"Where is Trevelyan, anyway?" interjected Summerville. "I'd have thought he'd have been here with knobs on, now that he's a member again."

Trevelyan had been strangely reticent to come back to the Club. I made a mental note to challenge him on it later. "I think he's enjoying The Dorchester's hospitality. But I'm sure he'll pop in at some point."

Summerville's brow furrowed for a moment, she flicked her eyes to Hendricks. I got the message: close the deal.

"Listen, old boy," I said insincerely, "it's time to put our differences aside. From what I understand, the Club has never needed its senior members more. I'm not too proud to say it again. I'm sorry."

Advantage Cornwall.

"Hendricks," Summerville school-marm'ed, "I take it Cornwall's apology is accepted."

Hendricks nodded slowly.

Game Cornwall.

THE DORCHESTER HOTEL BAR, LONDON, TWO HOURS LATER.

Summerville had reserved the entire bar so we could have a meeting away from the Club. Trevelyan was busy making his way through a platter of French pastries while

I smoked a *Three Times A Lady*, a smooth, caramel blend of sweet Virginian, Burley and Cavendish that I'd had the Scoundrels tobacconist whip up for contemplating sensational women.

Just then, Summerville swept in. "Hendricks is an insufferable prick, isn't he?"

"Quite so," I agreed, blowing smoke up to the ceiling.

"Thank you for apologising to him this afternoon. I know admitting fault doesn't come easily to you," she said.

"Think nothing of it."

"I don't know how much time you've had to follow the news while you were away," she said, "but things have moved on somewhat in the last few years. I thought this was a better place to fill you in on the details."

I was reluctant to admit how little I knew about the state of the world. I hadn't seen or read anything in the news for a long time. "Perhaps a recap would be helpful, Stephanie," I agreed.

"First things first," she said, "you know I've been standing in for Lunk as M.O.S of the Club until he fully recovered?"

"Yes."

"Well, it's been decided that I will now take over that role permanently."

"Congratulations, Stephanie," I said, getting up to shake her hand. "That's great, but what about Lunk?"

"Oh, I'm still here!" boomed Lunk's distinctive voice. Tiberius Lunk glided into the bar in his wheelchair. Considering he'd been shot in the spine and spent years fighting for his life in an iron lung, he looked well.

Trevelyan and I got up and greeted him enthusiastically.

"I'll still be around the Club," he said, "in an advisory capacity. But Stephanie's the M.O.S. now."

We had a brief catch-up about his recovery and what he'd been up to in the intervening years, but there was a sense it was all a preamble to the real reason we were there.

"So," I said, eventually, "I suppose you ought to brief us about Hansclapp?"

Summerville glanced across at Lunk. "You mean *Lord* Hansclapp."

I felt as if all the air had been sucked from my lungs. Trevelyan put down the platter of pastries. I could see his brain was registering a catastrophic malfunction, as it did whenever Hansclapp's name was mentioned.

"Lord Hansclapp?"

"'Fraid so," Summerville said, "He's been a busy boy since you've been away."

Trevelyan shook his head, "No, no, no!" He pushed the table away and rose to his feet, scanning the bar for something to destroy.

"Sit down, St. John," I said keeping my voice low. "Let's hear about it first."

Trevelyan sat down, gripping the table's edge. "Who in damn hell…" he said, his voice a deep growl, "made Hansclapp a Lord?"

"The Queen, obviously," said Lunk.

Summerville laid it out for us. Hansclapp had been productive over the years we'd spent on the streets.

He'd acquired vast wealth and bought up national newspapers, commercial television companies and radio stations. A word from his empire could now make or break a political career. He'd donated heavily to political campaigns and garnered favour with the government. The current Home Secretary certainly owed her rise to him. The Governor of the Bank of England had racked up gambling debts to the tune of a million, Summerville told us, all forgiven in exchange for a few nips and tucks to the exchange rate mechanism. Hansclapp had exploited legal loopholes to sidestep competition law and when challenged by the Monopolies and Mergers Commission, he had been ruthless in overturning the decision in the Court of Appeal. Enemies had met their deaths in terrible skiing accidents and choking incidents. Another's Bentley had unaccountably reversed over him, while he slept.

Then, abruptly, two years ago, at the age of sixty-two, Hansclapp had stepped away from all of his business commitments, handing total control over to his sister, Lady Marjorie of Nimbu Towers.

This allowed him to take up a seat in the House of Lords.

Trevelyan was in danger of eruption. He was pacing up and down the room, talking to himself. I found I'd lit two more cigarettes and was now smoking them simultaneously.

Summerville continued, "I'm afraid you haven't heard the worst of it yet."

"Go on."

"He's trying to join the Club."

Trevelyan stopped pacing and turned towards us, his face a deep shade of purple. "He WHAT?!" he shouted. Trevelyan picked up a brass lamp and hurled it across the room. It crashed through the window onto the street outside.

I turned to Summerville. "Give us a few days," I said, urgently. "We just need to come to terms with this and work out what we're going to do."

An occasional table soared through the air and smashed through another window. "But there's something I must do first," I said, "and I'm going to need some help."

"What is it?" Summerville said.

Another crash through the window as hotel security arrived.

"It's Titus. He's locked up in London Zoo. I need to break my boy out of that cage."

A bar stool sailed through the window.

Trevelyan continued to berserk around, but I asked the security to show some understanding. "He'll blow himself out in a minute," I said. "Perhaps we'll wait in this corner?"

Summerville had a word with the hotel manager, and we were allowed to stay on. She was not amused though. I said goodbye to her in the lobby, after I'd settled Trevelyan down.

"You need to get him under control," she said. "He's no use to me like that."

"It's Anais, of course," I told her. "He misses her so much."

Summerville nodded, and in a tender gesture that lived long in the memory, patted me on the shoulder, running her hand down my lapel to smooth the stretched fabric where St. John had grabbed me and thrown me against the wall just an hour before.

"Just spring Titus as fast as you can," she ordered. "Get the ape. Get control of Trevelyan. Then straight onto Hansclapp. OK?"

"Understood."

REGENT'S PARK, LONDON, FEBRUARY 1985

My hand-picked team of Scoundrels were dressed in black, crouched in the shadows of a bush in Regent's Park, less than fifty yards from London Zoo. I signalled a heads-in and the men silently gathered around. I always conducted the same ritual before every dangerous undertaking, to give myself valuable intel about my team's state of mind. In the comfort of a lounge bar, every chap is a hero. But put him behind enemy-lines at night, separate him from his platoon, then add a chasing pack of Dobermans and guards with flashlights, and you'll find that many men fall short of their own expectations. I now looked each and every one of them in the eye and asked myself the same two questions I

always posed, 'does this man have the right attitude?'
And, more importantly, 'is this man going to cost me the
mission?' My initial readings were not good. There were
seven of us in the team and judging by my reckoning,
nobody aside from myself was up for it, and six of them
could easily cost me the mission.

We were an odd bunch: Trevelyan was my seventh in
command, concerned with (c/w) Explosives & Ropes. He
seemed more preoccupied than usual, perhaps anxious
about how Titus might react when he saw him. It was
a fair concern. Titus loved Trevelyan, and after being
banged up for years he'd have a lot of pent-up sexual
energy to release.

Hendricks was c/w Surveillance & Exits. I hadn't
wanted to include him, but Summerville made me
consolidate our new-found goodwill by asking him
along. He'd accepted only after I'd agreed to pay his
travel costs and dry-cleaning expenses, which I thought
was a bit rich.

Then there was Chatsworth, a new Scoundrel –
twenty years old, five feet tall and as slender as a spiv's
necktie. He was c/w Recces & Locks. Chatsworth had
become a member after he attempted a break-in at the
Club. After he'd shinned up an eight-storey drainpipe,
avoided our electrified roof, the false skylights and the
pressure pads under the Kirkwood Window he was
leaving with a sack of silver plates when Jerwood caught
him in the neck with a blowpipe dart. After a quick
interview we realised he didn't have the disqualifications
and made him a member. This was his first undertaking

and he had been gee'ing himself up all day. Now he was a bit too gee'd up and behaving erratically. I handed him some beta blockers and told him to calm the fuck down.

Popsy O'Doherty was our S.W.P. – Scoundrel Without Portfolio, by now standard protocol for all infiltration and exfiltration undertakings. He'd replace any man who bought it on the job, or just roll up his sleeves and do whatever was required. After all, kidnapping a gorilla can be planned, but it cannot be planned perfectly.

My old mucker Fig Brondby, who'd recently returned to us after two decades marooned on a tiny desert island, when the plug popped out of the bathtub he'd been rowing from Hawaii to Tahiti, was in a new role which we thought was rather wet, c/w Health & Safety.

Finally, Dr Simeon Gotts was c/w Ents & Scran. Gotts had done a bloody good job in this regard, earlier in the day summoning us to the Nanny's Garden in the Park and treating us to a tremendous spread of beluga roe on freshly-skilleted blinis with soured cream, all washed down with tea from a samovar. He'd also brought a few bottles of claret for the non-tea drinkers, which was all of us.

We'd mustered for the break-in to the Zoo after a spirited game of rounders, and some ice cream from the café in the Inner Circle. We found a Laying Up Position in a large rhododendron bush and waited as the sun descended behind the treeline and the wardens locked up the park. Then we waited a few hours more to be sure that we were definitely alone.

It was on. I gave Chatsworth the nod and he scampered out of the bush and over the twelve-foot spiked railings as if they were a country stile. He did a quick sweep of our ingress zone and flashed his tactical torch to indicate there were no security patrols nearby. Phase one, complete. The rest of the team moved up to the railings, but unfortunately Chatsworth had made an error. He'd dropped inside the elephant enclosure, rather than the rabbit enclosure as we'd arranged. I gave a silent hand signal for him to get out. And then another to do so quick-smart, because the bull elephant had awoken and was looming out of the darkness behind him. Unfortunately this message was too complex to convey in the form of emergency hand signals. I don't know whether he couldn't see me or not, but he made no attempt to duck the flailing tusks. The elephant knocked him off his feet and repeatedly stamped on him until he resembled a pink paste.

It was a bad start.

I pinged Popsy to assume Chatsworth's role, and he was over the railings, into the correct enclosure, and had the side entrance gates open in under a minute and a half. Proper Scoundrel, Popsy.

Crouching low, we sprinted past the brush turkey enclosure and the parrot cages, without incident – apart from one of the parrots telling Fig to *phhharrk himself.*

We halted in the Eastern Underpass to regroup.

"Right, then," I said, "we've lost one man tonight, through no fault of our own. But let's make sure he's the last. We should honour Chatsworth's name by completing this undertaking."

"It's what he would have wanted," someone said, in the darkness.

We moved on. I'd seen Titus pull the heads off enough animals to know that birds have a particularly sensitive early warning system, so I'd planned our route to avoid running past the Eastern Aviary. This meant taking a wide loop past Otters, Flamingos and Okapi, all of which went well.

Fig, who'd drunk a lot of claret, was suddenly caught short, and needed to urinate. We stopped in the cover of the north side of the Butterfly House. Even on a good day, Fig couldn't go an hour without having a pee, on account of his prostate which was the size of a honeydew melon. He cracked open the door of the Butterfly House and went inside for a bit of privacy. This was the last time we saw him alive. After waiting outside for fifteen minutes he still hadn't emerged. Trevelyan went inside to get him and found Fig dead on the floor with his flies undone and his penis covered in butterflies. We'll never get to the bottom of what really happened, but the most likely scenario was that while Fig was peeing, a hungry venomous *Antimachus Swallowtail* was attracted by his nutritious stream of urine and mistook his glans for a rare orchid. Fig must have tried to brush it off, angering the butterfly so that it injected his penis with deadly serum. Fig's heart didn't stand a chance.

After this, we were all a little dejected. I felt moved to give my second inspirational speech of the evening, pointing out this was no-one's fault, especially mine.

"It's what they both would have wanted," said a doleful voice, although I couldn't tell who because London Zoo turns off all the lights at night and the entire site is pitch black.

We regrouped by the Penguin House. I pulled out the zoo map and illuminated it with a red lens torch. A brief argument ensued over the quickest way to get to the Ape House with Hendricks claiming he'd come a couple of years ago and it was definitely *this* way. Then Popsy started to complain that we hadn't seen any of the big cats yet and that they were the best. Then Simeon Gotts chipped in, moaning that he was tired and needed a sit down, and that London Zoo was 'different' to the last time he'd come. And by 'different' he meant 'not as good,' which really got my back up as it was a toss-up between bringing him or Ruff Puff, and I know Ruff Puff would have given his right arm to swap places. If he'd had a right arm.

Trevelyan didn't help matters by repeatedly pointing to the cafe icon on the map, saying, "it might still be open."

We pressed on, taking a minor detour via the African Savannah because I was actually a sucker for the big cats too. But even that was underwhelming because the lions were all hiding and we didn't even get to see them. If we hadn't illegally broken in, I'd have complained and asked for my money back.

By the time we arrived at the Ape House, we were another man down. Gotts had been adamant it was quicker via the Antipodean Birds Enclosure, but his short-cut through the cassowary paddock was his undoing. Grainy CCTV footage of the incident became infamous as a video nasty during the 80's, graphically showing Gotts being mangled by a pair of six-foot males. The banned footage revealed the birds scrabbling their powerful claws up Gotts' face until it resembled a steak tartare. And the VHS copy would later become part of the brief for Scoundrels on trips Down Under.

By now I was feeling a bit glum about our growing casualty list. Three dead Scoundrels before we'd even got to the objective. I'd have some explaining to do to Summerville, but that was a problem for later.

I gave the remaining team what I hoped would be my final motivational eulogy, reinforcing the fact that what had happened was nobody's fault in particular.

We'd reached the Ape House. Trevelyan nodded assent and passed me his knapsack containing the gelignite. He hustled off to do my bidding. I took a deep breath to calm my jangled nerves. It's never pleasant to see your colleagues die. But if they were going to, why couldn't one of them have been Hendricks, for Christ's sake? Life just isn't fair.

This was the tricky bit. The plan was to blow the doors off the Ape House, grab my boy and escape before the alarms were raised. I commando-rolled across the viewing area, landing on my feet in front of the heavy iron door. I began to tape the stick of gelignite to the handle. Titus' pen was one of the toughest cells in the Zoo, so I slapped another stick on for good luck. We'd only have one chance at this, after all. Then I ran the fuse twenty feet backwards towards the wall I'd use for cover. This took me past the reinforced glass windows that were Titus' only view of the world. The smudges and smears of a thousand grubby children's hands caked the bottom section of the window. Bloody hell, that must drive him mad, I thought. All those gurning little scallywags with their lollipops, tapping on the glass, demanding that he swing on the tyres for their amusement.

I peered through the window. I needed to attract Titus' attention so I could tell him what was about to happen. Years ago, I'd taught him the Yerkish ape lexigram language, and I hoped he'd still remember GET BACK BOOM-BOOM COMING, a sign I'd first taught him after a slow day dynamiting salmon when he was about seven years old.

And there he was, my boy. A big man now, with flecks of silver at the sides of his shapely head. He was sitting propped up against a pile of wooden pallets, cradling a little baby against his massive wiry chest. A lady gorilla – the baby's mother– was curled up at his feet. Daddy was doing the night shift.

Did this make me a grandfather? My heart burst with pride. The baby was asleep, but she stirred and began to mewl. Titus brushed a finger against her soft head back and forth. He cooed to her and lowered his lips to her shoulder for a soft kiss. The tiny baby settled immediately, burrowing into his chest for the warmth and comfort and security that a father provides.

A father provides. That's what a father does. I suddenly found that I had a peculiar lump in my throat. Yes, I had provided. I had been a wonderful father. I had given my boy Titus everything a young gorilla needed. 65 kgs of fresh fruit and vegetables a day. Space to run and play. A fine school. A butler. A pony. A handmade shotgun with extra wide trigger guard to allow for his thick sausagey fingers. But more than all of that, I'd provided Titus with *a home*.

And now, seeing Titus with his little baby daughter, I was suddenly struck by something.

It was Trevelyan, thumping me hard on the back. "Hurry up! What's the delay? Blow the door and bring him out."

But I was also struck by something else. This was now Titus' home. What right did I have to do this? Look at that lovely little girl there, nestling so tightly into the chest of my wonderful, warm-hearted boy. In that moment, I realised that if the signs in front of his cage were true, that if he really had sired over seventy-five baby gorillas from twenty-three different gorilla mummies, then taking him back to his old life would deprive many little gorillas of their own father.

I was paralysed by this sudden realisation. He was my boy. My lovely hairy lad who'd sit on my knee as we learned the alphabet. Well, 'A' at least, because after that he'd grow frustrated and tear the book in half. But those times had been so perfect, so full of love. My Titus. My son.

Tears were streaming down my face. Trevelyan looked at me, and instantly understood. "Having doubts?" he queried quietly.

I nodded, unable to speak.

Trevelyan chucked me on the arm. "Then let's get out of here, old man. Say your goodbyes. I'm going to give you..." he checked his watch, "...twelve seconds."

Trevelyan took the gelignite sticks from the door and began to wrap them back around the fuse wire. He stopped and turned to me. His voice was choked as he said, "you know, Victor, you've been a wonderful father, but you are right to let him go." He went back to winding the wire.

I turned back to the big window. Suddenly Titus was standing there on the other side of the glass, staring at me. His baby girl was still fast asleep. He showed her to me proudly and kissed her head again. Then he put his huge hand up to the glass and pressed his fingers to it. I put my hand up to.

I knew what I had to do. "Goodbye, Titus," I said, "goodbye my son,"

I signed to him that his baby girl was beautiful and then put my hand on my heart and kept it there.

And then I turned and walked away.

What happened next was a great shame, but I've decided to leave it out of the memoir to spare your blushes, Trevelyan, as you're looking like a bit of a duffer presently. You failed to de-rig the gelignite correctly, handing Popsy back a rucksack full of live explosives, ruining such a poignant moment. I was still wiping away the tears in my eyes, when Popsy and half the Ape House blew up.

I thank my stars that the little baby was unharmed and that Titus himself only lost a hand. The very hand, incidentally, that sits on my desk here at Hellcat, and that I still use as an ashtray.

Still, at least it meant London Zoo had to build a brand spanking new gorilla house – a much more spacious affair, with private dens and a water feature for Titus and his ever-expanding family.

It fills me with pride to learn that 'Guy', as they named him, was such a prolific shagger that now, just thirty years later, over 85% of zoo gorillas world-wide, share his genes. I never regretted my snap decision to leave him at London Zoo, although I missed him every day, and still miss him now.

Yours sincerely,
Major Victor Montgomery Cornwall.

Nimbu Towers
Pullen-under-Lyme
Gloucestershire
June 24th 2021

Dear Major,

I suppose you're right. It does simplify things somewhat if you miss out some of the awkward detailing around the destruction of the original gorilla house.

I suspect it was actually Hendricks who switched the fuses in my kit that night, perhaps hoping to blow up Titus and his beautiful new family, or even to end your days, and my days, prematurely. He may have hated you, but there was no love lost between us either.

I remember being actually quite reticent about returning to the Club after all those lost years. But I got fed up loafing around the Dorchester and decided to bite the bullet.

CHAPTER 14
BATTLE ARRAY

SCOUNDRELS CLUB, PICCADILLY, 1985

It was overwhelming at first. Aram Atsi picked me up and span me around, kissing my cheeks as if I were his brother returned from the war. There was more of him around the middle, and he was sporting another ill-advised neck tattoo, but the smile on his face and the tears in his eyes were unmistakable.

I stepped through the imposing black door and over the Club's threshold, with a long, controlled exhale. New wallpaper I see. Not sure about the fez they'd stuck on the Dead Frenchman, where the bloody hell was his original bicorne? Was nothing sacred?

But the more things had changed, the more they'd stayed the same. Joan the Coat Check Lady might have been wearing a bit more rouge than a decade before, but her twinkling eyes were still as bright and playful. As I jinked lightly up the Grand Staircase, I recognised the particular polish that they use on the banisters, Mr Sheen infused with black truffle oil. Just the aroma to get you in the mood for a whisky and one of Crozier's celebrated bar snacks. Which would I choose to break my long Blue Bar fast? A few strips of the Ouse pike jerky, perhaps? Or the deep-fried Cornish seagull wings. No! It had to be the devilled red-squirrel kidneys. I'd missed them the most. It would be bad form to order the lot, I reminded myself.

I skipped into the lounge and sidled up to the bar. The stools had been reupholstered in a *corduroy*, for God's sake. Who sanctioned that? Awful. Bugger it. The pike, the wings and the squirrel please. And put my whisky sour in a tankard. A hearty thump upon the back. Ouch. Hullo Maurice! Good lord, you look prosperous. Tumps, you great lummox, let's have a look at you. Hullo to you,

Stormington – like the moustaches, but get rid of the hairy nonsense on your chin, you look like you've felched a grizzly bear. Ponsonby! You elegant bastard. Beautiful ring I see. You finally got him to commit? Wonderful. Congratulations, and sorry I missed the ceremony. We're all still gorgeous, aren't we? To Scoundrels Club! We're very naughty boys! Cheers! Yes, I will have another of those, rather. See if Marwood– whoops, sorry, not Marwood, god rest 'im – see if… what's the barman's name? Yes, that's it. Knighthorn, old thing, will you ring the kitchen and beg a couple of fallow deer sausages in a bap? Good man.

I'd planned my return to the Club for a muggy Tuesday morning, wanting a quiet, even solitary, experience, to savour being back in the place I loved the best. But my appearance after such a long absence drew attention. Chaps crowded around me in the Blue Bar, with backslaps and arse-pinches, keen to hear my news. Prison? Quite a good laugh actually, once you got used to the dreadful nosh. A bit like this place in essence – nothing like as bad as sleeping next to Cornwall when he's been eating from the bins, what? Har, har, har. Yes, I've taken a few hits, it's true, but that's all squared away now. No complaints. Back in the bosom of the Club that made me. No, I do not want to buy your hooky Bernini, Maurice – you were trying to shift that before I got the boot! Go and ask an idiot instead. Hello Ruff Puff. What have you lost this time? Only a foot. No, tell me the story later, I want to savour it. Quality workmanship on that though, eh? What is it? Mahogany? Iroko! Wise choice.

It was a good hour of joshing and toasting before I could take myself off for a quiet read of the papers. I settled onto the ottoman, pleased to see the bullet hole was still present and correct. I rubbed a hand across the distressed fabric, rolling the loose threads with my calloused fingers. In 1923, T.E Lawrence had become exasperated with Ernest Hemingway's loud and detailed thoughts about the gearing mechanism on a Brough Superior SS 80, and had fired off a warning shot, missing Ernie's temple by a handspan. Hemingway realised his bad manners, roared with laughter and dedicated *The Sun Also Rises* to Lawrence. The round was still in the ottoman somewhere, lodged in a spring. It would be there in another hundred years. And another thousand after that. I settled back and let out a sigh of satisfaction.

It wasn't just good to be back. It was right.

Stuffinch materialised with the papers. "Good to see you again, sir," he murmured, a broad smile spread across his whiskered cheeks.

"And you too, Stuffinch," I nodded. "It's been a long sojourn."

"So I hear, sir." Stuffinch turned to leave me in peace, with a nod. But then he paused and grimaced, "I'd be remiss in neglecting to draw your attention to the foot of page four."

I opened *The Times*. The headline smacked me across the face like a duelling glove.

PRINCESS HENRIETTA AND LORD HANSCLAPP ANNOUNCE THEIR ENGAGEMENT.

Hansclapp proposes at Sandringham. Her
Majesty's corgi delivers twenty-carat ring
after whirlwind romance.

But it was when I got to the last paragraph of the article
that I really started to feel the red mist coming on:

Upon his marriage to Princess Henrietta,
Lord Hansclapp will become Lord
President of the Council, the fourth of the
Great Offices of State, entitling him to a
seat at Cabinet meetings, and to present the
affairs of government for Her Majesty's
approval. Princess Henrietta and Lord
Hansclapp are said to be delighted at the
prospect of setting up home in the grounds
of Windsor Castle.

I jumped up from the ottoman. All I'd wanted was a
peaceful morning with the papers, with a snifter in my
own bloody Club. Denied even this, I stalked over to
Summerville's office with murder on my mind.

SUMMERVILLE'S OFFICE, ONE MINUTE LATER

The moment I walked in, I heard the high-pitched
buzzing noise, but I ignored it. It must be a fly or the air-
conditioning unit, I thought. Lunk and Summerville were
deep in thought. "Is it checkmate?" asked Summerville.

Tiberius Lunk's wheelchair creaked as he shifted his weight and frowned. "No. It can only be checkmate if he's on the point of victory, which I don't think is true, yet at least. But Hansclapp's positioning is certainly commanding. I prefer a word from the game of *shatranj*."

"Which word?" I interrupted.

"Ahh Trevelyan, wonderful to see you," he smiled. "You look like you need a drink." Lunk motioned to the cocktail cabinet, where I took myself – and I noticed the buzzing sound again.

"The word I'm thinking of is Persian, تَعبِّيَة†. tabbiyya," continued Lunk. "I suppose the best sense of it is something like *battle array*. By joining the Royal Family, Hansclapp has set up a formidable position to become part of the Establishment in a way that cannot be undone or questioned. But surely there is more to his plans that that?"

"He's poised to strike," said Summerville, "wouldn't you say?"

"It seems so, but the trouble is," continued Lunk, "we have no clarity about what he really wants."

We mused for a second. Nobody really had anything else to go on just then.

I clinked a single ice cube into a splash of Bowmore '35 and noticed the buzzing noise again. I began to look around for its source. I'd been sensitive to high pitches ever since I took those whacks to the head during Snatch the Gander at Winstowe, and with age I'd become more and more attuned to annoyingly high sounds. I couldn't stand dog whistles for instance, nor the music of Kate Bush.

Cornwall burst in. He threw *The Times* onto the desk. "Have you seen this guff? What in hell's teeth is Hansclapp playing at now?"

His sudden and unexpected presence helped me see him with fresh eyes. Backlit by the bright sunlight from the window, his hairline had receded so much he looked like a fresco of St Francis of Assisi, but a St Francis who'd just walked in on the nuns showering, so bulged were his eyes. I suppose it was an effect of his overactive thyroid, brought on by smoking roll-ups with too much rat shit in them. He was still underweight and could have done with a few sessions in the Scoundrels gymnasium. A few pints of heavy cream would work wonders.

At that precise moment I worked out where the noise was coming from.

I stood up, finger to my lips, "Victor and I were just off down to the basement for a bit of a work-out."

Cornwall furrowed his brow at me, but played along. "Perhaps the pair of you would care to join us?"

I was pointing now. Pointing with both hands. One to my ear, and the other at the elephant's foot wastepaper basket in the corner…

Summerville was quick off the mark. "Well, I suppose a bit of physical exercise would do us all good," she said, at the same time edging over in her chair to the wastepaper basket.

"A fine idea, Trevelyan. I must admit I could do with a few stretches and whatnot," said Lunk. I span my fingers around each other, to encourage him to continue on this theme. "Regular training is one of those things that gets forgotten when you get too comfortable in a chair like this…"

As he waffled on in the same vein, Summerville crouched and examined the bin. She peered around the rim, and looked back at us, grimacing. With the point of a pencil, she indicated a tiny black circle, with a minute hair-like antennae, tucked into the lining. An audio bug. Every single word we were saying was being listened to.

"Well off we go then," I said, "perhaps a few rounds in the ring."

THE SCOUNDRELS GYMNASIUM, FIFTEEN MINUTES LATER.

Cornwall and I had stripped to the waist. Summerville was taping her fists with gauze, also stripped to the waist, as was Lunk, but his breasts were bigger. He'd run to fat over the last decade, and his fearsome Nigerian musculature rippled in a rather different way than it used to as he limbered up in his wheelchair, stretching his arms and rolling his shoulders. In contrast, Cornwall looked like a partially built xylophone, his skinny ribs poking through his sallow skin.

I don't know what I looked like, as there were too many scars and scrapes, bumps and bruises in the way to see.

"Where did you get that?" Lunk poked a livid horseshoe-shaped scar on my upper midriff.

"Kick from Shergar," I shrugged.

"And this?" Summerville had circled me and nodded to a long strip wound, running from left shoulder to lower back.

"Potosi mine. Collapsing tunnel."

"And that jagged one on your flank?"

"Removal of a troublesome kidney," I said, eyeballing Cornwall, who smiled sheepishly.

"And this?" Lunk pointed to a puncture wound in my upper thigh.

"Javelin injury. Winstowe. Sports day, 1935." Cornwall smiled sheepishly again.

"And what about that one?" Lunk asked gesturing to the crackled black skin that wrapped around my right forearm like a gauntlet.

"The fire. Anais."

A difficult silence.

"Of course," Lunk's head went down, and he did a couple of lightning-fast switches, wheeling his chair left and right, checking the machine's traction across the canvas.

The bell rang, and the horrible, nicotine-rinsed voice of Tug Malone coughed itself into life. "Are you fackers ganna chinwag ahl fackin' day, or are ya' ganna train?" Tug, leaning heavily on the scaffolding pole he used as a walking stick, was fed up with our chit-chat. "I'll remind yer, if yer in my ring, you're tearin' it ahp. An' if you're not tearin' it ahp, it's cos some cahnt's knocked yer aht. So git fackin' goin', yer banch av fackin' arse'oles."

The four of us were in the boxing ring of the Scoundrels' subterranean gym, directly beneath the

Club. We were, indeed, about to have a tear-up. I eyed my opponents, reminding myself of their strengths and weaknesses. In the world at large it was unusual for chaps in wheelchairs to fight the able-bodied as much as it was unusual for women to fight men, but at Scoundrels we knew those conventions to be wrongheaded and patronising. After all, a real fight is utterly pragmatic. It doesn't follow the Queensberry Rules, any more than arguments follow the rules of debating. It doesn't give a fig about weight classes and gender. Scoundrels know that if you're in a tight spot and things get frisky, you have to play to your strengths. And to play to your strengths, you have to know what they are, against opponents of all stripes. Why shouldn't a fellow use his own crutches as a weapon? Why on earth would a woman not use everything at her disposal – her high register, her sharpened fingernails, her lack of testicles. Scoundrels had to be ready to take out anyone, dwarf or giant, fatso or rake, at a moment's notice. Hence the old Scoundrels training tactic, *The Rumble,* a confection dating from the early 18th Century. All v. All, and a prize to the last man standing. Or woman. Or sitting.

The idea, I'm told, was later stolen by an American wrestling troupe who made a lot of money from it.

"Roight, yer shower of shite 'awks," spat Tug, "free, two, wahn… RUMBLE!"

He clanged the round bell. Cornwall sprinted for a wooden stave that was lying in the corner of the ring, but Tug clotheslined him with his scaffolding pole, and he slammed onto the canvas. Tug trod on his wrist.

"Mista Cornwall," he admonished, "I wouldn't 'ave fort yer'd fall for an ickle baby trick like that. Wos' wrong wiv yer?"

Meanwhile, Summerville had thrown herself at Lunk in his chair and struck him several times around the face and neck with sharp, quick elbows. He'd wheeled forward full tilt, catching her around the shins with the bumper bar. She collapsed to the ground, yelping. I could see what he was going to do, roll forward, tip himself up, and crash down onto her as she lay, smothering her with his formidable abdomen, so I jammed a bit of two-by-four into his nearest wheel, which checked its progress. Summerville span and rolled, bouncing to her feet, a wide smile on her handsome face. She wiped a frond of hair from her eye, nodded thanks and round-housed me on the ear as hard as she could.

I saw stars as I staggered away.

This was going to be fun. A four-way. Senior management only.

"So, he's bugged your office," called out Lunk to Summerville, as he rammed his chair into the back of Cornwall's knees, pulling his flailing body onto his lap.

"That means…" Summerville ducked an opportunistic swipe from me, "…that we've got another rat…" she replied, zeroing in on Cornwall and punching him in the chin six or seven times, "…in the house, no?"

"Seems likely," said Cornwall, lashing backward to catch Lunk in the mouth with the back of his head, and snatching both of Summerville's thin wrists. He was in the perfect position to headbutt her in the face, but she stuck her tongue out at him. He paused for a split second in surprise, which allowed her to lean in and knee him on the bridge of his nose instead. There was a horrible crack, and blood began to flow.

"I'd long thuspected dit," Lunk called as he threw Cornwall to the ground, elbowed me in the midriff and then sledgehammered his back fist into my adam's apple. "It can't be one of the new chaps, it's thomeone with a bit of pull."

I fell to one knee. Good lord, the power in Lunk's arms was off the charts. I suppose wheeling that chair was a perpetual workout. I'd have to watch out for tha – CLANG – Summerville hit me with the blunt end of a fire extinguisher that Tug had just chucked into the ring. Then, stylishly, she ripped out the red safety, and sprayed me with foam. I slipped around the canvas, trying to get back on my feet.

"What about our librarian?" I span onto my back, sweeping my feet through the foam, and slamming into Summerville's ankles. She crashed down on top of me, break-falling onto the meat of my thigh, deadening it.

"Tumps is a spent force," she mused, as I shoved her off me.

At the other side of the ring, Lunk had trapped Cornwall's fingers in the spokes of his right wheel, and was rocking back and forth to cause him maximum pain. "Did anyone used to knock around with Periford?" Cornwall wondered out loud, "you know, before Titus twisted his head off?"

I got low and charged Lunk, heaving his entire wheelchair over, and catapulting him through the lower ropes of the ring, and onto the floor beyond. Cornwall picked up the empty wheelchair and smashed me across the lower back with it, just as I was rebounding off the ropes. He leaned on the chair's back for a breather, but as he'd neglected to engage the chair's brakes it freewheeled away from him, sending him crashing down to the canvas.

"First thing I did was clean house, as soon as I took over," called Summerville, who was limping across the corner, with what looked like a nasty twisted ankle.

I staggered into the centre of the ring, intent on raising my arms and claiming victory as the last man standing. This was a mistake. In unison, Cornwall and Summerville launched themselves at me. Cornwall with about as much grace as a pregnant grey seal, and Summerville more effectively, pivoting on her uninjured ankle, skipping around behind me and looping a rusty bicycle chain around my neck.

"Has anyone tried to get rid of you as M.O.S, Stephanie?" I squeaked, booting Cornwall as hard as I could in the stomach as he tried to engage.

"Nope," called Summerville. Meanwhile Lunk had levered himself back into the ring. I lined up for another kick, but Cornwall grabbed me in a half-nelson, nodding to Summerville to get some digs in. She obliged with a blizzard of nasty *kapo-ken* strikes which seemed to find the spaces between my ribs every time. "Stephanie has an iron grip on the Club, she's unchallengeable," called Lunk.

From his corner of the ring, Tug threw a cleaning bucket at Summerville and it clanged off the side of her head. She hit the deck, bleeding from a cut to her cheekbone.

"Not in 'ere, she ain't," leered Tug. "She'd need eyes in the back of 'er 'ead."

Cornwall and I grappled above her in short tight circles. We didn't see that Lunk had somehow pulled himself back into his wheelchair, nor that he was now thundering across the canvas at us like an eighteen-wheeler. Summerville, Cornwall and I were all mown down at high speed. I cannoned into Victor, severely winded and threw my hand up in submission. I could see Cornwall had done the same. Summerville spat blood and slammed her hand against the canvas, tapping out.

"Lunk takes it," said Tug, admiringly. "Not bad fer an ironside."

I lay on the canvas, looking up at the crenelated visage that Tug Malone called a face.

BA-DANG, BA-DANG, BA-DANG, BA-DANG. My heart was hammering in my chest. I ached all over. My left eye was swollen and closed. I could taste blood in my mouth, and I wasn't even sure it was mine.

"Let that be a lesson to all 'a yer," said Tug, "cover all yer bases. Averwise yer fackin' askin' for it, aint' cha?"

"Wise words, Tug," said Summerville. "Now get me a pint of heavy cream, there's a love."

Tug shuffled off to fetch it. He was replaced by Summerville, lighting a cigarette from a small stock of *Little Lambs,* a simple blend of Turkish *canik* that the Scoundrels tobacconist had whipped up for violent interludes with chaps much bigger than her. She took a long drag and then crashed back down next to me. Together we stared at the ceiling. She passed the gasper to me, before lighting another.

"I'm not given to overblown predictions, Trevelyan," she said, exhaling.

"Neither am I."

"And I'm no spiritual, hippy-dippy type."

"Granted."

"But I've an image in my mind that keeps recurring in dreams and idle moments."

"Go on."

"I see you and Cornwall, and Hansclapp, standing in a triangle. I see a blade rushing through the air. It's a split-second, life-or-death thing. And then…"

"What?" I propped myself up on a bruised elbow.

"Death. I see death," she said.

"Whose?"

"That's the thing. I don't know."

I spat a wad of blood onto the canvas. "Well, I do," I said.

"So do I," Cornwall said. "Hansclapp's. We simply will not have it any other way."

I towelled myself as vigorously as the bruises allowed.

Tug had been watching me move during the fight and had some concerns. "It's yer fackin' skellington," he told me, "it's wonky as a nine-bob note, yer doss bastard."

He'd already called in the Club masseur, Efendi Jalawad, who went to work on my intercostals as if they were stiff keys on a church organ. Jalawad winced when he saw the state of my lower vertebrae, and made me smoke a full eighth of Moroccan hashish from the shisha pipe, so I could bear being crunched almost in half, and then straightened out again. Over the next two hours, a decade of jail cells and pavements were squeezed and pummelled and mashed and ground out of my trampled musculature.

I exited the gym a couple of inches taller than when I'd gone in. I mean that both literally and figuratively.

The evening papers were in the Blue Bar. I got to them before Stuffinch could warn me what was inside.

There on the front page was a paparazzi snap of Gruber Hansclapp, emerging from Annabel's nightclub, with an arm wrapped protectively around his royal bride-to-be. The headline, this time, was:

DEATH AT ANNABEL'S.

A man was found dead in the lavatories of Annabel's nightclub at 2AM last night, as Princess Henrietta and her fiancé Lord Hansclapp danced and drank the night away. The deceased, Mr Eustace Trevelyan of Nimbu Towers in Gloucestershire, was known to have had a pre-existing heart condition. He was not known to the Princess nor her fiancé. Police do not suspect foul play. Lord Hansclapp offered his condolences to the dead man's family.

There was only one way to read this. Retribution from Hansclapp. In his mind, we had disobeyed him by re-joining the Club, and this was his response.

Yours sincerely,
Major Arthur St. John Trevelyan.

Hellcat Manor
Great Trundleford
Devon
July 2nd 2021

Dear Major,

I remember that headline as if it were only yesterday. 'Condolences to the dead man's family,' indeed. Claptrap.

I'll keep my letter brief as we're about to go up a gear. A seminal moment this, in both of our fates.

CHAPTER 15
CORNWALL'S GAMBIT

THE BATH HOUSE, SCOUNDRELS CLUB, 1985

"You see this?" Trevelyan said, pointing to a scar above his left eyebrow. "That was Eustace. Silly fool came at me with one of Pa's medieval morning stars because I switcheroo'd a couple of chess pieces in a game he was playing against himself. I think I was six or seven." Trevelyan chuckled, incredulous at the memory. "One of the spikes lodged in my skull. Claret all over the floor. Ma just yanked the damn thing out and told me to put my finger on it until it stopped bleeding."

I carried on lathering my back with the sea sponge, nodding solemnly to show I was listening. Normally I would have told him to shut up so I could enjoy the steam in peace, but Trevelyan was in a reverie and it was my job to listen. After all, his brother had just died.

"And Eustace," Trevelyan continued, "just stood there staring at me, showing no emotion whatsoever."

"Uh-huh," I said, then held up the soap. "Are you going to actually use this?"

Trevelyan took the soap from me and plunged his head under the hot soapy water of the Club's communal hypocaust bath. His stringy, thinning hair floated across the surface like strands of seaweed in the Sargasso. Then he surfaced, exhaling noisily like a hippo, to take a lungful of air. He wiped back the straggles of his greying locks and settled into a funk, glowering at the water.

"I always liked Eustace," I said, just for something to say. "But I can't claim that I really knew him, if that makes sense."

"I don't think anybody really knew him," pondered Trevelyan. "Not even me. He never saw the point of having a younger brother. Pa told him numerous times that I was part of the family, but he didn't want to accept it. He lived within the confines of his own head. What the hell was he even doing in a nightclub?"

I didn't answer. No point. We both knew that Hansclapp, or Marjorie, or some other toerag in his network had befriended Eustace and lured him to Annabel's. His murder had been ruthless.

The door opened and Maurice Johncocktosen walked in, slapping about all over the place most unpleasantly. "Mind if I join you chaps?" he asked, not waiting for an answer before wading in.

"New tattoo, Maurice?" I enquired.

"Oh, that. D'you like it? Lost a bet with Ruff Puff, I'm afraid. The tattoo of his choice, site of his choice. He went for elephant ears, the cheeky devil."

Maurice rolled his eyes and then lay back in the hot water. "The trouble I get myself into," he mused, "still, I hear one can have them removed with a laser gun nowadays." Then, "ahh, Trevelyan, sorry to hear the news old chap," he said, "tough luck, that."

Trevelyan nodded thanks.

"Your brother would have come in handy for the Club next week. Bit of a chess genius, wasn't he?"

"He was," Trevelyan said.

"What's happening next week?" I asked.

"Haven't you heard? Someone's invoked the knave. The match is to be held on Monday."

"What chancer's done that?" Trevelyan asked.

"Ohh, that guy with all the newspapers," said Maurice. "You know, he's getting hitched soon, to a minor royal…"

Major, I remember being quite surprised that Maurice couldn't even bring Hansclapp's name to mind. But then, as far as the rest of the Club was concerned, Hansclapp wasn't a person of interest. We'd kept our struggle with him quiet for all these years. At first, this made sense for operational reasons. We, as well as Lunk, and later, Summerville, had been tight-lipped because of the rat in Scoundrels' house. And when that rat was trapped – when my boy pulled Periford's head off and shat down the stump of his neck – the connection was never made. Ditto when all of our money was taken on that fateful day in 1974. As far as the wider Club was concerned, Hansclapp was an unknown quantity.

The Knave's Gambit is a three-hundred-year-old addendum written into the Scoundrels Club Rules, by James II. Because membership to Scoundrels was so selective, it was designed as a backdoor way in – a very stiff and ungiving backdoor that was prohibitively difficult and expensive to prise open. James was concerned that amongst all the brawn in the Club, the soldiers, sailors, renegades, adventurers and sportsmen that made up the general membership, there was perhaps a lack of brain. He designed a method of offering a route to membership that cut through all the usual criteria. James decided that once a year, a non-club member could challenge The Club to a single game of chess – and if they won, membership was granted. To ward off unserious men there was an extortionate entry fee, redeemable should the challenger win.

Over the course of Scoundrels history only fourteen people have ever coughed up to invoke the gambit, and only three went on to become Scoundrels, Immanuel Kant, Charles Babbage, and Garry Kasparov in 1984. Famously, in consecutive years 1974 and 1975, both

Benny and Björn from ABBA gave it a crack, each stumping up the million-pound fee but failing dismally. I brokered those deals, and during that time developed a close friendship with the two men's wives. This led to an alleged threesome in a London hotel room, providing me with the inspiration for my achingly beautiful poem, 'Swedish Batteries' that can be found in the first volume of my memoirs. I am legally obliged to say though, that Agnetha and Anni-Frid have always denied any sexual congress took place, claiming they weren't even in London at that time, and they have been to the High Court to defend their reputations.

But if it wasn't Agnetha and Anni-Frid, it was one hell of a tribute act.

Trevelyan and I had rarely been this angry. The hinges on Summerville's door nearly came off their brackets. "We need an explanation, quick smart," I screamed, banging a fist down onto the desk.

"Calm down, Cornwall," Lunk said, looking up from his chair, where he and Summerville sat with a copy of *The Times*. "Take a seat."

"Hansclapp can NEVER become a member of this Club!" Trevelyan bellowed, his bovine noggin looming over Lunk. "We cannot allow him to make a play to join! It's unthinkable!"

The sight of Lunk in the wheelchair was a stark reminder of how close he had come to death. It may have been Fang's bullet that had ensured he would never walk again, but Hansclapp was the man who had loaded the gun and paid for the shot.

"Scoundrels Club was here before we were born, and it will be here after we're gone," Summerville said. "I'm sorry to say, we must abide by the rules, however distasteful the outcome."

Trevelyan was about to fire off another angry salvo, but I cut in. "I tell you what," I said, "I could do with a bloody great scotch if you've got one."

Lunk duly obliged, wheeling himself over to the drinks cabinet. He poured us each something brown and conciliatory.

For a while, we brooded in silence. It's rare for any Scoundrels meeting to ever be silent for more than a few seconds but in this instance there seemed to be nothing to say.

Eventually I said, "Can't we just refuse him on a technicality?"

"No. We've checked. His application is sound. He's paid the money and we're obliged to give him a match. Now we just have to make sure we win it," Lunk said.

"Do you know what kind of player Hansclapp is?" asked Summerville.

"No. But he'll be exceptional, I can guarantee it," I said.

Lunk, calm as always, said, "So who's our best player? We have a few decent ones to choose from."

"What about that new chap, Kasparov?" queried Trevelyan.

"Joan the Coat Check Lady beat him at draughts. We haven't seen him since. We think he's gone back to Russia," Lunk said.

This prompted a long and detailed discussion about the best sort of opponent for a man like Hansclapp, given that we didn't know anything about his game but that it was likely to be strategic, efficient and laden with nasty surprises. As ex-M.O.S., Lunk himself was not eligible, which was a shame as he combined an enyclopaedic knowledge of the game with a merciless killer instinct that meant his matches rarely went over two dozen moves. Summerville, who could destroy anyone at blitz, was out for the same reason. Trevelyan liked the creativity and chutzpah of Ruff Puff's play, but the rest of us considered him far too mercurial and easily drawn-out by an ambush. Tumps, our librarian, had taken some excellent victories over the years, but he did it by boring his opponents to death.

When the conversation was in danger of going in circles, I pitched in with my choice, although it hurt me to do so. My choice had bested Trevelyan and me in the past. He was our finest player in terms of aggression and verve, and he often seemed able to play two strategies out at once, drawing them together suddenly to pincer his opponent just when they felt they were making headway. He also had a refined set of bullyboy tactics when he was at the board, which could unsettle opponents and pull them into silly errors. Yes, here was the man for this undertaking, I argued. The problem was, I wasn't sure he'd want to do it. There was nothing in the rules that required a particular Scoundrel to step up and defend the Club.

And Hendricks rarely did anything he didn't want to do.

Despite my animosity towards him, if I was to pick a man to win a game against an unknown opponent, it would be Hendricks. He was a dirty bastard, who didn't just strive to win but also to break his rival's spirit and grind them into the dust so that they never, ever wanted to play against him again.

Hendricks won his games by playing 'total chess' – a term he'd coined for a range of aggressive tactics that made going up against him far more challenging. He was the only person I'd ever seen take an opponent out with a *reducer*, famously 'doing' Alain Brownsthorpe before an opening move had even been made. Alain was sitting down waiting for the game to begin, when Hendricks charged into the room with a two-footed, knee-high sliding tackle that ruptured Alain's anterior cruciate ligament and broke his tibia. The game was over before they'd even shaken hands. Hendricks was also the man who introduced sledging to chess, chiding his opponents about their wives' sexual indiscretions while they were trying to concentrate on their next move.

My problem was strategic. If I was to ask Hendricks to take on Hansclapp, I knew I would have to be subtle about it. If I was too eager, he'd sense my desperation, and then he'd refuse out of spite. I had to play it cool and use a bit of strategy to get him where I wanted him.

I found him in the seldom used, out-of-the-way Lapsang Bar on the fourth floor, drinking champagne with some of his chums on its elegant wrought iron balcony. He'd clearly heard that the Knave's Gambit had been invoked, and in his arrogance, assumed he'd be approached. His stock had risen now that the Club needed a player of his calibre and he was enjoying his moment in the sun.

"Cornwall!" he called knowingly, "please join us!"

I approached his table soberly, hands behind my back, head slightly downcast, a rueful expression on my face. He knew that I was not going to enjoy this overture one bit. He knew that I knew that I was going to ask him to play, and he knew that I knew that he knew this put him in an unassailable position.

There was chatter among his cronies as I approached. They were all saps as far I was concerned, cheap-seat spectators and fireside lapdogs whose names I barely bothered to remember. But, like a school of piranhas, they could still be tricky in numbers. And they gave Hendricks something else he craved: an audience.

He'd been around long enough to know something of my hatred of Hansclapp and now I was coming cap-in-hand for salvation. He wasn't going to let that pass without making me suffer for it. Nevertheless, I popped the question: would he represent the Club at the chessboard?

"You know I haven't played seriously for years," he said, stretching languidly. "Is there not another Scoundrel who can do it instead? Someone who's not quite as, what's the word, rusty?"

Aha. I see. He wants complimenting.

"Well, a talent like yours doesn't just die away, Hendricks," I oozed. "You're the one best placed to face Hansclapp, who is no slouch, as I understand it. And it's not just *me* saying so," I continued, "It's the Club. The whole Club needs you."

"Well, maybe, but…" Hendricks nodded to Jervis for another drink, "it's a lot of effort, isn't it? I mean, I was thinking about going skiing this weekend."

"It's July," I reminded him.

"Doesn't matter if you're on an Arctic glacier, though," he smiled. "And besides, I just think they should put someone in who…" he paused, looking around at his smirking cadre, dragging this out for effect, "…who actually cares about the outcome," then he added the kicker, "like Trevelyan."

I pretended to think about this. "Hmm, Trevelyan isn't the right player for this match," I mused. "He doesn't have your grit for middlegame positioning, nor your innate understanding of the opening."

Tewkesbury, a real gobshite, leaned in. "Hey chaps, I suppose tiddlywinks is more Trevelyan's game!" he laughed.

"I'd stay away from Trevelyan for a while if I were you, Tewkesbury," I said, holding his eye. Tewkesbury blanched.

"But seriously, Cornwall," Hendricks said, "would it really be the end of the world if this Hansclapp fellow gains membership?"

This remark really caught me off-balance. My blood pressure leapt to something like 370/360 and I sensed my temple vein bulging out like a length of anchor rope. Something was going to blow.

"You alright there, Cornwall?" said a pencil-thin wanker named Wexville, "you look a little scorched."

"Acid reflux, that's all," I said.

This was in danger of going south, but then Hendricks said something that gave me an idea. "If you're so invested in this, Cornwall, why don't you play him?"

With a flash I realised that it was Hendricks who was actually in the dark. Our mutual dislike of each other meant we hadn't played each other enough for him to work out how far behind him I was. Although I'd never actually beaten him, I'd once struggled to a draw. Plus, he'd seen me thrash Trevelyan, and given Lunk a run for his money, and knew that I was a capable player who could beat most in the Club, even if I wasn't that interested in the game. But that wasn't the issue. The issue was whether Hendricks thought I was confident enough to take on Hansclapp.

So I figured I'd do something I am world class at, every time.

I bluffed.

"You know what, Hendricks, that's not a bad idea. Maybe I *should* take him on myself. I seem to remember I gave you a run for your money last time we played."

Hendricks' smile evaporated. The cronies fell silent. "I don't think that's quite right," he retorted, taking a sip of champagne.

"Pretty sure I did," I said, nodding my head as I pretended to remember. "Anyway. If you're as busy as you say you are, then I'm probably the next best thing."

"That's not quite how I remember it, Cornwall. You—"

I cut him off. "And you're right," I continued. "It wouldn't even be the end of the world if Hansclapp became a Scoundrel. We're not adverse to admitting the odd arsehole, after all. Isn't that right, Tewkesbury?"

Tewkesbury opened his mouth but I shut him down with a passive aggressive face-palm. I cut to the chase. "We've no time to piss around here, I'm afraid. Summerville needs to know who's going to step out to bat. I see now that it should be me. After all, once I've sent Hansclapp packing they'll have to name another room after me."

I drained my glass, put it down on the table and turned to leave. "Thanks anyway, Hendricks, but I'll say you're not interested. Enjoy your skiing."

I made it as far as the door.

"Hang on there for a second, Victor…"

The central atrium in Scoundrels Club is a cavernous space surrounded by a sweeping staircase. It has held sporting events in the past, most notably the 1803 Scoundrels marathon, where runners completed one thousand and eighty-four laps of the tight circular track, but most of the time it's used as a thoroughfare. If you examine the floor you'll see it's laid with huge slabs of black and white Italian marble tiles, eight by eight. A chessboard.

Tonight, in the centre, a small table with two chairs was set, elevated on a dais, to create the sort of stage you'd expect at any first-rate chess venue like the elegant Tchaikovsky Hall in Moscow. Except that at Scoundrels Club, the mood was rather different than in the rest of the chess world. Rather than the subdued, cerebral atmosphere accepted as the norm, spectators at Scoundrels were encouraged to really cut loose.

This explains the five kilograms of house blend cocaine, sitting in a large brass dish at the foot of the staircase, into which members were expected to bury their faces as they passed. If cocaine was not your poison, you could avail yourself of one of the footlong *woolas,* which were rolled from pure Indonesian 'squidgy black' cannabis resin. Or you could simply get stuck into one of Jervis' takeaway cocktails, to celebrate the Knave's Gambit, available from all of the Club bars from midday. Jervis' signature mix was his *Bad Bishop* – it consisted of three shots of white rum, three shots of black rum, with a cherry and a mistletoe berry on top. As mistletoe berries are poisonous, the one side-effect was a potentially paralysing vegetative-state effect that lasted hours. This made them even more popular.

There was also pre-match entertainment. Tug Malone had been commissioned to set off his homemade firecrackers to really hype up the crowd. House band Rudi Kessler & His Rude Tubes had just finished a hypnotic hour-long bongo session and Joan the Coat Check Lady's three nieces were doing quite a bawdy belly dance inside the cage.

The cage? Yes.

To protect the players a tight wire mesh like a Victorian birdcage had been constructed around the table, as last time a bottle of stout had smacked Bjorn from ABBA on the jaw and he'd been knocked unconscious for fifteen minutes, during which Masterson took three pawns and a bishop from him.

Outside the cage, rows of seats were arranged in concentric circles for spectators to sit on, and, from the moment the match started, to pick up and throw around. These seats were chock-a-block hours before the scheduled start time. Chaps sat on each other's knees just to be at the centre of the action. Hijinks were expected, and widely encouraged. Bandu Tassletayle had been spotted with a trio of hungry otters on leads, which he was trying to encourage up any trouser leg that didn't have bicycle clips on it, and Maurice had bought some of his celebrated itchy-coo powder, a special edition with equal measures of black pepper and white pepper as well as the usual manganese sulphate, which was a devil if you got it in your eye.

At the back of the atrium, a giant chess board, twenty feet tall, had been erected vertically, to allow even more Scoundrels to follow the action from the stairs. Because of the no-holds-barred, carnival atmosphere, the board was already covered in filthy graffiti, and the remnants of a custard fight that Jangles Bowtoon had got going, debuting an ingenious stainless steel custard cannon of his own design.

With a few minutes to go before the match was due to start, the room was jam-packed, every inch of the surrounding staircases crammed with Scoundrels jostling for position and getting high as kites, but kites made of booze and drugs.

On the table was a Staunton chess set, built by Jaques of London, at Hendricks' request. I knew about their matchless quality because I had one myself, fashioned from a meteorite I'd dredged from the river Exe in Devon. They were works of art.

Trevelyan and I took our reserved seats, ringside. He was particularly twitchy at the thought of seeing Hansclapp in the Club and the riotous atmosphere wasn't helping his nerves. "Whatever happens, you need to stay calm!" I shouted, over the noise. "Maybe stay off the cocaine, today, eh?"

Trevelyan looked back at me, his jaw set hard.

"Have you got your hip flask?" I asked him.

He pulled it out of his breast pocket and offered it to me. "Not for me, for you," I told him.

The room was deafening. An empty bottle of Lafite shattered against the cage, and the shards cascaded down upon us. Trevelyan, as I feared, turned and launched himself at Noddy d'Busey, the thrower, and karate-chopped him viciously on both sides of the neck. Noddy went down like the sack of shit he was, and I grappled Trevelyan back to his seat. Mercifully for me, before he could relaunch, the room fell silent. A lone bugler, Fantohm-Waxwell, played a louche, jazz version of the Dawn Reveille under the Trafalgar Arch and on the last note, in strode Hendricks in an impeccable seersucker suit and Al Capone trilby, which he doffed to the braying crowd, who bellowed and began chanting his name.

HENDRICKS! HENDRICKS!
HENDRICKS! HENDRICKS!

It was this sort of acclaim that set a Scoundrel's soul on fire, for we are all, at root, showmen. For a moment I admit I felt a bit miffed that it wasn't me grandstanding my way around the chess cage.

Hendricks looked very relaxed. He acknowledged his legions of fans with a rather cool wave and took his seat. The crowd chanted for a while longer as eyes turned to the opposite end of the atrium, to the door under the Waterloo Arch. In anticipation, the room fell silent again.

"This is it," I said. Trevelyan was fiddling with the hip flask, grating his fingers nervously down its cheap, leatherette sides. He'd peeled much of the imitation tartan banding right off and was now scratching at the looping inscription on the base, which I caught a flash of. 'To A Fine Son, from Ma & Pa'.

It was, I realised, Eustace's old flask.

Gruber Hansclapp walked into Scoundrels Club. The crowd erupted again, this time, into a jeering chorus of:

WHO ARE YER?
WHO ARE YER?
WHO ARE YER?

A couple more bottles were thrown, smashing against the wire netting and showering glass onto the match table. From the corner of my eye, I saw Trevelyan cast Eustace's flask to the ground. He reached into his pocket and brought out a snub-nosed Webley Bull Dog .45 and cocked it. Quick smart, I jammed my thumb into the trigger space, and grabbed Trevelyan's tie with my other hand, pulling him around to face me. "Trevelyan, no!" I said it firmly, without shouting. I could see him debating whether to headbutt me or not, but he let out a strangled cry that was lost in the crowd noise and released the weapon, which I pocketed.

Hansclapp, sober suited, walked across the floor. He was unperturbed by the hostile crowd and stepped into the cage to take his seat. I shook my head in disbelief. I never could have imagined I'd ever see Hansclapp in our Club.

Then Marjorie walked in. The braying crowd faltered for a moment as they adjusted their monocles, their spectacles and their actual eyes.

Who was this gorgeous woman? Utterly beguiling in a red chiffon dress that was just this side of decent, she would have made a vicar bang his own font. She was ravishing still, perhaps more so, if that were possible. When Trevelyan had first met and married her, she had been the most feared Stasi spy in East Berlin, and as such was never an innocent, but with her new eyepatch and the scar down the side of her face, now she exuded a new kind of sexual allure.

Marjorie glided to a ring-side seat that happened to be next to Summerville, and they shared the polite nod and curt smile that very beautiful women reserve for each other.

"Get me out of here, Cornwall," Trevelyan said, "this is too much now."

"Don't move. Save it all for when Hendricks topples Hansclapp's king. Then we can go for him as he leaves."

We overheard a few lewd comments about Marjorie from younger Scoundrels, but I turned around and silenced them with my eyes. The crowd soon calmed down to let the game begin.

At the table, Hendricks stood up and offered his hand to his opponent, who grasped it.

"Oh god," I whispered. "Surely he isn't going to…"

Perhaps over-buoyed by the crowd, Hendricks went for one of his ridiculous signature power moves, a thing that had always rather revolted me for its sheer lack of class. Grasping Hansclapp's right hand tightly, he drew him in, and swung at him with the flat of his left hand, aiming to slap his ear or cheek quite hard, not so hard that it constituted an actual assault, but harder than a friendly shoulder punch merited. He called it his Tension Breaker, and it was often accompanied with a matey "look sharp" or "here comes the boom" or some other witless remark. It had burst the eardrum of many a young Scoundrel, who then had to pretend the senior man was only joshing, before making his excuses and getting off to see the nearest ENT surgeon.

But Hansclapp ducked so rapidly I only saw a blur. Hendricks' left hand swished harmlessly over his head, sending him off-balance, and in a millisecond Hansclapp had kidney punched Hendricks twice, with astonishing ferocity in his exposed midriff. I felt it. The crowd felt it, and a collective wince ran through the room. Then I saw that Hansclapp had on a set of brass knuckles, which he took off and dropped into his jacket pocket.

Hendricks was horribly winded, and coughed up a gobbet of blood, which he had to then spit into his handkerchief. He made a joke of it, but he was rattled. Hendricks was a chap who enjoyed making people feel uneasy, one of those who always needed others in his presence to be on the back foot, even if you were simply having a drink or going for dinner. Hansclapp had defused him utterly, and it had taken him less than a second.

I looked across to Summerville and Marjorie. They were chatting. What the hell would they be talking about? Marjorie spotted me looking, turned her head and fixed her steely blue eye on me, allowing it to linger. What? The nerve of the woman. She was actually giving me the glad eye. I was playing with fire, and yet I couldn't tear my gaze away. Dear lord she was a stunner. Trevelyan poked me in the ribs.

"Look away," he hissed at me. "Look away, now."

Marjorie parted her ruby lips and ran her tongue along the length of them. It was painful to rip my eyes from her, the sort of frisson I hadn't felt for many a year now. An image of Sayonara Fang flashed into my mind. A very private image that I won't share, but a bloody great one. I found myself wondering, would Marjorie be up for that sort of thing in the sack as well.

"The match is about to begin. White to play," called the arbiter. I snapped back into focus.

All eyes were now on the two players sat opposite each other. The arbiter started the clock. Hansclapp, playing as White, looked down at the board. What would be his first move?

Move 1
Hansclapp: pawn to d4

The move prompted no reaction from the crowd, after all it was a standard opening, probably the Nimzo-Indian Defence. Hansclapp tapped the top of the clock, clasped his hands together and rested his chin. Hendricks regarded him for a moment as if trying to see inside his head, then he looked down at the board and made a fast move.

Hendricks: knight to f6

His decisiveness caused a huge roar from the crowd. Farrington Steele let off a colossal airhorn he had hidden inside his bagpipes, deafening Ruff Puff and causing him to put one of his new iroko hands through a leaded window. The match was ON.

Move 2
Hansclapp: pawn to c4.

During this move, Hendricks yawned rudely and jostled the table with his knee so that every single piece rattled, displacing the massed ranks of Hansclapp's pieces from the centre of their squares. Hansclapp raised an eyebrow. Hendricks shifted his weight and did exactly the same thing again. Then:

Hendricks: pawn to e6.

This took just a few seconds, and Hendricks' swift response riled the crowd up. A raucous football terrace chant began from the staircase above. True to form it didn't make any concession to taste, referencing both of Hendrick's *bêtes noires*, his ruddy cheeks and the fate of his younger brother:

> HIS FACE,
> IS RED,
> HIS YOUNGER BROTHER'S DEAD
> HENDRIIIIIIIIIIICKS!!!
> HENDRIIIIIIIIIIICKS!!!

I shifted uncomfortably in my seat, as of course Hendricks Jr died at my own hand after a difficult evening at the Nelson Dinner in which he refused to pass the port. Now was not the time to dig all that up again. Not that Hendricks looked at all bothered. In response to the chant, he stood up and put his hand to his ear as if he'd just scored an excellent goal and wanted more from the crowd. They obliged with an even louder verse, to which Hendricks' started dancing.

> HE'S GREAT
> AT CHESS
> HIS UNCLE'S RUDOLPH HESS
> HENDRIIIIIIIIIIICKS!!!
> HENDRIIIIIIIIIIICKS!!!

Nasty dig that. Nobody wants a Nazi bigwig in the family, but Hendricks couldn't have cared less at this slur on his ancestry. He made a play at sitting down, and in pantomime style, indicated that he wasn't happy with his chair. He picked it up, brought it out of the cage, and walked up the stairs, shoulder-barging Scoundrels out of the way. Thirty seconds later he came back, with an identical chair…

…or so it seemed. He put this chair down in his place and sat on it. He was now sitting a full foot higher than his opponent. Hendricks puffed up his chest, beamed down at Hansclapp, and did the sort of silly little wave one would give a tiny child.

Hansclapp stared up, expressionless. His cold, dead eyes bored into Hendricks, who must have suddenly felt a lot less sure about how funny he was. So what did he do next? All he could do. More cavorting. He stood up again, walked to Hansclapp's chair and wobbled it, shaking his head extravagantly. He went off to get another chair for his opponent, and insisted he relinquish his old one. Without fuss, Hansclapp rose, not meeting anyone's eye.

The replacement chair Hendricks had fetched for Hansclapp was six inches shorter.

The spectators were falling about as if they were watching a Charlie Chaplin routine. In contrast, Hansclapp looked pained at these oafish goings-on. He glanced across at his sister Marjorie and shrugged.

After some more acting the goat, including mooning a chap in the front row, who promptly tried to plug his arsehole with an unopened Methuselah of champagne, Hendricks sat back down to focus on the game.

Move 3
Hansclapp: knight to f3
Hendricks: pawn to d5

Some wag who had done his homework started up another tune, which caught on like tinder in dry season. This time aimed at Hansclapp and to the tune of Harry Belafonte's calypso hit *Island in the Sun*:

OH, LITTLE AUSTRIAN,
WITH THE HOTTEST SISTER IN ALL THE
LANDS.
ALL OUR DAYS WE WILL SING IN PRAISE
OF THOSE MOST MAGNIFICENT
MAMMARY GLANDS.

Marjorie blushed at this and tossed her hair. Trevelyan began to breathe heavily. Then the same wag tried another verse. It was a little complex lyrically, and to be fair he did an excellent job with difficult scansion:

OH, SISTER OF THE AUSTRIAN
GIRLS LIKE YOU ARE SO VERY SPARSE
YOU SO YUMMY, FLIP YOU ON YOUR TUMMY
AND YOU LET ME TAKE YOU
RIGHT UP THE—

But he never got further than that, because Trevelyan snapped. He leapt three rows of chairs like Olympic high hurdles and got his hand down the singer's throat, pulling his tongue out from the root. The last word of the song – we'll never know what it was – was transposed into a horrific high-pitched screech as Trevelyan threw the man against a gigantic Ming floor pot and then set about him with his angry boots. Three Scoundrels had to pull him away. "That's my wife, you fucking, fucking, fucking, fucking cunt!" he screamed and stamped, incandescent, even by his standards.

It was at this point that Tug Malone let off another string of firecrackers.

Move 10.
Hansclapp: bishop to c4 (takes pawn)
Hendricks: bishop to b6

Something about this incident allowed the game to settle into a rhythm and the crowd became slightly less rowdy. There was a chess match to play, after all. Time began to tick away as the middlegame began. I coaxed Trevelyan back to our seats with a couple of sips from my own hip flask, and the singer was wheeled off to the San. From then on, I kept my eyes mostly on the viewing board at the back of the room. Although the carnival spirit continued around me, and the crowd cheered every gesture and grimace that Hendricks made, I focussed on the tactical battle, painting a picture of the game in my head.

Slowly, very slowly, a pattern began to emerge. The match appeared to be heading for a draw – a draw which would be no good for Hansclapp. If he wanted to be a Scoundrel, he had to win.

We adjourned for a comfort break. Hendricks wrote his next move on a piece of paper and the arbiter sealed it in a tiny envelope. The players stood up and disappeared through their respective doors.

"So far so good," I said to Trevelyan, patting him on the shoulder.

"So far so good?" Trevelyan replied, incredulous. "So far so good? That man is in OUR CLUB."

"The game, I mean. Looks like a draw."

Trevelyan didn't answer me. He was staring at Marjorie, who waved coquettishly at him, and then turned her back as a young blade offered to light her cigarette.

I got up and made my way to the exit to speak to Lunk, who had been watching from the back of the room the whole time. "Thoughts?"

"Hendricks is giving a good account of himself," I said, but Lunk seemed preoccupied and didn't immediately answer. "Is everything okay?" I enquired.

"I'm not sure."

"Is it about the game?" I asked.

"I think so," he said, "I can't put my finger on it."

"Well, a draw will do us fine," I said.

"Maybe that's it," Lunk chewed his lip. "A draw wouldn't be enough for Hansclapp."

"Then why do you still look worried?"

Lunk made no response. His brain was computing something and I knew better than to disrupt him.

The players were re-entering the cage. I hurried back to Trevelyan.

Move 11.
Hendricks: queen to d1 (takes queen)
Hansclapp: rook to d1 (takes queen)

The time ticked on. Still looked like a draw as they traded pieces of increasing importance.

Move 16.
Hansclapp: knight to d4
Hendricks: knight to d4 (takes knight)

It was fair to say that this match was not a classic. One might even call it boring. The noisy elements of the crowd had even started to sidle away into town or back into the Club bars, leaving a smaller band of chess purists to learn the outcome.

Move 16 revealed the true shape of the game, and the murmurings among the crowd were in agreement. This could only end in a draw. A few more trades and manoeuvres, and then:

Move 20.
Hansclapp: rook to d1 (takes rook)
Hendricks: rook to c8

Despite his earlier braggadocio and bully boy tactics, Hendricks had been rather sly: he'd choked the life out of this game, got it bogged down in the weeds and played what amounted to a tactical masterclass. He didn't have to win. He just needed not to lose. Hansclapp was going to fail in his attempt to become a Scoundrel. It was almost time to celebrate.

Then Hendricks made a blunder.

Move 29.
Hendricks: bishop to h2 (takes pawn)

He captured a 'poison' pawn, allowing his bishop to be trapped. It was such a schoolboy error that there were gasps of shock from the scattered spectators who were still watching. Trevelyan turned to me, ashen-faced. "What the hell just happened there?" he said.

I didn't reply. I couldn't speak.

From a position of comfort Hendricks had made a fatal error, and the stalemate was abruptly turned on its head. Hendricks' game began to unravel as he desperately tried to atone for his error, but Hansclapp sensed blood and we watched in horror as he took control of the board. For move after move he drew nearer to victory. He was like a boa constrictor that had seized its prey, and was slowly tightening around it, until it could breathe no more.

Move 42.
Hansclapp: king to h5.
Hendricks: king to f5.

Hendricks had the look of a beaten man, his hands were covering his face as reality bit, and he contemplated the error which had probably cost him the match. I looked at Trevelyan. "It's as we feared," I muttered.

Trevelyan put his head in his hands. From the corner of my eye, I saw Marjorie looking over at us again. She tilted her neck and allowed herself a little self-satisfied smile, and then turned back to look at the game.

Move 52.
Hansclapp: king to g5 (takes pawn)
Hendricks: king to c4

For several moves Hansclapp had been hunting Hendricks. Finally, at Move 56, he advanced his white king to d6 and Hendricks had no option.

Checkmate.

I felt numb all over. I couldn't believe this. Next to me, Trevelyan was staring into the abyss, motionless, paralysed. Neither of us spoke.

Hendricks studied the board for the last time, then he looked up at Hansclapp and nodded, his fate sealed. He slowly reached out and toppled his King over.

Gruber Hansclapp had won. He was now a Scoundrel.

I think I'll let you take it from here.

Yours sincerely,
Major Victor Montgomery Cornwall

Nimbu Towers
Pullen-under-Lyme
Gloucestershire
July 7th 2021

Dear Major,

Since we were taken on by the Club as teenagers,
Scoundrels has afforded us protection from all the horrors
of modern life, but with these events unfolding around us,
I have never felt so destabilised.

CHAPTER 16
CHECKMATED

SCOUNDRELS CLUB, LONDON, 1985

"Checkmate."
Checkmate.
CHECKMATE.
The word reverberated around my brain as if I'd
been sapped. With an infuriating smile, Hansclapp sat
back from the board, crossed his knees, examined his
fingernails and waited for Hendricks to offer him his
hand. Hendricks was a broken man. I wanted to throttle
the bastard. Surely he could have played a smarter
game, thought further ahead, dug deeper. That is what

Scoundrels are supposed to do, for goodness sake. When the chips are down you find something extra you didn't know you had, and BLOODY WELL get it DONE.

Hendricks clearly felt this himself. He stared at the carpet, unable to meet the eye of any member. Hansclapp sprang to his feet, seized his opponent's clammy hand to pump it up and down, and then discarded it like a used handkerchief. He marched over to Summerville. "How do we do this, Stephanie?" he oozed.

Summerville blanched. She was Stephanie to nobody, at least not inside the Club. "Welcome to Scoundrels Club, Lord Hansclapp," she hissed. "Perhaps you'll join me for a drink in the Blue Bar."

"I'd be delighted," crowed an exuberant Hansclapp, and offered Summerville his arm. She looked stunned at this second nasty breach. No Scoundrel had offered Summerville their arm since Jaswinder Sharm el Sheikh made that mistake and she'd sent him to establish a new clubhouse on the Kongsvegen glacier.

Summerville stalked off down the corridor alone. Hansclapp straightened his cuffs and followed her. The chess spectators drained away after them. There was a heavy silence. Cornwall held his head in his hands and uttered a single, solitary expletive. Then he loosened his Windsor knot and, in a gesture quite unprecedented, actually undid the top button of his shirt. I had never, ever seen him in such a state of despair.

I pulled out one of a small stock of *Filthy Shames*, a bitter little pick-me-up of Louisiana perique, too strong to be smoked pure – although I smoked them pure – which I'd had the Scoundrels tobacconist whip up for intolerable blows that must be taken on the chin. I offered Cornwall one and we smoked together for a time, considering the immediate prospect of sharing a bar with the man we hated most in the world.

When we got to the Blue Bar it was teeming with Scoundrels. Together we headed for the fireplace to warm ourselves and watch the cuckoo settle into the nest.

Over at the bar, Hansclapp was surrounded by younger Scoundrels in their twenties and thirties, unproven, unblooded, all of them, and eager to touch the hem of his garment. Hansclapp's success at the chessboard, and his reputation in the wider world, made him an interesting prospect, and there was plenty of clapping him on the back and shaking his hand. It made me sick. Hansclapp was telling a loud story, scotch casually in hand, about his fiancée, the Princess, and a polo game he'd just played. Chaps were falling about as his story progressed.

Stormington sidled over to us. "Hansclapp's in then. Bet you can't stomach that?"

"Quite right, Stormzy, it's as rum as it gets."

"Well, he's only gone and bought Maurice's Bernini off him," said an incredulous Stormington. Maurice had been trying to shift his horrible statue of the Fallen Madonna since about '45 when he'd hustled it back from Madrid in his kitbag.

"What did he give him for it?" I asked.

"Half a mill."

Cornwall spat out his scotch.

The light in the room faltered for a moment. The imposing figure of Aram Atsi had appeared at the Blue Bar door, carrying a wooden crate. Atsi looked around, and Hansclapp broke off his story to beckon him over. "Ahh!" he exclaimed, "it's arrived, good, good." The room fell into an expectant quiet.

Aram Atsi put the crate onto the bar and Hansclapp asked him to crowbar it open. "I hope that this will not be considered too gauche," he said to the room, "but in my own quiet way I am a bit of a vinophile. I love rare and unusual bottles from all over the globe. I know it is traditional for a new member to put something special behind the bar, is it not, Miss Summerville?"

Summerville nodded.

"So, I wanted to make a gift of some of my best bottles to the Club, to celebrate my membership. Mere gee-gaws, but perhaps diverting enough. Mr Atsi, would you kindly hand them to me please, one by one? Thank you."

There were a few murmurs from the room at this impromptu skit. Atsi levered the lid off the crate, removed a few handfuls of straw. He handed the first bottle to Hansclapp. It was brown glass, Edwardian in style and had no label.

"This bottle of James Martin I personally recovered from the wreck of the *S.S. Politician*, which you'll remember sank in 1941 off Eriskay in the Outer

Hebrides. It was bloody chilly down there, I can tell you, but perhaps my fault for planning the dive for January."

Mild laughter from the ranks. "It is one of only two bottles that I salvaged, but not to worry – for here is the other," he quipped. Atsi passed him the next bottle and Hansclapp held it up, a half-bottle of rectangular design.

"Ballantine's, a twelve-year-old, which would make it part of the 1929 release. I'm sorry I only have two of these to offer the Club," he said. "But at least each is unique."

What a load of nonsense. "As if he went down to the *Politician* himself," I whispered to Cornwall. "That sort of dive requires decades of planning."

As if reading my mind, Hansclapp put the two bottles on the bar and pulled a photograph from his breast pocket. "Here I am," he announced, passing the photo to a young Scoundrel at his side. "I rigged a rubber hose to pump hot water down inside my diving bell, which kept me alive just long enough to liberate them from the wreck." The young Scoundrel nodded and passed the photo around.

The crowd around Hansclapp was beginning to thicken, as chaps saw that something interesting was afoot. Atsi pulled out another bottle, the body of which was wrapped tightly in filthy hessian sacking which shed dust all over the floor.

"Next we have... ahh, yes, the Harewood Rum. Distilled in 1780 in Barbados and transported to England the next year, this was discovered in a dry well in Harewood House just last year."

I noticed Reverend Blunders-Hatch, the Club's ancient cellarmaster, craning his tortoise-like neck over the crowd of Scoundrels, hopping from one leg to the other and licking his flubbery lips.

"Now this one set me back a bit," scowled Hansclapp, looking around at his audience. "In fact, I had to buy the whole bloody house from Harewood, just to get hold of it!" The room erupted at this show of bullishness. "And don't worry if you're not quick enough for a taste of this one," he quipped. "There was a whole case! There are eleven more bottles to come. Just ask me nicely." More laughter.

I began to see something of the power of this terrible man, how he could charm and tease an audience, bending it to his will. And now he was warming to his theme. He snapped his fingers at Aram Atsi, who passed him another bottle from the crate. This one was an ancient clay gourd, with a new cork stoppering the spout. Hansclapp smoothed away some stalks of hay that clung to it and held it up for everyone to see.

"You may have read a few years ago about an archaeological dig to excavate the tomb of the Scorpion King, in Egypt. I kept it quiet at the time, but it was my expedition. We found sarcophagi, we found weapons, blah, blah, blah, so-on and so-forth. But what made the dig successful beyond my wildest dreams, gentlemen, is this wine." He shook the gourd, which made a sloshing sound.

"Tomb wine, meant for the Scorpion King's next life. It is over 4500 years old. In truth, it is perhaps a little piney, with an imbalance of honey – but maybe that's how they drank it back then!"

Another pathetic little witticism that got much too big a laugh.

"I thought," he continued, "that the Scorpion King's countryman Dr Shalwaz would like to try it first? Where are you, sir?"

Shalwaz was a popular Scoundrel, rotund, bookish and linen-suited, he'd made a few quid shifting antiquities from his homeland, having sold Cleopatra's bridal headdress to eleven different American millionairesses in the last year alone. Shalwaz cleared his throat theatrically.

"Here," shouted Hansclapp, "catch!" And he threw the ancient gourd across the room to Shalwaz, who jinked left and caught it with one hand, pulling the gourd into his chest as if he were at third slip.

"Ha! Good hands, Doctor," called Hansclapp. "My apologies for a poor throw. The honour is yours."

Shalwaz unstopped it and took a long swig. "Revolting!" he shouted as chaps wrestled the gourd off him and began to pass it around.

"Maybe it's corked!" called a wag.

"Shalwaz has the palate of an oxen, don't waste any more on him," shouted another, leaping on the first wag's back.

By now, chaps all over the room were roaring with laughter. This bloke Hansclapp, they were saying to one another, a bloody good egg, for sure. Top class booze and an adventuring spirit, just the sort of fellow we should have snapped up years ago! Why the hell hadn't he been recruited before now?

Atsi handed over another bottle. Hansclapp peered down at the label while pulling a handkerchief from his pocket and mopping his brow. "Ahhh! This is something I liberated a few years back. A reasonable drop of port."

He held up a dark bottle with a messy chalk mark on it. "1932, Castelo Soldado Sujo." Beside me, Cornwall froze. His jaw was clenched as tight as a sprung mantrap. "Does anyone know anything about this vintage?" Hansclapp surveyed the room, deliberately not looking in our direction. The room quietened down as everyone tried to work it out.

"I believe it's Portugal, the Douro Valley," Cornwall said, flatly.

Every man in the room turned to look at Cornwall.

Hansclapp's face lit up at this. "Yah, well done, Mr Cornwall. I take it you've been there?"

Cornwall didn't answer but smiled thinly. He hadn't ever been there and somehow Hansclapp knew it. Castelo Soldado Sujo was Brigadier Maximilian Cornwall's summer retreat. His father would come back home after a season spent alone at the Portuguese castle, shooting, making wine and sleeping with the local women. He'd arrive home with a few cases of young port chucked in the back of his Wolseley, and he'd have Cornwall lug them down to the cellars of Bluebell Manor. Each year Cornwall would clamour to be allowed to visit the Castelo with his father. Each year the Brigadier would look him up and down and say, "maybe next year."

Next year, as Cornwall had bitterly remarked, never came. So, this bottle could only have come from one place: Hellcat's cellars. Hansclapp must have removed it personally. A very private insult.

Cornwall reached up to unfasten his top button, before remembering he'd already done so.

"Easy, Victor," I murmured, "don't give him what he wants." Cornwall let out a long, slow breath and nodded once.

"And what's this?" Now Hansclapp held up a bottle of apple schnapps in a thin glass bottle. It was unlabelled and had a fully grown apple inside, still attached to the twigs and leaves of the tree it had grown on, like a ship in a bottle. "A bottle of schnapps from another estate I own." The glance he stole at me made me want to choke him.

When we were young, my brother Eustace and I used to put clear glass bottles onto the Nimbu orchard's apple blossoms, and, just occasionally, a fruit would grow inside the bottle. It was one of the only things I did together with Eustace when we were boys. This bottle had come from my own cellars at Nimbu Towers.

"I know this schnapps is of no particular class," goaded Hansclapp, "but it is humbly homemade, and quite delectable."

Hansclapp held the port and the schnapps up to the light. He had chosen these bottles for one reason only: a very private humiliation.

I took a step forward, but Cornwall gripped my arm. "No," he whispered.

I made do with eyeballing Hansclapp from across the room. Gradually, the red mist receded.

"The next bottle," he called, "is a very special one. In fact, gentlemen, a very special trio." Joan the Coat Check Lady was suddenly at the door, holding a tray upon which were balanced three bottles of scotch. Two were unopened, and the third was missing perhaps the top fifth. There was a collective intake of breath, and a path to Hansclapp was immediately made for Joan, as people realised the truth of the matter.

Three bottles of Glenavon Special Liqueur. Surely the rarest and most desirable whisky in the world.

As Joan made her way towards Hansclapp he turned to face us. "St. John Trevelyan, Victor Cornwall, I would like to say something, if I may."

The hubbub in the room died down until we could hear the distant sounds of the traffic on Piccadilly. Not many in the Club knew the truth of our fifty-year feud with Hansclapp, but most had heard a rumour or two.

"As you probably know, this is Glenavon Distillery's masterpiece, dating from 1852," said Hansclapp. "It is a titan amongst single malts, over one hundred and thirty years old. It is commonly believed there is only one bottle left – which I bought at auction for over £250,000 last year."

You could have heard a pin drop. This bottle of scotch was legendary.

"But I bought it only to put it with the other two bottles of Glenavon Special that I've owned for years. I know for a fact that these are the last three bottles in the world."

A ripple of excitement went around the room. Chaps were clamouring for space. Everyone wanted a grandstand view.

Hansclapp picked up a bottle of the Glenavon, and pulled off the grubby linen cork-cover, tossing it to the ground. Then he tugged out the cork stopper and threw that away too. Eyeballing us, he slowly turned it upside down. The amber liquid began to glug out of the bottle, splashing onto the carpet. "And tonight, in order to make peace with you, Victor, and you, St. John, I sacrifice them all."

Reverend Blunders-Hatch had gone completely pale, the adam's apple in his scrawny neck was rising and falling, and he was panting like an Alsatian at a church fete. The atmosphere was suddenly charged with a bizarre static as if every single object in the room had been rubbed with a balloon from that same church fete. All eyes were on Hansclapp, or Cornwall, or me. The dregs from the first bottle of Glenavon soaked into the carpet, and Hansclapp placed the empty bottle onto the bar. Then he began to uncork the second bottle. "Majors, I would like to make a sincere apology to you both."

Hansclapp upended the second bottle and it began to drain away. Blunders-Hatch, unable to contain himself any longer, suddenly screamed, "nooooo!" He lunged forward, shoulder-barging his way through the crowd and throwing himself onto the sopping carpet, trying to get his mouth under the amber stream.

Hansclapp kicked him once, very hard, in the head. The Reverend collapsed unconscious. The second bottle of whisky dribbled away to nothing, and Hansclapp put it on the bar with the first.

To an absolutely silent room, Hansclapp picked up the third almost-full bottle. Next to us Jerwood had suddenly materialised, and now he cleared his throat. He had a pair of tumblers on a silver tray. Each of the tumblers contained a generous dram of the Glenavon.

Hansclapp poured a similar dram into his own tumbler and upended the rest of the third and final bottle over the prone body of Blunders-Hatch. He put the empty bottle with the others on the bar.

Then he spoke, without breaking eye contact with us for even a second.

"Cornwall and Trevelyan, for the second time in my life, I find that I am the new boy. At Winstowe College you gave me a welcome that was far from warm. In the War, as expected given my nationhood, we found ourselves on opposite sides. You were worthy adversaries, and over the years I, in turn, have made some trouble for the pair of you. We have been putting each other's noses out of joint for half a century now. I want to thank you for the obstacles you have put in my way, for they have made me the great man I have become – a man with billions and a business empire. A man who is about to join this great nation's Royal Family. And a man who today can call himself *Scoundrel*. Trevelyan! Cornwall! Today we must make peace. For we are men of this Club, together. So, accept my apology for what has passed, and share these drinks with me."

It was nicely done. Reasonable, rueful, apologetic, decent. The speech of an affable man atoning for old misdemeanours. You could have cut the atmosphere in the Blue Bar with a knife as his voice echoed away, leaving his question hanging. I would have grabbed that knife and stabbed Hansclapp in the throat with it. What I couldn't do immediately was bring myself to answer him. There was a terribly awkward pause.

From somewhere deep inside myself I found the strength to pick up the tumbler, hold it up high, and say the worst words imaginable:

"Welcome to Scoundrels Club."

Cornwall croaked out the same toast, looking disgusted with himself as he did so. From the bar, Hansclapp raised his glass as well, his eyes shining in triumph.

We needed fresh air. We took a spin around the block, walking past the great plane trees that stood sentry to the side of the Club.

"This is an outrage," muttered Cornwall, through teeth so gritted I thought they'd shatter in his mouth.

We stopped at the service alley leading back to the Club's kitchens. I offered him a *Tough Break*, one of a small stock of Alabama soured brownleaf that I kept for unimaginably terrible developments. As he leaned forward to accept my light, I slapped him hard around the cheek, knocking the ciggie out of his mouth and over the balcony onto the street below.

"What the hell?"

"Your guard was down, Cornwall."

"And this is how you make your point?"

"You should slap me back! I deserve it as much as you do," I shouted back. "We've let the Devil in, man! Now he's doling out sweets to the kids."

Cornwall rubbed his cheek. "Come on, we both know he won't make it through the evening. The only question is who gets to put the knife in."

"Nobody puts the knife in," said a delicate voice behind us. Summerville spirited into view from out of the deep shadows of the alley. "That's non-negotiable. Not until we know what he's up to. Understood?"

"Come on, Stephanie," said Cornwall. "We've got a chance to end this once and for all, tonight. We can call it an accident."

"No," she replied. "Too much is unknown. We need to unpick everything Hansclapp's planned. This is clearly part of something bigger. Stay your hands, gentlemen. Instead, you're to get him to open up."

"Ply him with booze, is that what you're saying?" said Cornwall. "Hope his lips loosen?"

"Not just booze, maybe," I said frowning.

"Something else in mind?"

"Remember Maljeria?"

He saw immediately what the smart play was. "When is Hansclapp to be sworn in?"

"Midday tomorrow," said Summerville.

"Plenty of time," I said, draining my glass. "I'll make preparations."

"Good. Now get back in there," Summerville ordered, "and be on your best behaviour."

Back in the Blue Bar there was an impromptu knees-up taking place. Scoundrels kept standing Hansclapp drinks from his own bottles. The Reverend was sleeping it off in the Bone Jalopy. Two of the younger chaps had developed a primitive suction device, based on a Hopi ear candle, to try and get enough of the Glenavon out of the carpet for a measure each. It wasn't going well, and their attempt was collapsing into a recriminatory shoving match which would further degenerate into a formal duel within the hour, with one of them, I forget which, losing an earlobe.

In another corner of the bar, a game of bread roll cricket had started up, and in yet another, Maurice was trying to piece together the Bernini that Hansclapp had carelessly left on the piano, and which Batty Bratwurst had knocked over while demonstrating the correct way to strangle a wild turkey.

And through all this Cornwall and I did our best to look relaxed. Small talk. Bits of Club lore. Anecdotes Hansclapp wouldn't have heard before, about this expedition and that undertaking. All seemingly innocuous and off-the-cuff, but actually honed to make him feel we had given up and acquiesced. And that now he was *one of us*, inside the tent pissing out.

Cornwall made a good fist of a story about cooking up a storm at Wan Booli Camp at the end of the War. I followed up with some choice cuts about our long walk home and the time Cornwall took us a thousand miles

the wrong way with a short-cut through The Lebanon.
Then Cornwall chipped in with a great story about the
time I masqueraded as a corpse in order to steal a lewd
Picasso, and I retorted with a cheeky tale about the
ill-fated attempt on Everest. I was about to segue into
some reminiscences about Winstowe, when Hansclapp
suddenly slammed his tumbler onto the bar and snapped
his fingers at Jervis. "Three bottles of your oldest
Ardmore, hang the glasses."

Jervis began to see to it. "I've heard so much about
the splendid roof terrace, gentlemen," he said. "It would
be a fine thing if you would join me up there."

He was very drunk now, slurring and stumbling. It
would have been so easy to simply snuff out his candle.
But orders are orders. We made our way up the Grand
Staircase, past the Long Room and the Library to the
terrace. I thought the chill in the night air might bring
him to his senses after the bonhomie but out on the
terrace, looking out on London, he was no less friendly
– oddly more so.

"So, how does it feel to be joining the Royal Family?"
I asked him. "Do they expect a lot from you? A lot of
demands on your time?"

"Heavy is the head," he mused, "but I hope I might
lighten their load." He laughed to himself, stuffing his
knuckles into his mouth and biting them.

"What do you mean, Gruber?" I queried, slurring
theatrically to appear as drunk as him.

"They're prepared to take my money," he sneered,
taking a swig from the neck. "They think having a

billionaire who controls the newspapers will insulate them from what is coming."

"Oh yes? And what's coming?" Cornwall did a good job here, staring off into the distance, framing his question offhandedly, as if bored and drunk and hardly listening. Hansclapp caught his gaze and turned towards the view. It was a remarkably clear evening. The spring moon had clad our cruel mistress, London, in a shimmering iridescence so much more appealing than her usual grubby shroud. And we were getting a right eyeful. London was swathed in the sinuous boa of the River Thames and bedecked by jewels that caught the moonbeams – the roof of the Royal Academy, Nelson on his Column, and, far away, the dome of St Pauls Cathedral and the pale grey stone of the ancient Tower of London, glowing softly, a ghost of London's beginnings. It would have been beautiful, if the company hadn't been so grim.

Hansclapp stepped to the railing, took a deep breath and spread out his hands, godlike, as he surveyed the skyline. "Change," he slurred, "fundamental change. One might even say *revolutionary*."

"Yeh, the whole world is changing…" I mused, mock drunk.

"But not enough!" Hansclapp took a great swig from the neck of his Ardmore and threw the bottle down into the Piccadilly street. There was a squeal of brakes and the sound of a collision, but he paid it no mind. Instead, he swivelled on his heels to stare at the pair of us. "What's the legend?" He started to laugh, grabbed my bottle and swigged from it. His mind must have latched onto something, for what he said next didn't make any sense. "One day all the ravens will fly away," he smirked, "and we know what'll happen to the kingdom then."

"Not really," said Cornwall, yawning, "what, exactly?"

At this, something caused Hansclapp to collect himself and the peculiar, hallucinatory scene abruptly ended.

Hansclapp snapped back into focus and looked at his wristwatch. "A capital evening! Capital, capital!" His eyes shone. "I must get on. What is it you say, you Britons? Mind how you go."

And with that, Hansclapp clicked his heels in the Austrian style and marched away across the terrace, as fresh and alert as if he hadn't touched a drop all evening.

His Rolls Royce, parked insolently right outside the black doors of the Club, swept him away toward Park Lane, in the direction of Kensington Palace.

I was up at six the next morning, slipping silently from my usual attic bedroom in the Club. I'd been prop-drinking, to get Hansclapp drunk, but I still had a brutish headache.

I hotfooted it down to the second floor, and the Trophy Room. I checked left and right. I had the corridor to myself, so I snapped a pair of plastic gloves on and was about to move inside, when suddenly I heard soft footsteps on the pile carpet. I jammed my hands into my pockets and pretended to look at a picture. Around the corner came Hendricks.

Hendricks had let us down so badly over the Knave's Gambit that I prepared myself for a very difficult conversation. He considered turning on his heels but decided to tough it out and carried on toward me. "I can only say sorry," he said, surprising me with such a candid admission off the bat.

"I don't quite know what to say to you, Hendricks." I shrugged, so I didn't have to take my hands out of my pockets. "I've never wanted someone to win a chess match quite so much. I can't quite believe you spooned it."

"Neither can I. It's been…" he searched for the right word. "…humbling. Knocked me off my perch I suppose. I'm resigning my membership."

"What?"

"I've let everyone down. I was tasked to win. And I failed. It's that simple."

Again, this admission surprised me. "Bloody hell, Hendricks. Why quit the Club? I've been out there, and it's no picnic. Give it a couple of days before you decide, eh?" I'd never seen him looking so forlorn. He'd lost all the bravado that was at his core. What was left? Not much.

"I have a standing offer to become a Yeoman at the Tower of London, in my dotage. I think I'll do that, just for a quiet life."

"You're going to be a Beefeater?"

"I think so."

He was almost in tears, the poor bastard. It was awkward, seeing a man so sorry for himself, so I blustered, "Ah! I rather envy you."

"Not sure about that, but it's something. A duty I can discharge without stuffing anything up."

I couldn't think of a single kind thing to say, so I stared at my shoes.

"I've written my resignation to Summerville," he said, finally moving past me. "There's a Laphroaig of mine behind the Blue Bar. It's yours if you want it."

"Big of you."

"No hard feelings, Trevelyan. Mind how you go."

I didn't offer to shake hands. Neither did he. He strode off, head low. A broken man. Hansclapp had the ability to ruin anyone, even puffed-up arseholes like Hendricks.

The coast was clear. I slipped into the gloom of the Trophy Room, creeping past the snow leopard head and the X-rated print of the impossibly tessellated lesbians that M.C. Escher gave us for services rendered. Because of my broadness of beam, chaps tend to think of me as a bit of a lump who hits problems in the face to make them go away, but I can be dainty when required. Now I was in full stealth mode. I wanted this done and dusted before the fallow deer breakfast sausages were even in the pan.

I avoided the creaking floorboard and hopped over a fire bucket of unsorted gallantry medals which Tumps had been promising to put on the walls since the end of the War. I pulled the vial Cornwall had given me from my pocket. In the dark I could see the remaining inch of liquid at the bottom was glowing faintly. A good sign that there was still active ingredient left.

I arrived at my destination, a massive display case of burnished oak. The hand-blown glass panels warped the spidery handwriting of the document inside, but I could just about read the title: Club Orthodoxies.

Written after a debauched and drunken supper in 1635 by Charles I onto his own dinner napkin, it was stained with wine, blood and other unidentified substances. To a Scoundrel, this napkin occupied a space somewhere between the Domesday Book, the First Folio of Shakespeare and Playboy Magazine Number 1. It was the foundation the Club was built upon. It was what we stood for.

When he wrote it, Charles had been in a fix, beset by rebellious lords furious about his high spending and fending off enemies abroad. At court, the King was pulled this way and that by his various advisors, all jockeying for position. Bollocks to this, he decided. I'm the King! Charles shrugged off Parliament and began to rule on his own say-so, giving the royal finger to anyone who disagreed with him. But however bullish he was, he still needed friends.

One night Charles invited to dinner England's liveliest thinkers, drinkers, fighters, fornicators, roustabouts, raconteurs and ne'er-do-wells. Soon Charles was ranting to the room. How could he control an unruly kingdom and keep the King's Peace? How could he sort out mouthy dukes, and root out spies? Who could he send to seduce that Catalan princess he needed onside? Who might solve the highwayman problem on his forest roads? Who could he rely on to fix, well, whatever needed fixing?

For that, somebody said, you need a bunch of devastating bastards who thought fast, acted on the instant, and did extreme violence extremely well.

Charles liked this idea.

He liked it very, very much.

He scrawled out the statutes of a new Club that would solve his problems in pragmatic style. It would be *open to men of all classes, colours and creeds, who would remain free of the obligations of Tax and the Strictures of the Law, in return for the Undertaking of Missions for the Furtherance of The King, for England, and for Justice.*

That night, Scoundrels Club was born.

The King's Napkin was tatty as hell, ripped, smudged and torn, scrawled on, scuffed and lightly toasted with candle grease. Charles, or someone, had also drawn a cock and balls under his name, before later amending this into a griffin by adding claws and a little curved beak.

What I was doing right now was unutterably sacrilegious. If caught, I would certainly be slung out of the Club for a second time, and possibly throttled or run-through by a furious member, for Scoundrels touch the King's Napkin once and once only – on the day they join the Club.

Gingerly, I pulled the Napkin from its golden clips, and turned it over, emptying the only remaining vial of Bosphorus Phosphorus onto its underside and smeared it into all four corners. Then I reclipped the Napkin into the case, and gently closed the window.

Twelve seconds later I was sauntering back down the corridor, ready for sausages.

At midday sharp, Cornwall and I stood in front of the King's display case, surrounded by a cadre of hungover Scoundrels. After last night's raucous evening, it was a miracle anyone was there at all.

Hansclapp himself looked fresh-faced and affable, like an Olympian who has spent four years nobbling the opposition and is now waiting for the medal ceremony.

Summerville, in the corduroy plus-fours of the Membership and Operations Secretary, was all business too. You wouldn't have known just how much she detested Hansclapp from her welcoming smile, apart from the faintest pinch about her eyes. "Are we all ready, then?" she asked the room.

She creaked open the heavy glass door to reveal the King's Napkin. "The Orthodoxies, Mr Hansclapp," she intoned. "Are you familiar with this ceremony?"

Hansclapp inclined his head.

"Then please pick up the King's Napkin, clutch it tightly inside your right fist and make your Club Oaths."

Hansclapp reached up and pulled the Napkin from its golden clips. He took a moment to admire it, then bunched it tightly into his fist and held his fist up in front of him, at eye level.

He cleared his throat. "I declare, upon my honour,

that I will make myself the Club's Man for the furtherance of The King, of England and of Justice."

The next part of the ceremony may strike the layman as peculiar, but remember it was designed by a King at the end of a long and drunken evening, four hundred years ago.

"And will you now answer the King's Questions, as Charles himself asked them, on the night the Club was founded?"

"I will," he intoned.

"Gruber Hansclapp, soon to be Scoundrel, will you roll the Napkin up very small?" asked Summerville, making the traditional King's First Question.

"I will, if my King directs me," said Hansclapp.

"And will you stuff the Napkin up your arse?" asked Summerville.

"I will, if my King directs me," repeated Hansclapp.

"And will you remove the Napkin from your arse and rub the Napkin upon your noggin?" asked Summerville.

"I will, if my King directs me," replied Hansclapp.

Summerville paused, as if considering his responses. She strung this moment out as long as possible. After eyeballing the assembled members and rubbing her chin theatrically she finally replied, "then put the Napkin down, for you are now a man of the Scoundrels' Club. You are now a Scoundrel."

Hansclapp bowed deeply to Summerville, turned and unravelled the King's Napkin, and put it back into the display case. There were tears in his eyes, damn the bastard to hell.

I'd kept a count of how long Summerville had kept him holding the King's Napkin: 63 seconds, more than enough for the Bosphorus Phosphorus residue to seep into his skin. The question was, would it loosen his tongue? Would we find out what we needed to know, so that we could finally kill him?

More celebratory drinks in the bar, the Gaye Bar this time. Cornwall and I nodded brief congratulations to the new boy and took ourselves off to a window seat to lend weight to the lie that we were suffering terribly with hangovers. We sipped the *haejangguk* blood broth that Masterson ladled out from the bar on rough mornings-after, to watch events unfold.

After forty minutes of chat at the bar Hansclapp began to look distinctly peaky, his forehead glistening with sweat. Soon enough he made his excuses.

We followed him down the stairs, and onto Piccadilly. He walked unsteadily into St James' Park, taking off his topcoat and draping it over his arm, as if tremendously hot. He was soon struggling to walk, and we dropped back to tail him from fifty yards – about as relaxed a tail as one would ever do on foot.

Up ahead, Hansclapp staggered to a park bench, throwing his body down onto it, frightening a Norland nanny with a pram, who rushed off right away. We sauntered towards him. Cornwall clapped me on the back. "Bloody good job, St. John," he remarked. "He's had a good dose of the stuff alright. Look at him, he's buggered. Where shall we take him?

"Back to the gym," I suggested. I was looking forward to wrapping a bit of barbed wire around a scaffolding pipe and then wrapping that around Hansclapp. For the entire afternoon.

We were forty yards away. Hansclapp vomited into the rubbish bin next to the bench and then slumped back, wheezing heavily. He wrestled his tie from his neck and threw it down on the path. We approached more hurriedly now, keen to scoop him up and get him out of public view, in case some do-gooder offered assistance.

Twenty yards away. Hansclapp was folded over double, his shoulders wracked by a sudden coughing fit. He spat onto his own shoes.

Ten yards away. "Well I never," began Cornwall, jovially, looking forward to this, "if it isn't Gruber–"

Inside a second, Hansclapp sat upright and alert, eyes like ice. In his lap, was a .38 snub-nosed pistol, already cocked. "Oh dear," he said, "you walked into that one."

I said nothing. Cornwall said nothing. We'd been sloppy.

"I assume this is a chance encounter?" Hansclapp smoothed his hair with one hand, his grip on the pistol was steady.

My bowie knife was inaccessible, strapped to my calf. And as far as I knew, Cornwall was unarmed. His Fairburn-Sykes dagger was with the Scoundrels armourer after he'd bent the quillion.

"No sudden movements please,' said Hansclapp, "I wouldn't want there to be an accident." I could now see that we weren't alone, the muzzle of a rifle just visible, protruded from a bush twenty yards to our left.

"We've been here before, haven't we? When are you going to learn?" he tutted.

I told him, in no uncertain terms, where to go.

Hansclapp set his pistol down on the bench. "I wondered if you had kept a bit of Bosphorus Phosphorus for yourself when you destroyed my laboratory in Maljeria."

We didn't say anything.

"I began taking micro-doses some time ago," he said, picking up his tie from the ground and brushing it down. "I wasn't going to let it come to market unless I had immunity."

He finished knotting his half Windsor. "There! Every bit the respectable gentleman again."

There followed an awkward silence, then Cornwall spoke up, "So what happens now? You've taken your revenge, Hansclapp. You've seen us suffer. And now you're a Scoundrel. Where does it end?"

Hansclapp scratched his head as if the answer was obvious. "For most of my life," he said, "I was told I was not up to calibre for membership of Scoundrels. But now I see that it is the Scoundrels who are not up to my calibre."

He stood up from the park bench, "I'd hoped you'd prove more interesting adversaries, gentlemen, but you've never got anywhere near me. Don't worry, I'll put you out of your misery soon."

Then he walked away.

Cornwall and I trudged back to the Club, each lost in a world of anguish. It took me a while to access how exactly I was feeling, but then it came to me as we rounded the southern corner of Fortnum's and I saw the toy department window display. A toy soldier, banging a little toy drum. A teddy bear at a table, accepting a cup of toy tea in a little toy cup, served by an Aunt Jemima. That's it, I thought. We're *playthings*.

Hansclapp's playthings.

Before long we were back outside the Club. Aram Atsi had already got the door open. Out stepped Lunk and Summerville, as tense as I've ever seen either of them.

"Tiberius has it figured," Summerville said.

"I'm afraid we have a worse problem than we thought," Lunk added.

"What?"

"The chess match was rigged."

"Rigged! How do you know?" said Cornwall.

"Something didn't feel right when I was watching it. Something I couldn't put my finger on. Then it clicked. I finally saw the pattern. It was a match I'd seen before."

"Which one?" I asked.

"Spassky-Fischer, '72. They played an exact re-run of the opening game. Every single bloody move was the same. The game was a sham."

"So that means…" Cornwall said.

"…that Hendricks lost deliberately," I finished the sentence for him. Summerville continued the train of thought, "which means that Hendricks has been in league with Hansclapp all along. He sold us down the Thames."

"That sneaky bastard," said Cornwall. "I should have known."

This was all too confounding. "Are you sure?" I said, "I saw Hendricks earlier this morning. He told me he'd resigned his membership."

"Resigned?" said Lunk.

"He said he was going to work at the Tower of London."

"What? Why the hell would he do that?" said Cornwall, "unless…"

It all came to me with a sudden flash. "Yes. Of course! Hansclapp was drunk… He let it slip: *heavy hangs the crown.* He talked of ravens leaving the Tower, and the Kingdom falling."

"And? What else?" asked Summerville.

"Hansclapp's plan is the ultimate indignity for the nation," I blurted. "He's going to steal the Crown Jewels."

Lunk nodded slowly as if it made *some* sense. "Is it a deliberate signpost, d'you think?" he asked Summerville.

"Well, if it is, it's cack-handed," she snorted, "and entirely unsubtle."

"In that case, we must assume," concluded Lunk, "that this isn't a trail of breadcrumbs for us to follow. He must have made a mistake."

Over to you, Cornwall. Get on with it!

Yours sincerely,
Major Arthur St. John Trevelyan.

Hellcat Manor
Great Trundleford
Devon
July 12th 2021

Dear Major,

I won't slow things down with empty rhetoric, for as they say nowadays, shit was about to get real.

CHAPTER 17

TROUBLE AT THE TOWER

SCOUNDRELS CLUB, LONDON.
THE FOLLOWING DAY

We were back in Summerville's office the following day.

"I volunteer to go to the Tower and finish Hendricks off once and for all," I said, "I've been waiting for an excuse to end the bastard for years."

"I'm afraid not," Summerville replied, "he mustn't realise that we're on to them. Instead we have an opportunity to catch them in the act."

"So, what happens now?" asked Trevelyan.

"We put Hendricks and the Crown Jewels under surveillance. And we wait for as long as it takes."

"Sounds like that might take a while," I mused. I didn't relish the prospect of sitting in a bush in the grounds of the Tower for weeks, waiting for the burglary to happen.

Summerville seemed to read my mind. "I'm not suggesting an observation post," she paused, then added, "one of you needs to go undercover."

"Undercover as what?" Trevelyan asked.

"Raven Master. I've already made the call to fix it."

"Raven Master?" I queried.

"One of the Beefeaters, responsible for the welfare of the ravens at the Tower."

Trevelyan stepped forward, "I'd like to put myself forward for this one," he said, gamely.

"Really?" I said, giving him a curious look.

"Yep. Always fancied being a Beefeater as it happens. This one's got my name on it, if there are no objections."

"Fine by me," I said.

"Good, that's settled then," Summerville declared, "you'll still need a disguise. Ruff Puff will get to work on some prosthetics."

Trevelyan nodded his approval.

"What do you need me to do?" I asked.

"You'll be working closely with me and Lunk, running the intel between the Tower and the Club," Summerville replied.

"So strategic stuff, high-level analysis, crunching the numbers with the top brass in the big tent."

"If you like."

"I do like," I said, then added, "Congratulations

to the new Raven Master." I reached over and shook Trevelyan's hand.

"Good," Summerville said, "Trevelyan, we'll get you installed as soon as you're ready. Start working on your cover story."

I gave Trevelyan a few days to settle in at the Tower before paying a visit. Initially I couldn't find him, so I bought myself an ice cream and wandered around the white limestone walls, mingling with the tourists. I'd never really been before and I was quite enjoying reading all the information plaques about the history. There were several Beefeaters standing around looking fine in their red uniforms. Generally, they were a smart bunch, but there was one who stuck out like a sore thumb. He was a complete shambles. He had an ill-fitting uniform, covered in a tacky tartan trim that suggested Scottish heritage, but it looked like no regiment I'd ever seen. The chap was sweating heavily in the midday sun as he tried to enthuse a group of bored teenagers who were on a school trip. One shaved yob had snuck behind him and set alight to the hem of his tunic.

I lifted my sunglasses onto the top of my head. "I can see what you're doing there, you little sod," I said, "bugger off."

The Beefeater suddenly realised he was on fire and started frantically patting himself down. The kids ran off laughing.

"Sorry to disturb you," I said, "but where might I find the Raven Master?"

"Och, aye, the neeew boy, you saaaay?"

My heart sank. "Oh no. Trevelyan is that you?"

"Aye!"

I could barely contain my disappointment. Trevelyan looked like a complete numpty. Why he had styled himself as an elderly Scottish soldier, god only knows. Saying that, at least the disguise worked. He didn't look a bit like himself – except for being fat. Ruff Puff, the Scoundrels resident costumier, had performed a miracle with latex and make-up. If it hadn't been for Trevelyan's fruity, hopelessly overblown accent I would never have recognised him. The nose itself was an absolute work of art. Somehow Ruff Puff had been able to condense the entire backstory of Trevelyan's Scottish character into this one appendage. I knew nothing about him, and yet, somehow, I knew it all. It wasn't just any nose. It was a nose that belonged to the son of a Govan steelworker. It was the nose of a man who'd felt the red-hot burn of his faither's temper and had gone on to develop one of his own. This nose had burgled a hoose when it was a wee-un and been told to join the army by a sympathetic police constable. This nose had seen action, perhaps Suez or Aden and had carried the trauma of it since. This nose had been throon out of every pub in Glasgie and told to ne'er come back. This nose liked to drink. Och aye, this nose liked tae get blathered every night till eet shat ee-sel'. This wa' a nose that hud been locked out of the hoose every weekend, calling up to th' wife to be let in, begging fa' forgiveness. This wis a hooter that hud felt th' bane crack as anither jimmy drove his heed intae it efter spilling his dram. This hooter hud bin rearranged by gless efter goupin' at anither man's wee lassie. 'N' in efter years, this wis a hooter that knew th' loneliness o' swallyin ale alone in th' neuk o' a workin' man's club, watery-eyed 'n' singing 'shortenin' bread' quietly tae itself while ither, better men played darts.

Ruff Puff was an absolute genius and if I'd been wearing a cap I would have doffed it there and then. "The whole tartan flavour is a bit much, Trevelyan, to be honest, but your fake nose is terrific."

"That's my real nose," he said.

"..."

"That's the only bit Ruff Puff didn't touch."

There was a bit of an awkward pause, then I noticed a bird cage at his feet. It had a disconsolate raven inside. I took a bite of my ice cream.

"Settling in nicely, I see," I said, "enjoying it?"

"I'm loving it, Cornwall," he said, wheezing. "Absolutely loving being the new Raven Master."

He was perspiring heavily and seemed to have lost his full range of movement. "Are you all right in there, Trevelyan?" I whispered.

"Don't call me Trevelyan. I'm Sergeant MacDairmid."

"C'mon Trevelyan, don't be a dick."

"Ah said a'm Sergeant MacDairmid, dae ye ken? Ah'm method actin', eh? Ye either ca' me by mah name or ah will kick aff. Dae ye git me? A'm lou'in speakin' in Scots tae fowk."

"Fine. Whatever. I take it there's nothing to report?"

"Nothing, yet." Trevelyan bent down and gave the raven a mealworm that must have been secreted up his tartan sleeve.

"And how you are finding the evenings?"

"Easy. I'll brief you on what we need to do later but the jewels are safe during the day."

"Good. In that case I'll come back later after all the tourists have buggered off."

"Hang on, don't you want to meet the birds?"

"Not reall–"

But he started on his patter, although mercifully not in his ludicrous vernacular. "This little madam is called Diva. She's been at the Tower longer than any of the other ravens and as a result likes to get her own way." Trevelyan adopted a horrible kind of baby talk as he took her out of the cage, "Don't you, Diva? You naughty little missis." Diva tilted her head and made a coquettish cawing noise. For some reason he rewarded this underwhelming trick with a morsel of meat. Then he whispered, "She's my favourite, but don't tell the others."

"You sure you know what you're doing with these birds, Trevelyan?" I asked.

"They genuinely like me," he said, "I just keep them well fed and they behave themselves." There was some logic to this. After all, it was exactly the same tactic that I'd been using on him for the last fifty years.

"Anyway, Diva is one of seven birds we have here at the Tower…"

"Save it for the tourists, Trevelyan. I couldn't care less," I said. "Show me where the Jewels are kept."

"I can't rush Diva, Cornwall," continued Trevelyan. She needs half an hour out of the cage at lunch time. Like I said, she's a bit of a diva."

We'll never know if Diva was about to have a strop or not because at that moment my own bird, Majestic Death, the golden eagle I'd raised from a fledgling, closed in from downwind at around 180mph. For a microsecond, a huge, sweeping shadow cast us into shade and in the same instant Diva was dead, ripped from Trevelyan's arm and carried up onto the battlements in the eagle's vicious talons. Majestic Death pulled Diva's head off and started to eat it.

A few tourists, milling around the green, began to shout and point in dismay. A little girl started to sob.

"Christ! Cornwall! That's one of the Tower's ravens!" Trevelyan was beside himself. "You can't bring Majestic Death here!"

"I had to. She's giving Baxter hell at home. She needs exercise."

"Get her back in her cage, right now," he demanded. "You're supposed to be in charge here! It's your job to protect the bloody things."

"Make her come down!"

"She won't come down unless I can tempt her. Lend me another raven."

"No!"

"Just one, otherwise we'll never get her back." The crowd of tourists were agitated by what they were witnessing, and I could see Trevelyan feared an incident. "Give me the one you like the least," I said.

Trevelyan grumbled a bit more and then reached into a cage and pulled out another bird, a scrawny little bugger with a gammy eye.

"Be careful with him," he warned.

He handed me the raven and I held it high in the air and made the eagle call I'd perfected years ago, "arrkkkkkskkkksksksks."

Majestic Death spat out the remnants of Diva and launched herself off the battlements to swoop down towards us. Several of the crowd dived on the lawns as she buzzed them, and she raked a fat American tourist's bald head when he wasn't quick enough to the ground. I steeled myself as she closed in on me, her fearsome wings spread wide. Reflexively, my arsehole clenched, anticipating her impact… and at the last second, I pulled the proffered raven away, keeping my arm aloft, as a perch for Majestic Death to land on. "Good girl," I said as she settled her talons onto my forearm. "Now get the raven back in her cage."

But as I handed it back to Trevelyan, Madge, quick as a flash, lunged forward and crushed the raven's head with her beak. The smaller bird fluttered briefly and then toppled onto the grass. The little girl began to cry again.

"Nooooo!" screamed Trevelyan, forgetting his Scots.

"Bad girl!" I wagged a finger in Madge's face for emphasis and finished off with a deeper, louder, "NAUGHTY!"

Clearly, she didn't care for my tone. In her early years, I'd taken pains to maintain absolute authority so she knew who was boss, but now she was a cantankerous old bird and wouldn't tolerate being talked to like that. She adjusted herself on my gloved hand, reached out one leg and casually raked her razor-sharp talons down the length of my face. I knew it was bad immediately and I reeled back. The eagle sprung from my arm and lifted into the air, wheeling away. "Dammit, bird!" I shouted, overcome by the knife-like pains that had bent me double. I raised my left hand to cover the wound, but it was clear to me that she'd lanced my eyeball.

The little girl was now vomiting into the moat.

"She's blinded me!" I cried, trying to stem the flow of blood from my right socket. "Jeesus, Madge what have you done?"

"Och, she's caught you a good 'un there," Trevelyan said, "You okay?"

"Not really, no. I have an unbearable burning sensation in my lacerated eye. I'm blind, losing blood and need urgent medical help."

HARLEY STREET, LONDON. ONE HOUR LATER.

"You're lucky she missed your pupil," Von Hoffenhaus said. "You'll recover your sight, but you need ze eye to heal for a few veeks before using it. Vith rest, it'll be fine."

I let out a sigh of relief. "I hope I'll still have an eye for the ladies," I quipped.

"Vell, it depends…"

"That was a joke, doc. Pick up the pace." I was feeling bullish after this good news. "So, you're saying, rest up and just use the other one for a few weeks."

"Somsing like zat."

"How do you propose I do that, though? My right eye is a stubborn bugger and always wants to get involved with what the other one is doing."

"I suggest an eyepatch."

"An eyepatch?" I turned this over in my mind for a moment. Could I bring it off? Did I have the dash and elan for an eyepatch? Well, that wasn't even a real question. "Yeah, that'll suit me just fine."

Von Hoffenhaus bade me farewell. I stepped out of the surgery into the chill London air with only one thing on my mind – Purdey's. I flagged down a taxi. If I was to wear an eyepatch, I'd make sure I'd have a damn fine one. Nothing ostentatious or vulgar, something tasteful, maybe silk-lined, perhaps in pangolin skin or tiger fur.

A black cab pulled up to the side of the kerb.

"Purdey's, please." I said, opening the taxi door. And whether it was because my mind was pre-occupied or because of my blind right-side, I didn't see the lithe, hooded figure slip from the shadow of the building behind me and follow me into the back of the cab.

"Hello Victor," Sayonara Fang said, pressing a thin blade against my throat as I tried to sit down. She slammed the door shut and the taxi pulled away.

"*Sakura*," I whispered, "has death finally come to take me?"

"No, you fool. I've come to help you. But don't make any sudden movements. We need to talk."

My mind now turned to the last time we met. A furious sexual encounter in Maljeria where I abstained from the security of protection and ploughed her lady soil with my man seed.

"Dear Lord, I'm not a father, am I? Tell me it's not so! Sayonara, have I sired a child?"

Fang's blade softened on my skin for a moment, and I detected a minor chord of sadness in her. "No," she said, and then the pressure of the blade came back. "It's about Hansclapp. I know his plan. We need to talk in private."

"I see," I said. "Driver, forget Purdey's. Cornwall Terrace, Regents Park, please."

Fang was on edge. She checked every inch of my flat for surveillance devices, then drew the curtains and put the lights on low. I fixed us both a stiff drink while she carried out her sweep.

"Hendricks is working with Hansclapp," she said.

"We know," I replied. "Lunk figured out that the game was a re-run of the Spassky-Fischer match. Arrogant bastards. Hendricks quit the Club and is now a Beefeater at the Tower of London. Trevelyan is there keeping an eye on him."

"Your friend with the rubber lips?"

"Those lips aren't rubb—"

"He's in danger."

"Relax," I said, "Trevelyan sniffs danger like a dog sniffs its own faeces."

"No, Victor," she insisted. "He's in real danger."

"Listen Fang,' I said, "He may look like an idiot, and for the most part, be an idiot. But make no mistake, behind the brutish brow and Neanderthal gap between the eyes, lies a machine that has evolved to defend itself." Unexpectedly, I found myself stepping out to bat for Trevelyan's team. "Yes," I continued, "his final school report described him as feeble-minded. Yes, he's nearly got me killed more times than I care to remember. Yes, he's an infuriating son-of-a-bitch! But..." somehow Fang's comment had got under my skin and I was getting pretty worked up, "...in a dust-up between him and Hendricks, there's only going to be one winner."

Fang took a sip of her scotch. I continued to make my argument. "Aside from that, working with the ravens seems to give him solace. I've never seen a man happier in a Jacobean ruff. He's due a break after all he's been through."

Fang's eyes narrowed. "He's your friend and you're worried about him," she said.

Her comment disarmed me. I stuttered for a moment. "I don't have many people in my life, Fang, but Trevelyan has been a constant throughout."

I paused, as I suddenly found I had something in my eye. I went to the window to regroup. "What's happening here, Fang? Why are you helping me?" Fang drained her glass and handed it back to me, demanding a refill. "We better have another drink," she said.

We made love for the next seventy-two hours, only stopping for the odd comfort break or sachet of electrolyte salts. As we lay on my Egyptian cotton sheets on the third morning, I lit us a pair of *Dirty Weekends*, a savoury blend of Indonesian fine shag, and Afghan indica, that the Scoundrels tobacconist had whipped up for erotic marathons.

Fang told me everything. For years, she'd been addicted to Bosphorous Phosphorus and under its influence, was used by Hansclapp to carry out his bidding. She was clean now and had broken free from his iron grip.

"Tell me everything you know. What's he going to do next?" I asked.

"He's tasked me with stealing the Crown Jewels. That's why Hendricks is working at the Tower. It can only be done as an inside job."

"Why does Hansclapp want the Crown Jewels?"

Fang shrugged, "I don't know."

I rolled out of bed and got dressed.

The following day, I relayed everything I'd found out to Trevelyan, placing him on high alert at the Tower. If we were going to foil the forthcoming heist and catch Hansclapp and Hendricks in the act, then I had some more preparation to do.

Summerville suggested I find accommodation nearer the Tower, so Maurice kindly lent me his mews house by the Globe Theatre on the banks of the Thames. It was only a quarter mile away, but on the other side of the river. To cut my travelling time I bought a charming little motorboat that was moored at the pier outside the property and, with practice, I could do the whole journey in less than three minutes. Trevelyan wasn't impressed. Whenever I turned up, he seemed as if his nose was out of joint. And I'm talking metaphorically as well as physically. He was annoyed that I was living a fancy-free lifestyle, while he was spending his days cleaning up bird mess, admonishing the tourists for spitting on the grass and unblocking the Tower's ancient plumbing system. He'd stand in front of the raven cages defensively and would scan the skies looking for Majestic Death who would fly above my boat.

When Majestic Death did for a couple more ravens, he thrust a pager into my hand and told me in no uncertain terms to bugger off and stay buggered off, until he buzzed me for back-up. Apparently, there'd been calls between Buckingham Palace and the Fortress Guard, calling for him to be fired. And as there were only three ravens left – the lowest number since records began – he was statistically the worst Raven Master in history. I took pity on him and stayed away.

I asked Fang if she would like to move into the mews house with me. To my surprise and delight, she said yes.

This was a golden period. Weeks passed and I came the closest, since dating Fuffy, to being in a real relationship. It was a glimpse of a world that could have been, or still could be. We were like a couple of giddy teenagers. We went to the cinema together and held hands. We went to galleries and museums, chatting for hours and hours. And, for the first time, we talked about a potential future together. Fang would give up being an international assassin and become a conceptual artist and singer/ songwriter. I would grow a beard, leave Scoundrels and become a performance poet and jazz drummer. I felt myself changing in ways I would never have expected. I learnt to cook just so I could cook for her, I read more, just so I could tell her what I'd been reading. I noticed the world more, became more open and accepting of others. I'd even stopped swearing at the buskers who got in my way as I walked down the South Bank. Fang truly brought out the best in me. Sometimes in the evenings I'd pose for her nude while she sculpted me out of bits and bobs around the cottage – some pipe cleaners, a tangerine, a Cumberland sausage.

Life was good. We'd dine at the Savoy during the day, and retire to Heavy Betsy's for the evening, where we'd often make space for a few extra girls to spice up the party. Sometimes she'd let me watch. Sometimes she'd let me join in. Sometimes we'd all roll back to Maurice's and do unspeakably filthy things to each other on his soft furnishings.

Then one night, after about four months of bliss, it all came to an end.

Trevelyan paged me around one in the morning with a hasty message:

NOW.

A violent storm raged over London that night. I'd already unhooked the rope and dropped down into my boat, when Fang appeared on the jetty above me. "Go back inside!" I yelled, the rain streaking down my weather-beaten face. "I have to go."

Sheet lightning split open the black sky once again, followed by the crack of thunder. "I'm coming!" Fang declared.

"Please!" I shouted, "stay! This won't take long."

I knew she'd protest. Fang took orders from nobody, so I didn't wait for her reply. I spun the wheel and pushed the throttle forward, turning the boat on a sixpence. Looking back at the slight figure standing alone, long black hair billowing in the wind, a compulsion rose within me that I couldn't hold back. "Marry me, Sayonara Fang!" I shouted.

She raised a hand and called out, but another boom of thunder drowned out her response. I had not time to go back. As the prow of the boat rose out of the water, Majestic Death was already in the air above me. The boat's twin turbo engines made short work of the stretch of river to the Tower. I'd practiced this many times and shaved vital seconds off the journey, but I always knew I had a final timesaving manoeuvre reserved for when it really mattered. Rather than moor at the jetty, I shot past it, cranking the wheel hard left, aiming the craft at the Thames Wall. The boat ramped up the steps at the water's edge and crashed through the metal barriers at Tower Wharf. Above me, Majestic Death screeched and climbed higher into the sky. "Yes, go girl, fly!" I cried.

Another boom of thunder ruptured the night. The boat burst into flames as I leapt onto *terra firma* and sprinted towards the Water Gate. Looking up I saw Majestic Death was not circling in the holding pattern I'd taught her. We'd been building up to this moment for weeks, and I'd made it abundantly clear that her job was to identify potential threats to my life. Instead, she'd gone straight to Trevelyan's bird cages. "No! Madge! Not them!" I yelled after her. As she disappeared over the Tower Wall, I could hear the screech of the terrified ravens.

I reached the Water Gate and slotted the iron key I'd got from Trevelyan into the ancient wooden door. I was now inside the Outer Ward. Racing forward again, I selected another key which got me into the Inner Ward. Here I found the first sign of trouble. Two dead Beefeaters lay on the ground. High treason was underway.

I ran across the lawn to the Jewel House. The ravens continued to screech their distress, and no wonder. I saw that Majestic Death had picked their lock with her beak and was inside their cage, slaughtering them. A pang of loss knotted in my stomach, not for the ravens, but for the realisation that my beloved bird, so reliable in the past, couldn't be relied upon anymore.

Leaving the ravens to their fate, I arrived at the Jewel House. A flare burned on the steps outside. I stepped quietly inside.

Something was afoot. The sound of cutting equipment echoed up the stairwell. I raced down the spiral staircase and came across another door, leading to the Jewel Room. This was it. My blood was up. I was spoiling for this fight. Hendricks had damn near killed me in the desert, got me blackballed from the Club and had caused me a huge pain in the arse – literally. It was time to put an end to him and save Britannia in the process.

Silently I cocked my snub-nosed pistol with one hand while turning the door handle with the other. With the element of surprise, I stepped one pace back, then kicked the door open. "Caught you, you son-of-a-bitch!" I screamed. And then I saw it.

What I then witnessed was something no training could have ever prepared me for. It is burned into my memory. It will forever be, no matter how much hypnotherapy I undergo, one of the most horrific things I've ever seen.

I think I'll let you take over from here, Trevelyan, as you have some explaining to do. You know exactly what I mean.

Yours sincerely,
Major Victor Montgomery Cornwall.

Nimbu Towers
Pullen-under-Lyme
Gloucestershire
July 19th 2021

Dear Major,

Very good. I can see you want to wring every last drop of *bathos* from my perfectly reasonable response to the cards I was dealt.

With a bit of a run-up, I can put this whole thing into context and explain exactly why you found me in that compromising position.

CHAPTER 18
A MASTER OF DISGUISE

THE TOWER OF LONDON, DECEMBER 1985

My reputation at Scoundrels Club had always been that of consummate operator. Chaps knew you could chuck me into any situation, and I'd come up with the goods. I was the human equivalent of a Swiss Army knife, but instead of corkscrew, pliers and thing for taking stones out of horses' hooves, my tradecraft included hand-to-hand combat, lock-picking, bomb-making, seduction, codebreaking, surveillance, anti-surveillance, withstanding torture, torture, bushcraft, sniping, whispering campaigns, Argentinian tango and very accurate semaphore including the type where you use table tennis bats instead of flags. And if you asked me where I excelled most, I'd simply shrug and say, bashfully, that I excelled most at everything.

But if you really forced me to pick my greatest talent, I'd hold my hands up and admit that my greatest ability is as a master of disguise.

This term is horribly overused by pretenders like Victor Cornwall, whose imagination only extends as far as a glued-on moustache and a funny hat. But I'm the real deal. I spent a month as a Greek Orthodox nun on the island of Crete, watching for Soviet submarines from a ruined clocktower. I did three weeks as a terracotta warrior statue, standing stock still in the British Museum, waiting for a traitor to emerge. I've even masqueraded as an East-German photocopier behind enemy lines in Berlin. I'm a changeling, a chameleon, a man of a thousand faces. I can become a country parson, or a rock star, or the manager of Luton Town during the difficult January transfer market – and that one was without even knowing how many players you need in a soccer team, or any of the positions.

So, when Summerville pinged me to become the Raven Master at the Tower, I shrugged and said sure, if that's what you need me to do, I'll do it. And what's more, I'll enjoy it. And what's more, I'll be brilliant at it, because that's me all over. I know when to hold 'em, and when to fold 'em. I roll with the punches and I gather ye rosebuds while I may.

I thought I'd have to jostle with Cornwall for the role, but it turns out he wasn't up for it anyway. He can't really play anyone but himself. But he was content, as so often, to be my wingman, a back-up, in a supporting role. He was fine with this because he has plenty of other strengths, like...

> NOTE: Cornwall, I've ground to a halt here. Can you fill in a few things you are not bad at please, as nothing much springs to mind.

However, when I accepted the undertaking, I had no idea that this role would be my most challenging yet, nor that it would end in near-disaster. For at the Tower, I wasn't required to don a mere disguise, or even a disguise within a disguise. It was a disguise within a disguise that disguised something else entirely. Like a Russian doll – but where the bigger outer dolls don't just disguise a smaller doll, but something else that isn't a doll at all.

I arrived at the Office of the Yeoman Warders of Her Majesty's Royal Palace and Fortress the Tower of London at six o'clock in the morning, sweating like a pig that had just run an uphill marathon at high altitude on a tropical course.

I was kitted out in the complex Beefeater uniform, which consists of a knee-length woollen scarlet tunic in the Tudor style, scarlet knee breeches and thick stockings also in the Tudor style, with a Victorian tabard and outsized Tudor bonnet. It was a heavily embroidered get-up that, including belt and boots, weighed somewhere around 50lbs. I'd also been issued a light chainmail undervest, a must-have for those early months when the ravens might attack their new master without warning. This added another 18lbs. In addition to this, my duties with the birds required me to secrete another 5lbs of meat scraps about my person, to keep the seven ravens happy at all times. Then there was my cosh, 3lbs, and a seven-foot-long ceremonial pikestaff, weighing in at 6lbs. In all, I'd be lugging over 80lbs of kit and uniform as I paraded around the Tower, for twelve hours a day, as well as spending another three hours tending to the ravens after hours.

And that was my first level of disguise.

The second level was my actual physical identity, for which I needed to lean heavily on all my theatrical training. I couldn't work in the Tower as Arthur St. John Trevelyan, as it would have been a red flag to Hendricks, so each morning I would rise early and spend an hour with my latex mask, glue gun and make-up box, transforming myself into Parade Sergeant Falstaff MacDairmid of the Black Watch.

I'd workshopped *MacDairmid* at the Club's private theatre in Drury Lane, improvising long into the night with Maurice and Ruff Puff, starting on a blacked-out stage with one stark spotlight and adding detail only when it felt truly authentic. Only when I'd *done the work*. Gradually, MacDairmid took shape for me. For all of us. With his bulbous nose, portly frame and thick Glaswegian accent, he was a character I could now throw on like a cloak, a hard-drinking old warhorse who had served with distinction in France, Malay and Korea and also been involved in a few special operations that he didn't like to talk about. He'd got the job as a Beefeater, so rumour had it, after saving his colonel from assassination in Kuala Lumpur with a deft swipe of his claymore blade (3lbs), which nowadays he carried under his tunic. MacDairmid loved whisky, The Tower, tourists, being a Beefeater, whisky, ravens and whisky. He was never happier than when cooking up his white-hot chicken and whisky takari in the Tower kitchens. MacDairmid's dislikes were litter, gout, traitors to the Crown and large predatory birds.

But playing him was an epic challenge, especially in such a public arena. The latex facemask, full red beard, heavy gold sovereign rings, thick woollen kilt, sporran, tam o'shanter, deflated bagpipes and the bulky stomach-enhancing padding I needed to portray a man with liver disease added an extra 40lbs on top of the 80lbs I was already lugging..

Sgt Major Griff Bones, the Chief Yeoman Warder, took me down to Tower Green, where Anne Boleyn was executed in 1536, and bid me step inside the raven cage. He warned me to expect a proper initiation from the birds.

The ravens were silent as I stepped inside. All of a sudden, Diva, the grandmother of the group, swooped from her perch to land on my shoulder, where she bit off the bottom of my earlobe, and screeched as the blood flowed down my tunic. I ignored the blood, reached under my hat and pulled out a rotten weasel head for her. She stabbed it through the eye and fluttered back to her perch with her prize, sucking out the brain juice while keeping her bright eyes upon me.

Next, a huge raven came squawking at me, slapping me with his black wings. This was Keble, a right bruiser. He drilled his beak into my forehead several times, more woodpecker than raven. I pulled from my pocket a pot of chilled mouse ragu. Keble stopped drilling and slurped the ragu down, nodding his sleek head in appreciation. Turns out these were exactly the right moves. Show no pain. Give out fancy treats. Initiation passed. From that first morning the seven ravens loved me.

I got to know their personalities. As well as Diva, and the hard man, Keble, there was Tootsie – silly, flighty and cute as a button, and in stark contrast to the stern and unknowable Lady Josie, with her eyes that could turn you to stone. Then there was the daft ha'porth Charlie-Boy, the greedy, skew-eyed Dibble, who was always getting into hilarious scrapes and adventures in his endless quest for food. Finally, there was the rock-n-roll bad boy, Lord Lucan, whose unruly mess of black neck feathers made him look as if he were wearing a leather motorcycling jacket with the collar turned up.

My first week with the birds was a real education. I began to decipher the clicks and squeaks the birds made to each other, and some of the surprisingly courtly body language. Charlie-Boy, for instance, always forgot to defer to Diva at feeding time, but he'd suddenly remember his rank and make an Ek-a-ek-a-ek-a noise at her, hopping backwards so she could have the first helping of mashed squirrel guts with fox leg marmalade, as if saying 'sorry ma'am, sorry ma'am, sorry ma'am.' Then Dibble would steal a ribbon he fancied from Tootsie's stoop, and she'd make an indignant screech, 'Yaaahhh-kkkkaaarr' exactly as if she were a teenage girl whose little brother had hidden her hairdryer.

I loved them all, but there was a special place in my heart for Diva, who reminded me of my own dear ma. Her glossy wings and air of quiet dignity made her a huge hit with the crowds of tourists who thronged the Tower. Diva was a real matriarch, a queen, if you will.

Which is why, when Cornwall's malevolent eagle bit her head off and carried her corpse off to the top of the White Tower, it cut me to the quick. And I had some explaining to do to the Chief.

And when Dibble was murdered by the same eagle a few moments later, that explanation became twice as hard.

Sgt Major Bones gave me the sort of bollocking I'd not been in receipt of since I ran aground the *Hercules* cargo ship in 1961, by throwing the captain into the sea during a wrestling bout. "I don't know who the hell you really are, MacDairmid, but I do know nobody walks into the Raven Master's job like you did," he barked in my face, "so I know you're about something. But if any more of the birds get caught in your crossfire, I will tear your arsehole a new arsehole." And if he ever saw, Bones screamed, "that wanker with the ice cream," whom he suspected of being the eagle's owner, he'd "throttle him with his bare hands."

I apologised.

I promised it wouldn't happen again.

It did happen again.

The trouble was that Cornwall was bored. He was restless and fidgety and couldn't really get used to the idea that there was nothing for him to do but hurry up and wait. Waiting was never his strong suit. I had to contend with ever more disruptive visits that put me right off my duties. He'd insist on 'checking in' twice daily, sitting for hours alone on a bench until Hendricks had gone off duty, and it was time to buy another ticket and another ice cream, and sidle up to me for a progress report. The other Warders thought he was a sex pest with a predilection for big fellows in Tudor clothing, which is more common than you'd think. They wanted to sling him in a cell for a hard forty-eight, but I couldn't have that as Hendricks would have clocked him.

Then Cornwall became obsessed with how long it would take him to get to the Tower once the jewel heist was underway. He moved to a cottage across the river and bought a ridiculous red powerboat which he'd run up the Thames on full throttle, skidding dangerously around the busy river, timing himself with a stopwatch. Things came to a head when the wake from his craft washed several French schoolchildren into the Thames, and the lifeboat had to be called out.

Our undertaking was beginning to attract the sort of attention that jeopardised everything. Summerville stopped by to see me one evening about it. She'd had an unamused call from a contact at the M.O.D.

"What the hell's the matter with him?" she fumed. "Why the hell has be bought a powerboat? How is that 'undercover'?"

"That's the least of it," I mused. "He's threatening to get hold of a mini-sub so he can lie in wait at Traitor's Gate."

"Right," she shouted, "that's it. He's off the case. Maurice will stand in."

"No, no," I counselled. "It's true he is no good at being second fiddle, but I need him in my corner when the time comes."

Summerville assented, and threw her ice cream at a pigeon that waddled along the lawn. The pigeons were a rarity these days at the Tower, as Cornwall's eagle had scared them all away.

So I bought Cornwall a pager, and told him to stay away from the Tower, and that I'd contact him when I needed him. After a tricky first fortnight, things settled down and I concentrated on keeping the remaining two ravens safe.

Two ravens? Yes. Sadly, Majestic Death had torn Keble's beak off and used it to run Tootsie through, a bloody spectacle which occurred during a state visit by the Namibian PM. Three days later the frozen remains of Lady Josie were found on the roof of Wakefield Tower, with puncture marks to her breast. The Tower vet's post-mortem suggested that she'd been carried into the low troposphere by a predator, and once she'd frozen to death, simply discarded to fall back to earth.

THE TOWER OF LONDON, APRIL 1986

I had been in post for just over four months. Spring had sprung and five new raven juveniles – Spiky, Juno, Heston, Handsome Dan and Glynnis, were beginning to venture out onto the verdant lawns. For the first time in the Tower's history, Beefeaters had been issued with shotguns in case of eagle attack. It was deemed necessary after the Press had reported that England was threatened by a mysterious marauding bird that was murdering the ravens. Who was behind it? Was it sent by the Russians? The Chinese? Was it, perhaps, a bald eagle that flew from the US Embassy, a reminder of the 'special relationship'? All this conjecture only increased the pressure on me to foil the coming raid. If the Crown Jewels were nabbed now, it would be a PR disaster for Great Britain in the eyes of the rest of the world.

Even though I was disguised as MacDairmid, I'd taken care to stay well away from the other new boy, Hendricks, which was easy. He had developed a reputation as a rum cove. He drank alone in the Tower's private pub – the Keys – as soon as he came off duty, sinking pint after pint, whisky after whisky, remaining sullen during all attempts at communication by the lads. The Beefeaters are a boozy, sociable lot, and the atmosphere would improve after Hendricks staggered off to his quarters. Of course, I knew this was part of Hendricks' plan. It was easier for him to be alone in parts of the Tower – the Jewel Room, say. But perhaps there was something honest in his dour, gloomy disposition? I'd look over at him brooding and wonder if the deal he'd done with Hansclapp weighed heavily on him. As heavy as a crown.

It was a Friday night. We'd done the Locking Up ceremony, and the Tower was ours for the night. It was a remarkable place to be after all the tourists had gone. The lads were on the lash as usual in the Keys, six rounds down and singing the regimental songs. Hendricks, the misery guts, drank up and retired alone. When he'd gone, I excused myself for a wee – and to tail him from a safe distance.

"May ye never die a Beefeater!" I shouted to the lads from the door, as tradition dictated, tipping my massive Tudor hat to them.

I followed Hendricks as he negotiated the flagstones. He had a drunken stagger on him that I'd seen many a time at that other exclusive London club we knew so well; but as he rounded the east corner of the Tower, he straightened up, cricked his neck and quickened into a jog, all business.

I followed on, trying to close the gap. I wished I'd been able to get out of my cumbersome uniform earlier, but little Heston had a nasty head cold and I'd stayed to feed him the liquidized rat toddy he loved, and from there I'd gone straight to the Keys.

Hendricks was now moving fast across the lawns in front of the White Tower, in the direction of the Jewel House, and getting further away from me, so I decided to take a chance. I called out in my thick Glaswegian accent. "Ye a'richt thare, sur?"

I heard him curse faintly and stop dead. Silhouetted on the grass, he turned back to me, and gave a nod. I got closer. "Thought I heard something," he declared, "up here. The sound of breaking glass. Care to take a look with me, Yeoman?"

Classic Scoundrels move. Hendricks was springing a False Tonk on me: if surprised in the middle of a show, pretend there is an urgent problem, ask for help, join forces, and then bean him while he's helping to solve it.

"Aye, m'laddie, lead on t'whither ye heard tha' noise." At least that would put him in front of me where I could keep an eye on him.

We moved past the site of the Executioner's Block, over College Green towards the Gaoler's House, which was built into the massive inner wall. We stopped in the thick shadow that a forty-foot stone wall provides.

"What's that?" Hendricks crept a few paces ahead, dodging the vintner's barrels and low hedgerow. I followed him. A thick mountaineer's rope hung down the wall, with a few feet of spare at the bottom. Hendricks crept forward to investigate. There was the sense of swift movement behind me as a catlike figure flashed past my periphery. I turned in a reflex and caught a hard strike on the side of the head. It wasn't enough to knock me out, but I decided to slump down to the ground, as if unconscious. This was a hell of a risk, but one I thought it best to take. If they were in the business of slitting throats this evening, I'd have only to get my hand to my neck quick enough and I'd probably pull through. For now, I lay, immobilised, listening.

"Hendricks, dahling." Mwah. Mwah. A double air kiss. Her voice. Quintessentially British, with the East German poking through.

"Who's this old duffer?" said Marjorie, prodding me with her foot.

"Someone, in his day, I gather," said Hendricks, "but nobody to worry about. Look at the state of him."

"Shall I...?" I heard the metallic ring of a blade.

I could almost hear Hendricks thinking about it.

"Unnecessary," he said. "Let's go."

The noise of light steps, fast, off over the lawns again.

I rolled over and opened an eye, confirming my suspicions that they were heading for The Jewel House. I reached into my jerkin and pulled out the pager. I typed one word to Cornwall and sent the message:

NOW.

I picked myself up and followed on.

In the courtyard of the Jewel House, Edward Talbot, the Jewel Keeper, lay dying. His once merry eyes were glassing over, his neck slashed. I gave him a rueful nod and stepped over him, not having even a second to make him more comfortable. I had to stop the heinous crime taking place. It's what he would have wanted.

I rummaged in my uniform for a flare, lit it, and stuck it in the ground as a sign for Cornwall. I slipped through the studded Jewel House door and descended two flights of stairs to the underground stronghold which housed the Crown treasures. My heart was pumping madly, hammering in my chest like a Fusilier's drum. These next few minutes would count for everything.

The outer chamber was shrouded in darkness, but I quickly navigated past the glass cases containing the lesser treasures: the coronation robes, golden maces, brass bugles and swords of state. I knew exactly where I was heading, and as I got close to the end of the room, I could see that the massive steel vault doors that housed all the good jewellery were sprung wide open. But there was a surprise for me. I came upon a further body, that of Sergeant Bones.

He lay sprawled on the flagstones. Clearly, he had been surprised by Hendricks and Marjorie at an inopportune moment. He had jammed himself into the white satin dress that Queen Victoria wore in the coach to her Coronation in 1838, although his broad, hairy chest was far too wide to do it justice as he didn't have Victoria's décolletage. Sgt Bones was also wearing the pearl earrings that Victoria received from Prince Albert in 1847 and the Strawberry Leaf Tiara that she later gave to Princess Beatrice, although this wasn't displayed at its best either, perched on a bald head that had been smashed open, oozing blood and grey matter. I took a second to tuck the poor soul back in, saving the last vestiges of his dignity.

I could hear them ahead of me, inside the steel doors of the vault.

Perhaps I could slam the doors shut, trapping the thieves inside? I discounted this right away. The doors were twenty tonnes each. I could no more slam them quickly than I could decapitate a traitor with a triangle of brie. No, I would have to take Hendricks and Marjorie out another way, or at least delay until Cornwall got here to even up the numbers.

They were hard at work, cutting a circle into the armoured glass in front of the priceless symbols of the right to rule in Britain: St Edward's Crown, the Sovereign's Orb, The Imperial State Crown.

They were working quickly, Hendricks was taping the glass up, and Marjorie was grinding through it with the diamond blade. Her lithe, crouching, catsuit-clad figure took me aback. My wife.

This woman was, after everything, still my wife. Her glossy black hair was held back by a tight-fitting Alice band. My breath caught in my throat. With a rush of emotion, I knew that even after all she'd done: drugged me into marriage, taken my ancestral home, sent me to prison, I'd still have taken her back in a heartbeat, even if I would have hated myself for the rest of my life. She was still very, very, very, very attractive and really had a hold over me. But what to do? This woman, this astonishing beauty, was stealing the very symbols of Britain and in doing so, she was making all Britain a cuckold. The jewels that made Britain great were being snaffled away – for the benefit of herself and her despicable brother – to be locked in some private tower of theirs, rather than the much more reasonably priced and publicly accessible Tower they were in currently.

And when I saw, in the reflection of the glass she was destroying, the intense focus on her merciless face, her allure was stronger than ever. I had a moment of clarity. I realised that the only thing holding me back, was inside my own mind. Now I understood: to defeat Marjorie I had to banish the enchantment of her fiercely potent sexual allure.

Somehow, I had to perform an exorcism on myself, to expunge every last trace of the strange power she had over me. Damn you to hell, Marjorie! I thought, as I realised there was only one way I could break her spell forever.

A sense of calm descended over me as I moved to a corner and began to disrobe, ripping off my outer disguise, the Beefeater garb, knowing I'd never need it again. Off came the Victorian tabard, the Tudor tunic, breeches, stockings and bonnet, peeled away like the outer layers of an onion. Soon I was down to my inner disguise, the full highland military uniform of MacDairmid. That came off too. The kilt, sporran, tam o'shanter and the deflated bagpipes. I pulled away the excess stomach padding and dropped it, the belt and skean'dhu knife on to the discarded pile. In a final flourish, I tore off my latex mask.

I was Arthur St. John Trevelyan again.

Rolling my shoulders and cricking my neck, I felt free. For the first time in four months I could move unfettered. I was down to a pair of white cotton Y-fronts. I was shoeless, hatless, beardless – and entirely myself. Or so I thought.

But then, with a terrible clarity, I realised that wasn't true. Shedding my outer layers of disguise wasn't enough. I also needed to be free of the final layer: the disguise *inside my mind*. From the first time I had ever laid eyes on my Stasi bride, she had possessed my soul and my loins, holding me fast in her sexual tractor beam. For all these years, despite every terrible thing she'd ever done, I'd been trapped in a deep-rooted deception of the self. Even seeing her now, with stakes as high as they were, my monkey brain had taken control, and all I could think about was making love to her. It was clouding my judgement, making me weak at the very time I needed to be strong.

There was only one way to regain control of myself.

I had to have a wank.

I whipped off the Y-fronts and felt the breeze on my own bell tower. Less than forty feet away my ex-wife was stealing the Crown Jewels and I was helpless, at least until I could expend the desire I still had for her.

I took myself in hand and dived headfirst into my own sex vault, to summon an erotic collage of all of my greatest escapades with Marjorie. It may sound base to the reader, but I knew without a shadow of a doubt that this was the right move. How else could I be sure that my mind would be free, and able to focus on bringing this woman to justice? Images of Marjorie kaleidoscoped through my head, faster and faster. Her glistening abdomen as she emerged from my swimming pool in a leopard skin bikini; her full lips wrapping themselves around a plump cherry; dancing to her favourite song, Grace Jones' filthy disco masterpiece *Pull Up To The Bumper;* the turn of her head in the forests of Nimbu, as she throttled a squirrel that had got too close; the savage way she would tongue out the flesh from a soft-boiled egg.

Within a quarter of a second I was fully tumescent. And as soon as I had a lob-on I began hammering away like a cobbler buffing a new pair of brogues. This couldn't be a leisurely Sunday afternoon hand-job, but a furious, high-octane race to the chequered flag.

Time was of the essence, so I commenced phase two – a full ten minutes before I normally would. I began to lightly finger my ballsack with the nimbleness of a banjo-playing hillbilly. But there was a problem. The cold room had triggered genital preservation mode, rendering my scrotum about as sensitive as the husk on a winter coconut. My mighty oak had become a dead slug in my hand. I needed to warm it up. I dropped to a crouch and bent forward as much as my spine would allow, panting out warm breath towards my groin. Nothing. With a quick calculation, I concluded that I needed to raise the micro-climate around my ballbag to sixty-eight degrees – about the same temperature I keep red wine. It would require a rapid succession of breaths. I began controlled panting in a compound triple meter, and soon felt lightheaded, but it was beginning to work. The sordid slideshow in my mind had gone into overdrive, image replacing image replacing image. A rictus grin creased my face and I was drooling from my bottom lip as I hammered away.

I was close.

The world around me disappeared and I drifted, floating around in my own magical mystery wank-o-sphere. I slumped onto my side ever closer to my goal. As I began the final lap, I conjured up my favourite ever image of Marjorie, the one that never failed to get me over the line: her perfect breasts squashing down on the photocopier glass in the Stasi office, the first time I ever saw her. I was nearly there! So close! Keep smashing away, Trevelyan! Get there!

And…

And…

And…

Victor Cornwall leapt into the room. "Caught you, you son of a bitch!" he said.

From the vault, Marjorie's head turned in horror. Hendricks' head turned in horror. My head turned in horror. Cornwall looked at me in horror. It was horrible. It was also too late to divert. I lay there naked, pumping my memories of Marjorie all over the flagstones.

"For God's sake, man! Now is not the time!" he cried.

To his credit, he wasn't that fussed when I began to stammer out a convoluted explanation of my thinking. He simply shrugged, grabbed a medieval mace from the wall and passed it to me.

Together we charged into the vault.

You can see, Major, that I am prepared to *own* this episode, and style it out. My only regret is that you found my brilliantly pragmatic solution so amusing that you obtained the CCTV footage from the vault and sent it to the Club.

And I wish even more fervently that they didn't have an annual dinner on the anniversary of our battle at the Tower, in which they apparently watch this footage, evaluating my rushed and atypical performance.

But we cannot choose all the stories about us, I suppose.

Yours sincerely,
Major Arthur St. John Trevelyan

Hellcat Manor

Great Trundleford

Devon

July 25th 2021

Dear Major,

You might be surprised to learn my reaction to that was quite unexpected. May I congratulate you on a moving and beautiful depiction of a man haunted by desire.

As an aside, I've always felt that Emily Brontë missed the mark with *Wuthering Heights.* I now see that all it needed was a scene where Heathcliff thrashes one out to expel the ghost of Catherine. Not only would it have silenced his demons, but it would have improved the ending considerably.

CHAPTER 19
LADY VENGEANCE

I stormed into the Crown Jewels vault ready to kick some arse. "Caught you, you son-of-a-bitch!" I screamed, only to be confronted with the sight of Trevelyan beaming one off like he used to on the bottom bunk of our Winstowe dorm. Unexpected as that was, it was not the only thing that confounded me. Hendricks was not alone. He was with Marjorie.

Hendricks reacted instinctively. He picked up a wrench and, using it like a tomahawk, hurled it in my direction. I dived and rolled, springing up again to fire off a couple of rounds from my pistol. Behind me, Trevelyan yelped like a man whose bell-end had been thwacked with a wrench.

Unfortunately, my rounds missed Hendricks, putting a nasty dent in a silver state trumpet. I made a mental note to pay for the damage. A standoff followed. From my position behind one of the displays, I could see Hendricks and Marjorie, but was unable to get a clean shot away without putting myself in danger. I hissed at Trevelyan, "Bloody well hurry up and get your clothes back on!" I grabbed a medieval mace and threw it in his direction. "Use this!" I shouted. Trevelyan let out another scream as the spiked weapon landed on his lap. Hendricks' shoulder became visible and I fired again. I missed again. This time my round shattered the emerald that sits within the Sovereign's sceptre. That looked valuable, so I binned the previous mental note about paying for breakages. Casting the gun aside I grabbed the closest weapon I could find – the celebrated *Curtana*, or Sword of Mercy. This had been used at the coronation of every British monarch since James II, although there would be no mercy shown today.

Abandoning my cover, I charged. This caught Hendricks by surprise and he only just dodged my sword as it carved through the air towards his head, slamming into another exhibit.

On the other side of the room Trevelyan had snuck around to tackle Marjorie. Unfortunately, his sexual endeavours seemed to have drained him of energy. As he lunged at her, she slipped aside and sent him careening into one of the glass display cases. Marjorie turned to face him. From a sheath on her back, she produced two short swords and readied herself for battle. Trevelyan picked himself up off the floor and brushed away the fragments of glass.

"Dahling, I've been wanting to kill you since the day we were married," she said.

Trevelyan nodded sagely as if he already knew so. "We made a vow, my love, or so they tell me," he said, "till death do us part."

At this, Marjorie let out a guttural scream, the kind I suspect only a marriage to Trevelyan can provoke, and she attacked. Her twin blades whirled viciously through the air, feinting with one and slashing with the other. Trevelyan swung the mace in defence but from the outset it was clear he was in trouble. Marjorie was fresh and lithe, whereas he seemed laboured and clumsy, always a beat behind her. The poor sod was exhausted.

I was also in trouble. To my horror, I discovered that the Curtana was only a ceremonial weapon and bugger-all use in a real fight. Hendricks had picked up a functioning blade and was swatting away my thrusts with ease. I also had another disadvantage. This was my first fight since Majestic Death had damaged my eye and only now did I realise what a hindrance it was. Hendricks realised it too. He was using my blindside against me, feinting to my right and then attacking from my left. If his sword had been lighter and easier to manoeuvre, he might already have done for me. As it was, each strike got him a little bit closer. He was testing my field of vision, working out its boundaries. I saw that the only way I could win this was by going on the offensive, so with a blitzkrieg of aggressive strikes I forced him back past the glass cabinets and their treasures.

Now, backed up against the door, he grabbed the helmet from a suit of armour and chucked it at me, then slipped through the doorway and fled up the staircase.

I gave chase, leaping two stairs at a time to gain ground on him. I exited the Jewel House into torrential rain, just in time to see Hendricks running through the gates leading out to Tower Hill. I sprinted after him but was unable to keep him in my line of sight. This of course had been his plan all along. As I emerged through the doorway leading toward Traitors Gate a heavy blow came out of nowhere, striking me across my cheek. I was stunned. My whole world reeled, and I crashed down onto the sodden ground. A flash of lightning and a deafening thunderclap tore the night sky in two.

Hendricks stood over me. "Like the eyepatch, Cornwall," he sneered. "I'd heard your eagle had turned on you."

"I expect she'll turn on you in a minute," I said, "she's around here somewhere." Hendricks looked up to the sky for a half second which gave me the chance to scramble to my feet. He lunged at me again but telegraphed his movement just enough for me to read it. I brought my blade up to parry. The mention of Majestic Death gave me an idea. At his next attack I cried at the top of my voice, "kill, Majestic Death! Kill him!" Hendricks was panicked. He spun round and swiped at thin air with his blade. I closed in with a downward strike to his neck, but he saw me just in time, and struck the Curtana from my hand, in doing so losing his grip on his own weapon. Now we were both empty-handed. This levelled things up, or so I thought.

Hendricks reached into his back pocket and pulled out a butterfly knife.

"It's over, Cornwall," he snarled.

"No, it's over for you, Hendricks," I said, ducking as he slashed at me with the short blade. "Summerville knows you threw the game of chess. Spassky-Fischer '72."

"That was Gruber's idea," he said. The familiarity of the first name term brought bile to my throat. "It doesn't change our plan one bit."

"Your plan has failed," I goaded. "He's hung you out to dry. You're finished."

This riled him. He jabbed hard with his blade again.

I tried to block it but was fractionally too slow and his knife found a way through my defence. The blade caught me between my ribs. I knew right away I was in trouble. The wound wasn't deep, but it was a decent stab through the muscle. A sodden red patch of blood blossomed through my clothing.

I shuffled back and shrugged off my coat, wrapping it around my left forearm for padding. With no knife to hand I was at a significant disadvantage, but if I led with my left arm I might at least be able to protect myself a little. I heard my father's voice in my mind. "Victor, you can't be in a knife fight without getting cut." The trick, he would say, was to minimise the impact of your injuries. The winner was invariably the one who lost the least blood.

Hendricks slashed at me again. I raised my forearm to defend myself. The blade cut only the thick padding of my coat. We circled each other. He was still using my injured eye against me, feinting with his free hand and then going in on my blindside. He stabbed again, and this time punctured my defences, piercing the skin on my leading arm. Another cut. Blood leeched through the coat padding. I needed to act fast or I'd bleed out. Retreating, I unwound the coat from my arm, and, as I'd hoped, Hendricks charged at me with his blade outstretched. I threw the bloodied overcoat in his face and, as he swiped it away, I kicked the knife from his grasp and bulldozed into him.

We wrestled, each of us twisting and kicking, trying to find a pivot point for a throw. The grappling was stretching the wound in my ribs, and I could feel it bleeding freely. As a lightning flash illuminated the sky, I saw Trevelyan and Marjorie high on the battlements, locked in combat. Marjorie smashed him across the face with the handle of her sword, and, as he staggered backwards, he fell, disappearing from view.

My vision was blurring at the edges. With all I could muster, I drove my elbow into Hendricks' neck, and broke free from his grip, springing back to give myself space and time. But Hendricks was quick. He picked up the knife and advanced on me.

For the first time, I felt the cold realisation that I was going to lose this fight. I was going to die.

Then, a blur of movement behind him and I was flooded with relief. The tables had turned in an instant.

"You've still got time to surrender, Hendricks," I called.

He smiled and rolled his shoulders. "You've got some nerve, Cornwall, I'll grant you that, but I've waited a long time for this. I won't be denied."

"You will be denied," I said, "stupidity obviously runs in your family. You're making the same mistake your brother did. Never go into a knife fight with a Cornwall."

"Except you don't have a knife."

"No," I said, "but she does."

Sayonara Fang, my *sakura*, emerged out of the blackness, a spectre of death who had claimed so many lives. There was a brief flash of steel and a thin red line appeared at Hendricks' throat. In one fluid movement, Fang cleaned the katana on her sleeve and re-sheathed it. Hendricks realised he was dead. The red line widened as the blood began to flow.

"Goodbye, Hendricks," I said, "the Club won't miss you, and neither will I." His soul, if he had one, left him then. His arms fell to his side and he pitched forward, his body falling into the moat by Traitors' Gate.

I slumped down on the wet grass. I needed to patch myself up quickly or I'd go the same way as Hendricks. I looked up to the battlements as another flash of lightning lit up the sky, but I could see no sign of Trevelyan or Marjorie.

"Find Trevelyan," I gasped to Fang. "He needs your help."

Fang came in close and gently touched my face. She nodded and spirited away into the blackness. The rain hammered down as I began the painful process of turning my coat into a field dressing. My thoughts now turned to Hansclapp. Where was he? Was he somewhere nearby, in the shadows? Was all this merely a diversion for him to get into the Jewel House? A faint noise made me look up. Through the darkness I could see a slim figure walking towards me across the grass. Fang was coming back.

"Problem?" I called out.

"For you, yes, dear Victor," came the reply. It wasn't Fang's voice.

There was another flash of lightning and Marjorie was standing before me. Her swords were sheathed across her back and she carried a Yeoman's lance.

"My fool of a husband is finally dead," she said. The night sky lit her up again. I saw the prone body of Trevelyan lying at the foot of the Tower wall. Protecting my injured side, I struggled to stand, but I barely had the strength. It was pointless. I slumped back down and cradled my wound.

"You have me at a disadvantage, Marjorie. I'm injured and I have no weapon."

"I'll make this quick then," she said. She twirled the long spear in her hand until the business end was pointing at me. Then, like a javelin thrower she skipped a couple of paces and launched it directly at me with terrifying accuracy. It was so fast I had no time to react.

A metallic clang almost burst my eardrum as the spear was knocked off course at the last moment.

Sayonara stepped forward; her katana held high in the *Jodan No Kamae* stance.

Marjorie's eyes darted to the slight figure dressed in black, and for the first time I saw uncertainty. "You must be Lady Sayonara Fang," she said, and bowed slightly without taking her eyes from Fang's blade. "At last, we meet. An honour, please know that I hold you in high esteem."

"As you should. And now you'll find out why," Fang replied quietly.

"I don't know what he's offering you, but my brother will offer more."

"I'm not here for money, Marjorie," Fang said, "I'm here for love."

A jolt of electricity flashed through my chest. It was my charred and calcified heart skipping a beat, and for a second I thought Hendricks' blade had gone deeper than I'd realised, but no, this was no wound.

It was my *feelings*.

Her eyes locked on Marjorie, Fang spoke softly to me. "Trevelyan isn't dead, my love," she said. "But he needs you. Go to him while I cut this lady's head off."

Marjorie drew the two short swords that were sheathed across her back and dropped into a fighting stance. She looked rattled. In contrast, Fang held her katana in a loose two-handed grip and flowed back into *Sha No Kamae*, turning the sword behind her. For a few seconds, nothing happened. Fang stood calmly, as if contemplating nothing more stressful than a placid mountain stream, whereas Marjorie found the tension unbearable. She broke first, screaming out a shrill battle cry, and launched herself forward in attack. The ring of steel on steel echoed off the Tower walls.

I needed to get to Trevelyan, and when I did, I found him bloodied but alive, sprawled on the soaking grass. He looked dreadful. He was covered in cuts and abrasions, where he'd been bounced off the rough stone of the Tower's walls. His hair was matted with blood and sweat and whatever drama he'd been through was evidenced by the state of the Y-fronts which were his only remaining clothing. He opened his eyes. "Did we win?" he asked.

"We're getting there. Can you sit?"

Trevelyan eased himself up.

"Hendricks?" he said.

"Dead."

"Marjorie?"

"Fingers crossed. What about the Jewels?"

"They got the cases open, but they didn't take anything. We did it, Cornwall," he said, "we foiled the bastards."

There was a note of pride in his voice, which told me he'd be alright. "Any sign of Hansclapp?"

"No."

Majestic Death landed beside me. She was covered in raven feathers and gore. I looked apologetically to Trevelyan. He just shrugged. "Come on," I said, "this isn't over yet."

Under the stormy London sky, framed by the imposing structure of the Tower, Sayonara Fang and Marjorie Trevelyan were locked in mortal combat. To an untrained eye it may have looked like an even contest. Marjorie was a skilled fighter, and as ferocious as a tiger. She was more than a match for most people, including her husband, and myself, I expect. But Fang wasn't most people. She was death personified, and as she danced around the Stasi Captain, a blur of elegant motion, her blade, like a serpent's tongue, flicked out again and again. It was death by a thousand strikes.

We watched from the grass where Trevelyan lay, too exhausted to move. Marjorie circled around her adversary, and when she saw her husband sitting up, alive, the red mist descended. She cried out in fury and made a frenzied charge towards him.

Fang chose this moment to strike. With the poise and grace of a ninth *dan* prima ballerina, she pirouetted, bringing the katana around her head in a sweeping arc, to decapitate Marjorie with one clean blow.

Marjorie's head, like Anne Boleyn's before her, rolled across the royal turf.

Fang muttered something to herself, perhaps a prayer or an offering, then she ran to me. "How badly are you hurt?" she asked.

"Paper cuts, my love," I lied.

Fang didn't have a scratch on her. She'd dismantled Marjorie with, it seemed, almost no effort. She bent down to touch my face tenderly and we kissed. "I thought I was going to lose you," she said.

"Not this time," I replied.

To my left Trevelyan coughed up a gobbet of blood and spat it onto the grass. "Don't mind me," he said, regarding Fang suspiciously, "but I've just been kicked off the castle wall. Any chance of some assistance?"

In the pouring rain, Fang went to work on both of us, dressing our wounds using strips of fabric, torn from Hendricks' clothing. By the time she'd patched us up, I felt much brighter.

As she helped us to our feet, a thunderous crack tore through the darkness again, but this one was not from the heavens.

It was a rifle shot.

Fang lurched forward and fell into my arms knocking both of us over.

I looked into her eyes, which were wide with shock.

A trickle of blood ran from her lips.

She clutched my hand desperately but slowly her grip faded away. She was dying.

"No, no!" I screamed. "NOOOOOOO!"

She held my gaze, her lips parted and with her last breath, she said, "Yes, I will marry you, Victor Cornwall."

Then, she slipped away from me.

A figure marched through the darkness carrying the sniper rifle that had just shot Fang. It was Summerville.

"You're a lucky man, Major Cornwall," she said, "Sayonara Fang doesn't leave many men alive."

Then she looked down dismissively at the dead assassin. "That was for shooting Lunk, bitch."

I found I could say nothing, I just held Fang tightly in my arms.

A dark day indeed, Major. For the second time in my life I'd been denied the chance of love, but perhaps in the end it was for the best. Had Fang lived, the authorities would have never left her alone. Assassins don't get to have happy endings.

THE BALLAD OF SAYONARA FANG (1986)

Sleep now, my love,
And rest your tired eyes,
One day we'll be together,
At your dojo in the skies.

Over to you.

Yours sincerely,
Major Victor Montgomery Cornwall

Nimbu Towers
Pullen-under-Lyme
Gloucestershire
August 1st 2021

Dear Major,

Thank you for your thrilling account of the final act of my marriage from hell. As ever, it was packed full of the usual Cornwall narcissism. I had an epic sword fight with my *Stahlfrau,* at the Tower of London in a lightning storm (which was a lot more evenly matched than you suggest, by the way) and in your hands it was barely mentioned.

But for once that wasn't what rankled. What rankled was your account of Fang's fate. After Summerville shot her, I'll be damned if I didn't see her scrabble to her feet and disappear off into the night. Just thought I'd mention this as further evidence of your muddled mind. It's a good thing we're nearing the end of this biographical endeavour because senility is clearly knocking on your door demanding to be let in.

I'll push on, shall I? Here is:

CHAPTER 20
A PAIR OF C.A,H.N.T.S

The aftermath of all that swordplay and knifery left a bloody mess. A couple of searchlights left over from the Second World War were fired up, and soon the courtyards of the Tower were flooded in yellow sodium, and the various dismantled bodies cast long, thin shadows across the lawns. Cornwall and I were both knackered out from blood loss and battle fatigue. The Beefeaters rallied around us and one kind chap, the Gurkha Corporal Ranjat Gurung, stuck gaffer tape over my wounds, so I didn't lose more than three or four pints all told.

Sirens told us that the City Police had arrived, although Summerville soon bigfooted them into dropping back and forming a perimeter guard with her tales of cat-burglars threatening the Crown Jewels. The coroner's van arrived and began the grisly business of packing away the bodies into a Bedford van. First, they loaded up a body bag containing Sergeant Bones, still in Queen Victoria's dress. The coroner's assistants were speculating on the best way to get blood out of antique crushed velvet, an argument that continued as they loaded the corpses of Edward Talbot, the two Beefeater guards, and Hendricks. Finally, Marjorie's body bag was loaded into the van, which gave me a genuine sense of relief as I came to understand that she was actually, irrevocably, definitively dead. She was in two bags: a big one for her torso and, after they'd rummaged around for something appropriate, a leatherette sports hold-all for her head. Six bodies in total.

Not seven, Cornwall. Not Fang, see?

Cornwall and I gave an account of the evening to the Warden, and before too long we were back in the Keys being slapped on the back and quizzed about the details again and again: the murder of two Beefeaters, the discovery of the Crown Jewel heist, the fights, the death. All the stories about the Tower are hundreds of years old, and the lads were all for hearing a newly minted adventure. They even liked that I'd been masquerading as MacDairmid, taking this with good grace. We toasted the heroic way Edward Talbot met his death, and mused over the precise details of Bones' demise, but the pitch was that he'd been a bloody good egg with a unique passion for Queen Victoria and for historical fashions. And what, when all is said and done, is wrong with that?

Cornwall turned to me. "Eventful night," he remarked.

I shrugged. "Well done for killing that arsehole Hendricks."

He seemed very pleased about that, and then remarked that Nimbu Towers was mine again.

I snapped to attention. He was right! Nimbu Towers was Marjorie's, now deceased, and as her husband the estate would automatically pass back to me. I hadn't even considered this. I could write to Cacahuete and see if he'd come back from Mexico to resume his duties. This really was the most tremendous shot in the arm.

But I couldn't even take a moment to celebrate, for just then a smartly dressed fellow stepped into the doorway of the Keys. He was an impressive looking man, straight-backed, not a hair out of place – even though it was stupid o'clock in the morning. He scanned the room and zeroed in on the pair of us. One raised eyebrow was all it took for the Beefeaters to melt away. This chap's jet-black moustache was really quite something. I could feel Cornwall eyeballing it jealously, wondering at its bushiness, the straightness of the cut, and its sheer depth of field.

"Good morning gentleman," he said, "My name is Commander Peter Grassing, and I am the Queen's Private Secretary."

It had already been a long night so perhaps it wasn't surprising that Cornwall wasn't ready to let his guard down just yet. He responded with a raised glass and a cautious, 'Good morning, Commander." From the corner of my eye, I saw his hand move a few inches closer to Fang's katana.

Grassing smiled at this and gamely pulled up a chair, putting his hands up in a gesture of surrender.

"You can forget all that nonsense, chaps. I'm no threat at all." The laugh he gave us was authentic. "How about another whisky instead? You deserve it after what you've achieved tonight."

The barman put three large single malts in front of us.

"And snacks, barkeep!" chided Grassing. "These men require crisps and peanuts right away. What sort of pub is this?"

"The best in London, Commander," shot back the landlord.

"Oh, I know it, Jim," Grassing nodded, and turned to us. "Right. I've good news. Her Majesty was woken and told of events. She wishes to relay her thanks and appreciation for the foiling of this heinous crime," he said. "Obviously your discretion will be required. No word of this event must be spoken, for now, at least."

"What's there to say, Commander?" I confirmed, "all in the day's work of a Scoundrel."

"Indeed. Good to hear. Her Majesty requires me to bestow upon you both a Gratitude."

"A Gratitude?" I queried.

"Rare honour. Off the books. Bloody big privilege. Reserved for those who need a slap on the back for some magnificent service that needs to remain all secret squirrel."

Cornwall was leaning in to make sure he heard Grassing's every word. I realised I was doing the same.

"This Gratitude is a ruddy great trident of honour. Three prongs to it!" he roared, laughing at his own joke. "Prong One. It's the State Opening of Parliament tomorrow. And it's been a tradition since Guy Fawkes that the Yeomen carry out a security sweep of the cellars beforehand. This year, we'd like you to do it, agreed?"

"Naturally," I said.

"Good, because you'll both be well acquainted with the cellars by the morning, I believe." Grassing slid an ancient bronze key across the table. "Prong two. This is the key to the Parliament Wine Cellar, arguably the best stocked cellar in the world. Things in there you can't imagine. Her Majesty has granted you unfettered access from now on. You may help yourself to whatever you find. And trust me, there is much to find. Acceptable?"

"Acceptable," agreed Cornwall.

"Good." Grassing tossed back his scotch, pushed back his chair and said, "off we go, then."

"And the third prong, Commander?" I queried.

Grassing threw his hands in the air. "So sorry, yes, the most important part. The Queen requests your presence tomorrow after she's opened Parliament. She'd like to thank you."

"We'd be delighted," I replied.

"Are you sure we look presentable enough for her Majesty?" Cornwall asked, dusting himself down.

Grassing gave us the once-over. Cornwall's suit was heavily creased and sliced to ribbons at the sleeves. My bare chest was crudely bandaged with gaffer tape and smeared with mud and gore. My underpants were so stretched and soiled that they hung from my hips like an adult nappy. Grassing's moustache twitched once. "I'll have your tailors send something appropriate to Parliament for the morning. Savile Row?"

"Gieves," I replied.

"Same," said Cornwall.

"Leave it with me," he said, standing, "now, to the Palace."

As we stood, I instinctively picked up the medieval mace I'd used to battle Marjorie, and Cornwall picked up Fang's katana. Grassing eyed us wryly.

"Hopefully you'll have no need of those."

We swished down Fleet St in Grassing's Bentley in the peculiar serenity of the City in the small hours. I had a moment to reflect. The Parliamentary Cellar. Good lord. Finally, after all these years, we were about to be honoured as the heroes we were.

When a monarch grants a Gratitude, it can be anything they like.

In 1774, the future King William IV was almost kidnapped on the orders of George Washington in New York City. The holidaying Scoundrels' apiarist, Tranquilus Norton, overheard the kidnappers' scheme, got them drunk and delivered them to the bottom of the Hudson river. William gave Norton one hundred acres in Somerset, which came complete with a license for the only cannabis field in England. Norton spent the rest of his days gently stoned on the cannabis honey his bees produced.

In 1900, Edward VII, the playboy prince, was drinking with Jimothy Birchall, a Scoundrel. The King was bemoaning his difficult, overfilled schedule. Quite off the cuff, Jimothy came up with the concept of

'Sandringham Time', corresponding to UTC +00:30, and applying only to the royal estate at Sandringham. It gave the King half an hour each day for shooting, his favourite pursuit. Jimothy found himself appointed masseur to the British ladies' croquet squad at the Paris Olympics later that year. And those girls needed a lot of massages.

It was a month on the Royal Yacht Britannia for Barnes Wallis, fishing for marlin off the coast of Antigua, when King George wanted to applaud his special genius in designing the bouncing bomb.

And now we'd been given the keys to the Parliamentary Cellar, a place *nobody I'd ever met* had been.

We pulled up at College Green. Grassing pointed us towards an ancient porch in the service yard of the Palace of Westminster. Waiting there was the incumbent Gentleman Usher of the Black Rod, in splenetic mood. He'd been roused from a deep slumber and had thrown on his black robes and golden chain in a hurry.

"Cornwall? Trevelyan? This is most irregular. Follow!" he grumbled, before turning on his heel and leading us down a series of corridors. After a long route to the basement, Black Rod stopped at an iron-studded door.

"Well," he huffed, "I don't know what you've done to deserve this, but it must really have been something. This is the Parliamentary Wine Cellar. Don't ask me about it, I've never been allowed in."

Black Rod cleared his throat and read something out from a tiny scroll.

"Her Britannic Majesty bestows upon Majors Cornwall and Trevelyan the right to pass freely without let or hindrance within the Parliamentary cellars for as long as they wish forever more, for time immemorial, with no relinquishment, respite nor quarter. In the Name of Her Majesty, I, hereby grant to you *Cellar Access, Having No Termination.*

"Sounds official." I said, rubbing my hands together.

"It is," Black Rod straight batted. "Both of you are now C.A,H.N.T.s. I looked it up in the register," he said. "There's no instance of two cahnts being granted together." Black Rod smiled for the first time. "I suppose that makes you a pair of cahnts."

"Won't you come in and have one with us now?" Cornwall enquired.

Black Rod gritted his teeth. I could see him wavering. Then he sighed and made up his mind. "More than my job's worth," he said.

I shrugged and turned the bronze key in the lock. Behind us, Black Rod went up on his tiptoes to try and get a looksee inside the Cellar. Cornwall stepped inside after me, nodded politely and slammed the door in Black Rod's face.

I clicked on the light. The sight that met my eyes was glorious. It was the Sistine Chapel. It was the Swiss Alps on a clear day. It was La Gioconda holidaying at the Sea of Tranquility. This room has a beauty of its own, distilled. Of course, at the Club we were no stranger to good bottles, but this place was something else. I looked at Cornwall and nodded. He nodded back at me. I will always remember what he said next, for its peculiarity:

"Welcome to the pleasure dome."

After some back and forth we established that this was the name of an album by a popular band called *Frankie Goes to Hollywood* that Cornwall had been listening to, and the words just seemed apt to him. I didn't disagree. How could I? After all, our Queen had granted us the ultimate gift for a bon vivant: the lock-in to end all lock-ins.

The agony of choice. This phrase went around my head like a clanging bell as the splendour of the Parliamentary Cellar revealed itself to us. Talk about quality booze. This cellar had the lot. The place housed every notable concoction imaginable, from Tudor to modern. A bottle of *Vin de Constance* the Duke of Wellington found in the Emperor Napoleon's vacated tent at Waterloo. A Victorian small beer made from the urine of Nell Gwynne. A jug of *Kill the Bastard Redcoat Special Cask* recovered from William Wallace's hovel. A crate of porter that Pitt the Elder confiscated from Pitt the Younger because he was underage.

One surprise was the Top Shelf, a wooden counter that ran along the entire length of one wall, and which contained a repository of stuff too controversial or embarrassing to be displayed publicly, yet was too important to be thrown away.

We began to investigate. Cornwall took an exploratory bite from a musty object which was labelled as being the

Earl of Sandwich's original sandwich (cheese and pickle). At the back of the shelf was Queen Victoria's bedroom spittoon containing six of John Brown's used condoms.

I lit one of a small stock of Winston Churchill's cigars with a match from the box found in Guy Fawkes' pocket when he was apprehended. Everywhere you looked was something eye-opening, and none of it would ever see the light of day.

To our delight, we found the Klunghammer, Hitler's machine-engineered dildo that we'd liberated from his Black Forest fortress over forty years before. It was splendid to see it again. It stirred memories of throttling Nazis and crash-landing Spitfires, and I wondered if life could ever be that simple again.

An entire shelf was given over to ministerial red boxes. Gladstone's box contained a folder of high-grade nun porn and a greasy lump of brown stuff, which struck us as odd from such a public opponent of the Chinese opium trade. I had to throw it down a drain before Cornwall could ruin the evening by smoking it. Arthur Balfour's box had a graffiti cock and balls scratched on the front, complete with knobbly shaft, apparently rendered by Edward VII when Balfour left it on an occasional table to visit the lavatory.

We found a shelf of Nazi bottles, the spoils of war, and had fun reading out the notes on luggage labels that hung around their necks. We had a swig from the remnants of a bottle of rum Jesse Owens used to seduce Unity Mitford in the long jump pit at the Berlin Olympics, but it was disappointingly bland.

Later I was trying to get at an interesting pouch at the back of the shelf, (which actually turned out to be a pound of cocaine which had been smuggled in the diplomatic bag of T.E Lawrence). I couldn't quite reach, so I dragged a dusty barrel across the room to stand upon. Closer inspection of the barrel revealed that William Beatty had put Lord Nelson's body in it for the voyage back from Trafalgar when he was killed by a musket ball. It had 'spirit of wine' written in white chalk across the repaired cask lid, and it was still chock full of brandy.

"I'm having some of that," I said.

"Bit grim, no?" Cornwall was squeamish.

"Victor," I said, "years from now, you'll admit you had the chance to toast Nelson from the very brandy he came home in, and you passed it up, is that what you're saying?"

"When you put it like that…"

"Can't not?"

"Can't not."

We unstoppered a cask and a stream of brandy glugged out, which we decanted into a pair of tulip glasses. "To Lord Nelson," toasted Cornwall.

"To Lord Nelson, cheers!"

Down the hatch. The brandy was not an immediate classic. It had a whiff of the barnyard about it.

"Perhaps past it's best," I said, "but it's made tolerable by association."

"Well put," said Cornwall.

"Years from now," I mused, "will you admit you had the chance to make another toast with the very brandy

Nelson came home in, after you'd toasted Lord Nelson himself?"

"I suppose not," he said.

"What shall we drink to this time?" said Cornwall.

I considered this golden opportunity. "A pair of true British heroes," I ventured.

"Good show," nodded Cornwall. "We saved the Crown bloody Jewels."

"That's right," I answered him. "To the bastards that saved Great Britain!"

"To the bastards who saved Great Britain," he cried. "To us!"

"To us!"

The second measure tasted sweeter. I threw my glass into the corner of the room. Cornwall threw his glass into a different corner of the room.

I collapsed onto a dusty chaise longue upon which Lillie Langtry had done all her best work. Cornwall pulled up the chair Christine Keeler was photographed in after the Profumo Affair.

"I mean, we've always been heroes. But now we'll be finally *recognised*," I enthused, "and we'll probably get a knighthood."

"Knighthood minimum," said Cornwall, glassy-eyed. "Probably a peerage."

He got up and selected a bottle of *usquebaugh* that, the label said, Benjamin D'Israeli won from Sir Robert Peel betting on who could drink a policeman's helmet full of Thames water fastest. "Are you glad Marjorie's dead?" he asked.

It took me a while to marshall my thoughts, but when I did, I was emphatic. "She was the devil. What about Fang?" I asked. "Did you really ask her to marry you?"

Cornwall lapsed into silence as he thought about the second woman who had died in his arms immediately following his marriage proposal. "All these years, I thought it was my destiny to be a lone wolf," he brooded. "But as it turns out all I needed was…"

"A lady wolf?"

He shrugged. "Perhaps that's what I saw in her. But it doesn't matter now, does it? She's gone."

"To Sayonara Fang," I struggled to my feet and splashed a bit of plum wine – from a state dinner for the Emperor Showa in 1971 – into my mouth. "To Fang! The yin to your yang."

Cornwall toasted his love, but a darkness took hold of him. "Fang, the yin to my yang," he slurred, rolling off Keeler's chair and onto the floor. He can hold his liquor as much as any man, but he must have gone through the thick end of four bottles of wine, alongside all the treats and fancies this most peculiar night had brought.

I kicked him awake and watched as he moved unsteadily over to an electric blue suede Chesterfield that Princess Margaret had won off Elvis Presley in a game of Texas Hold 'Em. He swept it clear of bottles and slumped down onto the fabric.

"Funny thing," he slurred. "After all these years we've foiled Hansclapp's masterplan, and it boiled down to little more than a jewel heist."

I thought about this.

I may even have attempted a response.

But instead I decided to rest my eyes for a moment.

THE NEXT MORNING

I woke up with a racehorse stamping repeatedly on the top of my head with its specially sharpened hooves. My tongue was soldered to the roof of my mouth. Someone was operating a road drill on each of my eardrums. I was sweating heavily and my fever was running so hot I became convinced I had typhoid. My skin was trying to tear itself from my body to get away from the source of the agony. Worse still, sometime in the night Cornwall had lost control of his bowels and somehow managed to shit in my underpants. The chaise longue was a total write-off.

I knew all this before I'd even tried to open my eyes.

I opened my eyes.

Everything got one hundred times worse.

Cornwall staggered around the room like the victim of a serious road traffic accident. I wondered whether I should call him an ambulance but I couldn't remember the number. I vomited into my own lap and started to cry. Everything in the world was hopeless and I was entirely helpless and alone. It wasn't typhoid, I decided, but ebola.

I closed my eyes again, but the room spun like a funfair Wurlitzer. Then some good news: the drill stopped

– to reveal a horrible scraping noise that was much worse. Perhaps the ebola had turned all my bones and organs to glass, and I was shattering from the inside? No, it can't be that. What was it then? What was that infernal cacophony? I opened my eyes again. On the other side of the room, Cornwall was trying to get the foil off a bottle of champagne, and for some reason he'd chosen a medieval mace. But the elementary task of opening the bottle was beyond him, as his fingers were made of wet cardboard.

"Hair of the dog," he said, over again and again. Then he lost consciousness, his head crashing down forehead first onto the table.

I rolled over and attempted to die through will alone. It felt like I had been stung all over by… what's the worst animal that could sting you, I asked myself? A fox? Shouted my brain into the wrong end of my ears. No, foxes don't sting. A goose, then? I hate geese, I thought. I hate all animals. Why would they want to sting me, especially when I'm this close to death anyway? A long string of disconnected nonsense in this vein flooded my brain until Cornwall shat in my underpants again.

There was a knock at the door. With an agonised cry, Cornwall awoke. He got up and wrenched it open to reveal Black Rod holding a tray of coffee and warm rolls. The look he gave us was two parts empathy to one part contempt. "Your suits have arrived," he called inside, "but you might want to visit the cloakrooms before you put them on. It is a little close in here."

Black Rod took great pleasure in slamming the door as loudly as he possibly could. That bastard seemed to revel in making unacceptable noise. The sound was like a sledgehammer to the chest, and I snapped awake. Properly awake.

Of course! Our meeting with the Queen! And honours for being Britain's greatest heroes. Worth getting on with the day for all that. I undertook to pull myself together. Cornwall was right. There was only one thing that would improve matters – the hair of the dog that bit me.

I had to find the booze that caused this frightful mess and get it down my neck. My hangover would still be there, but something in the fresh intake of alcohol would loosen the stranglehold it had over me, enabling the next steps in the long road to recovery: coffee, bacon, hot shower, a bit of a cry.

I couldn't remember what I'd drunk. Then I did remember: I'd drunk everything. That was the problem. And for the hangover caused by a combination of grape, grain and everything in between, the only thing is a large glass of vintage port with a larger slug of whisky mixed in.

I staggered to my feet. That racehorse with the sharpened hooves had just completed another circuit and landed on me again. Then he stamped on me some more and tried to sting me with his special horse poison. With a start I realised I was still horribly drunk. Would the hair of the dog even work if I was horribly drunk?

I saw a cask of Members' port on the table, the standard booze they serve in the Parliamentary bars. It was already tapped. That'll sort me out, I thought. I staggered around the table, scooped up a glass and filled it almost to the brim. The electric light Black Rod had unkindly switched on was burning a bright hole in the single eye I could open, so I held up the full glass to blot it out.

I took a few deep breaths. I needed to force this entire glass down in one if it was going to have the desired effect.

There was a sudden scuffling noise to my left.

I raised the glass to my lips.

The glass flew across the room and disintegrated against the wall. Cornwall had smashed it out of my hand, the rotten sod. A good measure of the port splattered the old oak table. As it seeped away into the grainy, pitted surface a fluorescent blue residue remained.

"By god, look, man!" Cornwall was pointing in horror. "Bosphorus Phosphorus!"

"It can't be! There's none left!" I blurted, all my synapses suddenly firing at once, "It's Tyneside Cyanide!"

Cornwall kicked over the rest of the barrel of Members Ordinary. Its contents spilled across the brick floor, leaving the same ominous bluish glow.

"Stealing the Crown Jewels wasn't Hansclapp's plan at all," I shouted, ignoring my pulsing skull, "he's poisoned the MPs!"

Cornwall looked at me, aghast. "Anyone who's been drinking the port is now a walking, talking unexploded bomb!"

Cornwall shat in my pants again.

"With you in a minute," I said, "I really do need to sort this out first."

I have no words to add to this, Major.

Yours sincerely,

Major Arthur St. John Trevelyan

Hellcat Manor
Great Trundleford
Devon
August 4th 2021

Dear Major,

You could never handle your drink.

CHAPTER 21
GATECRASHING

The sound of a bugle playing a fanfare echoed down the stairwell and into the cellar. High above us, the State Opening of Parliament had begun. The Queen would be up there, along with every Lord, Lady and MP in the country. "Come on Trevelyan, we've got to stop this," I said, shrugging off my hangover as if it were a duelling cape. I picked up Fang's katana. Trevelyan grabbed the mace and followed me as I bounded up the stairs.

We burst into a busy lobby, full of the great and the good milling around. There was no way of knowing exactly who had been quaffing Tyneside Cyanide and who hadn't. Being here, we realised, was like stepping into a field of landmines, but landmines that wandered around slapping each other on the back. To make matters worse, every part of the building was rammed, for this was the most important day of the Parliamentary year. We hurried down the corridor towards the Peers Lobby, which was lined with MPs, four or five deep. As we pushed our way in to the House of Peers, several heads turned, their scowling faces hushing us to be quiet.

Through the doorway, I could see the Queen taking her place on the golden throne. And there, not more than ten yards away from her, was the newly ennobled Lord Gruber Hansclapp, dressed in scarlet woollen robes.

The Queen addressed the House. "My Lords, pray be seated." She gave the signal to Black Rod, his cue to summon the MPs to the House of Lords by rapping on the Commons door three times, an ancient ceremony that signifies the Commons independence from the Sovereign.

"If Black Rod has been drinking the port, one strike on that door, and he'll blow!" I murmured to Trevelyan, trying to slip through the crowd without jostling anyone, but the sheer volume of people made progress slow. Black Rod bowed to Her Majesty and began his long march down the corridor.

"Black Rod!" came the call as he passed through the Central Lobby. We needed to act decisively but we were hemmed in by the throng.

"Maybe if you get on my shoulders you can warn him," Trevelyan suggested. It wasn't a great plan, but it was the only one that sprung to mind. Trevelyan bent down on one knee and I clambered onto his shoulders. This wasn't new to us. We'd perfected this during many dormitory pillow fights back at Winstowe. Trevelyan would be *anchor*, while I'd be *up-top*. I'd had a few partners in my time but none were as steady as him. He was a big unit with a low centre of gravity. Some of the boys even refused to play with him, declaring him the biggest *anchor* they'd ever met.

Now, on his shoulders, I could see over the bobbing MPs heads, but several angry voices shouted out, calling for me to get down. Below me, Trevelyan held firm, but I knew I didn't have long to make an impact. I took in an enormous breath and bellowed with all my might, "STOPPPP!"

"Get down you bloody fool!" yelled one onlooker.

"Call security!" shouted somebody else.

I had a brief window to make my case and I needed to go for it, so I did. "YOUR MAJESTY, LORDS, LADIES, AND GENTLEMEN! YOU ARE ALL IN EXTREME DANGER! LORD HANSCLAPP IS PLANNING TO DESTROY US ALL!"

I looked across to a stony-faced Hansclapp. His fingers were pressed together, white and bloodless, suggesting an inner turmoil. He hadn't expected us to be here.

Below me, Trevelyan was having to fend off several MPs who were trying to pull me to the ground.

"HANSCLAPP HAS SPIKED THE PARLIAMENTARY PORT WITH AN UNSTABLE COMPOUND KNOWN AS TYNESIDE CYNANIDE!" I shouted. Even as I said it, I realised this was never going to work. I sounded like a madman, but I had no other option. "MANY OF YOU ARE HIGHLY EXPLOSIVE!

PLEASE LEAVE THE BUILDING IN AN ORDERLY MANNER!" I turned my attention to Black Rod, who had stopped his procession and yelled, "I BESEECH YOU SIR. DO NOT STRIKE THAT DOOR!"

"Somebody get him out of here," yelled a furious Norman Tebbit.

The hands clawing at Trevelyan finally overwhelmed him, and I was dragged to the ground.

Within seconds, the heavy mob arrived. Burly Westminster security guards, and a couple of the Queen's protection officers. I found myself pinned down on the flagstones with a knee in my back. I looked across to Trevelyan who had four guards sitting on top of him. A brief cheer went up from the crowd now that we'd been neutralised.

Black Rod gathered his composure and continued along the corridor towards the Commons doors.

We were hauled up off the floor to be handcuffed when Black Rod reached his objective. He raised his heavy rod and smashed it hard against the door.

He was blown to smithereens.

All hell broke loose.

Bodies were scattered around the blast radius as shrapnel passed through the closest bystanders. Some were killed instantly, others were horribly maimed. The MP for Runcorn South bled out from his severed leg stumps. The MP for Penzance stumbled around with a jagged shard of wood protruding from his skull. The attending police began pushing their way towards the bombsite, while everyone else began shoving their way out of the Chamber. It was bedlam. The MP for Norwich South was knocked over, sloshing the unstable Tyneside Cyanide that had formed in his guts, like a bolus of nitro-glycerine. When he hit the hard stone floor, the impact caused a supersonic shockwave to detonate. Half a dozen MPs were launched into the air. Shrieks of terror filled the halls as ruddy-cheeked Westminster backbenchers ran panicked towards the exits. But the exits had been locked.

Blood and viscera, hysteria and pandemonium. Pushing, shoving, trampling, and bloody, violent death. The Palace of Westminster was on fire. The most pragmatic of the MPs used this moment to settle scores with old rivals. The MP for Ruislip smashed the liberal peer Lord Jayson in the face with a briefcase and then stamped on his chest when he fell. She in turn was throttled by the MP for Cardiff West with the straps from her own handbag.

I shrugged off the police officer who had failed to cuff me and scrambled to my feet. "We need to get to the Queen!" I shouted to Trevelyan.

"To the Queen!" Trevelyan cried, wiping away a splash of gore from his face.

We surged forward, nimbly dodging through the sea of terrified members, each one of them a potentially lethal explosion, back towards the House of Peers.

As we weaved our way through, the Shadow Secretary of State for Health and Social Services, Robin Cook, stepped across our path. He was apoplectic, "You two are responsible for this!" he raged, "you'll be made to pay!" Trevelyan didn't hesitate and dropped him with a sharp right hook. We charged onwards as the world around us went up in flames, devising a crude early-warning system as we went. We had no way of knowing who'd been at the doctored port, so we steered clear of any MP that carried the warning signs of alcoholism. Unfortunately, that was most of them. Our system seemed to work. "Incoming!" shouted Trevelyan, "bulbous nose, spidery cheek veins, go left!"

"Clinically obese," I shouted back, "yellowy eyes from cirrhosis, turn right."

To our left, a lumbering walrus of an MP took a tumble down some steps. We hit the deck and covered our heads. God knows how much port he'd taken on board, but when his giant gut slammed onto the carpet, it caused a terrifying detonation with the same explosive power of a German sea mine.

Ahead of us, stalwart against the tide of fleeing politicians, a viscera-smeared Margaret Thatcher was ordering people to calm down and walk, like a sixth form prefect. Eventually she lost patience, took off her spectacles and headbutted Neil Kinnock as he ran past.

Knowing she was teetotal, we had no hesitation in barging Maggie out of the way – although she did catch Trevelyan a good one in the throat with her elbow. We broke through the threshold back into the House of Peers. I looked across to the golden throne. It was empty. The Queen must have been evacuated by her protection officers but we were just in time to catch sight of Hansclapp slipping through the door to the Royal Gallery – the Queen's private sitting room.

We jumped up onto the red leather seats and ran down the rows, leaping and dodging the confused and elderly peers, some of whom who were still sitting there in terror.

Two guards blocked our path, but we had no time to argue with them, we simply floored one each with brutal efficiency. We stormed through the door and heard three gunshots ring out from the next room. As we burst into the Royal Gallery, we found Hansclapp with a pistol in his hand and three dead officers. Worse still, the Queen was unprotected in the centre of the Gallery. He had just taken aim at her…

"HANDSCLAPP!" I boomed.

Hansclapp swivelled and fired a shot in our direction, sending us diving for cover. Trevelyan hurled the medieval mace at him, knocking the pistol from his hand. It skittered across the wooden floor, lodging under the body of one of the dead security men.

"It's over, Hansclapp!" I said, drawing Fang's katana.

The Queen, admirably calm, saw her moment. She stepped back to the edge of the room, isolating Hansclapp. Trevelyan and I began to close him down, cutting the space he had to manoeuvre to a few square metres. He crouched to pick up the discarded mace and slipped the leather strap onto his wrist and tested its weight.

"I'm afraid not, Cornwall," he said. "It is not over yet."

I raised Fang's katana and braced myself for combat. Trevelyan adopted a low wrestling stance, edging to Hansclapp's blindside, waiting for the right time to spring at him. Hansclapp sensed he was being closed in and shifted his bodyweight from right to left. In the split second he wasn't settled, I attacked, closing down the space between us and bringing the blade down in a clean overhead strike. I was quick but he parried, whirling his mace around his head, and launching it at my face. I brought the katana up just in time to block it, the mace's chain wrapping itself around my blade. With a sharp yank I tore the mace from Hansclapp's grip. Trevelyan saw his opening. He rushed forward and tackled Hansclapp around the midriff, taking him to the ground. Years of pent-up anger poured from Trevelyan as he meted out the most vicious beating. I wouldn't normally enjoy watching such savagery, but I didn't want to miss a second of this.

I realised the Queen was standing next to me.

"Are you unharmed, Ma'am?" I asked.

"Quite, thank you," she said.

I did not step in, as I thought it right that Trevelyan should have his vengeance. "This is for Anais," he screamed. Now he had his hands around Hansclapp's neck and was squeezing tighter and tighter. Hansclapp's face turned a deep shade of purple.

Hansclapp's struggling grew weaker as Trevelyan continued to strangle him. It was all but over, but we both neglected to notice that Hansclapp had scrabbled a throwing knife from his trouser pocket. Trevelyan let out a sudden roar as Hansclapp dragged the blade across his wrists. Blood poured from Trevelyan's wounds but still he held on. But then Hansclapp stabbed up at his neck. Had it landed it would have been a fatal blow. Trevelyan blocked the blade but in doing so overbalanced. Hansclapp twisted free and from the floor, kneed Trevelyan in the groin, following up with the judo throw, *Tomoe Nage*, flipping Trevelyan over his head to crash into a fireplace.

Astonishingly, Hansclapp was on his feet in an instant. I raced in for the kill, but I was forced to pull up short. Hansclapp was smiling at me through his bloodied teeth. He held the spiteful little throwing knife in his hand and in his sights was the Queen, an unmissable distance away. I hurled myself in front of the Queen to cover her, spreading my arms to make myself as large a target possible.

"Like I said," Hansclapp sneered, "this is not over yet." He backed his way out of the room.

Trevelyan staggered up. He was furious with himself. "I should have bloody killed him," he said, "I had him in my hands!"

"You'll get your chance," I said. I turned to the Queen. "Sorry about this, ma'am, we must pursue Lord Hansclapp."

The Queen nodded.

I darted after him, Trevelyan right behind me. Hansclapp was right. This was not over yet.

Yours sincerely,
Major Victor Montgomery Cornwall

Nimbu Towers
Pullen-under-Lyme
Gloucestershire
8th August, 2021

Dear Major,

Good. Well done. Moving swiftly on:

CHAPTER 22

LULLABY FOR A MADMAN

"Help is on its way, Ma'am," I said to the Queen, as I picked up the mace and ran after Cornwall in pursuit of Hansclapp through the narrow, panelled corridors of the Palace of Westminster. He'd only had perhaps a ten second head start as he burst from the Royal Gallery, but he was quick and knew the terrain.

Up ahead I saw him leap over the corpse of an unfortunate Lord, whose body blocked the entire width of the corridor. His stomach had exploded, and black blood dripped grimly from the ceiling. As we passed by, Cornwall tripped over a severed arm still encased in a tattered ermine sleeve, but he regained his balance and pushed on. Ahead of us, Hansclapp skidded around a corner and sprinted away again, desperate to make his escape.

After a few more turns, the corridor opened up into a tiled vestibule, and from there we pushed through a pair of swinging doors into the House of Peers, with its rows of red leather seats.

We charged into the devastated chamber, expecting to see Hansclapp disappearing out of the other end of it – but he had vanished. Where the hell had he gone? He wouldn't have had time to get away. He had to be in here somewhere.

"Cover that exit," I shouted to Cornwall, and he ran to the far doors – the only other way our quarry could escape – and bound the heavy brass door handles with cord that he hacked from the curtains with the katana. I ripped away more cord and tied up the doors near me. The House of Peers was now locked down, but finding and incapacitating Hansclapp would be a challenge, and we had to do it quickly before the resourceful cur found another way to escape. "He's in here! Stay by the doors and I'll flush him out," I shouted to Cornwall.

The explosions had annihilated the chamber. It was a midden of charred benches, shattered glass and papers. Smoke billowed from fires smouldering on the carpets, making it difficult to see. The room had the eerie atmosphere of a battlefield when all the killing has been done. There were too many bodies to count. Some had been blown up beyond recognition, reduced to nothing more than seared, gristly lumps of meat, while other victims were intact, with no discernible injuries save blood trickling from their mouths. Those poor souls must have had only had a few sips of the doctored port, but the Tyneside Cyanide had still detonated with enough power to rupture their stomachs. The smell of blood and burnt flesh was heavy in the air.

There was no sign of Hansclapp. But we knew he was here. Time to flush him out. I crept along the rows of red leather seats, heart hammering in my chest. Could he have ducked behind one of the benches? Was there a storage cupboard he could have hidden in? I made my way through the smoke. He still had the throwing knife he'd used to threaten the Queen, so I wrapped my arms across my chest to protect my vital organs, in case he suddenly launched it at me from wherever he was hiding. Although there were two of us, the fact that we were hunting him put us at a tactical disadvantage. On top of that, I reminded myself, a dangerous bastard like Hansclapp could have armed himself further, or even set a trap since he'd got into the chamber.

Cornwall and I needed to change the paradigm with a bit of Scoundrels tradecraft. I had a glimmer of an idea, but it sounded ridiculous even as it crystallised in my mind. But nothing better presented itself, and time was short. "Cornwall," I called, "what was that song Gruber used to sing about his pet bull?"

Cornwall caught my drift. From his sentry post at the far doors, almost invisible through the smoke, he began to sing:

The sun now fades
Beyond white-topped hills
It's time to go to bed.

His rich alto lent *Wiegenlied fur ein Stier*, Hansclapp's own *Lullaby to a Bull*, a maudlin air as it echoed around the Lords' chamber:

> *Here is fresh hay,*
> *To prevent the chill.*
> *I've made some*
> *Farmhouse bread.*

As Cornwall sang, I crept along the twisted, snarled up benches, stepping carefully over dead MPs, checking each one carefully. I wasn't sure what kind of reaction this would provoke in Hansclapp, perhaps nothing, but I'd knew he'd loved his little pet bull more than life itself.

From the far side of the room, Cornwall began the next verse.

> *So sleep little Stier,*
> *And rest your eyes.,*
> *You've had a busy day.*
> *Dream your dream*
> *For I'll be here,*
> *To keep the cold at bay.*

I switched to the other side of the room, moving stealthily, alive to anything that might betray Hansclapp's whereabouts. So far he'd managed to stay hidden, but the song was about to reach it's emotional denouement:

I love you! I love you!
I love my little bull.

What was that? Towards the end of this line, I heard a tiny sound behind me. It was a strangulated choke of rage, instantly stifled, from across the chamber. I turned on my heels. I couldn't make out anything through the smoke, so I looked at Cornwall. He had one hand to his ear, telling me he'd heard it too. He was pointing, insistently, over and over, to a spot on the ground about ten yards ahead of me.

Cornwall sang the last lines of Gruber's boyhood song, and as we did so I craned forward to try and focus on what he was pointing at.

I love you! I love you!
I love you, little bull.

By the time the last line of the lullaby died away I'd managed to get closer. Now I could make out a mess of sprawled body parts, the side of a red bench with the stuffing burst out, and broken shards of blood-soaked wood. And there, obscured by all this, he was lying, spreadeagled on the thick blue carpet, as still and silent as a desert snake. Hansclapp was pretending to be a corpse. He'd managed to peel the tattered remnants from the face and scalp of an unlucky victim and laid it on top of his own. He had been waiting for me to pass by, when, I suppose, he would have jumped up and slit my throat with his knife.

I beckoned Cornwall over to me. Together we moved closer but took care not to move too quietly.

"Nothing," I said, and swore loudly. "How the hell did he escape?"

"Damn him, he must have got through the far door," said Cornwall, furiously, as he counted down from three on his fingers...

At zero, I slammed my full weight down on to Hansclapp. A quarter of a second before I made impact, he sensed me and tried to roll away, but it was too late. I landed with my elbow hard on his temple. He went limp. The knife fell from his hand.

Two minutes later, Hansclapp was trussed with more curtain cord, and double bound with a couple of neckties whose owners wouldn't need them anymore. His feet were tied tight enough to cut off the circulation, and his hands were fastened behind him.

I slapped him awake and wiped his blood from my hands. Cornwall and I moved over to a red bench and sat, side by side, looking down at our captive.

I sighed long and hard, allowing some of the tension to drain from my body. We'd done it. After all these years, Gruber Hansclapp was no longer a threat.

Gradually, he eased himself up to lean against the lowest stair that led to the golden throne.

"So, Gruber, it's over," I said.

"Don't be so sure," he sneered, and spat out a gobbet of blood.

"I'm sure," I said. "You may have blown up a few MPs, but you have failed."

"Failed?" Hansclapp began to laugh. "On the contrary," he coughed and spat out more blood. "I have so loved antagonising you and ruining your privileged, petty little lives, but I have known all along that it doesn't matter."

"What are you talking about?" I asked.

"Ruining the pair of you has been nothing more than a sideline for me. My target has always been the very society that created you. A society made from lies, that allow public schoolboys to grow up to become men like you, built on a foundation of nothing more than class and privilege. The more I learned about your silly, pompous island, the more my hatred grew. The Royals, the Lords, the self-serving prejudice, the elitism. So I fought back! Ever since you slaughtered my little Hermanus I decided to bring Britannia to destruction."

Hansclapp hacked up more blood. "But as I say, it doesn't matter. I realised I didn't need to destroy anything at all…" He spat onto the floor, "…as Britain has been destroying itself for years."

"Bollocks!" I shouted. "That's a load of bloody nonsense!"

"You think so? You used to rule the world," he smirked, "but your Empire is dead, and now the whole world is laughing at you."

Cornwall was riled. "Of course you would say that, Gruber, because you're only capable of hate. Britain isn't dying, it's changing. Britain was great, is great, and will continue to be great, long after we're all dead."

"Which for you will be very soon," I reminded him.

With that, Cornwall lifted Hansclapp's head up by his chin, and punched him very hard in the face. Hansclapp's lights went out again.

Cornwall turned to me. "Smoke?"

"What are they?"

Cornwall passed me a *Jolly Good Show*, a blend of Virginian fine shag, rose petals and spring laurel buds that the Scoundrels tobacconist had whipped up for telling it how it is.

"What shall we do with him?"

Cornwall mulled this over, "drop him off a bridge?"

"Could do..." I said, contemplating this.

"Or take him down to Hellcat and have a pair of stallions tear him apart?"

"Perhaps..."

"Actually, that'd be too quick, he deserves worse," he said.

I didn't respond.

Cornwall continued, "A while back you told me you wanted to be the one that snuffed out his candle. Well, now's your chance."

I looked down at the inert body of our nemesis. I was surprised at my indecision on this matter. I suddenly felt numb and unfocussed. "I've imagined nothing else but vengeance these last fifteen years," I said, "but now we're here, I find myself asking..." My voice trailed off.

"Asking what?" Cornwall said.

"Whether killing him actually *is* vengeance. I'm wondering what Anais would want me to do."

Cornwall thought about this as he blew a cloud of blue smoke into the air.

"I see," he said.

I stared down at the broken man before us. His eyes were swollen shut. His face was a mess of blood and bruises, but behind them, I saw only the scheming schoolboy who had dogged our days at Winstowe and wrecked much of our lives afterwards.

"I think Anais would want to lock him up in a very dark hole for the rest of his life," I said. "I'm not sure she'd want me to sully my hands with his blood."

Cornwall thought about this. "I suspect you're right," he said, stubbing out his smoke. "I'll do it. Pass me the katana."

"Not a chance, Victor. She may not have wanted me to kill him, but I do," I said, indignantly, snatching up the katana and unsheathing it.

"Give it here, St. John," said Cornwall. "I'm killing him."

"You *said*, in the hotel in La Paz, that when the time came *I could do it*."

"Well, I've changed my mind…" Cornwall made a grab for the katana. "That was before I spent ten years eating rat shit for breakfast. Give it here!"

I threw the katana onto a bench behind me and shoved him. "No chance."

He shoved me back and tried to get past me to pick it up. I am unsure how this all would have developed, but at that moment a tiny door, hidden in the side of a panelled wall, creaked open. The Queen peered out.

Cornwall and I stopped arguing. "Your Majesty!"

"Ma'am, we thought you'd left the building!"

"Has Lord Hansclapp been incapacitated?" she queried.

"Yes Ma'am," I said.

The Queen stepped out into the chamber. Her gown was slightly askew, but her crown was still firmly on top of her head. Underneath it, she looked fragile and careworn.

"You are the same chaps that saved the Crown Jewels last night, aren't you?"

"Yes, Ma'am," Cornwall said.

"I owe you both a debt of gratitude, but for now I ought to get back to the Palace. Would you provide your Queen with an escort?"

"Certainly Ma'am," I said.

"Wait, then, while I gather my things." The Queen went back through the secret door.

Cornwall sidled towards me. "Definitely a peerage each," he whispered.

"At minimum. And statues on Whitehall."

"We saved Britannia. I'm not sure there's even a medal for something as heroic as that."

"Yet," I corrected him.

"Yet," Cornwall agreed, nodding.

It shames me to say that we both became slightly giddy with this prospect. We had finally bested the man who had destroyed our lives and were about to be richly rewarded for doing so.

That's the thing about hubris. When it comes, it comes hard and heavy.

For we didn't see that Hansclapp had regained consciousness, dislocated his own elbow and managed to free one of his hands...

We didn't see that he had located his knife and cut himself free of the cords...

We didn't realise that he had picked up the discarded katana...

And we didn't see that we were about to be decapitated.

I don't know what it was that pricked our ears. A creak of floorboard. A disturbance in the air. A heartbeat. Whatever it was, we both turned as the katana blade sliced through the air towards our throats.

Our guard was down.

There was no time to react.

We were going to die.

BOOM!

A gunshot.

Hansclapp's forehead exploded, spattering blood and bone fragments all over us. He slumped to the ground.

As we wiped blood from our eyes, through the pistol smoke, we saw her. The Queen, gun in hand.

"Your... your Majesty," I cried.

"You saved us!" Cornwall said.

"My pleasure," said her Majesty, lowering the gun.

The far doors were broken open by firemen, and the room began filling with security staff, police, ambulance crews and anxious ladies-in-waiting. Within seconds a small army had surrounded the Queen.

I looked at the dead body of Gruber Hansclapp. I saw grey matter seeping from his shattered forehead. He was definitely dead, his eyes as cold as they'd been when he was alive.

"What's that?" I queried, still jittery from our near-death experience. I pointed at Hansclapp's left hand. In his hand was a remote switch, with a tiny transmitting unit.

It was flashing red.

Bugger.

Through all the commotion and hullabaloo, nobody seemed to notice that the crown, which the Queen still wore, was beeping.

Crack on then! What are you waiting for?

Yours sincerely,

Major Arthur St. John Trevelyan

Hellcat Manor
Great Trundleford
Devon
11th August 2021

Dear Major,

I won't slow down the end of our story with all the things you got wrong in that bit, but suffice to say, it wasn't you who saw the bomb-crown first, it was me. I'll take it from here:

CHAPTER 23

HEAVY HANGS THE CROWN

The crown was beeping.

"Silence!" I yelled, and every face in the chamber turned to look at me. "Listen!" The hullabaloo ceased. "The Crown!"

Beep. Beep. BEEP. BEEP.

Hansclapp's grand plan suddenly made sense. The crown was a bomb! Of course, this was it all along! Hansclapp wasn't trying to *steal* the Crown Jewels after all. He had been priming the Crown with a bomb, to make sure the Queen would be killed, even if she escaped Parliament.

The Queen reached up to take the crown off.

"Ma'am, please don't move!" I called. "Your crown will be rigged to explode."

The Queen froze. Several of her retinue began to edge nervously away from her.

"We need to get it out of here, quick smart," Trevelyan said.

"How? Even if we can move it, we'll never get it clear of the building in time. Lord knows how much explosive will be stashed inside it."

We'd run out of time. We'd run out of options. We'd failed to protect her Majesty.

There was an enormous crash as the giant circular stained-glass window above us shattered into a million pieces, and a familiar shape scythed through the air, spiralling down, looming larger and larger. And as she descended, her sharp, discordant cry filled the air.

– ARRAAAKAAAKKA –

The sound echoed off the ornate stonework like a dragon's scream. It was deafening. I watched in awe at her grace, her power, her total command of the air, as she took the measure of us all. Now this ancient hall was her domain. Everywhere was Majestic Death's domain.

It was a sight that gladdened, and at the same time, broke my heart, for I could no longer control her. She swooped low over our heads and tossed me something from her beak. It rolled to a stop at my feet, and I saw the bloodied head of the last Tower raven, a present for me.

Did that mean the Kingdom was about to fall?

– ARRAKKKAAAKAKKKAAAARRR –

she cried, as she flexed her enormous talons and came to rest on the top edge of a golden lectern. She folded her mighty wings and turned her head to eyeball me.

"Easy girl," I said softly. The assembled crowd remained rooted to the spot. The bomb in the crown continued to beep. Majestic Death swivelled her gaze to the noise, fixing the Queen in her menacing glare.

"Is this your bird, Major Cornwall?" asked the Queen.

"As much as one can own an eagle, yes, Ma'am."

"She's watching me," said the Queen.

Trevelyan tugged my arm. "She doesn't look right, Cornwall," he murmured.

But I saw something different, a glint in my girl's eye, something beyond intelligence. It was as if she was communicating telepathically with me. And suddenly it became clear to me what she was thinking. "Your Majesty," I called, "please do not move a muscle, whatever happens."

The beeps were now getting faster.

I looked into Majestic Death's eyes and nodded solemnly. "Yes, my girl," I said, "that is what you must do."

"Cornwall! What are you saying?" Trevelyan didn't know her like I did.

"Fetch it, girl!" I cried. Majestic Death launched into the air, beating her wings until she'd risen high above us, an archangel of salvation. Then she tucked her wings in and hurtled towards the Queen with the speed of a heat-seeking missile. A howl of terror went up from the people in the room as her talons flashed out towards our Monarch. Instinctively I flinched, screwing my eyes shut, hoping I hadn't got this horribly wrong.

But when I opened them again, the crown was no longer on the Queen's head.

Majestic Death wheeled away, the bomb crown in her grip, but we were not out of danger yet. I had to deliver her final instruction, something I'd not used in years. "Majestic Death!" I called, "fly to the sun!" I pointed to the sky, just as I had when I trained her all those years ago at Hellcat. "Fly to the sun!"

She pumped her powerful wings, twice, three times, taking her up, up, up, out of the shattered window and into the bright sky.

"The terrace!" I called. Trevelyan and I raced through the lobby and out onto the deserted terrace overlooking the river Thames.

Majestic Death was still climbing and climbing. Up, up, up, higher and higher, carrying the danger away.

I shielded my eyes from the glare of the sun, my heart aching at the sight of my beautiful girl flying to her death.

Trevelyan placed a calming hand on my shoulder. "There's nothing you could have done, old friend," he said sympathetically.

"I could have locked her cage door," I said.

"Yes, you could have done that," he replied awkwardly. "But instead," he said, trying to sound enigmatic and wise, "you set her free, and that is the greatest gift of all."

I gave him a curious look. His words, kind as they were, coincided with the low whumping sound of Majestic Death exploding in a colossal fireball that filled the London sky. The crown had indeed been stuffed full of plastic explosive. It would have brought down the entire House.

A single tear rolled down my face. She had saved us all. My wonderful killing machine, who enjoyed nothing more than slashing a man's jugular at two hundred miles per hour, had showed me that she did have a heart after all.

Her name and her fate were intertwined forever. Truly, a Majestic Death.

Well that's the Booker Prize sewn up. That was a magnificent piece of writing you must agree. Not a dry eye in the house. Over to you.

Yours sincerely,
Major Victor Montgomery Cornwall

Nimbu Towers,
Pullen-under-Lyme,
Gloucestershire,
14th August 2021

Dear Major,

I don't wish to sound ungrateful, but I think we're in
danger of being upstaged by an eagle. Perhaps we
should have those two idiots look at this during the edit.
    Anyway, on with the story.

CHAPTER 24
CAVEAT EMPTOR

The cover-up operation began immediately. Over seventy
MPs had exploded, and the Palace of Westminster was
in terrible shape. A press release was put out lamenting
'a significant fire in the Parliament kitchens, with many
victims.' The square mile around Whitehall was cordoned
off, and all residents removed to hotels. The imminent
danger had passed, and Hansclapp was dead, but there
was a lot of work to be done to ensure that no one found
out how close the Queen had come to being murdered.

    Cornwall and I were hustled into a Daimler and
driven up to Buckingham Palace. We were escorted into
a drawing room and instructed to wait. We were poured

Earl Grey by a foxy lady-in-waiting. We'd both have preferred whisky, but it wasn't offered.

After several minutes, Commander Grassing, the Queen's private secretary, strolled in. He was in a garrulous mood. "Well done gentlemen!" he said shaking both of our hands vigorously. "Twice in a bloody row! This is unparalleled! I hope you made the most of the Parliamentary Cellar last night, but I've a feeling you are in for some more special treats, what?"

"Happy to be of service, Commander," I said.

Grassing nodded approvingly. "The Queen will join us presently. You saved her life, saved the House and saved the very structures that this country is built upon. Thank you."

"It was nothing really," said Cornwall, trying and failing to sound modest.

The Queen entered, followed, a few paces behind, by the Duke of Edinburgh.

"Majors Cornwall and Trevelyan," said the Queen. "Thank you. This country is greatly in your debt." I inclined my head as if it were all in a day's work. "Had it not been for your dogged determination, bravery and heroism who knows what would have lain ahead for the country and the monarchy."

The Duke of Edinburgh nodded sagely as he regarded us.

"How does one repay fellows for saving their Queen?" she mused. Now we were getting onto the good bit.

Cornwall spoke up. "If I may be so bold, Ma'am, I'd like to have a go at answering that."

"It was a rhetorical question, Major Cornwall," she deadpanned.

"Of course, Ma'am," Cornwall said, zipping it.

The Queen made a subtle brushing motion with her hand and the room emptied until we, the Queen and the Duke were alone. Now her voice hardened.

"No one must know what I did," she said.

"Ma'am?"

"No one must know of this, none of it," she repeated.

I began to feel a little uneasy.

"Tell me Major Cornwall, what fate befell Lord Hansclapp?"

"Well…Ma'am," he said, stumbling, "I believe…" Cornwall wasn't sure what the Queen wanted him to say, and after a bit more footling, he blurted, "…that he… turned the gun on himself?"

The Queen's gaze fell upon me. "Is that how you remember it, Major Trevelyan?" Thirty-five years of facing down Prime Ministers had sharpened her interview technique very considerably.

"…Errr, yes, Ma'am." I said, "Lord Hansclapp knew the game was up… and, ahem, clearly he couldn't face spending the rest of his life in prison… so… he killed himself."

"Nonsense. Hansclapp died in the fire. It was very sad," she said, not sadly at all.

I nodded. Cornwall nodded.

"You were the only ones who saw what happened in that room. I won't speak of it again. Will you?"

"Ma'am," I said. "There's really no need to be concerned on that front. We can be trusted."

"Can you be trusted, Major Cornwall?"

"One hundred percent, Ma'am," he said.

Just then the Duke of Edinburgh sat bolt upright in his chair, his brow furrowing. He leaned forward and looked at us with new eyes.

"Wait a damn second!" he shouted, leaping to his feet, "you're the two fuckers that sold me that bloody horse! Shergar was supposed to sire my wife a champion!"

"Did he not?" I asked innocently.

"Did he bollocks!" shouted the Duke, working up a proper head of steam. "That horse turned out to be three hundred grand's worth of nothing. He couldn't even get a semi!"

"I'm sorry about that, sir," cut in Cornwall, "but what is it that they say?"

The world seemed to turn in slow motion as Cornwall added a phrase that haunts me to this day, perhaps the daftest and most tone-deaf response of all time:

"...caveat emptor."

"Buyer beware?" The Duke was apoplectic. "Are you telling me it was *my fault*?"

Cornwall decided, too late, to keep his own counsel.

"The vet told me he couldn't sire any little baby Shergars," shouted the Duke, "because some bastard had fused his balls together!"

Cornwall nodded towards me. "He did that, with a twenty-four-volt battery as we crossed the Irish sea."

"What kind of arsehole sells someone a jaffa racehorse?" The Duke kicked a chair over, and marched over to the drinks cabinet, pouring himself a treble with an extra one thrown in, which he glugged back in two swallows.

The Queen pursed her lips. "Gentlemen, in light of this new information, I can see that I'd better have a rethink," she said.

Caveat emptor, you said! To the Duke of Edinburgh! *Caveat* bloody *emptor*. Words fail me. Shame they didn't fail you.

    Go on then…finish our story.

Yours sincerely,
Major Arthur St. John Trevelyan

Hellcat Manor
Great Trundleford
Devon
17th August 2021

Dear Major,

And so, we come to the gut-wrenching finale. I hope you're ready to relive this, Major, as its strong stuff.

CHAPTER 25
HER MAJESTY'S PLEASURE

The Queen and the Duke left the room.

For a few minutes we sat on the sofa, wondering what our immediate future would bring. Ominously, soldiers began filing into the room, occupying positions at both doors.

The Queen returned and sat down, followed as ever by the Duke. "I thank you once again for your service to this country. Your actions have saved hundreds of lives, including mine," she said, "but based on new information that has come to light, I have decided something you might find hard to take."

I felt as though the air was being drawn from my lungs. "Ma'am?"

The Queen continued, "Lord Hansclapp's attack can never be revealed. It would be so damaging to the future of the Royal Household that the greatest service you, as Scoundrels, could perform for me now, is, simply, to do nothing. For men of action like yourselves, no doubt you will find this intolerable. But, given your mendaciousness, and the fact that you both have comfortable abodes, I decree that you shall be confined to them, and allowed no contact with the outside world, including each other."

"For how long?" I asked.

"Thirty years."

"WHAT?"

"WHAT?"

"You will be free to do as you please in 2016," she continued, "but of course you will be well into your nineties by then. On that date you'll be free to leave your homes, gentlemen, should you still be alive. Let me say again that I am eternally grateful for what you have done for Great Britain, and for me. You should consider yourselves heroes for the sacrifice you are making."

"But, Ma'am..." I was going to remonstrate, but soldiers began to crowd around me. One seized my arm. I shoved him hard in the chest and he fell backwards over a table filled with photographs of corgis. I could see the same rough treatment was happening to Trevelyan, who was jostling and bouncing around as soldiers tried to strongarm him.

"Cornwall, what's happening here? I don't understand," he called.

"We've just saved your life!" I shouted at Her Majesty. "We've just saved the bloody country!"

"Take them away please," ordered the Duke, with a malevolent grin.

The soldiers stepped it up a gear in order to subdue us. A scuffle ensued. I was just breaking one soldier's wrist when another one hooked his forearm around my throat. Trevelyan lamped a couple of early enthusiasts, but two others got behind him and pitched him forward onto a sofa, where he was put in an armlock. More guards joined the melee, and as I twisted from their grip, my prized pocket watch – a gift from the Sultan of Brunei – fell from my jacket and was kicked away. More guards entered the fray and soon we were overpowered, and thereafter neither Trevelyan nor I put up as much of a fight. How could we have done? These were British troops, and we were Scoundrels, bound by the laws of our own Club to do the Queen's bidding.

And so, the guards separated us and tore us away from each other. Trevelyan reached out to me, his hands grabbing at thin air, "Cornwall!" he cried.

I reached out to him, "Trevelyan!"

Trevelyan was taken to the door on the far side of the room. I was pulled towards the near door. Just before Trevelyan disappeared, he glanced back over his shoulder and our eyes met for the last time.

"But we're heroes!" I cried. "We're bloody heroes!"

Then the soldiers swept a black cloth bag over Trevelyan's head, and, just as abruptly, my world was plunged into darkness too.

That was thirty-five years ago. It was the last time that I saw my friend Major Arthur St. John Trevelyan.

So, there you have it. That's the whole story. It feels damn good to get it off my chest.

As for the house arrest? Well, the first year was hard. But not as hard as the last few have been. Your recollections of that night at the Tower were better than I thought they'd be. You were right. Fang did survive Summerville's bullet. She lived with me at Hellcat for twenty-eight happy years. Baxter was ordained as a Shinto minister and married us in the Library. On our wedding night, I took the biggest gamble of my life, and discarded my mammoth-tusk condom. I never needed it again.

The old girl died a couple of years before I first wrote to you. I miss her terribly. After she'd gone, I wanted nothing more than for the world to know my story – and Fang's, and of course, yours. I took the liberty of laying Sayonara next to Anais. They're both looked over by a lovely cherry blossom tree that I planted myself. I think you'll approve.

Now that these memoirs are concluded, I'll have a bit of time on my hands. I'm planning to get Baxter to take me up to the Club next week. He's still driving the Bentley although he's registered blind. I'm curious to see whether the place has changed at all.

So how about it then? A meet up, at Scoundrels? I rather like the idea of taking up our old seats in the Blue Bar, sinking a few interesting measures from the top shelf, and chatting about old times.

After all, we have plenty more stories to tell.

Your old friend,
Victor

Nimbu Towers
Pullen-under-Lyme
Gloucestershire
20th August 2021

Dear Victor,

Yes. I'd like that a lot.

Your old friend,
St. John

ACKNOWLEDGEMENTS

It is difficult to underplay our relief at finally getting to the end of Cornwall and Trevelyan's tale, which has blighted our lives since we signed for the Majors' first manuscript with the motorcycle courier (we are sure this was Baxter, or Cacahuete) thereby entering us into an unbreakable contract to publish. We have squabbled endlessly over who actually signed the thing, but we're equally at fault.

We'd like to thank Bill Godber at Turnaround, as well as Ian West, Claire Thompson, Liam Konemann, Julie Thelot and Jim Crowley. We'd also like to thank Martin Usborne, of Hoxton Mini Press, for his sage advice and support; Esther Harris for her strategic genius; Gieves & Hawkes for a memorable launch party at 1 Savile Row; Chelsea Taylor and Joe Shillito for their indefatigable production support; Daniel Barnett at CPI; Mel Adkins, Tollon Adkins and Julie O'Doherty for their forensic attention to the text; the artist Michael Gambriel for a superb set of covers; and our very own Massingberd, Tom Palmer.

We've met some wonderfully supportive booksellers along the way and are grateful for their support. Special mention to the excellent Daniel Matthews and inestimable Steven Hevey of Foyles; to and to the combined brilliance of Grace Barrett, Rosie Beaumont-Thomas, Michael Callanan, Dr Amy Crawford, Abbey Guessis, Jo Halpin, Paul Holding, Heather James, Sam Jarvis, Robin Mawhood, Sarah McGhee, Katie Mosscrop and Paul Simpson, all of Waterstones, for their repeatedly warm welcomes and support in stores.

Special thanks must also go to our exceptional agent, Charlie Campbell at CCLA, who has provided mission support since Volume One; to Emily Hayward-Whitlock at The Artists'

Partnership; and to Thorsten Schumacher, Lars Sylvest, Whitney Sudler-Smith and Levi Woodward at Rocket Science, who have decided, despite our sternest warnings, to begin mixing it up with the Majors to bring their story to the screen.

Inevitably, over the last few years many friends, relatives and colleagues have also been drawn into the Majors' toxic orbit, so we'd like to apologise, in no particular order to Peter Chinn, Rufus Radcliffe, Mike Crowe, William Peak, Christopher Peak, Alex Macdonald, Anthony Jarman, Tom Fleming, Pete Duncan, Frank Brinkley, Hephzibah Anderson, Shelley Squire, Chris Hide, Julia Hide, Paul O'Doherty, Dave Webster and indeed anyone who attended a pub or café in Brockley, Enfield or the West End of London between 2014 and 2021 and heard the Major's horrible tales being discussed.

Also, a very special thanks to Hana, George and Matilda Crowe; and to Jane, Molly and Jack Peak for making room for the Majors, on countless evenings, at our dinner tables.

And a note to you, the reader. Be aware that the Majors are no longer confined to their estates, so there's a chance you might bump into them. If you ever find yourself in Mayfair or St James's and happen upon a couple of elderly gentlemen in good suits bickering on a bench or comparing the size of their swordsticks, by all means offer to buy them a drink. They'll almost certainly tell you a tall story in return. Trust us, there are plenty that didn't make it into these three volumes. But on no account sign your name to anything they give you.

Our final thanks are directed to Majors Cornwall and Trevelyan themselves. It's no exaggeration to say that you've changed our lives, but we do hope you stay true to your word, and never, ever contact us again.

Duncan Crowe & James Peak,
London, November 2021